Harold Pinter

Harold Pinter was born in London in 1930. He lived
with Antonia Fraser from 1975 and they married in
1980. In 1995 he won the David Cohen British
Literature Prize, awarded for a lifetime's achievement in
literature. In 1996 he was given the Laurence Olivier
Award for a lifetime's achievement in theatre. In 2002 he
was made a Companion of Honour for services to
literature. In 2005 he was awarded the Nobel Prize in
Literature and, in the same year, the Wilfred Owen
Award for Poetry and the Franz Kafka Award (Prague).
In 2006 he was awarded the Europe Theatre Prize and,
in 2007, the highest French honour, the Légion
d'honneur. He died in December 2008.

HAROLD PINTER

The Short Plays

with a foreword by
Antonia Fraser

FABER & FABER

This collection first published in 2018
by Faber and Faber Limited
Bloomsbury House
74–77 Great Russell Street
London WC1B 3DA

Typeset by Country Setting, Kingsdown, Kent CT14 8ES
Printed and bound in Great Britain
by CPI Group (UK) Ltd, Croydon CR0 4YY

Harold Pinter is hereby identified as author of this work
in accordance with Section 77 of the Copyright, Designs
and Patents Act 1988

All rights whatsoever in this work are strictly reserved
and applications for permission for performance etc.
should be made in advance, before rehearsals begin, to
Judy Daish Associates Limited, 2 St Charles Place,
London W10 6EG

A CIP record for this book is available from the British Library

ISBN 978-0-571-34991-3

FSC
www.fsc.org
MIX
Paper from
responsible sources
FSC® C020471

2 4 6 8 10 9 7 5 3 1

Contents

Foreword

The exciting project of publishing (and performing) the totality of Harold's one-act plays is a most appropriate way of marking the tenth anniversary of his death on 24 December 2018.

The whole atmosphere around Harold changed when he was writing. The process, whether the subject was grim or humorous (or a mixture of both), filled him with happiness from the first sudden image to ignite his imagination to the exploration that then took place, often transforming that first image into something very different.

I shall never forget watching *The Lover* on television in 1963, ten years before we met. I was in bed, and the bedside television was a new treat. The plot, with its sudden amazing twist concerning the husband and the lover (which one critic failed to spot), held me in its spell from the challenging opening line. *The Collection*, which I saw on stage, was similarly both thrilling and mysterious: what really happened? As with many of Harold's plays I change my mind . . .

The writing of *Celebration* (his last play) is a perfect example of the way Harold's work altered during the writing process. A discomforting experience with raucous diners at the neighbouring table in a favourite restaurant started him off. When we were on holiday in Dorset, he began to write. Then Harold laid the play down for a moment, saying the original characters were too unpleasant, before grabbing it again, saying that fresh characters had 'walked into his mind' and demanded their place. From then on he wrote frantically, finished the play, as he thought, and got into bed – before getting out again, feeling the Waiter had more to say and that 'I must listen'.

This is a project of which Harold himself would have heartily approved.

Antonia Fraser
June 2018

THE ROOM

The Room first published by
Methuen & Co. 1960
© FPinter Limited, 1959, 1960

The Room was first presented at the University of Bristol Department of Drama on 15 May 1957 with the following cast:

BERT HUDD	Claude Jenkins
ROSE HUDD	Susan Engel
MR KIDD	Henry Woolf
MR SANDS	David Davies
MRS SANDS	Auriol Smith
RILEY	George Odlum

Directed by Henry Woolf

The Room was subsequently presented at the Hampstead Theatre Club on 21 January, 1960, with the following cast:

BERT HUDD	Howard Lang
ROSE	Vivien Merchant
MR KIDD	Henry Woolf
MR SANDS	John Rees
MRS SANDS	Auriol Smith
RILEY	Thomas Baptiste

Directed by Harold Pinter

The Room was then presented at the Royal Court
Theatre on 8 March 1960 with the following cast:

BERT HUDD   Michael Brennan
ROSE HUDD   Vivien Merchant
MR KIDD   John Cater
MR SANDS   Michael Caine
MRS SANDS   Anne Bishop
RILEY   Thomas Baptiste

Directed by Anthony Page

Characters

BERT HUDD
a man of fifty

ROSE
a woman of sixty

MR KIDD
an old man

MR SANDS
MRS SANDS
a young couple

RILEY

Scene: a room in a large house. A door down right. A gas-fire down left. A gas-stove and sink, up left. A window up centre. A table and chairs, centre. A rocking-chair, left centre. The foot of a double-bed protrudes from alcove, up right.

BERT *is at the table, wearing a cap, a magazine propped in front of him.* ROSE *is at the stove.*

ROSE Here you are. This'll keep the cold out.

She places bacon and eggs on a plate, turns off the gas and takes the plate to the table.

It's very cold out, I can tell you. It's murder.

She returns to the stove and pours water from the kettle into the teapot, turns off the gas and brings the teapot to the table, pours salt and sauce on the plate and cuts two slices of bread. BERT *begins to eat.*

That's right. You eat that. You'll need it. You can feel it in here. Still, the room keeps warm. It's better than the basement, anyway.

She butters the bread.

I don't know how they live down there. It's asking for trouble. Go on. Eat it up. It'll do you good.

She goes to the sink, wipes a cup and saucer and brings them to the table.

If you want to go out you might as well have something inside you. Because you'll feel it when you get out.

She pours milk into the cup.

Just now I looked out of the window. It was enough for me. There wasn't a soul about. Can you hear the wind?

She sits in the rocking-chair.

I've never seen who it is. Who is it? Who lives down there? I'll have to ask. I mean, you might as well know, Bert. But whoever it is, it can't be too cosy.

Pause.

I think it's changed hands since I was last there. I didn't see who moved in then. I mean the first time it was taken.

Pause.

Anyway, I think they've gone now.

Pause.

But I think someone else has gone in now. I wouldn't like to live in that basement. Did you ever see the walls? They were running. This is all right for me. Go on, Bert. Have a bit more bread.

She goes to the table and cuts a slice of bread.

I'll have some cocoa on when you come back.

She goes to the window and settles the curtain.

No, this room's all right for me. I mean, you know where you are. When it's cold, for instance.

She goes to the table.

What about the rasher? Was it all right? It was a good one, I know, but not as good as the last lot I got in. It's the weather.

She goes to the rocking-chair, and sits.

Anyway, I haven't been out. I haven't been so well. I didn't feel up to it. Still, I'm much better today. I don't know about you though. I don't know whether you ought to go out. I mean, you shouldn't, straight after you've been laid up. Still. Don't worry, Bert. You go. You won't be long.

She rocks.

It's good you were up here, I can tell you. It's good you weren't down there, in the basement. That's no joke. Oh, I've left the tea. I've left the tea standing.

She goes to the table and pours tea into the cup.

No, it's not bad. Nice weak tea. Lovely weak tea. Here you are. Drink it down. I'll wait for mine. Anyway, I'll have it a bit stronger.

She takes a plate to the sink and leaves it.

Those walls would have finished you off. I don't know who lives down there now. Whoever it is, they're taking a big chance. Maybe they're foreigners.

She goes to the rocking-chair and sits.

I'd have pulled you through.

Pause.

There isn't room for two down there, anyway. I think
there was one first, before he moved out. Maybe
they've got two now.

She rocks.

If they ever ask you, Bert, I'm quite happy where I am.
We're quiet, we're all right. You're happy up here. It's
not far up either, when you come in from outside. And
we're not bothered. And nobody bothers us.

Pause.

I don't know why you have to go out. Couldn't you
run it down tomorrow? I could put the fire in later.
You could sit by the fire. That's what you like, Bert, of
an evening. It'll be dark in a minute as well, soon.

She rocks.

It gets dark now.

She rises and pours out tea at the table.

I made plenty. Go on.

She sits at table.

You looked out today? It's got ice on the roads. Oh,
I know you can drive. I'm not saying you can't drive.
I mentioned to Mr Kidd this morning that you'd be
doing a run today. I told him you hadn't been too

grand, but I said, still, he's a marvellous driver. I wouldn't mind what time, where, nothing, Bert. You know how to drive. I told him.

She wraps her cardigan about her.

But it's cold. It's really cold today, chilly. I'll have you some nice cocoa on for when you get back.

She rises, goes to the window, and looks out.

It's quiet. Be coming on for dark. There's no one about.

She stands, looking.

Wait a minute.

Pause.

I wonder who that is.

Pause.

No. I thought I saw someone.

Pause.

No.

She drops the curtain.

You know what though? It looks a bit better. It's not so windy. You'd better put on your thick jersey.

She goes to the rocking-chair, sits and rocks.

This is a good room. You've got a chance in a place like this. I look after you, don't I, Bert? Like when they offered us the basement here I said no straight off.

I knew that'd be no good. The ceiling right on top of you. No, you've got a window here, you can move yourself, you can come home at night, if you have to go out, you can do your job, you can come home, you're all right. And I'm here. You stand a chance.

Pause.

I wonder who has got it now. I've never seen them, or heard of them. But I think someone's down there. Whoever's got it can keep it. That looked a good rasher, Bert. I'll have a cup of tea later. I like mine a bit stronger. You like yours weak.

A knock at the door. She stands.

Who is it?

Pause.

Hallo!

Knock repeated.

Come in then.

Knock repeated.

Who is it?

Pause. The door opens and MR KIDD *comes in.*

MR KIDD I knocked.

ROSE I heard you.

MR KIDD Eh?

ROSE We heard you.

MR KIDD Hallo, Mr Hudd, how are you, all right?
I've been looking at the pipes.

ROSE Are they all right?

MR KIDD Eh?

ROSE Sit down, Mr Kidd.

MR KIDD No, that's all right. I just popped in, like,
to see how things were going. Well, it's cosy in here,
isn't it?

ROSE Oh, thank you, Mr Kidd.

MR KIDD You going out today, Mr Hudd? I went
out. I came straight in again. Only to the corner, of
course.

ROSE Not many people about today, Mr Kidd.

MR KIDD So I thought to myself, I'd better have a
look at those pipes. In the circumstances. I only went
to the corner, for a few necessary items. It's likely to
snow. Very likely, in my opinion.

ROSE Why don't you sit down, Mr Kidd?

MR KIDD No, no, that's all right.

ROSE Well, it's a shame you have to go out in this
weather, Mr Kidd. Don't you have a help?

MR KIDD Eh?

ROSE I thought you had a woman to help.

MR KIDD I haven't got any woman.

ROSE I thought you had one when we first came.

13

MR KIDD No women here.

ROSE Maybe I was thinking of somewhere else.

MR KIDD Plenty of women round the corner. Not here though. Oh no. Eh, have I seen that before?

ROSE What?

MR KIDD That.

ROSE I don't know. Have you?

MR KIDD I seem to have some remembrance.

ROSE It's just an old rocking-chair.

MR KIDD Was it here when you came?

ROSE No, I brought it myself.

MR KIDD I could swear blind I've seen that before.

ROSE Perhaps you have.

MR KIDD What?

ROSE I say, perhaps you have.

MR KIDD Yes, maybe I have.

ROSE Take a seat, Mr Kidd.

MR KIDD I wouldn't take an oath on it though.

BERT *yawns and stretches, and continues looking at his magazine.*

No, I won't sit down, with Mr Hudd just having a bit of a rest after his tea. I've got to go and get mine going in a minute. You're going out then, Mr Hudd? I was just looking at your van. She's a very nice little van, that. I notice you wrap her up well for the cold. I don't blame you. Yes, I was hearing you go off, when was it, the other morning, yes. Very smooth. I can tell a good gear-change.

ROSE I thought your bedroom was at the back, Mr Kidd.

MR KIDD My bedroom?

ROSE Wasn't it at the back? Not that I ever knew.

MR KIDD I wasn't in my bedroom.

ROSE Oh, well.

MR KIDD I was up and about.

ROSE I don't get up early in this weather. I can take my time. I take my time.

Pause.

MR KIDD This was my bedroom.

ROSE This? When?

MR KIDD When I lived here.

ROSE I didn't know that.

MR KIDD I will sit down for a few ticks.

He sits in the armchair.

ROSE Well, I never knew that.

MR KIDD Was this chair here when you came?

ROSE Yes.

MR KIDD I can't recollect this one.

Pause.

ROSE When was that then?

MR KIDD Eh?

ROSE When was this your bedroom?

MR KIDD A good while back.

Pause.

ROSE I was telling Bert I was telling you how he could drive.

MR KIDD Mr Hudd? Oh, Mr Hudd can drive all right. I've seen him bowl down the road all right. Oh yes.

ROSE Well, Mr Kidd, I must say this is a very nice room. It's a very comfortable room.

MR KIDD Best room in the house.

ROSE It must get a bit damp downstairs.

MR KIDD Not as bad as upstairs.

ROSE What about downstairs?

MR KIDD Eh?

ROSE What about downstairs?

MR KIDD What about it?

ROSE Must get a bit damp.

MR KIDD A bit. Not as bad as upstairs though.

ROSE Why's that?

MR KIDD The rain comes in.

Pause.

ROSE Anyone live up there?

MR KIDD Up there? There was. Gone now.

ROSE How many floors you got in this house?

MR KIDD Floors. (*He laughs.*) Ah, we had a good few of them in the old days.

ROSE How many have you got now?

MR KIDD Well, to tell you the truth, I don't count them now.

ROSE Oh.

MR KIDD No, not now.

ROSE It must be a bit of a job.

MR KIDD Oh, I used to count them, once. Never got tired of it. I used to keep a tack on everything in this house. I had a lot to keep my eye on, then. I was able for it too. That was when my sister was alive. But I lost track a bit, after she died. She's been dead some time now, my sister. It was a good house then. She was a capable woman. Yes. Fine size of a woman too. I think she took after my mum. Yes, I think she took after my old mum, from what I can recollect. I think my mum was a Jewess. Yes, I wouldn't be surprised to learn that she was a Jewess. She didn't have many babies.

ROSE What about your sister, Mr Kidd?

MR KIDD What about her?

ROSE Did she have any babies?

MR KIDD Yes, she had a resemblance to my old mum, I think. Taller, of course.

ROSE When did she die then, your sister?

MR KIDD Yes, that's right, it was after she died that I must have stopped counting. She used to keep things in very good trim. And I gave her a helping hand. She was very grateful, right until her last. She always used to tell me how much she appreciated all the – little things – that I used to do for her. Then she copped it. I was her senior. Yes, I was her senior. She had a lovely boudoir. A beautiful boudoir.

ROSE What did she die of?

MR KIDD Who?

ROSE Your sister.

Pause.

MR KIDD I've made ends meet.

Pause.

ROSE You full at the moment, Mr Kidd?

MR KIDD Packed out.

ROSE All sorts, I suppose?

MR KIDD Oh yes, I make ends meet.

ROSE We do, too, don't we, Bert?

   Pause.

Where's your bedroom now then, Mr Kidd?

MR KIDD Me? I can take my pick. *(Rising.)* You'll be going out soon then, Mr Hudd? Well, be careful how you go. Those roads'll be no joke. Still, you know how to manipulate your van all right, don't you? Where you going? Far? Be long?

ROSE He won't be long.

MR KIDD No, of course not. Shouldn't take him long.

ROSE No.

MR KIDD Well then, I'll pop off. Have a good run, Mr Hudd. Mind how you go. It'll be dark soon too. But not for a good while yet. Arrivederci.

   He exits.

ROSE I don't believe he had a sister, ever.

   She takes the plate and cup to the sink. BERT *pushes his chair back and rises.*

All right. Wait a minute. Where's your jersey?

   She brings the jersey from the bed.

Here you are. Take your coat off. Get into it.

   She helps him into his jersey.

Right. Where's your muffler?

19

She brings a muffler from the bed.

Here you are. Wrap it round. That's it. Don't go too fast, Bert, will you? I'll have some cocoa on when you get back. You won't be long. Wait a minute. Where's your overcoat? You'd better put on your overcoat.

He fixes his muffler, goes to the door and exits. She stands, watching the door, then turns slowly to the table, picks up the magazine, and puts it down. She stands and listens, goes to the fire, bends, lights the fire and warms her hands. She stands and looks about the room. She looks at the window and listens, goes quickly to the window, stops and straightens the curtain. She comes to the centre of the room, and looks towards the door. She goes to the bed, puts on a shawl, goes to the sink, takes a bin from under the sink, goes to the door and opens it.

ROSE Oh!

MR *and* MRS SANDS *are disclosed on the landing.*

MRS SANDS So sorry. We didn't mean to be standing here, like. Didn't mean to give you a fright. We've just come up the stairs.

ROSE That's all right.

MRS SANDS This is Mr Sands. I'm Mrs Sands.

ROSE How do you do?

MR SANDS *grunts acknowledgement.*

MRS SANDS We were just going up the stairs. But you can't see a thing in this place. Can you, Toddy?

MR SANDS Not a thing.

ROSE What were you looking for?

MRS SANDS The man who runs the house.

MR SANDS The landlord. We're trying to get hold of the landlord.

MRS SANDS What's his name, Toddy?

ROSE His name's Mr Kidd.

MRS SANDS Kidd, Was that the name, Toddy?

MR SANDS Kidd? No, that's not it.

ROSE Mr Kidd. That's his name.

MR SANDS Well, that's not the bloke we're looking for.

ROSE Well, you must be looking for someone else.

Pause.

MR SANDS I suppose we must be.

ROSE You look cold.

MRS SANDS It's murder out. Have you been out?

ROSE No.

MRS SANDS We've not long come in.

ROSE Well, come inside, if you like, and have a warm.

They come into the centre of the room.

(*Bringing the chair from the table to the fire.*) Sit down here. You can get a good warn.

MRS SANDS Thanks. (*She sits.*)

ROSE Come over by the fire, Mr. Sands.

MR SANDS No, it's all right. I'll just stretch my legs.

MRS SANDS Why? You haven't been sitting down.

MR SANDS What about it?

MRS SANDS Well, why don't you sit down?

MR SANDS Why should I?

MRS SANDS You must be cold.

MR SANDS I'm not.

MRS SANDS You must be. Bring over a chair and sit down.

MR SANDS I'm all right standing up, thanks.

MRS SANDS You don't look one thing or the other standing up.

MR SANDS I'm quite all right, Clarissa.

ROSE Clarissa? What a pretty name.

MRS SANDS Yes, it is nice, isn't it? My father and mother gave it to me.

Pause.

You know, this is a room you can sit down and feel cosy in.

MR SANDS (*looking at the room*) It's a fair size, all right.

MRS SANDS Why don't you sit down, Mrs –

ROSE Hudd. No thanks.

MR SANDS What did you say?

ROSE When?

MR SANDS What did you say the name was?

ROSE Hudd.

MR SANDS That's it. You're the wife of the bloke you mentioned then?

MRS SANDS No, she isn't. That was Mr Kidd.

MR SANDS Was it? I thought it was Hudd.

MRS SANDS No, it was Kidd. Wasn't it, Mrs Hudd?

ROSE That's right. The landlord.

MRS SANDS No, not the landlord. The other man.

ROSE Well, that's his name. He's the landlord.

MR SANDS Who?

ROSE Mr Kidd.

Pause.

MR SANDS Is he?

MRS SANDS Maybe there are two landlords.

Pause.

MR SANDS That'll be the day.

MRS SANDS What did you say?

MR SANDS I said that'll be the day.

Pause.

ROSE What's it like out?

MRS SANDS It's very dark out.

MR SANDS No darker than in.

MRS SANDS He's right there.

MR SANDS It's darker in than out, for my money.

MRS SANDS There's not much light in this place, is there, Mrs Hudd? Do you know, this is the first bit of light we've seen since we came in?

MR SANDS The first crack.

ROSE I never go out at night. We stay in.

MRS SANDS Now I come to think of it, I saw a star.

MR SANDS You saw what?

MRS SANDS Well, I think I did.

MR SANDS You think you saw what?

MRS SANDS A star.

MR SANDS Where?

MRS SANDS In the sky.

MR SANDS When?

MRS SANDS As we were coming along.

MR SANDS Go home.

24

MRS SANDS What do you mean?

MR SANDS You didn't see a star.

MRS SANDS Why not?

MR SANDS Because I'm telling you. I'm telling you
you didn't see a star.

Pause.

ROSE I hope it's not too dark out. I hope it's not too
icy. My husband's in his van. He doesn't drive slow
either. He never drives slow.

MR SANDS (*guffawing*) Well, he's taking a big chance
tonight then.

ROSE What?

MR SANDS No – I mean, it'd be a bit dodgy driving
tonight.

ROSE He's a very good driver.

Pause.

How long have you been here?

MRS SANDS I don't know. How long have we been
here, Toddy?

MR SANDS About half an hour.

MRS SANDS Longer than that, much longer.

MR SANDS About thirty-five minutes.

ROSE Well, I think you'll find Mr Kidd about
somewhere. He's not long gone to make his tea.

MR SANDS He lives here, does he?

ROSE Of course he lives here.

MR SANDS And you say he's the landlord, is he?

ROSE Of course he is.

MR SANDS Well, say I wanted to get hold of him, where would I find him?

ROSE Well – I'm not sure.

MR SANDS He lives here, does he?

ROSE Yes, but I don't know –

MR SANDS You don't know exactly where he hangs out?

ROSE No, not exactly.

MR SANDS But he does live here, doesn't he?

Pause.

MRS SANDS This is a very big house, Toddy.

MR SANDS Yes, I know it is. But Mrs Hudd seems to know Mr Kidd very well.

ROSE No, I wouldn't say that. As a matter of fact, I don't know him at all. We're very quiet. We keep ourselves to ourselves. I never interfere. I mean, why should I? We've got our room. We don't bother anyone else. That's the way it should be.

MRS SANDS It's a nice house, isn't it? Roomy.

ROSE I don't know about the house. We're all right, but I wouldn't mind betting there's a lot wrong with this house.

She sits in the rocking-chair.

I think there's a lot of damp.

MRS SANDS Yes, I felt a bit of damp when we were in the basement just now.

ROSE You were in the basement?

MRS SANDS Yes, we went down there when we came in.

ROSE Why?

MRS SANDS We were looking for the landlord.

ROSE What was it like down there?

MR SANDS Couldn't see a thing.

ROSE Why not?

MR SANDS There wasn't any light.

ROSE But what was – you said it was damp?

MRS SANDS I felt a bit, didn't you, Tod?

MR SANDS Why? Haven't you ever been down there, Mrs Hudd?

ROSE Oh yes, once, a long time ago.

MR SANDS Well, you know what it's like then, don't you?

ROSE It was a long time ago

MR SANDS You haven't been here all that long, have you?

ROSE I was just wondering whether anyone was living down there now.

MRS SANDS Yes. A man.

ROSE A man?

MRS SANDS Yes.

ROSE One man?

MR SANDS Yes, there was a bloke down there, all right.

He perches on the table.

MRS SANDS You're sitting down!

MR SANDS (*jumping up*) Who is?

MRS SANDS You were.

MR SANDS Don't be silly. I perched.

MRS SANDS I saw you sit down.

MR SANDS You did not see me sit down because I did not sit bloody well down. I perched!

MRS SANDS Do you think I can't perceive when someone's sitting down?

MR SANDS Perceive! That's all you do. Perceive.

MRS SANDS You could do with a bit more of that instead of all that tripe you get up to.

MR SANDS You don't mind some of that tripe!

MRS SANDS You take after your uncle, that's who you take after!

MR SANDS And who do you take after?

MRS SANDS (*rising*) I didn't bring you into the world.

MR SANDS You didn't what?

MRS SANDS I said, I didn't bring you into the world.

MR SANDS Well, who did then? That's what I want to know. Who did? Who did bring me into the world?

She sits, muttering. He stands, muttering.

ROSE You say you saw a man downstairs, in the basement?

MRS SANDS Yes, Mrs Hudd, you see, the thing is, Mrs Hudd, we'd heard they'd got a room to let here, so we thought we'd come along and have a look. Because we're looking for a place, you see, somewhere quiet, and we knew this district was quiet, and we passed the house a few months ago and we thought it looked very nice, but we thought we'd call of an evening, to catch the landlord, so we came along this evening. Well, when we got here we walked in the front door and it was very dark in the hall and there wasn't anyone about. So we went down to the basement. Well, we got down there only due to Toddy having such good eyesight really. Between you and me, I didn't like the look of it much, I mean the feel,

we couldn't make much out, it smelt damp to me.
Anyway, we went through a kind of partition, then
there was another partition, and we couldn't see
where we were going, well, it seemed to me it got
darker the more we went, the further we went in, I
thought we must have come to the wrong house. So I
stopped. And Toddy stopped. And then this voice
said, this voice came – it said – well, it gave me a bit
of a fright, I don't know about Tod, but someone
asked if he could do anything for us. So Tod said we
were looking for the landlord and this man said the
landlord would be upstairs. Then Tod asked was there
a room vacant. And this man, this voice really, I think
he was behind the partition, said yes there was a room
vacant. He was very polite, I thought, but we never
saw him, I don't know why they never put a light on.
Anyway, we got out then and we came up and we
went to the top of the house. I don't know whether it
was the top. There was a door locked on the stairs, so
there might have been another floor, but we didn't see
anyone, and it was dark, and we were just coming
down again when you opened your door.

ROSE You said you were going up.

MRS SANDS What?

ROSE You said you were going up before.

MRS SANDS No, we were coming down.

ROSE You didn't say that before.

MRS SANDS We'd been up.

30

MR SANDS We'd been up. We were coming down.

Pause.

ROSE This man, what was he like, was he old?

MRS SANDS We didn't see him.

ROSE Was he old?

Pause.

MR SANDS Well, we'd better try to get hold of this landlord, if he's about.

ROSE You won't find any rooms vacant in this house.

MR SANDS Why not?

ROSE Mr Kidd told me. He told me.

MR SANDS Mr Kidd?

ROSE He told me he was full up.

MR SANDS The man in the basement said there was one. One room. Number seven he said.

Pause.

ROSE That's this room.

MR SANDS We'd better go and get hold of the landlord.

MRS SANDS (*rising*) Well, thank you for the warm-up, Mrs Hudd. I feel better now.

ROSE This room is occupied.

MR SANDS Come on.

31

MRS SANDS Goodnight, Mrs Hudd. I hope your husband won't be too long. Must be lonely for you, being all alone here.

MR SANDS Come on.

They go out. ROSE *watches the door close, starts towards it, and stops. She takes the chair back to the table, picks up the magazine, looks at it, and puts it down. She goes to the rocking-chair, sits, rocks, stops, and sits still. There is a sharp knock at the door, which opens. Enter* MR KIDD.

MR KIDD I came straight in.

ROSE Mr Kidd! I was just going to find you. I've got to speak to you.

MR KIDD Look here, Mrs Hudd, I've got to speak to you. I came up specially.

ROSE There were two people in here just now. They said this room was going vacant. What were they talking about?

MR KIDD As soon as I heard the van go I got ready to come and see you. I'm knocked out.

ROSE What was it all about? Did you see those people? How can this room be going? It's occupied. Did they get hold of you, Mr Kidd?

MR KIDD Get hold of me? Who?

ROSE I told you. Two people. They were looking for the landlord.

MR KIDD I'm just telling you. I've been getting ready to come and see you, as soon as I heard the van go.

ROSE Well then, who were they?

MR KIDD That's why I came up before. But he hadn't gone yet. I've been waiting for him to go the whole weekend.

ROSE Mr Kidd, what did they mean about this room?

MR KIDD What room?

ROSE Is this room vacant?

MR KIDD Vacant?

ROSE They were looking for the landlord.

MR KIDD Who were?

ROSE Listen, Mr Kidd, you are the landlord, aren't you? There isn't any other landlord?

MR KIDD What? What's that got to do with it? I don't know what you're talking about. I've got to tell you, that's all. I've got to tell you. I've had a terrible weekend. You'll have to see him. I can't take it any more. You've got to see him.

Pause.

ROSE Who?

MR KIDD The man. He's been waiting to see you. He wants to see you. I can't get rid of him. I'm not a young man, Mrs Hudd, that's apparent. It's apparent. You've got to see him.

ROSE See who?

MR KIDD The man. He's downstairs now. He's been there the whole weekend. He said that when Mr Hudd went out I was to tell him. That's why I came up before. But he hadn't gone yet. So I told him. I said he hasn't gone yet. I said, well when he goes, I said, you can go up, go up, have done with it. No, he says, you must ask her if she'll see me. So I came up again, to ask you if you'll see him.

ROSE Who is he?

MR KIDD How do I know who he is? All I know is he won't say a word, he won't indulge in any conversation, just – has he gone? That and nothing else. He wouldn't even play a game of chess. All right, I said, the other night, while we're waiting I'll play you a game of chess. You play chess, don't you? I tell you, Mrs Hudd, I don't know if he even heard what I was saying. He just lies there. It's not good for me. He just lies there, that's all, waiting.

ROSE He lies there, in the basement?

MR KIDD Shall I tell him it's all right, Mrs Hudd?

ROSE But it's damp down there.

MR KIDD Shall I tell him it's all right?

ROSE That what's all right?

MR KIDD That you'll see him.

ROSE See him? I beg your pardon, Mr Kidd. I don't know him. Why should I see him?

34

MR KIDD You won't see him?

ROSE Do you expect me to see someone I don't know? With my husband not here too?

MR KIDD But he knows you, Mrs Hudd, he knows you.

ROSE How could he, Mr Kidd, when I don't know him?

MR KIDD You must know him.

ROSE But I don't know anybody. We're quiet here. We've just moved into this district.

MR KIDD But he doesn't come from this district. Perhaps you knew him in another district.

ROSE Mr Kidd, do you think I go around knowing men in one district after another? What do you think I am?

MR KIDD I don't know what I think.

He sits.

I think I'm going off my squiff.

ROSE You need rest. An old man like you. What you need is rest.

MR KIDD He hasn't given me any rest. Just lying there. In the black dark. Hour after hour. Why don't you leave me be, both of you? Mrs Hudd, have a bit of pity. Please see him. Why don't you see him?

ROSE I don't know him.

MR KIDD You can never tell. You might know him.

ROSE I don't know him.

MR KIDD (*rising*) I don't know what'll happen if you don't see him.

ROSE I've told you I don't know this man!

MR KIDD I know what he'll do. I know what he'll do. If you don't see him now, there'll be nothing else for it, he'll come up on his own bat, when your husband's here, that's what he'll do. He'll come up when Mr Hudd's here, when your husband's here.

ROSE He'd never do that.

MR KIDD He would do that. That's exactly what he'll do. You don't think he's going to go away without seeing you, after he's come all this way, do you? You don't think that, do you?

ROSE All this way?

MR KIDD You don't think he's going to do that, do you?

Pause.

ROSE He wouldn't do that.

MR KIDD Oh yes. I know it.

Pause.

ROSE What's the time?

MR KIDD I don't know.

Pause.

ROSE Fetch him. Quick. Quick!

MR KIDD goes out. She sits in the rocking-chair. After a few moments the door opens. Enter a blind Negro. He closes the door behind him, walks further, and feels with a stick till he reaches the armchair. He stops.

RILEY Mrs Hudd?

ROSE You just touched a chair. Why don't you sit in it?

He sits.

RILEY Thank you.

ROSE Don't thank me for anything. I don't want you up here. I don't know who you are. And the sooner you get out the better.

Pause.

(*Rising.*) Well, come on. Enough's enough. You can take a liberty too far, you know. What do you want? You force your way up here. You disturb my evening. You come in and sit down here. What do you want?

He looks about the room.

What are you looking at? You're blind, aren't you? So what are you looking at? What do you think you've got here, a little girl? I can keep up with you. I'm one ahead of people like you. Tell me what you want and get out.

RILEY My name is Riley.

ROSE I don't care if it's – What? That's not your name. That's not your name. You've got a grown-up woman in this room, do you hear? Or are you deaf too? You're not deaf too, are you? You're all deaf and dumb and blind, the lot of you. A bunch of cripples.

Pause.

RILEY This is a large room.

ROSE Never mind about the room. What do you know about this room? You know nothing about it. And you won't be staying in it long either. My luck. I get these creeps come in, smelling up my room. What do you want?

RILEY I want to see you.

ROSE Well you can't see me, can you? You're a blind man. An old, poor blind man. Aren't you? Can't see a dickeybird.

Pause.

They say I know you. That's an insult, for a start. Because I can tell you, I wouldn't know you to spit on, not from a mile off.

Pause.

Oh, these customers. They come in here and stink the place out. After a handout. I know all about it. And as for you saying you know me, what liberty is that? Telling my landlord too. Upsetting my landlord. What do you think you're up to? We're settled down here, cosy, quiet, and our landlord thinks the world of us,

38

we're his favourite tenants, and you come in and drive
him up the wall, and drag my name into it! What
did you mean by dragging my name into it, and my
husband's name? How did you know what our name
was?

Pause.

You've led him a dance, have you, this weekend?
You've got him going, have you? A poor, weak old
man, who lets a respectable house. Finished. Done for.
You push your way in and shove him about. And you
drag my name into it.

Pause.

Come on, then. You say you wanted to see me. Well,
I'm here. Spit it out or out you go. What do you want?

RILEY I have a message for you.

ROSE You've got what? How could you have a
message for me, Mister Riley, when I don't know you
and nobody knows I'm here and I don't know
anybody anyway. You think I'm an easy touch, don't
you? Well, why don't you give it up as a bad job? Get
off out of it. I've had enough of this. You're not only
a nut, you're a blind nut and you can get out the way
you came.

Pause.

What message? Who have you got a message from?
Who?

RILEY Your father wants you to come home.

39

Pause.

ROSE Home?

RILEY Yes.

ROSE Home? Go now. Come on. It's late. It's late.

RILEY To come home.

ROSE Stop it. I can't take it. What do you want? What do you want?

RILEY Come home, Sal.

Pause.

ROSE What did you call me?

RILEY Come home, Sal.

ROSE Don't call me that.

RILEY Come, now.

ROSE Don't call me that.

RILEY So now you're here.

ROSE Not Sal.

RILEY Now I touch you.

ROSE Don't touch me.

RILEY Sal.

ROSE I can't.

RILEY I want you to come home.

ROSE No.

RILEY With me.

ROSE I can't.

RILEY I waited to see you.

ROSE Yes.

RILEY Now I see you.

ROSE Yes.

RILEY Sal.

ROSE Not that.

RILEY So, now.

   Pause.

So, now.

ROSE I've been here.

RILEY Yes.

ROSE Long.

RILEY Yes.

ROSE The day is a hump. I never go out.

RILEY No.

ROSE I've been here.

RILEY Come home now, Sal.

   *She touches his eyes, the back of his head and his
   temples with her hands. Enter BERT.*

   *He stops at the door, then goes to the window and
   draws the curtains. It is dark. He comes to the
   centre of the room and regards the woman.*

41

BERT I got back all right.

ROSE (*going towards him*) Yes.

BERT I got back all right.

Pause.

ROSE Is it late?

BERT I had a good bowl down there.

Pause.

I drove her down, hard. They got it dark out.

ROSE Yes.

BERT Then I drove her back, hard. They got it very icy out.

ROSE Yes.

BERT But I drove her.

Pause.

I sped her.

Pause.

I caned her along. She was good. Then I got back. I could see the road all right. There was no cars. One there was. He wouldn't move. I bumped him. I got my road. I had all my way. There again and back. They shoved out of it. I kept on the straight. There was no mixing it. Not with her. She was good. She went with me. She don't mix it with me. I use my hand. Like that. I get hold of her. I go where I go. She took me there. She brought me back.

Pause.

I got back all right.

He takes the chair from the table and sits to the left of RILEY's *chair, close to it. He regards the* RILEY *for some moments. Then with his foot he lifts the armchair up.* RILEY *falls on to the floor. He rises slowly.*

RILEY Mr Hudd, your wife –

BERT Lice!

He strikes RILEY, *knocking him down, and then kicks his head against the gas-stove several times.* RILEY *lies still,* BERT *walks away.*

Silence.

ROSE *stands clutching her eyes.*

ROSE Can't see. I can't see. I can't see.

Blackout.

Curtain.

THE DUMB WAITER

The Dumb Waiter was first presented at Hampstead Theatre Club on 21 January 1960, with the following cast:

BEN   Nicholas Selby
GUS   George Tovey

Directed by James Roose-Evans

This production transferred to the Royal Court Theatre, London, on 8 March 1960, with the same cast.

The Dumb Waiter was produced for BBC Televison on 23 July 1985, with the following cast:

BEN   Colin Blakely
GUS   Kenneth Cranham

Directed by Kenneth Ives

Characters

BEN

GUS

Scene: a basement room. Two beds, flat against the back wall. A serving hatch, closed, between the beds. A door to the kitchen and lavatory, left. A door to a passage, right.

BEN *is lying on a bed, left, reading a paper.* GUS *is sitting on a bed, right, tying his shoelaces, with difficulty. Both are dressed in shirts, trousers and braces.*

Silence.

GUS *ties his laces, rises, yawns and begins to walk slowly to the door, left. He stops, looks down, and shakes his foot.*

BEN *lowers his paper and watches him.* GUS *kneels and unties his shoe-lace and slowly takes off the shoe. He looks inside it and brings out a flattened matchbox. He shakes it and examines it. Their eyes meet.* BEN *rattles his paper and reads.* GUS *puts the matchbox in his pocket and bends down to put on his shoe. He ties his lace, with difficulty.* BEN *lowers his paper and watches him.* GUS *walks to the door, left, stops, and shakes the other foot. He kneels, unties his shoe-lace, and slowly takes off the shoe. He looks inside it and brings out a flattened cigarette packet. He shakes it*

nd examines it. Their eyes meet. BEN *rattles his paper
and reads.* GUS *puts the packet in his pocket, bends
down, puts on his shoe and ties the lace.*

He wanders off, left.

BEN *slams the paper down on the bed and glares after
him. He picks up the paper and lies on his back,
reading.*

Silence.

*A lavatory chain is pulled twice off, left, but the lavatory
does not flush.*

Silence.

GUS *re-enters, left, and halts at the door, scratching his
head.*

BEN *slams down the paper.*

BEN Kaw!

He picks up the paper.

What about this? Listen to this.

He refers to the paper.

A man of eighty-seven wanted to cross the road. But
there was a lot of traffic, see? He couldn't see how he
was going to squeeze through. So he crawled under a
lorry.

GUS He what?

BEN He crawled under a lorry. A stationary lorry.

GUS No?

BEN The lorry started and ran over him.

GUS Go on!

BEN That's what it says here.

GUS Get away.

BEN It's enough to make you want to puke, isn't it?

GUS Who advised him to do a thing like that?

BEN A man of eighty-seven crawling under a lorry!

GUS It's unbelievable.

BEN It's down here in black and white.

GUS Incredible.

Silence. GUS *shakes his head and exits.* BEN *lies back and reads.*

The lavatory chain is pulled once off left, but the lavatory does not flush.

BEN *whistles at an item in the paper.*

GUS *re-enters.*

I want to ask you something.

BEN What are you doing out there?

GUS Well, I was just –

BEN What about the tea?

GUS I'm just going to make it.

BEN Well, go on, make it.

GUS Yes, I will. (*He sits in a chair. Ruminatively.*)
He's laid on some very nice crockery this time, I'll say
that. It's sort of striped. There's a white stripe.

  BEN *reads.*

It's very nice. I'll say that.

  BEN *turns the page.*

You know, sort of round the cup. Round the rim. All
the rest of it's black, you see. Then the saucer's black,
except for right in the middle, where the cup goes,
where it's white.

  BEN *reads.*

Then the plates are the same, you see. Only they've
got a black stripe – the plates – right across the middle.
Yes, I'm quite taken with the crockery.

BEN (*still reading*) What do you want plates for?
You're not going to eat.

GUS I've brought a few biscuits.

BEN Well, you'd better eat them quick.

GUS I always bring a few biscuits. Or a pie. You
know I can't drink tea without anything to eat.

BEN Well, make the tea then, will you? Time's getting
on.

  GUS *brings out the flattened cigarette packet and
  examines it.*

GUS You got any cigarettes? I think I've run out.

He throws the packet high up and leans forward to catch it.

I hope it won't be a long job, this one.

Aiming carefully, he flips the packet under his bed.

Oh, I wanted to ask you something.

BEN (*slamming his paper down*) Kaw!

GUS What's that?

BEN A child of eight killed a cat!

GUS Get away.

BEN It's a fact. What about that, eh? A child of eight killing a cat!

GUS How did he do it?

BEN It was a girl.

GUS How did she do it?

BEN She –

He picks up the paper and studies it.

It doesn't say.

GUS Why not?

BEN Wait a minute. It just says – 'Her brother, aged eleven, viewed the incident from the toolshed.'

GUS Go on!

BEN That's bloody ridiculous.

Pause.

GUS I bet he did it.

BEN Who?

GUS The brother.

BEN I think you're right.

Pause.

(*Slamming down the paper.*) What about that, eh? A kid of eleven killing a cat and blaming it on his little sister of eight! It's enough to -

He breaks off in disgust and seizes the paper.

GUS *rises.*

GUS What time is he getting in touch?

BEN *reads.*

What time is he getting in touch?

BEN What's the matter with you? It could be any time. Any time.

GUS (*moves to the foot of* BEN's *bed*) Well, I was going to ask you something.

BEN What?

GUS Have you noticed the time that tank takes to fill?

BEN What tank?

GUS In the lavatory.

BEN No. Does it?

GUS Terrible.

BEN Well, what about it?

GUS What do you think's the matter with it?

BEN Nothing.

GUS Nothing?

BEN It's got a deficient ballcock, that's all.

GUS A deficient what?

BEN Ballcock.

GUS No? Really?

BEN That's what I should say.

GUS Go on! That didn't occur to me.

GUS *wanders to his bed and presses the mattress.*

I didn't have a very restful sleep today, did you? It's not much of a bed. I could have done with another blanket too.

He catches sight of a picture on the wall.

Hello, what's this?

(*Peering at it.*) 'The First Eleven.' Cricketers. You seen this, Ben?

BEN (*reading*) What?

GUS The first eleven.

BEN What?

GUS There's a photo here of the first eleven.

BEN What first eleven?

GUS (*studying the photo*) It doesn't say.

BEN What about that tea?

GUS They all look a bit old to me.

GUS *wanders downstage, looks out front, then all about the room.*

I wouldn't like to live in this dump. I wouldn't mind if you had a window, you could see what it looked like outside.

BEN What do you want a window for?

GUS Well, I like to have a bit of a view, Ben. It whiles away the time.

He walks about the room.

I mean, you come into a place when it's still dark, you come into a room you've never seen before, you sleep all day, you do your job, and then you go away in the night again.

Pause.

I like to get a look at the scenery. You never get the chance in this job.

BEN You get your holidays, don't you?

GUS Only a fortnight.

BEN (*lowering the paper*) You kill me. Anyone would think you're working every day. How often do we do a job? Once a week? What are you complaining about?

GUS Yes, but we've got to be on tap though, haven't we? You can't move out of the house in case a call comes.

BEN You know what your trouble is?

GUS What?

BEN You haven't got any interests.

GUS I've got interests.

BEN What? Tell me one of your interests.

Pause.

GUS I've got interests.

BEN Look at me. What have I got?

GUS I don't know. What?

BEN I've got my woodwork. I've got my model boats. Have you ever seen me idle? I'm never idle. I know how to occupy my time, to its best advantage. Then when a call comes, I'm ready.

GUS Don't you ever get a bit fed up?

BEN Fed up? What with?

Silence.

BEN *reads.* GUS *feels in the pocket of his jacket, which hangs on the bed.*

GUS You got any cigarettes? I've run out.

The lavatory flushes off left.

There she goes.

GUS *sits on his bed.*

No, I mean, I say the crockery's good. It is. It's very nice. But that's about all I can say for this place. It's worse than the last one. Remember that last place we were in? Last time, where was it? At least there was a wireless there. No, honest. He doesn't seem to bother much about our comfort these days.

BEN When are you going to stop jabbering?

GUS You'd get rheumatism in a place like this, if you stay long.

BEN We're not staying long. Make the tea, will you? We'll be on the job in a minute.

GUS *picks up a small bag by his bed and brings out a packet of tea. He examines it and looks up.*

GUS Eh, I've been meaning to ask you.

BEN What the hell is it now?

GUS Why did you stop the car this morning, in the middle of that road?

BEN (*lowering the paper*) I thought you were asleep.

GUS I was, but I woke up when you stopped. You did stop, didn't you?

Pause.

In the middle of that road. It was still dark, don't you remember? I looked out. It was all misty. I thought perhaps you wanted to kip, but you were sitting up dead straight, like you were waiting for something.

BEN I wasn't waiting for anything.

GUS I must have fallen asleep again. What was all that about then? Why did you stop?

BEN (*picking up the paper*) We were too early.

GUS Early? (*He rises.*) What do you mean? We got the call, didn't we, saying we were to start right away. We did. We shoved out on the dot. So how could we be too early?

BEN (*quietly*) Who took the call, me or you?

GUS You.

BEN We were too early.

GUS Too early for what?

Pause.

You mean someone had to get out before we got in?

He examines the bedclothes.

I thought these sheets didn't look too bright. I thought they ponged a bit. I was too tired to notice when I got in this morning. Eh, that's taking a bit of a liberty, isn't it? I don't want to share my bed-sheets. I told you things were going down the drain. I mean, we've always had clean sheets laid on up till now. I've noticed it.

BEN How do you know those sheets weren't clean?

GUS What do you mean?

BEN How do you know they weren't clean? You've spent the whole day in them, haven't you?

GUS What, you mean it might be my pong? (*He sniffs sheets.*) Yes. (*He sits slowly on bed.*) It could be my pong, I suppose. It's difficult to tell. I don't really know what I pong like, that's the trouble.

BEN (*referring to the paper*) Kaw!

GUS Eh, Ben.

BEN Kaw!

GUS Ben.

BEN What?

GUS What town are we in? I've forgotten.

BEN I've told you. Birmingham.

GUS Go on!

He looks with interest about the room.

That's in the Midlands. The second biggest city in Great Britain. I'd never have guessed.

He snaps his fingers.

Eh, it's Friday today, isn't it? It'll be Saturday tomorrow.

BEN What about it?

GUS (*excited*) We could go and watch the Villa.

BEN They're playing away.

GUS No, are they? Caarr! What a pity.

BEN Anyway, there's no time. We've got to get straight back.

GUS Well, we have done in the past, haven't we?
Stayed over and watched a game, haven't we? For a
bit of relaxation.

BEN Things have tightened up, mate. They've
tightened up.

GUS *chuckles to himself.*

GUS I saw the Villa get beat in a cup-tie once. Who
was it against now? White shirts. It was one-all at
half-time. I'll never forget it. Their opponents won by
a penalty. Talk about drama. Yes, it was a disputed
penalty. Disputed. They got beat two-one, anyway,
because of it. You were there yourself.

BEN Not me.

GUS Yes, you were there. Don't you remember that
disputed penalty?

BEN No.

GUS He went down just inside the area. Then they
said he was just acting. I didn't think the other bloke
touched him myself. But the referee had the ball on
the spot.

BEN Didn't touch him! What are you talking about?
He laid him out flat!

GUS Not the Villa. The Villa don't play that sort of
game.

BEN Get out of it.

Pause.

63

GUS Eh, that must have been here, in Birmingham.

BEN What must?

GUS The Villa. That must have been here.

BEN They were playing away.

GUS Because you know who the other team was? It was the Spurs. It was Tottenham Hotspur.

BEN Well, what about it?

GUS We've never done a job in Tottenham.

BEN How do you know?

GUS I'd remember Tottenham.

> BEN *turns on his bed to look at him.*

BEN Don't make me laugh, will you?

> BEN *turns back and reads.* GUS *yawns and speaks through his yawn.*

GUS When's he going to get in touch?

> *Pause.*

Yes, I'd like to see another football match. I've always been an ardent football fan. Here, what about coming to see the Spurs tomorrow?

BEN (*tonelessly*) They're playing away.

GUS Who are?

BEN The Spurs.

GUS Then they might be playing here.

BEN Don't be silly.

GUS If they're playing away they might be playing
here. They might be playing the Villa.

BEN (*tonelessly*) But the Villa are playing away.

Pause. An envelope slides under the door, right.
GUS *sees it. He stands, looking at it.*

GUS Ben.

BEN Away. They're all playing away.

GUS Ben, look here.

BEN What?

GUS Look.

BEN *turns his head and sees the envelope. He*
stands.

BEN What's that?

GUS I don't know.

BEN Where did it come from?

GUS Under the door.

BEN Well, what is it?

GUS I don't know.

They stare at it.

BEN Pick it up.

GUS What do you mean?

BEN Pick it up!

GUS *slowly moves towards it, bends and picks it up.*

What is it?

GUS An envelope.

BEN Is there anything on it?

GUS No.

BEN Is it sealed?

GUS Yes.

BEN Open it.

GUS What?

BEN Open it!

GUS *opens it and looks inside.*

What's in it?

GUS *empties twelve matches into his hand.*

GUS Matches.

BEN Matches?

GUS Yes.

BEN Show it to me.

GUS *passes the envelope.* BEN *examines it.*

Nothing on it. Not a word.

GUS That's funny, isn't it?

BEN It came under the door?

GUS Must have done.

BEN Well, go on.

GUS Go on where?

BEN Open the door and see if you can catch anyone outside.

GUS Who, me?

BEN Go on!

GUS *stares at him, puts the matches in his pocket, goes to his bed and brings a revolver from under the pillow. He goes to the door, opens it, looks out and shuts it.*

GUS No one.

He replaces the revolver.

BEN What did you see?

GUS Nothing.

BEN They must have been pretty quick.

GUS *takes the matches from his pocket and looks at them.*

GUS Well, they'll come in handy.

BEN Yes.

GUS Won't they?

BEN Yes, you're always running out, aren't you?

GUS All the time.

BEN Well, they'll come in handy then.

GUS Yes.

BEN Won't they?

GUS Yes, I could do with them. I could do with them too.

BEN You could, eh?

GUS Yes.

BEN Why?

GUS We haven't got any.

BEN Well, you've got some now, haven't you?

GUS I can light the kettle now.

BEN Yes, you're always cadging matches. How many have you got there?

GUS About a dozen.

BEN Well, don't lose them. Red too. You don't even need a box.

GUS *probes his ear with a match.*

(*Slapping his hand.*) Don't waste them! Go on, go and light it.

GUS Eh?

BEN Go and light it.

GUS Light what?

BEN The kettle.

GUS You mean the gas.

BEN Who does?

GUS You do.

BEN (*his eyes narrowing*) What do you mean, I mean the gas?

GUS Well, that's what you mean, don't you? The gas.

BEN (*powerfully*) If I say go and light the kettle I mean go and light the kettle.

GUS How can you light a kettle?

BEN It's a figure of speech! Light the kettle. It's a figure of speech!

GUS I've never heard it.

BEN Light the kettle! It's common usage!

GUS I think you've got it wrong.

BEN (*menacing*) What do you mean?

GUS They say put on the kettle.

BEN (*taut*) Who says?

They stare at each other, breathing hard.

(*Deliberately.*) I have never in all my life heard anyone say put on the kettle.

GUS I bet my mother used to say it.

BEN Your mother? When did you last see your mother?

GUS I don't know, about –

69

HAROLD PINTER

BEN Well, what are you talking about your mother for?

They stare.

Gus, I'm not trying to be unreasonable. I'm just trying to point out something to you.

GUS Yes, but –

BEN Who's the senior partner here, me or you?

GUS You.

BEN I'm only looking after your interests, Gus. You've got to learn, mate.

GUS Yes, but I've never heard –

BEN (*vehemently*) Nobody says light the gas! What does the gas light?

GUS What does the gas –?

BEN (*grabbing him with two hands by the throat, at arm's length*) The kettle, you fool!

GUS *takes the hands from his throat.*

GUS All right, all right.

Pause.

BEN Well, what are you waiting for?

GUS I want to see if they light.

BEN What?

GUS The matches.

He takes out the flattened box and tries to strike.

No.

He throws the box under the bed. BEN *stares at him.*

GUS *raises his foot.*

Shall I try it on here?

BEN *stares.* GUS *strikes a match on his shoe. It lights.*

Here we are.

BEN (*wearily*) Put on the bloody kettle, for Christ's sake.

BEN *goes to his bed, but, realising what he has said, stops and half turns. They look at each other.* GUS *slowly exits, left.* BEN *slams his paper down on the bed and sits on it, head in hands.*

GUS (*entering*) It's going.

BEN What?

GUS The stove.

GUS *goes to his bed and sits.*

I wonder who it'll be tonight.

Silence.

Eh, I've been wanting to ask you something.

BEN (*putting his legs on the bed*) Oh, for Christ's sake.

GUS No. I was going to ask you something.

He rises and sits on BEN's *bed.*

BEN What are you sitting on my bed for?

GUS *sits.*

What's the matter with you? You're always asking me questions. What's the matter with you?

GUS Nothing.

BEN You never used to ask me so many damn questions. What's come over you?

GUS No, I was just wondering.

BEN Stop wondering. You've got a job to do . Why don't you just do it and shut up?

GUS That's what I was wondering about.

BEN What?

GUS The job.

BEN What job?

GUS (*tentatively*) I thought perhaps you might know something.

BEN *looks at him.*

I thought perhaps you –1 mean – have you got any idea – who it's going to be tonight?

BEN Who what's going to be?

They look at each other.

GUS (*at length*) Who it's going to be.

Silence.

BEN Are you feeling all right?

GUS Sure.

BEN Go and make the tea.

GUS Yes, sure.

> GUS *exits, left,* BEN *looks after him. He then takes his revolver from under the pillow and checks it for ammunition.* GUS *re-enters.*

The gas has gone out.

BEN Well, what about it?

GUS There's a meter.

BEN I haven't got any money.

GUS Nor have I.

BEN You'll have to wait.

GUS What for?

BEN For Wilson.

GUS He might not come. He might just send a message. He doesn't always come.

BEN Well, you'll have to do without it, won't you?

GUS Blimey.

BEN You'll have a cup of tea afterwards. What's the matter with you?

GUS I like to have one before.

BEN *holds the revolver up to the light and polishes it.*

BEN You'd better get ready anyway.

GUS Well, I don't know, that's a bit much, you know, for my money.

He picks up a packet of tea from the bed and throws it into the bag.

I hope he's got a shilling, anyway, if he comes. He's entitled to have. After all, it's his place, he could have seen there was enough gas for a cup of tea.

BEN What do you mean, it's his place?

GUS Well, isn't it?

BEN He's probably only rented it. It doesn't have to be his place.

GUS I know it's his place. I bet the whole house is. He's not even laying on any gas now either.

GUS *sits on his bed.*

It's his place all right. Look at all the other places. You go to this address, there's a key there, there's a teapot, there's never a soul in sight – (*He pauses.*) Eh, nobody ever hears a thing, have you ever thought of that? We never get any complaints, do we, too much noise or anything like that? You never see a soul, do you? – except the bloke who comes. You ever noticed that? I wonder if the walls are sound-proof. (*He touches the wall above his bed.*) Can't tell. All you do

74

is wait, eh? Half the time he doesn't even bother to put in an appearance, Wilson.

BEN Why should he? He's a busy man.

GUS (*thoughtfully*) I find him hard to talk to, Wilson. Do you know that, Ben?

BEN Scrub round it, will you?

Pause.

GUS There are a number of things I want to ask him. But I can never get round to it, when I see him.

Pause.

I've been thinking about the last one.

BEN What last one?

GUS That girl.

BEN *grabs the paper, which he reads.*

(*Rising, looking down at* BEN.) How many times have you read that paper?

BEN *slams the paper down and rises.*

BEN (*angrily*) What do you mean?

GUS I was just wondering how many times you'd –

BEN What are you doing, criticising me?

GUS No, I was just –

BEN You'll get a swipe round your earhole if you don't watch your step.

GUS Now look here, Ben –

BEN I'm not looking anywhere! (*He addresses the room.*) How many times have I –! A bloody liberty!

GUS I didn't mean that.

BEN You just get on with it, mate. Get on with it, that's all.

BEN *gets back on the bed.*

GUS I was just thinking about that girl, that's all.

GUS *sits on his bed.*

She wasn't much to look at, I know, but still. It was a mess though, wasn't it? What a mess. Honest, I can't remember a mess like that one. They don't seem to hold together like men, women. A looser texture, like. Didn't she spread, eh? She didn't half spread. Kaw! But I've been meaning to ask you.

BEN *sits up and clenches his eyes.*

Who clears up after we've gone? I'm curious about that. Who does the clearing up? Maybe they don't clear up. Maybe they just leave them there, eh? What do you think? How many jobs have we done? Blimey, I can't count them. What if they never clear anything up after we've gone.

BEN (*pityingly.*) You mutt. Do you think we're the only branch of this organisation? Have a bit of common. They got departments for everything.

GUS What cleaners and all?

76

BEN You birk!

GUS No, it was that girl made me start to think –

*There is a loud clatter and racket in the bulge of
wall between the beds, of something descending.
They grab their revolvers, jump up and face the
wall. The noise comes to a stop. Silence. They look
at each other.* BEN *gestures sharply towards the
wall.* GUS *approaches the wall slowly. He bangs it
with his revolver. It is hollow.* BEN *moves to the
head of his bed, his revolver cocked.* GUS *puts his
revolver on his bed and pats along the bottom of
the centre panel. He finds a rim. He lifts the panel.
Disclosed is a serving-hatch, a 'dumb waiter'. A
wide box is held by pulleys.* GUS *peers into the
box. He brings out a piece of paper.*

BEN What is it?

GUS You have a look at it.

BEN Read it.

GUS (*reading*) Two braised steak and chips. Two sago
puddings. Two teas without sugar.

BEN Let me see that. (*He takes the paper.*)

GUS (*to himself*) Two teas without sugar.

BEN Mmnn.

GUS What do you think of that?

BEN Well –

The box goes up. BEN *levels his revolver.*

GUS Give us a chance! They're in a hurry, aren't they?

BEN *re-reads the note.* GUS *looks over his shoulder.*

That's a bit – that's a bit funny, isn't it?

BEN (*quickly*) No. It's not funny. It probably used to be a café here, that's all. Upstairs. These places change hands very quickly.

GUS A café?

BEN Yes.

GUS What, you mean this was the kitchen, down here?

BEN Yes, they change hands overnight, these places. Go into liquidation. The people who run it, you know, they don't find it a going concern, they move out.

GUS You mean the people who ran this place didn't find it a going concern and moved out?

BEN Sure.

GUS Well, who's got it now?

Silence.

BEN What do you mean, who's got it now?

GUS Who's got it now? If they moved out, who moved in?

BEN Well, that all depends –

The box descends with a clatter and bang. BEN *levels his revolver.* GUS *goes to the box and brings out a piece of paper.*

GUS (*reading*) Soup of the day. Liver and onions. Jam tart.

A pause. GUS *looks at* BEN. BEN *takes the note and reads it. He walks slowly to the hatch.* GUS *follows.* BEN *looks into the hatch but not up it.* GUS *puts his hand on* BEN's *shoulder.* BEN *throws it off.* GUS *puts his finger to his mouth. He leans on the hatch and swiftly looks up it.* BEN *flings him away in alarm.* BEN *looks at the note. He throws his revolver on the bed and speaks with decision.*

BEN We'd better send something up.

GUS Eh?

BEN We'd better send something up.

GUS Oh! Yes. Yes. Maybe you're right.

They are both relieved at the decision.

BEN (*purposefully*) Quick! What have you got in that bag?

GUS Not much.

GUS goes to the hatch and shouts up it.

Wait a minute!

BEN Don't do that!

GUS examines the contents of the bag and brings them out, one by one.

GUS Biscuits. A bar of chocolate. Half a pint of milk.

BEN That all?

GUS   Packet of tea.

BEN   Good.

GUS   We can't send the tea. That's all the tea we've got.

BEN   Well, there's no gas. You can't do anything with it, can you?

GUS   Maybe they can send us down a bob.

BEN   What else is there?

GUS   (*reaching into bag*) One Eccles cake.

BEN   One Eccles cake?

GUS   Yes.

BEN   You never told me you had an Eccles cake.

GUS   Didn't I?

BEN   Why only one? Didn't you bring one for me?

GUS   I didn't think you'd be keen.

BEN   Well, you can't send up one Eccles cake, anyway.

GUS   Why not?

BEN   Fetch one of those plates.

GUS   All right.

GUS *goes towards the door, left, and stops.*

Do you mean I can keep the Eccles cake then?

BEN   Keep it?

GUS Well, they don't know we've got it, do they?

BEN That's not the point.

GUS Can't I keep it?

BEN No, you can't. Get the plate.

> GUS *exits, left.* BEN *looks in the bag. He brings out a packet of crisps. Enter* GUS *with a plate.*

(*Accusingly, holding up the crisps.*) Where did these come from?

GUS What?

BEN Where did these crisps come from?

GUS Where did you find them?

BEN (*hitting him on the shoulder*) You're playing a dirty game, my lad!

GUS I only eat those with beer!

BEN Well, where were you going to get the beer?

GUS I was saving them till I did.

BEN I'll remember this. Put everything on the plate.

> *They pile everything on to the plate. The box goes up without the plate.*

Wait a minute!

> *They stand.*

GUS It's gone up.

BEN It's all your stupid fault, playing about!

GUS What do we do now?

BEN We'll have to wait till it comes down.

BEN puts the plate on the bed, puts on his shoulder holster, and starts to put on his tie.

You'd better get ready.

GUS goes to his bed, puts on his tie, and starts to fix his holster.

GUS Hey, Ben.

BEN What?

GUS What's going on here?

Pause.

BEN What do you mean?

GUS How can this be a café?

BEN It used to be a café.

GUS Have you seen the gas stove?

BEN What about it?

GUS It's only got three rings.

BEN So what?

GUS Well, you couldn't cook much on three rings, not for a busy place like this.

BEN (*irritably*) That's why the service is slow!

BEN puts on his waistcoat.

GUS Yes, but what happens when we're not here? What do they do then? All these menus coming down and nothing going up. It might have been going on like this for years.

BEN *brushes his jacket.*

What happens when we go?

BEN *puts on his jacket.*

They can't do much business.

The box descends. They turn about. GUS *goes to the hatch and brings out a note.*

GUS (*reading*) Macaroni Pastitsio. Ormitha Macarounada.

BEN What was that?

GUS Macaroni Pastitsio. Ormitha Macarounada.

BEN Greek dishes.

GUS No.

BEN That's right.

GUS That's pretty high class.

BEN Quick before it goes up.

GUS *puts the plate in the box.*

GUS (*calling up the hatch*) Three McVitie and Price! One Lyons Red Label! One Smith's Crisps! One Eccles cake! One Fruit and Nut!

BEN Cadbury's.

GUS (*up the hatch*) Cadbury's!

BEN (*handing the milk*) One bottle of milk.

GUS (*up the hatch*) One bottle of milk! Half a pint! (*He looks at the label.*) Express Dairy! (*He puts the bottle in the box.*)

   The box goes up.

Just did it.

BEN You shouldn't shout like that.

GUS Why not?

BEN It isn't done.

   BEN *goes to his bed.*

Well, that should be all right, anyway, for the time being.

GUS You think so, eh?

BEN Get dressed, will you? It'll be any minute now.

   GUS *puts on his waistcoat.* BEN *lies down and looks up at the ceiling.*

GUS This is some place. No tea and no biscuits.

BEN Eating makes you lazy, mate. You're getting lazy, you know that? You don't want to get slack on your job.

GUS Who me?

BEN Slack, mate, slack.

GUS Who me? Slack?

BEN Have you checked your gun? You haven't even checked your gun. It looks disgraceful, anyway. Why don't you ever polish it?

GUS rubs his revolver on the sheet. BEN takes out a pocket mirror and straightens his tie.

GUS I wonder where the cook is. They must have had a few, to cope with that. Maybe they had a few more gas stoves. Eh! Maybe there's another kitchen along the passage.

BEN Of course there is! Do you know what it takes to make an Ormitha Macarounada?

GUS No, what?

BEN An Ormitha –! Buck your ideas up, will you?

GUS Takes a few cooks, eh?

GUS puts his revolver in its holster.

The sooner we're out of this place the better.

He puts on his jacket.

Why doesn't he get in touch? I feel like I've been here years. (*He takes his revolver out of its holster to check the ammunition.*) We've never let him down though, have we? We've never let him down. I was thinking only the other day, Ben. We're reliable, aren't we?

He puts his revolver back in its holster.

Still, I'll be glad when it's over tonight.

He brushes his jacket.

I hope the bloke's not going to get excited tonight, or anything. I'm feeling a bit off. I've got a splitting headache.

Silence.

The box descends, BEN *jumps up.*

GUS *collects the note.*

(*Reading.*) One Bamboo Shoots, Water Chestnuts and Chicken. One Char Siu and Beansprouts.

BEN Beansprouts?

GUS Yes.

BEN Blimey.

GUS I wouldn't know where to begin.

He looks back at the box. The packet of tea is inside it. He picks it up.

They've sent back the tea.

BEN (*anxious*) What'd they do that for?

GUS Maybe it isn't tea-time.

The box goes up. Silence.

BEN (*throwing the tea on the bed, and speaking urgently*) Look here. We'd better tell them.

GUS Tell them what?

BEN That we can't do it, we haven't got it.

GUS All right then.

BEN Lend us your pencil. We'll write a note.

GUS, *turning for a pencil, suddenly discovers the speaking-tube, which hangs on the right wall of the hatch facing his bed.*

GUS What's this?

BEN What?

GUS This.

BEN (*examining it*) This? It's a speaking-tube.

GUS How long has that been there?

BEN Just the job. We should have used it before, instead of shouting up there.

GUS Funny I never noticed it before.

BEN Well, come on.

GUS What do you do?

BEN See that? That's a whistle.

GUS What, this?

BEN Yes, take it out. Pull it out.

GUS *does so.*

That's it.

GUS What do we do now?

BEN Blow into it.

GUS Blow?

BEN It whistles up there if you blow. Then they know you want to speak. Blow.

GUS *blows. Silence.*

GUS (*tube at mouth*) I can't hear a thing.

BEN Now you speak! Speak into it!

GUS *looks at* BEN, *then speaks into the tube.*

GUS The larder's bare!

BEN Give me that!

He grabs the tube and puts it to his mouth.

(*Speaking with great deference.*) Good evening. I'm sorry to – bother you, but we just thought we'd better let you know that we haven't got anything left. We sent up all we had. There's no more food down here.

He brings the tube slowly to his ear.

What?

To mouth.

What?

To ear. He listens. To mouth.

No, all we had we sent up.

To ear. He listens. To mouth.

Oh, I'm very sorry to hear that.

To ear. He listens. To GUS.

The Eccles cake was stale.

He listens. To GUS.

The chocolate was melted.

He listens. To GUS.

88

The milk was sour.

GUS What about the crisps?

BEN (*listening*) The biscuits were mouldy.

He glares at GUS. *Tube to mouth.*

Well, we're very sorry about that.

Tube to ear.

What?

To mouth.

What?

To ear.

Yes. Yes.

To mouth.

Yes certainly. Certainly. Right away.

To ear. The voice has ceased. He hangs up the tube.

(*Excitedly.*) Did you hear that?

GUS What?

BEN You know what he said? Light the kettle! Not put on the kettle! Not light the gas! But light the kettle!

GUS How can we light the kettle?

BEN What do you mean?

GUS There's no gas.

BEN (*Clapping hand to head*) Now what do we do?

GUS What did he want us to light the kettle for?

BEN For tea. He wanted a cup of tea.

GUS He wanted a cup of tea! What about me? I've been wanting a cup of tea all night!

BEN (*despairingly*) What do we do now?

GUS What are we supposed to drink?

BEN *sits on his bed, staring.*

What about us?

BEN *sits.*

I'm thirsty too. I'm starving. And he wants a cup of tea. That beats the band, that does.

BEN *lets his head sink on to his chest.*

I could do with a bit of sustenance myself. What about you? You look as if you could do with something too.

GUS *sits on his bed.*

We send him up all we've got and he's not satisfied. No, honest, it's enough to make the cat laugh. Why did you send him up all that stuff? (*Thoughtfully.*) Why did I send it up?

Pause.

Who knows what he's got upstairs? He's probably got a salad bowl. They must have something up there.

They won't get much from down here. You notice
they didn't ask for any salads? They've probably got a
salad bowl up there. Cold meat, radishes, cucumbers.
Watercress. Roll mops.

Pause.

Hardboiled eggs.

Pause.

The lot. They've probably got a crate of beer too.
Probably eating my crisps with a pint of beer now.
Didn't have anything to say about those crisps, did
he? They do all right, don't worry about that. You
don't think they're just going to sit there and wait for
stuff to come up from down here, do you? That'll get
them nowhere.

Pause.

They do all right.

Pause.

And he wants a cup of tea.

Pause.

That's past a joke, in my opinion.

He looks over at BEN, *rises, and goes to him.*

What's the matter with you? You don't look too
bright. I feel like an Alka-Seltzer myself.

BEN *sits up.*

BEN (*in a low voice*) Time's getting on.

91

GUS I know. I don't like doing a job on an empty stomach.

BEN (*wearily*) Be quiet a minute. Let me give you your instructions.

GUS What for? We always do it the same way, don't we?

BEN Let me give you your instructions.

> GUS *sighs and sits next to* BEN *on the bed. The instructions are stated and repeated automatically.*

When we get the call, you go over and stand behind the door.

GUS Stand behind the door.

BEN If there's a knock on the door you don't answer it.

GUS If there's a knock on the door I don't answer it.

BEN But there won't be a knock on the door.

GUS So I won't answer it.

BEN When the bloke comes in –

GUS When the bloke comes in –

BEN Shut the door behind him.

GUS Shut the door behind him.

BEN Without divulging your presence.

GUS Without divulging my presence.

BEN He'll see me and come towards me.

GUS He'll see you and come towards you.

BEN He won't see you.

GUS (*absently*) Eh?

BEN He won't see you.

GUS He won't see me.

BEN But he'll see me.

GUS He'll see you.

BEN He won't know you're there.

GUS He won't know you're there.

BEN He won't know you're there.

GUS He won't know I'm there.

BEN I take out my gun.

GUS You take out your gun.

BEN He stops in his tracks.

GUS He stops in his tracks.

BEN If he turns round –

GUS If he turns round –

BEN You're there.

GUS I'm here.

   BEN *frowns and presses his forehead.*

You've missed something out.

BEN I know. What?

GUS I haven't taken my gun out, according to you.

BEN You take your gun out –

GUS After I've closed the door.

BEN After you've closed the door.

GUS You've never missed that out before, you know that?

BEN When he sees you behind him –

GUS Me behind him –

BEN And me in front of him –

GUS And you in front of him –

BEN He'll feel uncertain –

GUS Uneasy.

BEN He won't know what to do.

GUS So what will he do?

BEN He'll look at me and he'll look at you.

GUS We won't say a word.

BEN We'll look at him.

GUS He won't say a word.

BEN He'll look at us.

GUS And we'll look at him.

BEN Nobody says a word.

Pause.

GUS What do we do if it's a girl?

BEN We do the same.

GUS Exactly the same?

BEN Exactly.

Pause.

GUS We don't do anything different?

BEN We do exacdy the same.

GUS Oh.

GUS *rises, and shivers.*

Excuse me.

He exits through the door on the left. BEN *remains sitting on the bed, still. The lavatory chain is pulled once off left, but the lavatory does not flush.*

Silence.

GUS *re-enters and stops inside the door, deep in thought. He looks at* BEN, *then walks slowly across to his own bed. He is troubled. He stands, thinking. He turns and looks at* BEN. *He moves a few paces towards him.*

(*Slowly in a low, tense voice.*) Why did he send us matches if he knew there was no gas?

Silence.

BEN *stares in front of him.* GUS *crosses to the left side of* BEN, *to the foot of his bed, to get to his other ear.*

95

BEN Why did he send us matches if he knew there was no gas?

BEN *looks up.*

Why did he do that?

BEN Who?

GUS Who sent us those matches?

BEN What are you talking about?

GUS *stares down at him.*

GUS (*thickly*) Who is it upstairs?

BEN (*nervously*) What's one thing to do with another?

GUS Who is it, though?

BEN What's one thing to do with another?

BEN *fumbles for his paper on the bed.*

GUS I asked you a question.

BEN Enough!

GUS (*with growing agitation*) I asked you before. Who moved in? I asked you. You said the people who had it before moved out. Well, who moved in?

BEN (*hunched*) Shut up.

GUS I told you, didn't I?

BEN (*standing*) Shut up!

GUS (*feverishly*) I told you before who owned this place, didn't I? I told you.

BEN *hits him viciously on the shoulder.*

I told you who ran this place, didn't I?

BEN *hits him viciously on the shoulder.*

(*Violently.*) Well, what's he playing all these games for? That's what I want to know. What's he doing it for?

BEN What games?

GUS (*passionately, advancing*) What's he doing it for? We've been through our tests, haven't we? We got right through our tests, years ago, didn't we? We took them together, don't you remember, didn't we? We've proved ourselves before now, haven't we? We've always done our job. What's he doing all this for? What's the idea? What's he playing these games for?

The box in the shaft comes down behind them. The noise is this time accompanied by a shrill whistle, as it falls. GUS *rushes to the hatch and seizes the note.*

(*Reading.*) Scampi!

He crumples the note, picks up the tube, takes out the whistle, blows and speaks.

We've got nothing left! Nothing! Do you understand?

BEN *seizes the tube and flings* GUS *away. He follows* GUS *and slaps him hard, back-handed, across the chest.*

BEN Stop it! You maniac!

GUS But you heard!

BEN (*savagely*) That's enough! I'm warning you!

Silence.

BEN *hangs the tube. He goes to his bed and lies down. He picks up his paper and reads.*

Silence.

The box goes up.

They turn quickly, their eyes meet. BEN *turns to his paper.*

Slowly GUS *goes back to his bed, and sits.*

Silence.

The hatch falls back into place.

They turn quickly, their eyes meet. BEN *turns back to his paper.*

Silence.

BEN *throws his paper down.*

BEN Kaw!

He picks up the paper and looks at it.

Listen to this!

Pause.

What about that, eh?

Pause.

Kaw!

Pause.

Have you ever heard such a thing?

GUS   (*dully*) Go on!

BEN   It's true.

GUS   Get away.

BEN   It's down here in black and white.

GUS   (*very low*) Is that a fact?

BEN   Can you imagine it.

GUS   It's unbelievable.

BEN   It's enough to make you want to puke, isn't it?

GUS   (*almost inaudible*) Incredible.

BEN *shakes his head. He puts the paper down and rises. He fixes the revolver in his holster.*

GUS *stands up. He goes towards the door on the left.*

BEN   Where are you going?

GUS   I'm going to have a glass of water.

He exits. BEN *brushes dust off his clothes and shoes. The whistle in the speaking-tube blows. He goes to it, takes the whistle out and puts the tube to his ear. He listens. He puts it to his mouth.*

BEN   Yes.

To ear. He listens. To mouth.

Straight away. Right.

To ear. He listens. To mouth.

Sure we're ready.

To ear. He listens. To mouth.

Understood. Repeat. He has arrived and will be coming in straight away. The normal method to be employed. Understood.

To ear. He listens. To mouth.

Sure we're ready.

To ear. He listens. To mouth.

Right.

He hangs the tube up.

Gus!

He takes out a comb and combs his hair, adjusts his jacket to diminish the bulge of the revolver. The lavatory flushes off left. BEN *goes quickly to the door, left.*

Gus!

The door right opens sharply, BEN *turns, his revolver levelled at the door.*

GUS *stumbles in.*

He is stripped of his jacket, waistcoat, tie, holster and revolver. He stops, body stooping, his arms at his sides. He raises his head and looks at BEN.

A long silence.

They stare at each other.

Curtain.

A SLIGHT ACHE

A Slight Ache first published by
Methuen & Co. 1961
© FPinter Limited, 1961, 1966, 1968

A Slight Ache was first performed on the BBC Third Programme on 9 July 1959, with the following cast:

EDWARD   Maurice Denham
FLORA   Vivien Merchant

Directed by Donald McWhinnie

The play was first presented on stage by Michael Codron at the Arts Theatre, London, on 18 January 1961, and subsequently at the Criterion Theatre, with the following cast:

EDWARD   Emlyn Williams
FLORA   Alison Leggat
MATCHSELLER   Richard Briers

Directed by Donald McWhinnie

It was revived at the Young Vic in June 1987 with the following cast:

EDWARD   Barry Foster
FLORA   Jill Johnson
MATCHSELLER   Malcolm Ward

Directed by Kevin Billington

It was revived on the Lyttelton stage of the National Theatre, London, on 13 September 2008, in a double bill with *Landscape*. The cast was as follows:

EDWARD   Simon Russell Beale
FLORA   Clare Skinner
MATCHSELLER   Jamie Beamish

Directed by Iqbal Khan

Characters

EDWARD

FLORA

MATCHSELLER

A country house, with two chairs and a table laid for breakfast at the centre of the stage. These will later be removed and the action will be focused on the scullery on the right and the study on the left, both indicated with a minimum of scenery and props. A large well-kept garden is suggested at the back of the stage with flower beds, trimmed hedges, etc. The garden gate, which cannot be seen by the audience, is off right.

FLORA *and* EDWARD *are discovered sitting at the breakfast table.* EDWARD *is reading the paper.*

FLORA Have you noticed the honeysuckle this morning?

EDWARD The what?

FLORA The honeysuckle.

EDWARD Honeysuckle? Where?

FLORA By the back gate, Edward.

EDWARD Is that honeysuckle? I thought it was . . . convolvulus, or something.

FLORA But you know it's honeysuckle.

EDWARD I tell you I thought it was convolvulus.

Pause.

FLORA It's in wonderful flower.

EDWARD I must look.

FLORA The whole garden's in flower this morning. The clematis. The convolvulus. Everything. I was out at seven. I stood by the pool.

EDWARD Did you say – that the convolvulus was in flower?

FLORA Yes.

EDWARD But good God, you just denied there was any.

FLORA I was talking about the honeysuckle.

EDWARD About the what?

FLORA (*calmly*) Edward – you know that shrub outside the toolshed . . .

EDWARD Yes, yes.

FLORA That's convolvulus.

EDWARD That?

FLORA Yes.

EDWARD Oh

> *Pause.*

I thought it was japonica.

FLORA Oh, good Lord no.

EDWARD Pass the teapot, please.

> *Pause. She pours tea for him.*

I don't see why I should be expected to distinguish between these plants. It's not my job.

FLORA You know perfectly well what grows in your garden.

EDWARD Quite the contrary. It is clear that I don't.

Pause.

FLORA (*rising*) I was up at seven. I stood by the pool. The peace. And everything in flower. The sun was up. You should work in the garden this morning. We could put up the canopy.

EDWARD The canopy? What for?

FLORA To shade you from the sun.

EDWARD Is there a breeze?

FLORA A light one.

EDWARD It's very treacherous weather, you know.

Pause.

FLORA Do you know what today is?

EDWARD Saturday.

FLORA It's the longest day of the year.

EDWARD Really?

FLORA It's the height of summer today.

EDWARD Cover the marmalade.

FLORA What?

EDWARD Cover the pot. There's a wasp. (*He puts the paper down on the table.*) Don't move. Keep still. What are you doing?

FLORA Covering the pot.

EDWARD Don't move. Leave it. Keep still.

Pause.

Give me the *Telegraph*.

FLORA Don't hit it. It'll bite.

EDWARD Bite? What do you mean, bite? Keep still

Pause.

It's landing.

FLORA It's going in the pot.

EDWARD Give me the lid.

FLORA It's in.

EDWARD Give me the lid.

FLORA I'll do it.

EDWARD Give it to me! Now . . . Slowly . . .

FLORA What are you doing?

EDWARD Be quiet. Slowly . . . carefully . . . on . . . the . . . pot! Ha-ha-ha. Very good.

He sits on a chair to the right of the table.

FLORA Now he's in the marmalade.

EDWARD Precisely.

Pause. She sits on a chair to the left of the table and reads the Telegraph.

FLORA Can you hear him?

EDWARD Hear him?

FLORA Buzzing.

EDWARD Nonsense. How can you hear him? It's an earthenware lid

FLORA He's becoming frantic.

EDWARD Rubbish. Take it away from the table.

FLORA What shall I do with it?

EDWARD Put it in the sink and drown it.

FLORA It'll fly out and bite me.

EDWARD It will not bite you! Wasps don't bite. Anyway, it won't fly out. It's stuck. It'll drown where it is, in the marmalade.

FLORA What a horrible death.

EDWARD On the contrary

Pause.

FLORA Have you got something in your eyes?

EDWARD No. Why do you ask?

FLORA You keep clenching them, blinking them.

EDWARD I have a slight ache in them.

FLORA Oh, dear.

EDWARD Yes, a slight ache. As if I hadn't slept.

FLORA Did you sleep, Edward?

EDWARD Of course I slept. Uninterrupted. As always.

FLORA And yet you feel tired.

EDWARD I didn't say I felt tired. I merely said I had a slight ache in my eyes.

FLORA Why is that, then?

EDWARD I really don't know

Pause.

FLORA Oh goodness!

EDWARD What is it?

FLORA I can see it. It's trying to come out.

EDWARD How can it?

FLORA Through the hole. It's trying to crawl out, through the spoon-hole.

EDWARD Mmmnn, yes. Can't do it, of course.

Silent pause.

Well, let's kill it, for goodness' sake.

FLORA Yes, let's. But how?

EDWARD Bring it out on the spoon and squash it on a plate.

FLORA It'll fly away. It'll bite.

EDWARD If you don't stop saying that word I shall leave this table.

FLORA But wasps do bite.

EDWARD They don't bite. They sting. It's snakes . . . that bite.

FLORA What about horseflies?

Pause.

EDWARD (*to himself*) Horseflies suck

Pause.

FLORA (*tentatively*) If we . . . if we wait long enough, I suppose it'll choke to death. It'll suffocate in the marmalade.

EDWARD (*briskly*) You do know I've got work to do this morning, don't you? I can't spend the whole day worrying about a wasp.

FLORA Well, kill it.

EDWARD You want to kill it?

FLORA Yes.

EDWARD Very well. Pass me the hot water jug.

FLORA What are you going to do?

EDWARD Scald it. Give it to me.

She hands him the jug. Pause.

Now . . .

FLORA (*whispering*) Do you want me to lift the lid?

EDWARD No, no, no. I'll pour down the spoon hole. Right . . . down the spoon-hole.

FLORA Listen!

EDWARD What?

FLORA It's buzzing.

EDWARD Vicious creatures

Pause.

Curious, but I don't remember seeing any wasps at all, all summer, until now. I'm sure I don't know why. I mean, there must have been wasps.

FLORA Please.

EDWARD This couldn't be the first wasp, could it?

FLORA Please.

EDWARD The first wasp of summer? No. It's not possible.

FLORA Edward.

EDWARD Mmmmnnn?

FLORA Kill it.

EDWARD Ah, yes. Tilt the pot. Tilt. Aah . . . down here . . . right down . . . blinding him . . . that's . . . it.

FLORA Is it?

EDWARD Lift the lid. All right, I will. There he is! Dead. What a monster. (*He squashes it on a plate.*)

FLORA What an awful experience.

EDWARD What a beautiful day it is. Beautiful. I think

I shall work in the garden this morning. Where's that canopy?

FLORA It's in the shed.

EDWARD Yes, we must get it out. My goodness, just look at that sky. Not a cloud. Did you say it was the longest day of the year today?

FLORA Yes.

EDWARD Ah, it's a good day. I feel it in my bones. In my muscles. I think I'll stretch my legs in a minute. Down to the pool. My God, look at that flowering shrub over there. Clematis. What a wonderful . . . (*He stops suddenly.*)

FLORA What?

Pause.

Edward, what is it?

Pause.

Edward . . .

EDWARD (*thickly*) He's there.

FLORA Who?

EDWARD (*low, murmuring*) Blast and damn it, he's there, he's there at the back gate

FLORA Let me see.

She moves over to him to look. Pause

(*Lightly.*) Oh, it's the matchseller.

EDWARD He's back again.

FLORA But he's always there.

EDWARD Why? What is he doing there?

FLORA But he's never disturbed you, has he? The man's been standing there for weeks. You've never mentioned it.

EDWARD What is he doing there?

FLORA He's selling matches, of course.

EDWARD It's ridiculous. What's the time?

FLORA Half past nine.

EDWARD What in God's name is he doing with a tray full of matches at half past nine in the morning?

FLORA He arrives at seven o'clock.

EDWARD Seven o'clock?

FLORA He's always there at seven.

EDWARD Yes, but you've never . . . actually seen him arrive?

FLORA No, I . . .

EDWARD Well, how do you know he's . . . not been standing there all night?

 Pause.

FLORA Do you find him interesting, Edward?

EDWARD (*casually*) Interesting? No. No, I . . . don't find him interesting.

116

FLORA He's a very nice old man, really.

EDWARD You've spoken to him?

FLORA No. No, I haven't spoken to him. I've nodded.

EDWARD (*pacing up and down*) For two months he's been standing on that spot, do you realise that? Two months. I haven't been able to step outside the back gate.

FLORA Why on earth not?

EDWARD (*to himself*) It used to give me great pleasure, such pleasure, to stroll along through the long grass, out through the back gate, pass into the lane. That pleasure is now denied me. It's my own house, isn't it? It's my own gate.

FLORA I really can't understand this, Edward.

EDWARD Damn. And do you know I've never seen him sell one box? Not a box. It's hardly surprising. He's on the wrong road. It's not a road at all. What is it? It's a lane, leading to the monastery. Off everybody's route. Even the monks take a short cut to the village, when they want to go . . . to the village. No one goes up it. Why doesn't he stand on the main road if he wants to sell matches, by the front gate? The whole thing's preposterous.

FLORA (*going over to him*) I don't know why you're getting so excited about it. He's a quiet, harmless old man, going about his business. He's quite harmless.

EDWARD I didn't say he wasn't harmless. Of course he's harmless. How could he be other than harmless?

117

Fade out and silence.

FLORA's *voice, far in the house, drawing nearer.*

FLORA (*off*) Edward, where are you? Edward? Where are you, Edward?

She appears.

Edward?

Edward, what are you doing in the scullery?

EDWARD (*looking through the scullery window*) Doing?

FLORA I've been looking everywhere for you. I put up the canopy ages ago. I came back and you were nowhere to be seen. Have you been out?

EDWARD No.

FLORA Where have you been?

EDWARD Here.

FLORA I looked in your study. I even went into the attic.

EDWARD (*tonelessly*) What would I be doing in the attic?

FLORA I couldn't imagine what had happened to you. Do you know it's twelve o'clock?

EDWARD Is it?

FLORA I even went to the bottom of the garden, to see if you were in the toolshed.

118

EDWARD (*tonelessly*) What would I be doing in the toolshed?

FLORA You must have seen me in the garden. You can see through this window.

EDWARD Only part of the garden.

FLORA Yes.

EDWARD Only a corner of the garden. A very small corner.

FLORA What are you doing in here?

EDWARD Nothing. I was digging out some notes, that's all.

FLORA Notes?

EDWARD For my essay.

FLORA Which essay?

EDWARD My essay on space and time.

FLORA But . . . I've never . . . I don't know that one.

EDWARD You don't know it?

FLORA I thought you were writing one about the Belgian Congo.

EDWARD I've been engaged on the dimensionality and continuity of space . . . and time . . . for years.

FLORA And the Belgian Congo?

EDWARD (*shortly*) Never mind about the Belgian Congo.

Pause.

FLORA But you don't keep notes in the scullery.

EDWARD You'd be surprised. You'd be highly surprised.

FLORA Good Lord, what's that? Is that a bullock let loose? No. It's the matchseller! My goodness, you can see him . . . through the hedge. He looks bigger. Have you been watching him? He looks . . . like a bullock.

Pause.

Edward?

Pause.

(*Moving over to him.*) Are you coming outside? I've put up the canopy. You'll miss the best of the day. You can have an hour before lunch.

EDWARD I've no work to do this morning.

FLORA What about your essay? You don't intend to stay in the scullery all day, do you?

EDWARD Get out. Leave me alone

A slight pause.

FLORA Really Edward. You've never spoken to me like that in all your life.

EDWARD Yes, I have.

FLORA Oh, Weddie. Beddie-Weddie . . .

EDWARD Do not call me that!

FLORA Your eyes are bloodshot.

EDWARD Damn it.

FLORA It's too dark in here to peer . . .

EDWARD Damn.

FLORA It's so bright outside.

EDWARD Damn.

FLORA And it's dark in here.

Pause.

EDWARD Christ blast it!

FLORA You're frightened of him.

EDWARD I'm not.

FLORA You're frightened of a poor old man. Why?

EDWARD I am not!

FLORA He's a poor, harmless old man.

EDWARD Aaah my eyes.

FLORA Let me bathe them.

EDWARD Keep away

Pause.

(*Slowly.*) I want to speak to that man. I want to have a word with him

Pause.

It's quite absurd, of course. I really can't tolerate something so . . . absurd, right on my doorstep. I shall not tolerate it. He's sold nothing all morning. No one passed. Yes. A monk passed. A non-smoker. In a loose garment. It's quite obvious he was a non-smoker but still, the man made no effort. He made no effort to clinch a sale, to rid himself of one of his cursed boxes. His one chance, all morning, and he made no effort.

Pause.

I haven't wasted my time. I've hit, in fact, upon the truth. He's not a matchseller at all. The bastard isn't a matchseller at all. Curious I never realised that before. He's an impostor. I watched him very closely. He made no move towards the monk. As for the monk, the monk made no move towards him. The monk was moving along the lane. He didn't pause, or halt, or in any way alter his step. As for the matchseller – how ridiculous to go on calling him by that title. What a farce. No, there is something very false about that man. I intend to get to the bottom of it. I'll soon get rid of him He can go and ply his trade somewhere else. Instead of standing like a bullock . . . a bullock, outside my back gate.

FLORA But if he isn't a matchseller, what is his trade?

EDWARD We'll soon find out.

FLORA You're going out to speak to him?

EDWARD Certainly not! Go out to *him*? Certainly . . . not. I'll invite him in here. Into my study. Then we'll . . . get to the bottom of it.

FLORA Why don't you call the police and have him removed?

He laughs. Pause.

Why don't you call the police, Edward? You could say
he was a public nuisance. Although I . . . I can't say
I find him a nuisance.

EDWARD Call him in.

FLORA Me?

EDWARD Go out and call him in

FLORA Are you serious?

Pause.

Edward, I could call the police. Or even the vicar.

EDWARD Go and get him.

She goes out. Silence.

EDWARD *waits.*

FLORA (*in the garden*) Good morning.

Pause.

We haven't met. I live in this house here. My husband
and I.

Pause.

I wonder if you could . . . would you care for a cup
of tea?

Pause.

Or a glass of lemon? It must be so dry, standing here.

Pause.

123

Would you like to come inside for a little while? It's much cooler. There's something we'd very much like to . . . tell you, that will benefit you. Could you spare a few moments? We won't keep you long.

Pause.

Might I buy your tray of matches, do you think? We've run out, completely, and we always keep a very large stock. It happens that way, doesn't it? Well, we can discuss it inside. Do come. This way. Ah now, do come. Our house is full of curios, you know. My husband's been rather a collector. We have goose for lunch. Do you care for goose?

She moves to the gate.

Come and have lunch with us. This way. That's . . . right. May I take your arm? There's a good deal of nettle inside the gate.

The MATCHSELLER *appears.*

Here. This way. Mind now. Isn't it beautiful weather? It's the longest day of the year today.

Pause.

That's honeysuckle. And that's convolvulus. There's clematis. And do you see that plant by the conservatory? That's japonica.

Silence. She enters the study.

FLORA He's here.

EDWARD I know.

FLORA He's in the hall.

EDWARD I know he's here. I can smell him.

FLORA Smell him?

EDWARD I smelt him when he came under my window. Can't you smell the house now?

FLORA What are you going to do with him, Edward? You won't be rough with him in any way? He's very old. I'm not sure if he can hear, or even see. And he's wearing the oldest –

EDWARD I don't want to know what he's wearing.

FLORA But you'll see for yourself in a minute, if you speak to him.

EDWARD I shall

  Slight pause.

FLORA He's an old man. You won't . . . be rough with him?

EDWARD If he's so old, why doesn't he seek shelter . . . from the storm?

FLORA But there's no storm. It's summer, the longest day . . .

EDWARD There was a storm, last week. A summer storm. He stood without moving, while it raged about him.

FLORA When was this?

EDWARD He remained quite still, while it thundered all about him

Pause.

FLORA Edward . . . are you sure it's wise to bother about all this?

EDWARD Tell him to come in.

FLORA I . . .

EDWARD Now.

She goes and collects the MATCHSELLER.

FLORA Hullo. Would you like to go in? I won't be long. Up these stairs here.

Pause.

You can have some sherry before lunch.

Pause.

Shall I take your tray? No. Very well, take it with you. Just . . . up those stairs. The door at the . . .

She watches him move.

The door . . .

Pause.

The door at the top. I'll join you . . . later.

She goes out.

The MATCHSELLER *stands on the threshold of the study.*

EDWARD (*cheerfully*) Here I am. Where are you?

Pause.

126

Don't stand out there, old chap. Come into my study.
(*He rises.*) Come in.

   The MATCHSELLER *enters.*

That's right. Mind how you go. That's . . . it. Now.
make yourself comfortable. Thought you might like
some refreshment, on a day like this. Sit down, old
man. What will you have? Sherry? Or what about a
double scotch? Eh?

   Pause.

I entertain the villagers annually, as a matter of fact.
I'm not the squire, but they look upon me with some
regard. Don't believe we've got a squire here any
more, actually. Don't know what became of him. Nice
old man he was. Great chess-player, as I remember.
Three daughters. The pride of the county. Flaming red
hair. Alice was the eldest. Sit yourself down, old chap.
Eunice I think was number two. The youngest one was
the best of the bunch. Sally. No, no, wait a minute,
no, it wasn't Sally, it was . . . Fanny. Fanny. A flower.
You must be a stranger here. Unless you lived here
once, went on a long voyage and have lately returned.
Do you know the district?

   Pause.

Now, now, you mustn't . . . stand about like that.
Take a seat. Which one would you prefer? We have a
great variety, as you see. Can't stand uniformity. Like
different seats, different backs. Often when I'm
working, you know, I draw up one chair, scribble a

few lines, put it by, draw up another, sit back, ponder, put it by . . . (*Absently*.) Sit back . . . put it by . .

Pause.

I write theological and philosophical essays . .

Pause.

Now and again I jot down a few observations on certain tropical phenomena – not from the same standpoint, of course. (*Silent pause.*) Yes. Africa, now. Africa's always been my happy hunting ground. Fascinating country. Do you know it? I get the impression that you've . . . been around a bit. Do you by any chance know the Membunza Mountains? Great range south of Katambaloo. French Equatorial Africa, if my memory serves me right. Most extraordinary diversity of flora and fauna. Especially fauna. I understand in the Gobi Desert you can come across some very strange sights. Never been there myself. Studied the maps though. Fascinating things, maps

Pause.

Do you live in the village? I don't often go down, of course. Or are you passing through? On your way to another part of the country? Well, I can tell you, in my opinion you won't find many prettier parts than here. We win the first prize regularly, you know, the best kept village in the area. Sit down.

Pause.

I say, can you hear me?

Pause.

I said, I say, can you hear me?

Pause.

You possess most extraordinary repose, for a man of
your age, don't you? Well, perhaps that's not quite the
right word . . . repose. Do you find it chilly in here?
I'm sure it's chillier in here than out. I haven't been
out yet, today, though I shall probably spend the whole
afternoon working, in the garden, under my canopy,
at my table, by the pool

Pause.

Oh, I understand you met my *wife*? Charming
woman, don't you think? Plenty of grit there, too.
Stood by me through thick and thin, that woman. In
season and out of season. Fine figure of a woman she
was, too, in her youth. Wonderful carriage, flaming
red hair. (*He stops abruptly.*)

Pause.

Yes, I . . . I was in much the same position myself then
as you are now, you understand. Struggling to make
my way in the world. I was in commerce too. (*With a
chuckle.*) Oh, yes, I know what it's like – the weather,
the rain, beaten from pillar to post, up hill and down
dale . . . the rewards were few . . . winters in hovels . . .
up till all hours working at your thesis . . . yes, I've
done it all. Let me advise you. Get a good woman to
stick by you. Never mind what the world says. Keep
at it. Keep your shoulder to the wheel. It'll pay
dividends.

Pause

(*With a laugh.*) You must excuse my chatting away like this. We have few visitors this time of the year. All our friends summer abroad. I'm a home bird myself. Wouldn't mind taking a trip to Asia Minor, mind you, or to certain lower regions of the Congo, but Europe? Out of the question. Much too noisy. I'm sure you agree. Now look, what will you have to drink? A glass of ale? Curaçao Fockink Orange? Ginger beer? Tia Maria? A Wachenheimer Fuchsmantel Reisling Beeren Auslese? Gin and it? Chateauneuf-du-Pape? A little Asti Spumante? Or what do you say to a straightforward Piesporter Goldtropfschen Feine Auslese (Reichsgraf von Kesselstaff)? Any preference?

Pause.

You look a trifle warm. Why don't you take off your balaclava? I'd find that a little itchy myself. But then I've always been one for freedom of movement. Even in the depth of winter I wear next to nothing.

Pause.

I say, can I ask you a personal question? I don't want to seem inquisitive but aren't you rather on the wrong road for matchselling? Not terribly busy, is it? Of course you may not care for petrol fumes or the noise of traffic. I can quite understand that.

Pause.

Do forgive me peering but is that a glass eye you're wearing?

Pause.

Do take off your balaclava, there's a good chap, put your tray down and take your ease, as they say in this part of the world. (*He moves towards him.*) I must say you keep quite a good stock, don't you? Tell me, between ourselves, are those boxes full, or are there just a few half-empty ones among them? Oh yes, I used to be in commerce. Well now, before the good lady sounds the gong for petit déjeuner will you join me in an aperitif? I recommend a glass of cider. Now . . . just a minute . . . I know I've got some – Look out! Mind your tray!

The tray falls, and the matchboxes.

Good God, what . . .?

Pause.

You've dropped your tray.

Pause. He picks the matchboxes up

(*Grunts.*) Eh, these boxes are all wet. You've no right to sell wet matches, you know. Uuuuugggh. This feels suspiciously like fungus. You won't get very far in this trade if you don't take care of your goods. (*Grunts, rising.*) Well, here you are.

Pause.

Here's your tray.

He puts the tray into the matchseller's hands, and sits. Pause.

Now listen, let me be quite frank with you, shall I?
I really cannot understand why you don't sit down.
There are four chairs at your disposal. Not to mention
the hassock. I can't possibly talk to you unless you're
settled. Then and only then can I speak to you. Do
you follow me? You're not being terribly helpful.
(*Slight pause.*) You're sweating. The sweat's pouring
out of you. Take off that balaclava

   Pause.

Go into the corner then. Into the corner. Go on. Get
into the shade of the corner. Back. Backward

   Pause.

Get back!

   Pause.

Ah, you understand me. Forgive me for saying so, but
I had decided that you had the comprehension of a
bullock. I was mistaken. You understand me perfecdy
well. That's right. A little more. A little to the right.
Aaah. Now you're there. In shade, in shadow. Good-o.
Now I can get down to brass tacks. Can't I?

   Pause.

No doubt you're wondering why I invited you into
this house? You may think I was alarmed by the look
of you. You would be quite mistaken. I was not
alarmed by the look of you. I did not find you at all
alarming. No, no. Nothing outside this room has ever
alarmed me. You disgusted me, quite forcibly, if you
want to know the truth.

Pause.

Why did you disgust me to that extent? That seems to be a pertinent question. You're no more disgusting than Fanny, the squire's daughter, after all. In appearance you differ but not in essence. There's the same . . .

Pause.

The same . . .

Pause.

(*In a low voice.*) I want to ask you a question. Why do you stand outside my back gate, from dawn till dusk, why do you pretend to sell matches, why . . .? What is it, damn you. You're shivering. You're sagging. Come here, come here . . . mind your tray!

EDWARD *rises and moves behind a chair.*

Come, quick quick. There. Sit here. Sit . . . sit in this.

The MATCHSELLER *stumbles and sits. Pause.*

Aaaah! You're sat. At last. What a relief. You must be tired. (*Slight pause.*) Chair comfortable? I bought it in a sale. I bought all the furniture in this house in a sale. The same sale. When I was a young man. You too, perhaps. You too, perhaps.

Pause.

At the same time, perhaps!

Pause.

(*Muttering.*) I must get some air. I must get a breath of air.

133

He goes to the door.

Flora!

FLORA Yes?

EDWARD (*with great weariness*) Take me into the garden.

Silence. They move from the study door to a chair under a canopy.

FLORA Come under the canopy.

EDWARD Ah. (*He sits.*)

Pause.

The peace. The peace out here.

FLORA Look at our trees.

EDWARD Yes.

FLORA Our own trees. Can you hear the birds?

EDWARD No, I can't hear them.

FLORA But they're singing, high up, and flapping.

EDWARD Good. Let them flap.

FLORA Shall I bring your lunch out here? You can have it in peace, and a quiet drink, under your canopy.

Pause.

How are you getting on with your old man?

EDWARD What do you mean?

134

FLORA What's happening? How are you getting on with him?

EDWARD Very well. We get on remarkably well. He's a little . . . reticent. Somewhat withdrawn. It's understandable. I should be the same, perhaps, in his place. Though, of course, I could not possibly find myself in his place.

FLORA Have you found out anything about him?

EDWARD A little. A little. He's had various trades, that's certain. His place of residence is unsure. He's . . . he's not a drinking man. As yet, I haven't discovered the reason for his arrival here. I shall in due course . . . by nightfall.

FLORA Is it necessary?

EDWARD Necessary?

FLORA (*quickly sitting on the right arm of the chair*) I could show him out now, it wouldn't matter. You've seen him, he's harmless, unfortunate . . . old, that's all. Edward – listen – he's not here through any . . . design, or anything, I know it. I mean, he might just as well stand outside our back gate as anywhere else. He'll move on. I can . . . make him. I promise you. There's no point in upsetting yourself like this. He's an old man, weak in the head . . . that's all.

Pause.

EDWARD You're deluded.

FLORA Edward –

EDWARD (*rising*) You're deluded. And stop calling me Edward.

FLORA You're not still frightened of him?

EDWARD Frightened of him? Of him? Have you seen him?

Pause.

He's like jelly. A great bullockfat of jelly. He can't see straight. I think as a matter of fact he wears a glass eye. He's almost stone deaf . . . almost . . . not quite. He's very nearly dead on his feet. Why should he frighten me? No, you're a woman, you know nothing. (*Slight pause.*) But he possesses other faculties. Cunning. The man's an imposter and he knows I know it.

FLORA I'll tell you what. Look. Let me speak to him. I'll speak to him.

EDWARD (*quietly*) And I know he knows I know it.

FLORA I'll find out all about him, Edward. I promise you I will.

EDWARD And he knows I know.

FLORA Edward! Listen to me! I can find out all about him, I promise you. I shall go and have a word with him now. I shall . . . get to the bottom of it.

EDWARD You? It's laughable.

FLORA You'll see – he won't bargain for me. I'll surprise him. He'll . . . he'll admit everything.

EDWARD (*softly*) He'll admit everything, will he?

FLORA You wait and see, you just –

EDWARD (*hissing*) What are you plotting?

FLORA I know exactly what I shall –

EDWARD What are you plotting?

He seizes her arms.

FLORA Edward, you're hurting me!

Pause.

(*With dignity.*) I shall wave from the window when I'm ready. Then you can come up. I shall get to the truth of it, I assure you. You're much too heavy-handed, in every way. You should trust your wife more, Edward. You should trust her judgement, and have a greater insight into her capabilities. A woman . . . a woman will often succeed, you know, where a man must invariably fail.

Silence. She goes into the study.

Do you mind if I come in?

The door closes.

Are you comfortable?

Pause.

Oh, the sun's shining directly on you. Wouldn't you rather sit in the shade?

She sits down.

It's the longest day of the year today, did you know that? Actually the year has flown. I can remember Christmas and that dreadful frost. And the floods!

137

I hope you weren't here in the floods. We were out of danger up here, of course, but in the valleys whole families I remember drifted away on the current. The country was a lake. Everything stopped. We lived on our own preserves, drank elderberry wine, studied other cultures.

Pause.

Do you know, I've got a feeling I've seen you before, somewhere. Long before the flood. You were much younger. Yes, I'm really sure of it. Between ourselves, were you ever a poacher? I had an encounter with a poacher once. It was a ghastly rape, the brute. High up on a hillside cattle track. Early spring. I was out riding on my pony. And there on the verge a man lay – ostensibly injured, lying on his front, I remember, possibly the victim of a murderous assault, how was I to know? I dismounted, I went to him, he rose, I fell, my pony took off, down to the valley. I saw the sky through the trees, blue. Up to my ears in mud. It was a desperate battle.

Pause.

I lost.

Pause.

Of course, life was perilous in those days. It was my first canter unchaperoned.

Pause.

Years later, when I was a Justice of the Peace for the county, I had him in front of the bench. He was there for poaching. That's how I know he was a poacher. The evidence though was sparse, inadmissible, I acquitted him, letting him off with a caution. He'd grown a red beard, I remember. Yes. A bit of a stinker.

Pause.

I say, you are perspiring, aren't you? Shall I mop your brow? With my chiffon? Is it the heat? Or the closeness? Or confined space? Or . . . ?

She goes over to him.

Actually, the day is cooling. It'll soon be dusk. Perhaps it is dusk. May I? You don't mind?

Pause. She mops his brow.

Ah, there, that's better. And your cheeks. It is a woman's job, isn't it? And I'm the only woman on hand. There.

Pause. She leans on the arm of chair.

(*Intimately.*) Tell me, have you a woman? Do you like women? Do you ever . . . think about women?

Pause.

Have you ever . . . stopped a woman?

Pause.

I'm sure you must have been quite attractive once. (*She sits.*) Not any more, of course. You've got a vile smell. Vile. Quite repellent, in fact.

Pause.

139

Sex, I suppose, means nothing to you. Does it ever occur to you that sex is a very vital experience for other people? Really, I think you'd amuse me if you weren't so hideous. You're probably quite amusing in your own way. (*Seductively.*) Tell me all about love. Speak to me of love.

Pause.

God knows what you're saying at this very moment. It's quite disgusting. Do you know when I was a girl I loved . . . I loved . . . I simply adored . . . what *have* you got on, for goodness sake? A jersey? It's clogged. Have you been rolling in mud? (*Slight pause.*) You haven't been rolling in mud, have you? (*She rises and goes over to him.*) And what have you got under your jersey? Let's see. (*Slight pause.*) I'm not tickling you, am I? No. Good . . . Lord, is this a vest? That's quite original. Quite original. (*She sits on the arm of his chair.*) Hmmnn, you're a solid old boy, I must say. Not at all like a jelly. All you need is a bath. A lovely lathery bath. And a good scrub. A lovely lathery scrub.

Pause.

Don't you? It will be a pleasure. (*She throws her arms round him.*) I'm going to keep you. I'm going to keep you, you dreadful chap, and call you Barnabas. Isn't it dark, Barnabas? Your eyes, your eyes, your great big eyes.

Pause.

My husband would never have guessed your name. Never. (*She kneels at his feet. Whispering.*) It's me you

140

were waiting for, wasn't it? You've been standing
waiting for me. You've seen me in the woods, picking
daisies, in my apron, my pretty daisy apron, and you
came and stood, poor creature, at my gate, till death
us do part. Poor Barnabas. I'm going to put you to
bed. I'm going to put you to bed and watch over you.
But first you must have a good whacking great bath.
And I'll buy you pretty little things that will suit you.
And little toys to play with. On your deathbed. Why
shouldn't you die happy?

A shout from the hall.

EDWARD Well?

Footsteps upstage.

Well?

FLORA Don't come in.

EDWARD Well?

FLORA He's dying.

EDWARD Dying? He's not dying.

FLORA I tell you, he's very ill.

EDWARD He's not dying! Nowhere near. He'll see you
cremated.

FLORA The man is desperately ill!

EDWARD Ill? You lying slut. Get back to your trough!

FLORA Edward . . .

EDWARD (*violently*) To your trough!

She goes out. Pause.

(*Coolly.*) Good evening to you. Why are you sitting in the gloom? Oh, you've begun to disrobe. Too warm? Let's open these windows, then, what?

He opens the windows.

Pull the blinds.

He pulls the blinds.

And close . . . the curtains . . . again.

He closes the curtains.

Ah. Air will enter through the side chinks. Of the blinds. And filter through the curtains. I hope. Don't want to suffocate, do we?

Pause.

More comfortable? Yes. You look different in darkness. Take off all your togs, if you like. Make yourself at home. Strip to your buff. Do as you would in your own house.

Pause.

Did you say something?

Pause.

Did you say something?

Pause.

Anything? Well then, tell me about your boyhood. Mmnn?

Pause.

What did you do with it? Run? Swim? Kick the ball?
You kicked the ball? What position? Left back?
Goalie? First reserve?

Pause.

I used to play myself. Country house matches, mostly.
Kept wicket and batted number seven.

Pause.

Kept wicket and batted number seven. Man called –
Cavendish, I think had something of your style.
Bowled left arm over the wicket, always kept his cap
on, quite a dab hand at solo whist, preferred a good
round of prop and cop to anything else.

Pause.

On wet days when the field was swamped.

Pause.

Perhaps you don't play cricket.

Pause.

Perhaps you never met Cavendish and never played
cricket. You look less and less like a cricketer the more
I see of you. Where did you live in those days? God
damn it, I'm entitled to know something about you!
You're in my blasted house, on my territory, drinking
my wine, eating my duck! Now you've had your fill
you sit like a hump, a mouldering heap. In my room.
My den. I can rem . . . (*He stops abruptly.*)

Pause.

You find that funny? Are you grinning?

Pause.

(*In disgust.*) Good Christ, is that a grin on your face?
(*Further disgust.*) It's lopsided. It's all – down on one
side. You're grinning. It amuses you, does it? When
I tell you how well I remember this room, how well
I remember this den. (*Muttering.*) Ha. Yesterday now,
it was clear, clearly defined, so clearly.

Pause.

The garden, too, was sharp, lucid, in the rain, in the
sun.

Pause.

My den, too, was sharp, arranged for my purpose . . .
quite satisfactory.

Pause.

The house too, was polished, all the banisters were
polished, and the stair rods, and the curtain rods.

Pause.

My desk was polished, and my cabinet.

Pause.

I was polished. (*Nostalgic.*) I could stand on the hill
and look through my telescope at the sea. And follow
the path of the three-masted schooner, feeling fit, well
aware of my sinews, their suppleness, my arms lifted
holding the telescope, steady, easily, no trembling, my

aim was perfect, I could pour hot water down the
spoon-hole, yes, easily, no difficulty, my grasp firm,
my command established, my life was accounted for, I
was ready for my excursions to the cliff, down the
path to the back gate, through the long grass, no need
to watch for the nettles, my progress was fluent, after
my long struggling against all kinds of usurpers,
disreputables, lists, literally lists of people anxious to
do me down, and my reputation down, my command
was established, all summer I would breakfast, survey
my landscape, take my telescope, examine the
overhanging of my hedges, pursue the narrow lane
past the monastery, climb the hill, adjust the lens, *(He
mimes a telescope.)* watch the progress of the three-
masted schooner, my progress was as sure, as fluent . . .

Pause. He drops his arms.

Yes, yes, you're quite right, it is funny.

Pause.

Laugh your bloody head off! Go on. Don't mind me.
No need to be polite.

Pause.

That's right.

Pause.

You're quite right, it is funny. I'll laugh with you!

He laughs.

Ha-ha-ha! Yes! You're laughing with me, I'm laughing
with you, we're laughing together!

He laughs and stops.

(*Brightly.*) Why did I invite you into this room? That's your next question, isn't it? Bound to be.

Pause.

Well, why not, you might say? My oldest acquaintance. My nearest and dearest. My kith and kin. But surely correspondence would have been as satisfactory . . . more satisfactory? We could have exchanged postcards, couldn't we? What? Views, couldn't we? Of sea and land, city and village, town and country, autumn and winter . . . clocktowers . . . museums . . . citadels . . . bridges . . . rivers . . .

Pause.

Seeing you stand, at the back gate, such close proximity, was not at all the same thing.

Pause.

What are you doing? You're taking off your balaclava . . . you've decided not to. No, very well then, all things considered, did I then invite you into this room with express intention of asking you to take off your balaclava, in order to determine your resemblance to – some other person? The answer is no, certainly not, I did not, for when I first saw you you wore no balaclava. No headcovering of any kind, in fact. You looked quite different without a head – I mean without a hat – I mean without a headcovering, of any kind. In fact every time I have seen you you have looked quite different to the time before.

Pause.

Even now you look different. Very different.

Pause.

Admitted that sometimes I viewed you through dark glasses, yes, and sometimes through light glasses, and on other occasions bare-eyed, and on other occasions through the bars of the scullery window, or from the roof, the roof, yes in driving snow, or from the bottom of the drive in thick fog, or from the roof again in blinding sun, so blinding, so hot, that I had to skip and jump and bounce in order to remain in one place. Ah, that's good for a guffaw, is it? That's good for a belly laugh? Go on, then. Let it out. Let yourself go, for God's . . . (*He catches his breath.*) You're crying . . .

Pause.

(*Moved.*) You haven't been laughing. You're crying.

Pause.

You're weeping. You're shaking with grief. For me. I can't believe it. For my plight. I've been wrong.

Pause.

(*Briskly.*) Come, come, stop it. Be a man. Blow your nose for goodness sake. Pull yourself together.

He sneezes.

Ah.

He rises. Sneeze.

Ah. Fever. Excuse me.

He blows his nose.

I've caught a cold. A germ. In my eyes. It was this morning. In my eyes. My eyes.

Pause. He falls to the floor.

Not that I had any difficulty in seeing you, no, no, it was not so much my sight, my sight is excellent – in winter I run about with nothing on but a pair of polo shorts – no, it was not so much any deficiency in my sight as the airs between me and my object – don't weep – the change of air, the currents obtaining in the space between me and my object, the shades they make, the shapes they take, the quivering, the eternal quivering – please stop crying – nothing to do with heat-haze. Sometimes, of course, I would take shelter, shelter to compose myself. Yes, I would seek a tree, a cranny of bushes, erect my canopy and so make shelter. And rest. (*Low murmur.*) And then I no longer heard the wind or saw the sun. Nothing entered, nothing left my nook. I lay on my side in my polo shorts, my fingers lightly in contact with the blades of grass, the earthflowers, the petals of the earthflowers flaking, lying on my palm, the underside of all the great foliage dark, above mc, but it is only afterwards I say the foliage was dark, the petals flaking, then I said nothing, I remarked nothing, things happened upon me, then in my times of shelter, the shades, the petals, carried themselves, carried their bodies upon me, and nothing entered my nook, nothing left it.

Pause.

But then, the time came. I saw the wind. I saw the
wind, swirling, and the dust at my back gate, lifting,
and the long grass, scything together . . . (*Slowly,
in horror.*) You *are* laughing. You're laughing. Your
face. Your body. (*Overwhelming nausea and horror.*)
Rocking . . . gasping . . . rocking . . . shaking . . .
rocking . . . heaving . . . rocking . . . You're laughing
at me! Aaaaahhhh!

The MATCHSELLER *rises. Silence.*

You look younger. You look extraordinarily . . . youthful.

Pause.

You want to examine the garden? It must be very
bright, in the moonlight. (*Becoming weaker.*) I would
like to join you . . . explain . . . show you . . . the
garden . . . explain . . . The plants . . . where I run . . .
my track . . . in training . . . I was number one sprinter
at Howells . . . when a stripling . . . no more than a
stripling . . . licked . . . men twice my strength . . .
when a stripling . . . like yourself.

Pause.

(*Flatly.*) The pool must be glistening. In the moonlight.
And the lawn. I remember it well. The cliff. The sea.
The three-masted schooner.

Pause.

(*With great, final effort – a whisper.*) Who are you?

FLORA (*off*) Barnabas?

Pause.

She enters.

Ah, Barnabas. Everything is ready.

   Pause.

I want to show you my garden, your garden. You must see my japonica, my convolvulus . . . my honeysuckle, my clematis.

   Pause.

The summer is coming. I've put up your canopy for you. You can lunch in the garden, by the pool. I've polished the whole house for you.

   Pause.

Take my hand.

   Pause. The MATCHSELLER *goes over to her.*

Yes. Oh, wait a moment.

   Pause.

Edward. Here is your tray.

   She crosses to EDWARD *with the tray of matches, and puts it in his hands. Then she and the* MATCHSELLER *start to go out as the curtain falls slowly.*

A NIGHT OUT

A Night Out was first transmitted on the BBC Third Programme on 1 March 1960, with the following cast:

ALBERT STOKES	Barry Foster
MRS STOKES	Mary O'Farrell
SEELEY	Harold Pinter
KEDGE	John Rye
BARMAN AT THE COFFEE STALL	Walter Hall
OLD MAN	Norman Wynne
MR KING	David Bird
MR RYAN	Norman Wynne
GIDNEY	Nicholas Selby
JOYCE	Jane Jordan Rogers
EILEEN	Auriol Smith
BETTY	Margaret Hotine
HORNE	Hugh Dickson
BARROW	David Spenser
THE GIRL	Vivien Merchant

Produced by Donald McWhinnie

The play was subsequently gransmitted by ABC
Armchair Theatre on 24 April 1960, with the
following cast:

ALBERT STOKES	Tom Bell
MRS STOKES	Madge Ryan
SEELEY	Harold Pinter
KEDGE	Philip Locke
BARMAN AT THE COFFEE STALL	Edmond Bennett
OLD MAN	Gordon Phillott
MR KING	Arthur Lowe
MR RYAN	Edward Malin
GIDNEY	Stanley Meadows
JOYCE	José Read
EILEEN	Maria Lennard
BETTY	Mary Duddy
HORNE	Stanley Segal
BARROW	Walter Hall
THE GIRL	Vivien Merchant

Produced by Philip Saville

Characters

ALBERT STOKES

MRS STOKES
his mother

SEELEY

KEDGE

BARMAN AT THE COFFEE STALL

OLD MAN

MR KING

MR RYAN

GIDNEY

JOYCE

EILEEN

BETTY

HORNE

BARROW

THE GIRL

Act One

SCENE ONE

The kitchen of MRS. STOKES' *small house in the south of London. Clean and tidy.*

ALBERT, *a young man of twenty-eight, is standing in his shirt and trousers, combing his hair in the kitchen mirror over the mantelpiece. A woman's voice calls his name from upstairs. He ignores it, picks up a brush from the mantelpiece and brushes his hair. The voice calls again. He slips the comb in his pocket, bends down, reaches under the sink and takes out a shoe duster. He begins to polish his shoes.* MRS STOKES *descends the stairs, passes through the hall and enters the kitchen.*

MOTHER Albert, I've been calling you. (*She watches him.*) What are you doing?

ALBERT Nothing.

MOTHER Didn't you hear me call you, Albert? I've been calling you from upstairs.

ALBERT You seen my tie?

MOTHER Oh, I say, I'll have to put the flag out.

ALBERT What do you mean?

MOTHER Cleaning your shoes, Albert? I'll have to put the flag out, won't I?

157

ALBERT *puts the brush back under the sink and begins to search the sideboard and cupboard.*

What are you looking for?

ALBERT My tie. The striped one, the blue one.

MOTHER The bulb's gone in Grandma's room.

ALBERT Has it?

MOTHER That's what I was calling you about. I went in and switched on the light and the bulb had gone.

She watches him open the kitchen cabinet and look into it.

Aren't those your best trousers, Albert? What have you put on your best trousers for?

ALBERT Look, Mum, where's my tie? The blue one, the blue tie, where is it? You know the one I mean, the blue striped one, I gave it to you this morning.

MOTHER What do you want your tie for?

ALBERT I want to put it on. I asked you to press it for me this morning. I gave it to you this morning before I went to work, didn't I?

She goes to the gas stove, examines the vegetables, opens the oven and looks into it.

MOTHER (*gently*) Well, your dinner'll be ready soon. You can look for it afterwards. Lay the table, there's a good boy.

ALBERT Why should I look for it afterwards? You know where it is now.

MOTHER You've got five minutes. Go down to the cellar, Albert, get a bulb and put it in Grandma's room, go on.

ALBERT (*irritably*) I don't know why you keep calling that room Grandma's room, she's been dead ten years.

MOTHER Albert!

ALBERT I mean, it's just a junk room, that's all it is.

MOTHER Albert, that's no way to speak about your Grandma, you know that as well as I do.

ALBERT I'm not saying a word against Grandma –

MOTHER You'll upset me in a minute, you go on like that.

ALBERT I'm not going on about anything.

MOTHER Yes, you are. Now why don't you go and put a bulb in Grandma's room and by the time you come down I'll have your dinner on the table.

ALBERT I can't go down to the cellar, I've got my best trousers on, I've got a white shirt on.

MOTHER You're dressing up tonight, aren't you? Dressing up, cleaning your shoes, anyone would think you were going to the Ritz.

ALBERT I'm not going to the Ritz.

MOTHER (*suspiciously*) What do you mean, you're not going to the Ritz?

ALBERT What do you mean?

159

MOTHER The way you said you're not going to the Ritz, it sounded like you were going somewhere else.

ALBERT (*wearily*) I am.

MOTHER (*shocked surprise*) You're going out?

ALBERT You know I'm going out. I told you I was going out. I told you last week. I told you this morning. Look, where's my tie? I've got to have my tie. I'm late already. Come on, Mum, where'd you put it?

MOTHER What about your dinner?

ALBERT (*searching*) Look . . . I told you . . . I haven't got
the . . . wait a minute . . . ah, here it is.

MOTHER You can't wear that tie. I haven't pressed it.

ALBERT You have. Look at it. Of course you have. It's beautifully pressed. It's fine.

He ties the tie.

MOTHER Where are you going?

ALBERT Mum, I've told you, honestly, three times. Honestly, I've told you three times I had to go out tonight.

MOTHER No, you didn't.

ALBERT *exclaims and knots the tie.*

I thought you were joking.

ALBERT I'm not going . . . I'm just going to Mr King's. I've told you. You don't believe me.

MOTHER You're going to Mr King's?

ALBERT Mr Ryan's leaving. You know Ryan. He's
leaving the firm. He's been there years. So Mr King's
giving a sort of party for him at his house . . . well,
not exactly a party, not a party, just a few . . . you
know . . . anyway, we're all invited. I've got to go.
Everyone else is going. I've got to go. I don't want to
go, but I've got to.

MOTHER (*bewildered, sitting*) Well, I don't know . . .

ALBERT (*with his arm round her*) I won't be late. I
don't want to go. I'd much rather stay with you.

MOTHER Would you?

ALBERT You know I would. Who wants to go to Mr
King's party?

MOTHER We were going to have our game of cards.

ALBERT Well, we can't have our game of cards.

Pause.

MOTHER Put the bulb in Grandma's room, Albert.

ALBERT I've told you I'm not going down to the
cellar in my white shirt. There's no light in the cellar
either. I'll be pitch black in five minutes, looking for
those bulbs.

MOTHER I told you to put a light in the cellar. I told
you yesterday.

ALBERT Well, I can't do it now.

MOTHER If we had a light in the cellar you'd be able to see where those bulbs were. You don't expect me to go down to the cellar?

ALBERT I don't know why we keep bulbs in the cellar!

Pause.

MOTHER Your father would turn in his grave if he heard you raise your voice to me. You're all I've got, Albert. I want you to remember that. I haven't got anyone else. I want you . . . I want you to bear that in mind.

ALBERT I'm sorry . . . I raised my voice.

He goes to the door.

(*Mumbling.*) I've got to go.

MOTHER (*following*) Albert!

ALBERT What?

MOTHER I want to ask you a question.

ALBERT What?

MOTHER Are you leading a clean life?

ALBERT A clean life?

MOTHER You're not leading an unclean life, are you?

ALBERT What are you talking about?

MOTHER You're not messing about with girls, are you? You're not going to go messing about with girls tonight?

162

ALBERT Don't be so ridiculous.

MOTHER Answer me, Albert. I'm your mother.

ALBERT I don't know any girls.

MOTHER If you're going to the firm's party, there'll be girls there, won't there? Girls from the office?

ALBERT I don't like them, any of them.

MOTHER You promise?

ALBERT Promise what?

MOTHER That . . . that you won't upset your father.

ALBERT My father? How can I upset my father? You're always talking about upsetting people who are dead!

MOTHER Oh, Albert, you don't know how you hurt me, you don't know the hurtful way you've got, speaking of your poor father like that.

ALBERT But he is dead.

MOTHER He's not! He's living! (*Touching her breast.*) In here! And this is his house!

  Pause.

ALBERT Look, Mum, I won't be late . . . and I won't . . .

MOTHER But what about your dinner? It's nearly ready.

ALBERT Seeley and Kedge are waiting for me. I told you not to cook dinner this morning. (*He goes to the stairs.*) Just because you never listen . . .

He runs up the stairs and disappears. She calls after him from the hall.

MOTHER Well, what am I going to do while you're out? I can't go into Grandma's room because there's no light. I can't go down to the cellar in the dark, we were going to have a game of cards, it's Friday night, what about our game of rummy?

SCENE TWO

A coffee stall by a railway arch. A wooden bench is situated a short distance from it. SEELEY *and* KEDGE, *both about* ALBERT's *age, are at the counter, talking to the* BARMAN. *An* OLD MAN *leans at the corner of the counter.*

SEELEY Give us a cheese roll as well, will you?

KEDGE Make it two.

SEELEY Make it two.

BARMAN Two cheese rolls.

SEELEY What are these, sausages?

BARMAN Best pork sausages

SEELEY (*to* KEDGE) You want a sausage?

KEDGE (*shuddering*) No, thanks.

SEELEY Yes, you're right.

BARMAN Two cheese rolls. What about these sausages, you want them or don't you?

SEELEY Just the rolls, mate.

BARMAN Two tea, two rolls, makes one and eightpence.

SEELEY *gives him half a crown.*

KEDGE There'll be plenty to eat at the party.

SEELEY I'll bet.

OLD MAN Eh! (*They turn to him.*) Your mate was by here not long ago.

SEELEY Which mate?

OLD MAN He had a cup of tea, didn't he, Fred? Sitting over there he was, on the bench. He said he was going home to change but to tell you he'd be back.

KEDGE Uh-uh.

OLD MAN Not gone more than above forty-five minutes.

BARMAN One and eight from half a dollar leaves you ten pennies.

OLD MAN Anyway, he told me to tell you when I see you he was coming back.

KEDGE Thanks very much.

SEELEY Well, I hope he won't be long. I don't want to miss the booze.

KEDGE You think there'll be much there, do you?

OLD MAN Yes, he was sitting over there.

KEDGE Who was?

OLD MAN Your mate.

SEELEY Oh yes.

OLD MAN Yes, sitting over there he was. Took his cup of tea and went and sat down, didn't he, Fred? He sat there looking very compressed with himself.

KEDGE Very what?

OLD MAN Compressed. I thought he was looking compressed, didn't you, Fred?

BARMAN Depressed. He means depressed.

SEELEY No wonder. What about that game on Saturday, eh?

KEDGE You were going to tell me. You haven't told me yet.

BARMAN What game? Fulham?

SEELEY No, the firm. Firm's got a team, see? Play on Saturdays.

BARMAN Who'd you play?

SEELEY Other firms.

BARMAN You boys in the team, are you?

KEDGE Yes. I've been off sick though. I didn't play last week.

BARMAN Sick, eh? You want to try one of my sausages, don't he, Henry?

OLD MAN Oh, ay, yes.

KEDGE What happened with the game, then?

They move to the bench.

SEELEY Well, when you couldn't play, Gidney moved Albert to left back.

KEDGE He's a left half.

SEELEY I know he's a left half. I said to Gidney myself, I said to him, look, why don't you go left back, Gidney? He said, no, I'm too valuable at centre half.

KEDGE He didn't, did he?

SEELEY Yes. Well, you know who was on the right wing, don't you? Connor.

KEDGE Who? Tony Connor?

SEELEY No. You know Connor. What's the matter with you? You've played against Connor yourself.

KEDGE Oh – whatsisname – Micky Connor.

SEELEY Yes.

KEDGE I thought he'd given up the game.

SEELEY No, what are you talking about? He plays for the printing works, plays outside right for the printing works.

KEDGE He's a good ballplayer, that Connor, isn't he?

SEELEY Look. I said to Albert before the kick off, Connor's on the right wing, I said, play your normal game. I told him six times before the kick off.

KEDGE What's the good of him playing his normal game? He's a left half, he's not a left back.

SEELEY Yes, but he's a defensive left half, isn't he? That's why I told him to play his normal game. You don't want to worry about Connor, I said, he's a good ballplayer but he's not all that good.

KEDGE Oh, he's good, though.

SEELEY No one's denying he's good. But he's not all that good. I mean, he's not tip-top. You know what I mean?

KEDGE He's fast.

SEELEY He's fast, but he's not all that fast, is he?

KEDGE (*doubtfully*) Well, not all that fast . . .

SEELEY What about Levy? Was Levy fast?

KEDGE Well, Levy was a sprinter.

SEELEY He was a dasher, Levy. All he knew was run.

KEDGE He could move.

SEELEY Yes, but look how Albert played him! He cut him off, he played him out the game. And Levy's faster than Connor.

KEDGE Yes, but he wasn't so clever, though.

SEELEY Well, what about Foxall?

KEDGE Who? Lou Foxall?

SEELEY No, you're talking about Lou Fox, I'm talking about Sandy Foxall.

KEDGE Oh, the winger.

SEELEY Sure. He was a very smart ballplayer, Foxall. But what did Albert do? He played his normal game. He let him come. He waited for him. And Connor's not as clever as Foxall.

KEDGE He's clever though.

SEELEY Gawd blimey, I know he's clever, but he's not as clever as Foxall, is he?

KEDGE The trouble is, with Connor, he's fast too, isn't he?

SEELEY But if Albert would have played his normal game! He played a game foreign to him.

KEDGE How many'd Connor get?

SEELEY He made three and scored two.

Pause. They eat.

KEDGE No wonder he's depressed, old Albert.

SEELEY Oh, he was very depressed after the game, I can tell you. And of course Gidney was after him, of course. You know Gidney.

KEDGE That birk.

Pause.

OLD MAN Yes, he was sitting over where you are now, wasn't he, Fred? Looking very compressed with himself. Light-haired bloke, ain't he?

SEELEY Yes, light-haired.

SCENE THREE

The house.

ALBERT *is coming down the stairs. He is wearing his jacket. He goes towards the door. His* MOTHER *calls from the kitchen and goes into the hall.*

MOTHER Albert! Where are you going?

ALBERT Out.

MOTHER Your dinner's ready.

ALBERT I'm sorry. I haven't got time to have it.

MOTHER Look at your suit. You're not going out with your suit in that state, are you?

ALBERT What's the matter with it?

MOTHER It needs a good brush, that's what's the matter with it. You can't go out like that. Come on, come in here and I'll give it a brush.

ALBERT It's all right . . .

MOTHER Come on.

They go into the kitchen. She gets the brush.

Turn round. No, stand still. You can't go out and disgrace me, Albert. If you've got to go out you've got to look nice. There, that's better.

She dusts his jacket with her hands and straightens his tie.

I didn't tell you what I made for you, did I? I made it specially. I made Shepherd's Pie tonight.

ALBERT (*taking her hand from his tie*) The tie's all right.

He goes to the door.

Well, ta-ta.

MOTHER Albert! Wait a minute. Where's your handkerchief?

ALBERT What handkerchief?

MOTHER You haven't got a handkerchief in your breast pocket.

ALBERT That doesn't matter, does it?

MOTHER Doesn't matter? I should say it does matter. Just a minute. (*She takes a handkerchief from a drawer.*) Here you are. A nice clean one. (*She arranges it in his pocket.*) You mustn't let me down, you know. You've got to be properly dressed. Your father was always properly dressed. You'd never see him out without a handkerchief in his breast pocket. He always looked like a gentleman.

SCENE FOUR

The coffee stall.

KEDGE *is returning from the counter zvith two teas.*

KEDGE Time we were there.

SEELEY We'll give him five minutes.

KEDGE I bet his mum's combing his hair for him, eh?

He chuckles and sits.

You ever met her, Seeley?

SEELEY Who?

KEDGE His . . . mother.

SEELEY Yes.

KEDGE What's she like?

SEELEY (*shortly*) She's all right.

KEDGE All right, is she?

SEELEY I told you. I just said she was all right.

Pause.

KEDGE No, what I mean is, he always gets a bit niggly when she's mentioned, doesn't he? A bit touchy. You noticed that?

SEELEY (*unwillingly*) Yes.

KEDGE Why's that, then?

SEELEY I don't know. What're you asking me for?

KEDGE I don't know. I just thought you might . . . sort of . . . well, I mean, you know him better than I do, don't you?

Pause.

Of course, he don't let much slip, does he, old Albert?

SEELEY No, not much.

KEDGE He's a bit deep really, isn't he?

SEELEY Yes, he's a bit deep.

Pause.

KEDGE Secretive.

SEELEY (*irritably*) What do you mean, secretive? What are you talking about?

KEDGE I was just saying he was secretive.

SEELEY What are you talking about? What do you mean, he's secretive?

KEDGE You said yourself he was deep.

SEELEY I said he was deep. I didn't say he was secretive!

ALBERT *walks through the railway arch across to the bench.*

KEDGE Hullo, Albert.

ALBERT Hullo.

KEDGE That's a nice bit of clobber you've got on there.

SEELEY Very fair, very fair.

KEDGE Yes, fits you like a glove.

SEELEY Well, come on, catch a thirty-six round the corner.

173

ALBERT Wait a minute, I . . . I don't think I feel like going, actually.

KEDGE What are you talking about?

ALBERT I don't feel like it, that's all.

SEELEY What, with all that drink laid on?

ALBERT No, I've just got a bit of a headache.

OLD MAN That's the bloke! That's the bloke was here before, isn't it, Fred? I gave them your message, son.

ALBERT Oh . . . thanks.

OLD MAN Didn't I?

KEDGE You did, you did, mate.

SEELEY Well, what's going on, you coming or what?

ALBERT (*touching his forehead*) No, I feel a bit . . . you know . . .

KEDGE Don't you know who'll be there tonight, Albert?

ALBERT Who?

KEDGE Joyce.

ALBERT Joyce? Well, what about it?

KEDGE And Eileen.

ALBERT Well, so what?

KEDGE And Betty. Betty'll be there. They'll all be there.

SEELEY Betty? Who's Betty?

KEDGE Betty? What do you mean? You don't know Betty?

SEELEY There's no girl in the office called Betty.

KEDGE Betty! The dark bit! The new one. The one that came in last week. The litde one, in the corner!

SEELEY Oh, her. Is her name Betty? I thought it was –

KEDGE Betty. Her name's Betty.

SEELEY I've been calling her Hetty.

Pause.

KEDGE Anywhat, she'll be there. She's raring to go, that one.

ALBERT Well, you go then, I'll . . .

KEDGE Albert, what's the matter with you, mate? It's wine, women and song tonight.

ALBERT I see them every day, don't I? What's new in that?

KEDGE You frightened Gidney'll be after you, then, because of the game?

ALBERT What do you mean?

KEDGE Go on, everyone has a bad game, Albert.

ALBERT Yes, they do, don't they?

KEDGE I played against Connor myself once. He's tricky. He's a very tricky ballplayer.

ALBERT Yes.

SEELEY Clever player, Connor.

ALBERT What's Gidney got to do with it, Kedge?

KEDGE Well, you know what he is.

ALBERT What?

KEDGE Well, he's captain of the team, isn't he, for a bang-off?

ALBERT You think –?

SEELEY Oh, scrub round it, will you? It's late –

ALBERT You think I'm frightened of Gidney?

KEDGE I didn't say you were –

SEELEY Gidney's all right. What's the matter with Gidney?

ALBERT Yes. What's wrong with him?

KEDGE Nothing. There's nothing wrong with him. He's a nice bloke. He's a charmer, isn't he?

SEELEY The cream of the cream. Well, come on, you coming or what?

ALBERT Yes, all right. I'll come.

SEELEY Just a minute. I'll get some fags.

He goes to the counter, ALBERT *and* KEDGE *are left standing.*

(*To the* BARMAN.) Twenty 'Weights', mate.

KEDGE *regards* ALBERT.

KEDGE How's your mum, Albert?

ALBERT All right.

KEDGE That's the idea.

BARMAN Only got 'Woods'.

SEELEY They'll do.

ALBERT (*quietly*) What do you mean, how's my Mum?

KEDGE I just asked how she was, that's all.

ALBERT Why shouldn't she be all right?

KEDGE I didn't say she wasn't.

ALBERT Well, she is.

KEDGE Well, that's all right then, isn't it?

ALBERT What are you getting at?

KEDGE I don't know what's the matter with you tonight, Albert.

SEELEY (*returning*) What's up now?

ALBERT Kedge here, suddenly asks how my mother is.

KEDGE Just a friendly question, that's all. Gaw! You can't even ask a bloke how his mother is now without him getting niggly!

ALBERT Well, why's he suddenly ask –?

SEELEY He was just asking a friendly question, mate. What's the matter with you?

Pause.

ALBERT Oh.

SEELEY Well, how is she, then?

ALBERT She's fine. What about yours?

SEELEY Fine. Fine.

Pause.

KEDGE Mine's fine too, you know. Great. Absolutely great. A marvel for her age, my mother is. Of course, she had me very late.

Pause.

SEELEY Well? Are you coming or not? Or what?

KEDGE I'm coming.

ALBERT (*following*) I'm coming.

SCENE FIVE

The kitchen. The MOTHER *is putting* ALBERT'*s dinner into the oven. She takes the alarm clock from the mantelpiece and puts it on the table. She takes out a pack of cards, sits at the table and begins to lay out a game of patience. Close up of her, broodingly setting out the cards. Close up of the clock. It is seven forty-five.*

Act Two

SCENE ONE

The lounge of MR KING'*s house. The party is in progress.* KEDGE *and* BETTY *are dancing. Music comes from a radiogram.* MR KING, *an urbane man in his fifties,* GIDNEY, *the chief accountant, in his late twenties,* SEELEY *and* ALBERT, *are standing in a group.* JOYCE *and* EILEEN *are at the table which serves as a bar. Two men and a woman of indeterminate age sit holding drinks.* HORNE *and* BARROW, *two young clerks, stand by the door.* MR RYAN, *the old man, sits in the centre of the room, smiling.*

JOYCE You enjoying the party, Mr Ryan?

RYAN *nods and smiles.*

EILEEN (*pleasantly*) Enjoying the party, are you?

He nods, winks and smiles.

KING I recommend a bicycle, honestly. It really keeps you up to the mark. Out in the morning, on the bike, through the town . . . the air in your lungs, muscles working . . . you arrive at work . . . you arrive at work fresh . . . you know what I mean? Uplifted.

GIDNEY Not so good in the rain.

KING Refreshes you! Clears the cobwebs. (*He laughs.*)

SEELEY You don't walk to work, do you, Gidney?

GIDNEY Me? I've got the car.

KING I drive too, of course, but I often think seriously of taking up cycling again. I often think very seriously about it, you know.

JOYCE (*to* RYAN) Nice party, isn't it, Mr Ryan?

RYAN *nods and inclines his head, smiling.*

KEDGE (*dancing*) You dance like a dream, Betty, you know that?

BETTY (*shyly*) I don't.

KEDGE You do. Honest. Like a dream. Like a dream come true.

BETTY You're just saying that.

KING Well, Kedge looks all right again, doesn't he? What was the matter with him? I've forgotten.

SEELEY Stomach trouble.

KING Not enough exercise. (*To* KEDGE.) You'll have to see you get more exercise, Kedge!

KEDGE (*passing*) You never said a truer word, Mr King.

SEELEY Well, he don't look in bad trim to me, Mr King.

They laugh.

KING I must admit it.

GIDNEY He'll never get to the last lap with that one, I can tell you.

KING (*smiling*) Now, now, you young men, that's quite enough of that. No more of that.

GIDNEY (*pleasantly*) What are you laughing at, Stokes?

ALBERT What?

GIDNEY Sorry. I thought you were laughing.

ALBERT I was laughing. You made a joke.

GIDNEY Oh yes, of course. Sorry.

   Pause.

Well, we've got Kedge back at left back next Saturday.

KING Yes. Excuse me.

SEELEY That's a lovely pair of shoes you're wearing, Gidney.

GIDNEY Do you think so?

SEELEY Oh, they're the best, the very best, aren't they, Albert? Gidney always wears a nice pair of shoes, doesn't he, you noticed that? That's one thing I'll say about you, Gidney – you carry your feet well.

EILEEN A mambo! Who's going to dance?

SEELEY I'll give it a trot.

   SEELEY *and* EILEEN *dance.*

GIDNEY Don't you dance, Stokes?

ALBERT Yes, sometimes.

GIDNEY Do you? You will excuse me, won't you?

ALBERT Yes.

ALBERT *is left standing.*

KING Well, Ryan, enjoying the party?

RYAN *nods, smiles.*

Nice to see a lot of young people enjoying themselves, eh?

RYAN *nods, smiles.*

Of course, it's all in your honour, old man. Let's fill you up. I'll be the oldest man in the office after you've gone.

GIDNEY *and* JOYCE, *whispering.*

JOYCE No. Why should I?

GIDNEY Go on. Just for a lark.

JOYCE What for?

GIDNEY For a lark. Just for a lark.

JOYCE You've got an evil mind, you have.

GIDNEY No, it'll amuse me, that's all. I feel like being amused.

JOYCE Well, I'm not going to.

GIDNEY Gah, you wouldn't know how to, anyway.

JOYCE Oh, wouldn't I?

GIDNEY (*taking her arm*) Get hold of Eileen, don't tell her I told you though, and go over and lead him a dance, just lead him a dance, that's all, see what he does. I want to see his reaction, that's all, I just want to see how he takes it.

JOYCE What, in front of everyone else, in front of – ?

GIDNEY Just talk to him, talk to him. I don't mean anything else, do I?

JOYCE What do I get if I do?

GIDNEY A toffee apple.

JOYCE Oh, really? Thank you.

GIDNEY I'll take you for a ride in the car. Honest.

SEELEY (*dancing*) Hullo, Mr Ryan. Enjoying the party?

EILEEN You dance well, don't you?

SEELEY I was going in for ballet once.

EILEEN Go on!

SEELEY Yes, true. They offered me the leading part in *Rigoletto*. When I was a boy soprano.

EILEEN You're making it up.

GIDNEY (*to* JOYCE) No, he just irritates me, that bloke. I . . . I haven't got any time for a bloke like that.

JOYCE He's just quiet, that's all.

GIDNEY Well, see if you can wake him up.

KING (*to* BETTY) Well, Miss Todd, it hasn't taken you long to get to know everyone, has it?

BETTY Oh no, Mr King.

KEDGE I've taken her under my wing, Mr King.

KING So I noticed.

KEDGE Yes, I've been teaching her all about mortality tables. I told her in case of fire or burglary commission and damages come to her.

KING I would hardly take Kedge's word as gospel, Miss Todd.

KEDGE You know I've got the best interests of the firm at heart, Mr King.

GIDNEY (*drinking, with* JOYCE) Anyway, I'm thinking of moving on. You stay too long in a place you go daft. After all, with my qualifications I could go anywhere.

He sees ALBERT *at the bar.*

Couldn't I, Stokes?

ALBERT What?

GIDNEY I was saying, with my qualifications I could go anywhere. I could go anywhere and be anything.

ALBERT So could I.

GIDNEY Could you? What qualifications have you got?

ALBERT Well, I've got a few, you know.

GIDNEY Listen! Do you know that Chelsea wanted to sign me up a few years ago? They had a scout down to one of our games. They wanted to sign me up. And I'll tell you another thing as well. I could turn professional cricketer any day I wanted to, if I wanted to.

ALBERT Then why don't you?

GIDNEY I don't want to.

JOYCE You'd look lovely in white.

GIDNEY These people who talk about qualifications. Just makes me laugh, that's all.

KEDGE (*in the corner of the room, in an armchair with* BETTY) Oh, you're lovely. You're the loveliest thing on four wheels.

KING (*to* HORNE *and* BARROW, *by the door*) Well, I hope you'll both be in the team soon yourselves. I think it's a very good thing we've . . . that the firm's got a football team. And a cricket team, of course. It shows we look on the lighter side of things too. Don't you agree?

HORNE Oh yes, Mr King.

BARROW Yes, Mr King.

KING Also gives a sense of belonging. Work together and play together. Office work can become so impersonal. We like to foster . . . to foster something . . . very different. You know what I mean?

HORNE Oh yes, Mr King.

BARROW Yes, Mr King.

KING You interested in sailing, by any chance? You're quite welcome to come down to my boat at Poole any weekend – do a bit of sailing along the coast.

HORNE Oh, thank you, Mr King.

BARROW Thank you, Mr King.

JOYCE *and* EILEEN, *whispering.*

JOYCE (*slyly*) Eh, what about going over and cheering up old Albert?

EILEEN What for?

JOYCE Well, he looks a bit gloomy, don't he?

EILEEN I don't want to go over. You go over.

JOYCE No, come on. You come over.

EILEEN What for?

JOYCE Cheer him up. For a bit of fun.

EILEEN Oh, you're awful.

JOYCE Come on. Come over.

KING (*to* RYAN) Can I fill your glass, Ryan?

RYAN *nods, and smiles.*

Can't leave you without a drink, can we? The guest of honour.

JOYCE *and* EILEEN *sit either side of* ALBERT *on a divan.*

JOYCE Mind if we join you?

186

ALBERT Oh, hullo.

EILEEN Enjoying the party?

JOYCE What are you sitting all gloomy about?

ALBERT I'm not gloomy, I'm just sitting, drinking.
Feel a bit tired, actually.

JOYCE Why, what have you been doing?

ALBERT Nothing.

JOYCE You just said you were tired. Eh, move up, I'm
on the edge.

ALBERT Sorry.

EILEEN Eh, mind out, you're squashing me.

ALBERT Oh . . .

JOYCE You squash her, she won't mind.

EILEEN (*laughing*) Oh, Joyce!

   GIDNEY, *with a smile, watching.*

JOYCE Come on, tell us, what are you tired about?

ALBERT Oh, just work, I suppose.

JOYCE I've been working too. I'm not tired. I love
work. Don't you, Eileen? (*She leans across him to
speak.*)

EILEEN Oh yes, I love work.

ALBERT No, I'm not tired, really. I'm all right.

EILEEN He looks tired.

JOYCE You've been living it up. Women.

EILEEN I'll bet.

JOYCE Females.

The girls giggle.

ALBERT (*with an uncertain smile*) No, I wouldn't . . .

EILEEN Eh, mind your drink. My best taffeta.

JOYCE He's not bad looking when you get close.

EILEEN Quite nice when you get close.

ALBERT Thanks for the compliment.

EILEEN You got a flat of your own?

ALBERT No. Have you?

EILEEN (*forlornly*) No.

JOYCE You live with your mother, don't you?

ALBERT Yes.

JOYCE Does she look after you all right, then?

ALBERT Yes, she . . . (*He stands.*) I'm just going to the bar.

JOYCE So are we.

EILEEN Me too.

They follow.

KING Well, now everyone . . .

JOYCE I'm having gin.

ALBERT Gin? Wait a minute . . .

KING Just a minute, everyone, can I have your attention?

GIDNEY (*to* JOYCE) Didn't make much impression, did you?

JOYCE Didn't I?

KING Just for a moment, please . . .

GIDNEY Eh, Stokes, pay attention, will you?

ALBERT What?

GIDNEY Mr King wants your attention.

KING I'd just like to propose a toast to our guest of honour, Mr Ryan. Gidney!

GIDNEY Yes?

ALBERT Here's your gin, then.

JOYCE Thanks.

KING (*to* GIDNEY) Go and get Kedge out of that corner, will you? Now, as you know, we're all gathered here tonight to pay our respects to our old friend and colleague, Mr Ryan . . .

> KEDGE *and* BETTY *are locked together in the*
> *armchair.* GIDNEY *taps* KEDGE *on the shoulder.*

GIDNEY Mr King wants to know if you'll honour the party with your presence.

KEDGE (*jumping up*) Oh, sorry.

BETTY, *thrown off, falls. He picks her up.*

Sorry.

KING We've all known Mr Ryan for a very long time. Of course, I've known him myself much longer than anyone here –

KEDGE For he's a jolly good fellow –

KING Wait! Very glad for your enthusiasm, Mr Kedge. Your heart, I am quite sure, is in the right place.

General laughter.

ALBERT, EILEEN, JOYCE, SEELEY *and* GIDNEY *stand in a group around* MR RYAN's *chair.*

But please allow me to toast Mr Ryan first and then the floor is yours. Well, as I was saying, the whole department is here tonight to pay tribute to a man who from time immemorial has become, how shall I put it, the very core of our litde community. I remember Mr Ryan sitting at his very own desk the first time my father brought me into the office –

A sharp scream and stiffening from EILEEN. *All turn to her.*

Good heavens!

GIDNEY What is it?

AD LIB What's happened? Eileen, what's the matter?

EILEEN Someone touched me!

JOYCE Touched you?

EILEEN Someone touched me! Someone –!

BETTY What did he do?

KEDGE Touched you? What did he do?

JOYCE What did he do, Eileen?

EILEEN He . . . he . . . he took a liberty!

KEDGE Go on! Who did?

> EILEEN *turns and stares at* ALBERT. *Silence. All stare at* ALBERT.

ALBERT What are you looking at me for?

GIDNEY (*muttering*) Good God . . .

> *Tense, embarrassed pause.*

HORNE (*at the door, whispering*) What did he do, touch her?

BARROW (*open-mouthed*) Yes.

HORNE (*wide-eyed*) Where?

> *They look at each other, open-mouthed and wide-eyed.*

ALBERT What are you looking at me for?

KING Please, now . . . can we possibly . . . I mean . . .

EILEEN (*in a voice of reproach, indignation and horror*) Albert!

ALBERT What do you mean?

SEELEY How does she know it was Albert?

191

KEDGE Wonder what he did. Made her jump didn't he?

ALBERT Now look, wait a minute, this is absolutely ridiculous –

GIDNEY Ridiculous, eh? I'll say it is. What do you think you're up to?

EILEEN Yes, I was just standing there, suddenly this hand . . .

JOYCE I could tell he was that sort.

The camera closes on MR RYAN's *hand, resting comfortably on his knee, and then to his face which, smiling vaguely, is inclined to the ceiling. It must be quite clear from the expression that it was his hand which strayed.*

GIDNEY Come out here, Albert.

ALBERT Don't pull me. What are you doing?

SEELEY How do you know it was him?

ALBERT (*throwing off gidney's hand*) Let go of me!

SEELEY What are you pulling him for?

GIDNEY You keep out of this.

KING (*nervously*) Now please let me continue my toast, ladies and gendemen. Really, you must settle this elsewhere.

SEELEY We don't even know what he's supposed to have done.

ALBERT I didn't do anything.

GIDNEY We can guess what he did.

KING (*at speed*) We are all collected here tonight in honour of Mr Ryan and to present him with a token of our affection –

JOYCE (*to* ALBERT) You snake!

SEELEY Well, what did he do? What's he supposed to have done?

ALBERT She doesn't know what she's talking about.

SEELEY Come on, what's he supposed to have done, Eileen, anyway?

EILEEN Mind you own business.

JOYCE You don't think she's going to tell you, do you?

GIDNEY Look, Seeley, why don't you shut up?

SEELEY Now don't talk to me like that, Gidney.

ALBERT Don't worry about him, Seeley.

KING As I have been trying to say –

JOYCE You come over here, Eileen, sit down. She's upset, aren't you?

EILEEN (*to* SEELEY) So would you be!

KING Miss Phipps, would you mind composing yourself?

EILEEN Composing myself!

GIDNEY Come outside a minute, Albert.

KING As I have been trying to say –

KEDGE (*brightly*) I'm listening, Mr King!

KING What?

KEDGE I'm listening. I'm with you.

KING Oh, thank you. Thank you, my boy.

ALBERT I'm going, anyway.

ALBERT *goes into the hall, followed by* GIDNEY *and* SEELEY. *The door shuts behind them.*

GIDNEY Wait a minute, Stokes.

ALBERT What do you want?

GIDNEY I haven't been satisfied with your . . . sort of . . . behaviour for some time, you know that, don't you?

ALBERT You haven't . . . you haven't what?

GIDNEY For instance, there was that bloody awful game of football you played when you threw the game away last Saturday that I've got on my mind, besides one or two other things!

SEELEY Eh look, Gidney, you're talking like a prize –

GIDNEY (*viciously*) I've told you to keep out of this.

ALBERT (*tensely*) I'm going, anyway.

GIDNEY Wait a minute, let's have it out. What do you think you're up to?

ALBERT Look, I've told you –

GIDNEY What did you think you were doing with that girl?

ALBERT I didn't touch her.

GIDNEY I'm responsible for that girl. She's a good friend of mine. I know her uncle.

ALBERT Do you?

SEELEY You know, you're being so stupid, Gidney –

GIDNEY Seeley, I can take you any day, you know that, don't you?

SEELEY Go on!

GIDNEY Any day.

SEELEY You can take me any day?

GIDNEY Any day.

SEELEY Well, go on, then. Go on . . . if you can take me . . .

ALBERT Seeley –

SEELEY No, if he says he can take me, if he can take me any day . . .

The door opens slightly, HORNE *and* BARROW *peer out.*

ALBERT Gidney, why don't you . . . why don't you get back to the party?

GIDNEY I was telling you, Albert –

ALBERT Stokes.

GIDNEY I was telling you, Albert, that if you're going to behave like a boy often in mixed company –

ALBERT I told you my name's Stokes!

GIDNEY Don't be childish, Albert.

A sudden silence. MR KING's *voice from the room.*

KING . . . and for his unfailing good humour and
cheeriness, Mr Ryan will always be remembered at
Hislop, King and Martindale!

Scattered applause. HORNE, *caught by their stares,
shuts the door hastily.*

ALBERT (*going to the door*) Goodnight.

GIDNEY (*obstructing him*) Go back and apologise.

ALBERT What for?

GIDNEY For insulting a lady. Mate. A lady.
Something to do with breeding. But I suppose you're
too bloody backward to know anything about that.

ALBERT You're talking right out of your hat.

SEELEY Right out of the bowler.

GIDNEY (*to* SEELEY) No one invited you out here,
did they?

SEELEY Who invited you?

GIDNEY I'm talking to this man on behalf of the
firm! Unless I get a satisfactory explanation I shall
think seriously about recommending his dismissal.

ALBERT Get out of my way, will you?

GIDNEY Acting like an animal all over the place –

ALBERT Move out of it!

GIDNEY (*breathlessly*) I know your trouble.

ALBERT Oh, yes?

GIDNEY Yes, sticks out a mile.

ALBERT Does it?

GIDNEY Yes.

ALBERT What's my trouble then?

GIDNEY (*very deliberately*) You're a mother's boy. That's what you are. That's your trouble. You're a mother's boy.

> ALBERT *hits him. There is a scuffle,* SEELEY *tries to part them. The three rock back and forth in the hall: confused blows, words and grunts.*
>
> *The door of the room opens. Faces.* MR KING *comes out.*

KING What in heaven's name is going on here!

> *The scuffle stops. A short silence,* ALBERT *opens the front door, goes out and slams it behind him. He stands on the doorstep, breathing heavily, his face set.*

SCENE TWO

The kitchen.

MRS STOKES *ij asleep, her head resting on the table, the cards disordered. The clock ticks. It is twelve o'clock. The front door opens slowly.* ALBERT *comes*

in, closes the door softly, stops, looks across to the
open kitchen door, sees his mother, and begins to creep
up the stairs with great stealth. The camera follows
him. Her voice stops him.

MOTHER Albert!

He stops.

Albert! Is that you?

She goes to the kitchen door.

What are you creeping up the stairs for? Might have
been a burglar. What would I have done then?

He descends slowly.

Creeping up the stairs like that. Give anyone a fright.
Creeping up the stairs like that. You leave me in the
house all alone . . . (*She stops and regards him.*) Look
at you! Look at your suit. What's the matter with
your tie, it's all crumpled, I pressed it for you this
morning. Well, I won't even ask any questions. That's
all. You look a disgrace.

He walks past her into the kitchen, goes to the sink
and pours himself a glass of water. She follows him.

What have you been doing, mucking about with girls?

She begins to pile the cards.

Mucking about with girls, I suppose. Do you know
what the time is? I fell asleep, right here at this table,
waiting for you. I don't know what your father would
say. Coming in this time of night. It's after twelve
o'clock. In a state like that. Drunk, I suppose. I

suppose your dinner's ruined. Well, if you want to make a convenience out of your own home, that's your business. I'm only your mother, I don't suppose that counts for much these days. I'm not saying any more. If you want to go mucking about with girls, that's your business.

She takes his dinner out of the oven.

Well, anyway, you'll have your dinner. You haven't eaten a single thing all night.

She places a plate on the table and gets knife and fork. He stands by the sink, sipping water.

I wouldn't mind if you found a really nice girl and brought her home and introduced her to your mother, brought her home for dinner, I'd know you were sincere, if she was a really nice girl, she'd be like a daughter to me. But you've never brought a girl home here in your life. I suppose you're ashamed of your mother.

Pause.

Come on, it's all dried up. I kept it on a low light. I couldn't even go up to Grandma's room and have a look round because there wasn't any bulb, you might as well eat it.

He stands.

What's the matter, are you drunk? Where did you go, to one of those pubs in the West End? You'll get into serious trouble, my boy, if you frequent those places, I'm warning you. Don't you read the papers?

Pause.

I hope you're satisfied, anyway. The house in darkness,
I wasn't going to break my neck going down to that
cellar to look for a bulb, you come home looking like
I don't know what, anyone would think you gave me
a fortune out of your wages. Yes. I don't say anything,
do I? I keep quiet about what you expect me to
manage on. I never grumble. I keep a lovely home,
I bet there's none of the boys in your firm better fed
than you are. I'm not asking for gratitude. But one
things hurts me, Albert, and I'll tell you what it is.
Not for years, not for years, have you come up to me
and said, Mum, I love you, like you did when you
were a little boy. You've never said it without me
having to ask you. Not since before your father died.
And he was a good man. He had high hopes of you.
I've never told you, Albert, about the high hopes he
had of you. I don't know what you do with all your
money. But don't forget what it cost us to rear you,
my boy, I've never told you about the sacrifices we
made, you wouldn't care, anyway. Telling me lies
about going to the firm's party. They've got a bit of
respect at that firm, that's why we sent you there, to
start off your career, they wouldn't let you carry on
like that at one of their functions. Mr King would
have his eye on you. I don't know where you've been.
Well, if you don't want to lead a clean life it's your
lookout, if you want to go mucking about with all
sorts of bits of girls, if you're content to leave your
own mother sitting here till midnight, and I wasn't
feeling well, anyway, I didn't tell you because I didn't

want to upset you, I keep things from you, you're the
only one I've got, but what do you care, you don't
care, you don't care, the least you can do is sit down
and eat the dinner I cooked for you, specially for you,
it's Shepherd's Pie –

> ALBERT *lunges to the table, picks up the clock and
> violently raises it above his head. A stifled scream
> from the* MOTHER.

Act Three

SCENE ONE

The coffee stall, shuttered.

ALBERT *is leaning against it. He is sweating. He is holding the butt of a cigarette. There is a sound of a foot on gravel. He starts, the butt burns his hand, he drops it and turns. A girl is looking at him. She smiles.*

GIRL Good evening.

Pause.

What are you doing?

Pause.

What are you doing out at this time of night?

She moves closer to him.

I live just round the corner.

He stares at her.

Like to? Chilly out here, isn't it? Come on.

Pause.

Come on.

He goes with her.

SCENE TWO

The GIRL'*s room. The door opens. She comes in. Her manner has changed from the seductive. She is brisk and nervous.*

GIRL Come in. Don't slam the door. Shut it gently. I'll light the fire. Chilly out, don't you find? Have you got a match?

He walks across the room.

Please don't walk so heavily. Please. There's no need to let . . . to let the whole house know you're here. Life's difficult enough as it is. Have you got a match?

ALBERT No, I . . . I don't think I have.

GIRL Oh, God, you'd think you'd have a match.

He walks about.

I say, would you mind taking your shoes off? You're really making a dreadful row. Really, I can't bear . . . noisy . . . people.

He looks at his shoes, begins to untie one. The girl searches for matches on the mantelpiece, upon which are a number of articles and objects, including a large alarm clock.

I know I had one somewhere.

ALBERT I've got a lighter.

GIRL You can't light a gas fire with a lighter. You'd burn your fingers.

She bends down to the hearth.

Where are the damn things? This is ridiculous. I die without the fire. I simply die. (*She finds the box.*) Ah, here we are. At last.

She turns on the gas fire and lights it. He watches her. She puts the matchbox on the mantelpiece and picks up a photo.

Do you like this photo? It's of my litde girl. She's staying with friends. Rather fine, isn't she? Very aristocratic features, don't you think? She's at a very select boarding school at the moment, actually. In . . . Hereford, very near Hereford. (*She puts the photo back.*) I shall be going down for the prize day shortly. You do look idiotic standing there with one shoe on and one shoe off. All lopsided.

ALBERT *pulls at the lace of his other shoe. The lace breaks. He swears shortly under his breath.*

GIRL (*sharply*) Do you mind not saying words like that?

ALBERT I didn't . . .

GIRL I heard you curse.

ALBERT My lace broke.

GIRL That's no excuse.

ALBERT What did I say?

GIRL I'm sorry, I can't bear that sort of thing. It's just . . . not in my personality.

ALBERT I'm sorry.

GIRL It's quite all right. It's just . . . something in my nature. I've got to think of my daughter, too, you know.

She crouches by the fire.

Come near the fire a minute. Sit down.

He goes towards a small stool.

Not on that! That's my seat. It's my own stool. I did the needlework myself. A long time ago.

He sits in a chair, opposite.

Which do you prefer, electric or gas? For a fire, I mean?

ALBERT (*holding his forehead, muttering*) I don't know.

GIRL There's no need to be rude, it was a civil question. I prefer gas. Or a log fire, of course. They have them in Switzerland.

Pause.

Have you got a headache?

ALBERT No.

GIRL I didn't realise you had a lighter. You don't happen to have any cigarettes on you, I suppose?

ALBERT No.

GIRL I'm very fond of a smoke. After dinner. With a glass of wine. Or before dinner, with sherry.

She stands and taps the mantelpiece, her eyes roaming over it.

You look as if you've had a night out. Where have you been? Had a nice time?

ALBERT Quite . . . quite nice.

GIRL (*sitting on the stool*) What do you do?

ALBERT I . . . work in films.

GIRL Films? Really? What do you do?

ALBERT I'm an assistant director.

GIRL Really? How funny. I used to be a continuity girl. But I gave it up.

ALBERT (*tonelessly*) What a pity.

GIRL Yes, I'm beginning to think you're right. You meet such a good class of people. Of course, now you say you're an assistant director I can see what you mean. I mean, I could tell you had breeding the moment I saw you. You looked a bit washed out, perhaps, but there was no mistaking the fact that you had breeding. I'm extremely particular, you see. I do like a certain amount of delicacy in men . . . a certain amount . . . a certain degree . . . a certain amount of refinement. You do see my point? Some men I couldn't possibly entertain. Not even if I was . . . starving. I don't want to be personal, but that word you used, when you broke your lace, it made me shiver, I'm just not that type, made me wonder if you were as well bred as I thought . . .

He wipes his face with his hand.

You do look hot. Why are you so hot? It's chilly. Yes, you remind me . . . I saw the most ghasdy horrible fight before, there was a man, one man, he was sweating . . . sweating. You haven't been in a fight, by any chance? I don't know how men can be so bestial. It's hardly much fun for women, I can tell you. I don't want someone else's blood on my carpet.

ALBERT *chuckles.*

What are you laughing at?

ALBERT Nothing.

GIRL It's not in the least funny.

ALBERT *looks up at the mantelpiece. His gaze rests there.*

What are you looking at?

ALBERT (*ruminatively*) That's a nice big clock.

It is twenty past two.

GIRL (*with fatigue*) Yes, it's late, I suppose we might as well . . . Haven't you got a cigarette?

ALBERT No.

GIRL (*jumping up*) I'm sure I have, somewhere. (*She goes to the table.*) Yes, here we are, I knew I had. I have to hide them. The woman who comes in to do my room, she's very light-fingered. I don't know why she comes in at all. Nobody wants her, all she does is spy on me, but I'm obliged to put up with her, this room is serviced. Which means I have to pay a pretty penny.

She lights her cigarette.

It's a dreadful area, too. I'm thinking of moving. The neighbourhood is full of people of no class at all. I just don't fit in.

ALBERT Is that clock right?

GIRL People have told me, the most distinguished people, that I could go anywhere. You could go anywhere, they've told me, you could be anything. I'm quite well educated, you know. My father was a . . . he was a military man. In the Army. Actually it was a relief to speak to you. I haven't . . . spoken to anyone for some hours.

ALBERT *suddenly coughs violently.*

Oh, please don't do that! Use your handkerchief!

He sighs, and groans.

What on earth's the matter with you? What have you been doing tonight?

He looks at her and smiles.

ALBERT Nothing.

GIRL Really?

She belches.

Oh, excuse me. I haven't eaten all day. I had a tooth out. Hiccoughs come from not eating, don't they? Do you . . . do you want one of these?

She throws him a cigarette, which he slowly lights.

I mean, I'm no different from any other girl. In fact, I'm better. These so-called respectable girls, for instance, I'm sure they're much worse than I am. Well, you're an assistant director – all your continuity girls and secretaries, I'll bet they're . . . very loose.

ALBERT Uh.

GIRL Do you know what I've actually heard? I've heard that respectable married women, solicitors' wives, go out and pick men up when their husbands are out on business! Isn't that fantastic? I mean, they're supposed to be . . . they're supposed to be respectable!

ALBERT (*muttering*) Fantastic.

GIRL I beg your pardon?

ALBERT I said it was fantastic.

GIRL It is. You're right. Quite fantastic. Here's one thing, though. There's one thing that's always fascinated me. How far do men's girl friends go? I've often wondered. Pause. Eh?

ALBERT Depends.

GIRL Yes, I suppose it must.

Pause.

You mean on the girl?

ALBERT What?

GIRL You mean it depends on the girl?

ALBERT It would do, yes.

GIRL Quite possibly. I must admit that with your continuity girls and secretaries, I don't see why you . . . had to approach me. . . . Have you been on the town tonight, then? With a continuity girl?

ALBERT You're a bit . . . worried about continuity girls, aren't you?

GIRL Only because I've been one myself. I know what they're like. No better than they should be.

ALBERT When were you a . . .?

GIRL Years ago! (*Standing.*) You're nosey, aren't you?

She goes to the window.

Sometimes I wish the night would never end. I like sleeping. I could sleep . . . on and on.

ALBERT *stands and picks up the clock.*

Yes, you can see the station from here. All the trains go out, right through the night.

He stares at the clock.

I suppose we might as well . . . (*She turns and sees him.*) What are you doing? (*She crosses to him.*) What are you doing with that clock?

He looks at her, slowly.

Mmnn?

ALBERT Admiring it.

GIRL It's a perfectly ordinary clock. Give me it. I've seen too many people slip things into their pockets before now, as soon as your back's turned. Nothing personal, of course. (*She puts it back.*) Mind your ash! Don't spill it all over the floor! I have to keep this carpet immaculate. Otherwise the charlady, she's always looking for excuses for telling tales. Here. Here's an ashtray. Use it, please.

She gives it to him. He stares at her.

Sit down. Sit down. Don't stand about like that. What are you staring at me for?

He sits. She studies him.

Where's your wife?

ALBERT Nowhere.

She stubs her cigarette.

GIRL And what film are you making at the moment?

ALBERT I'm on holiday.

GIRL Where do you work?

ALBERT I'm a freelance.

GIRL You're . . . rather young to be in such a . . . high position, aren't you?

ALBERT Oh?

GIRL (*laughs*) You amuse me. You interest me. I'm a bit of a psychologist, you know. You're very young to be – what you said you were. There's something childish in your face, almost retarded. (*She laughs.*) I do like that word. I'm not being personal, of course . . . just being . . . psychological. Of course, I can see you're one for the girls. Don't know why you had to pick on me, at this time of night, really rather forward of you. I'm a respectable mother, you know, with a child at boarding school. You couldn't call me . . . anything else. All I do, I just entertain a few gentlemen, of my own choice, now and again. What girl doesn't?

> *His hand screws the cigarette. He lets it fall on the carpet.*

(*Outraged.*) What do you think you're doing?

> *She stares at htm.*

Pick it up! Pick that up, I tell you! It's my carpet!

> *She lunges towards it.*

It's not my carpet, they'll make me pay –

> *His hand closes upon hers as she reaches for it.*

What are you doing? Let go. Treating my place like a pigsty. (*She looks up at him as he bends over her.*) Let me go. You're burning my carpet!

ALBERT (*quietly, intensely*) Sit down.

GIRL How dare you?

ALBERT Shut up. Sit down.

GIRL (*struggling*) What are you doing?

ALBERT (*erratically, trembling, but with quiet command*) Don't scream. I'm warning you.

He lifts her by her wrist and presses her down on to the stool.

No screaming. I warn you.

GIRL What's the –?

ALBERT (*through his teeth*) Be quiet. I told you to be quiet. Now you be quiet.

GIRL What are you going to do?

ALBERT (*seizing the clock from the mantelpiece*) Don't muck me about!

She freezes with terror.

See this? One crack with this . . . just one crack . . . (*Viciously.*) Who do you think you are? You talk too much, you know that. You never stop talking. Just because you're a woman you think you can get away with it. (*Bending over her.*) You've made a mistake, this time. You've picked the wrong man.

He begins to grow in stature and excitement, passing the clock from hand to hand.

You're all the same, you see, you're all the same, you're just a dead weight round my neck. What makes you think . . .

He begins to move about the room, at one point half crouching, at another standing upright, as if exercising his body.

213

What makes you think you can . . . tell me . . . yes . . . It's the same as this business about the light in Grandma's room. Always something. Always something. (*To her.*) My ash? I'll put it where I like! You see this clock? Watch your step. Just watch your step.

GIRL Stop this. What are you –?

ALBERT (*seizing her wrist, with trembling, controlled violence*) Watch your step! (*Stammering.*) I've had – I've had – I've had – just about enough. Get it? . . . You know what I did?

He looks at her and chuckles.

Don't be so frightened.

GIRL I . . .

ALBERT (*casually*) Don't be so frightened.

He squats by her, still holding the clock.

I'm just telling you. I'm just telling you, that's all. (*Breathlessly.*) You haven't got any breeding. She hadn't either. And what about those girls tonight? Same kind. And that one. I didn't touch her!

GIRL (*almost inaudible*) What you been doing?

ALBERT I've got as many qualifications as the next man. Let's get that quite . . . straight. And I got the answer to her. I got the answer to her, you see, tonight. . . . I finished the conversation . . . I finished it . . . I finished her . . .

She squirms. He raises the clock.

With this clock! (*Trembling.*) One . . . crack . . . with . . . this. . . clock . . . finished! (*Thoughtfully.*) Of course, I loved her, really.

He suddenly sees the photograph on the mantelpiece, puts the clock down and takes it. The GIRL *half rises and gasps, watching him. He looks at the photo curiously.*

Uhhh? . . . Your daughter? . . . This a photo of your daughter? . . . Uuuh? (*He breaks the frame and takes out the photo.*)

GIRL (*rushes at him*) Leave that!

ALBERT (*dropping the frame and holding the photo*) Is it?

The girl grabs at it. albert clutches her wrist. He holds her at arm's length.

GIRL Leave that! (*Writhing.*) What? Don't – it's mine!

ALBERT (*turns the photo over and reads back*) 'Class Three Classical, Third Prize, Bronze Medal, Twickenham Competition, nineteen thirty-three.'

He stares at her. The girl stands, shivering and whimpering.

You liar. That's you.

GIRL It's not!

ALBERT That's not your daughter. It's you! You're just a fake, you're just all lies!

GIRL Scum! Filthy scum!

ALBERT, *twisting her wrist, moves suddenly to her. The* GIRL *cringing, falls back into her chair.*

ALBERT (*warningly*) Mind how you talk to me. (*He crumples the photo.*)

GIRL (*moans*) My daughter. My little girl. My little baby girl.

ALBERT Get up.

GIRL No . . .

ALBERT Get up! Up!

She stands.

Walk over there, to the wall. Go on! Get over there. Do as you're told. Do as I'm telling you. I'm giving the orders here.

She walks to the wall.

Stop!

GIRL (*whimpering*) What . . . do you want me to do?

ALBERT Just keep your big mouth closed, for a start.

He frowns uncertainly.

Cover your face!

She does so. He looks about, blinking.

Yes. That's right. (*He sees his shoes.*) Come on, come on, pick up those shoes. Those shoes! Pick them up!

She looks for the shoes and picks them up.

That's right. (*He sits.*) Bring them over here. Come on. That's right. Put them on.

He extends his foot.

GIRL You're . . .

ALBERT On! Right on. That's it. That's it. That's more like it. That's . . . more like it! Good. Lace them! Good.

He stands. She crouches.

Silence.

He shivers and murmurs with the cold. He looks about the room.

ALBERT It's cold.

Pause.

Ooh, it's freezing.

GIRL (*whispering*) The fire's gone.

ALBERT (*looking at the window*) What's that? Looks like light. Ooh, it's perishing. (*Looks about, muttering.*) What a dump. Not staying here. Getting out of this place.

He shivers and drops the clock. He looks down at it. She too. He kicks it across the room.

(*With a smile, softly.*) So you . . . bear that in mind. Mind how you talk to me.

He goes to door, then turns.

(*Flipping half a crown to her.*) Buy yourself a seat . . . buy yourself a seat at a circus.

He opens the door and goes.

SCENE THREE

The house.

The front door opens. ALBERT *comes in, a slight smile on his face. He saunters across the hall into the kitchen, takes off his jacket and throws it across the room. The same with his tie. He sits heavily, loosely, in a chair, his legs stretched out. Stretching his arms, he yawns luxuriously, scratches his head with both hands and stares ruminatively at the ceiling, a smile on his face. His mother's voice calls his name.*

MOTHER (*from the stairs*) Albert!

> *His body freezes. His gaze comes down. His legs slowly come together. He looks in front of him.*

> *His* MOTHER *comes into the room, in her dressing gown. She stands, looking at him.*

Do you know what the time is?

> *Pause.*

Where have you been?

> *Pause.*

(*Reproachfully, near to tears.*) I don't know what to say to you, Albert. To raise your hand to your own mother. You've never done that before in your life. To threaten your own mother.

> *Pause.*

That clock would have hurt me, Albert. And you'd

have been . . . I know you'd have been very sorry.
Aren't I a good mother to you? Everything I do is . . .
is for your own good. You should know that. You're
all I've got.

*She looks at his slumped figure. Her reproach turns
to solicitude.*

(*Gently.*) Look at you. You look washed out. Oh, you
look . . . I don't understand what could have come
over you.

She takes a chair and sits close to him.

Listen, Albert, I'll tell you what I'm going to do. I'm
going to forget it. You see? I'm going to forget all
about it. We'll have your holiday in a fortnight. We
can go away.

She strokes his hand.

We'll go away . . . together.

Pause.

It's not as if you're a bad boy . . . you're a good boy
. . . I know you are . . . it's not as if you're really bad,
Albert, you're not . . . you're not bad, you're good . . .
you're not a bad boy, Albert, I know you're not . . .

Pause.

You're good, you're not bad, you're a good boy . . .
I know you are . . . you are, aren't you?

NIGHT SCHOOL

Night School was transmitted by Associated Rediffusion Television on 21 July 1960 with the following cast:

ANNIE	Iris Vandeleur
WALTER	Milo O'Shea
MILLY	Jane Eccles
SALLY	Vivien Merchant
SOLTO	Martin Miller
TULLY	Bernard Spear

Directed by Joan Kemp-Welch

It was subsequently broadcast on the BBC Third Programme on 25 September 1966 in the version printed here, with the following cast:

ANNIE	Mary O'Farrell
WALTER	John Hollis
MILLY	Sylvia Coleridge
SALLY	Prunella Scales
SOLTO	Sydney Tafler
TULLY	Preston Lockwood
BARBARA	Barbara Mitchell
MAVIS	Carol Marsh

Directed by Guy Vaesen

Characters

ANNIE

WALTER

MILLY

SALLY

SOLTO

TULLY

BARBARA

MAVIS

Living room.

ANNIE Look at your raincoat. It's on the floor.

WALTER I'll hang it up. I'll take the case upstairs, eh?

ANNIE Have your tea. Go on, have your tea. Don't worry about taking the case upstairs. Pause.

WALTER Lovely cake.

ANNIE Do you like it? I've had to lay off cake. They was giving me heartburn. Go on, have another piece.

WALTER Ah well, the place looks marvellous.

ANNIE I gave it a nice clean out before you came.

  Pause.

Well, Wally, how did they treat you this time, eh?

WALTER Marvellous.

ANNIE I didn't expect you back so soon. I thought you was staying longer this time.

WALTER No, I wasn't staying longer.

ANNIE Milly's not been well.

WALTER Oh? What's the matter with her?

ANNIE She'll be down in a minute, she heard you come.

WALTER I brought some chocolates for her.

ANNIE I can't stand chocolates.

WALTER I know that. That's why I didn't bring any for you.

ANNIE You remembered, eh?

WALTER Oh, yes.

ANNIE Yes, she's been having a rest upstairs. All I do, I run up and down them stairs all day long. What about the other day? I was up doing those curtains, I came over terrible. Then she says I shouldn't have done them that way. I should have done them the other way.

WALTER What's the matter with the curtains?

ANNIE She says they're not hanging properly. She says I should have done them the other way. She likes them the other way. She lies up there upstairs. I'm older than she is.

Annie pours herself and Walter more tea.

I went out and got that cake the minute we got your letter.

WALTER (*sighing*) Ah, you know, I've been thinking for months . . . you know that? . . . months . . . I'll come back here . . . I'll lie on my bed . . . I'll see the curtains blowing by the window . . . I'll have a good rest, eh?

ANNIE There she is, she's moving herself. You got a bit of the sun.

WALTER I'm going to take it easy for a few weeks.

ANNIE You should. It's silly. You should have a rest for a few weeks. *Pause.*

WALTER How's Mr Solto?

ANNIE He's still the best landlord in the district. You wouldn't get a better landlord in any district.

WALTER You're good tenants to him.

ANNIE He's so kind. He's almost one of the family. Except he doesn't live here. As a matter of fact, he hasn't been to tea for months.

WALTER I'm going to ask him to lend me some money.

ANNIE She's coming down.

WALTER What's a couple of hundred to him? Nothing.

ANNIE (*whispering*) Don't say a word about the curtains.

WALTER Eh?

ANNIE Don't mention about the curtains. About the hanging. About what I told you about what she said about the way I hung the curtains. Don't say a word. Here she comes.

Milly enters.

WALTER (*kissing her*) Aunty Milly.

MILLY Did she give you a bit of cake?

WALTER Marvellous cake.

MILLY I told her to go and get it.

WALTER I haven't had a bit of cake like that for nine solid months.

MILLY It comes from down the road.

WALTER Here you are, Aunty, here's some chocolates.

MILLY He didn't forget that I like chocolates.

ANNIE He didn't forget that I don't like chocolates.

MILLY Nutty? Are they nutty?

WALTER I picked them specially for the nuts. They were the nuttiest ones they had there.

ANNIE Sit down,

MILLY Don't stand up.

MILLY I've been sitting down, I've been lying down. I got to stand up now and again.

WALTER You haven't been so well, eh?

MILLY Middling. Only middling.

ANNIE I'm only middling as well.

MILLY Yes, Annie's only been middling.

WALTER Well, I'm back now, eh?

MILLY How did they treat you this time?

WALTER Very well. Very well.

MILLY When you going back?

WALTER I'm not going back.

MILLY You ought to be ashamed of yourself, Walter, spending half your life in prison. Where do you think that's going to get you?

WALTER Half my life? What do you mean? Twice, that's all.

ANNIE What about Borstal?

WALTER That doesn't count.

MILLY I wouldn't mind if you ever had a bit of luck, but what happens? Every time you move yourself they take you inside.

WALTER I've finished with all that, anyway.

MILLY Listen, I've told you before, if you're not clever in that way you should try something else, you should open up a little business – you could get the capital from Solto, he'll lend you some money. I mean, every time you put a foot outside the door they pick you up, they put you inside. What's the good of it?

ANNIE You going to have a jam tart, Wally?

WALTER Sure.

MILLY (*eats*) Where'd you get the jam tarts?

ANNIE Round the corner.

MILLY Round the corner? I thought I told you to get them down the road.

ANNIE He didn't have any down the road.

MILLY Why, he'd run out?

ANNIE I don't know if he'd made any today.

MILLY What are they like?

WALTER Lovely.

He takes another. Eats. Pause.

MILLY I've had to lay off tarts, haven't I, Annie?

ANNIE They was giving her heartburn.

MILLY I had to lay off. I had to lay right off tarts, since just after Easter.

ANNIE I bet you never had a tart in prison, Wally.

WALTER No, I couldn't lay my hands on one.

Pause.

MILLY Well? Have you told him?

ANNIE Told him what?

MILLY You haven't told him?

WALTER Told me what?

MILLY Eh?

ANNIE No, I haven't.

MILLY Why not?

ANNIE I wasn't going to tell him.

WALTER Tell me what?

MILLY You said you was going to tell him.

ANNIE I didn't have the pluck.

WALTER What's going on here? What's all this?
  Pause.

ANNIE Have a rock cake, Wally.

WALTER No, thanks. I'm full up.

ANNIE Go on, have a rock cake.

WALTER No, I've had enough. Honest.

MILLY Have a rock cake, come on.

WALTER I can't, I'm full up!

ANNIE I'll go and fill the pot.

MILLY I'll go.

ANNIE You can't go, come on, give me the pot. You
can't go, you're not well.

MILLY I'll go, come on, give me the pot.

ANNIE I made the tea, why shouldn't I fill the pot?

MILLY Can't I fill the pot for my own nephew!

WALTER Now listen, what have you got to tell me –
what's the matter? I come home from prison, I been
away nine months, I come home for a bit of peace and
quiet to recuperate. What's going on here?

MILLY Well . . . we've let your room.

WALTER You've what?

ANNIE We've let your room.

Pause.

MILLY Look, Wally, don't start making faces. How could we help ourselves?

Pause.

WALTER You've done what?

ANNIE We missed you.

MILLY It gave us a bit of company.

ANNIE Of course it did . . .

MILLY It gave us a helping hand . . .

ANNIE You spend half your time inside, we don't know when you're coming out . . .

MILLY We only get the pension.

ANNIE That's all we got, we only got the pension.

MILLY She pays good money, she pays thirty-five and six a week . . .

ANNIE She's down here every Friday morning with the rent.

MILLY And she looks after her room, she's always dusting her room.

ANNIE She helps me give a bit of a dust round the house.

234

MILLY On the weekends . . .

ANNIE She leaves the bath as good as new . . .

MILLY And you should see what she's done to her room.

ANNIE Oh, you should see how she's made the room.

MILLY She's made it beautiful, she's made it really pretty . . .

ANNIE She's fitted up a bedside table lamp in there, hasn't she?

MILLY She's always studying books . . .

ANNIE She goes out to night school three nights a week.

MILLY She's a young girl.

ANNIE She's a very clean girl.

MILLY She's quiet . . .

ANNIE She's a homely girl . . .

  Pause.

WALTER What's her name?

ANNIE Sally . . .

WALTER Sally what?

MILLY Sally Gibbs.

WALTER How long has she been here?

MILLY She's been here about – when did she come?

ANNIE She came about . . .

MILLY Four months about . . . she's been here . . .

WALTER What does she do, for a living?

MILLY She teaches at a school.

WALTER A school teacher!

MILLY Yes.

WALTER A school teacher! In my room.
   Pause.

ANNIE Wally, you'll like her.

WALTER She's sleeping in my room!

MILLY What's the matter with the put-u-up? You can have the put-u-up in here.

WALTER The put-u-up? She's sleeping in my bed.

ANNIE She's bought a lovely coverlet, she's put it on.

WALTER A coverlet? I could go out now, I could pick up a coverlet as good as hers. What are you talking about coverlets for?

MILLY Walter, don't shout at your aunt, she's deaf.

WALTER I can't believe it. I come home after nine months in a dungeon.

ANNIE The money's been a great help.

WALTER Have I ever left you short of money?

MILLY Yes!

WALTER Well . . . not through my own fault. I've always done my best.

MILLY And where's it got you?

WALTER What's this, you reproaching me?

ANNIE Your aunt's not one to go around reproaching people, Walter.

MILLY Live and let live, that's my motto.

ANNIE And mine.

MILLY It's always been my motto, you ask anyone.

WALTER Listen, you don't understand. This is my home. I live here. I've lived in that room for years –

ANNIE On and off.

WALTER You're asking me to sleep on that put-u-up? The only person who ever slept on that put-u-up was Aunty Gracy. That's why she went to America.

MILLY She slept in it for five years with Uncle Alf, Grace did. They never had a word of complaint.

WALTER Uncle Alf! Honest, this has knocked me for . . . for six. I can't believe it. But I'll tell you one thing about that bed she's sleeping in.

ANNIE What's the matter with it?

WALTER There's nothing the matter with it. It's mine, that's all – I bought it.

ANNIE So he did, milly MILLY You? I thought I bought it.

237

ANNIE That's right. You did. I remember.

WALTER You bought it, you went out and chose it, but who gave you the money to buy it?

ANNIE Yes, he's right. He did.

WALTER I mean . . . what's happened to my damn things? What's happened to my case? The one I left here?

ANNIE Well, she didn't mind us leaving your things in the cupboard, did she, Milly?

WALTER Things? That's my life's work!

Pause.

She'll have to go, that's all.

MILLY She's not going.

WALTER Why not?

ANNIE She's not going to go.

MILLY I should say not. She's staying.

Pause.

WALTER (*with fatigue*) Why can't she sleep on the put-u-up?

ANNIE Put a lovely girl like that on the put-u-up? In the dining room?

WALTER She's lovely, is she?

MILLY You should see the beauty cream on her dressing table.

WALTER My dressing table.

MILLY I like a girl who looks after herself.

ANNIE She gives herself a good going over every night.

MILLY She's never out of the bath. Morning and night. On the nights she goes to night school, she has one before she goes out; other nights she has it just before she goes to bed.

WALTER Well, she couldn't have it after she's gone to bed, could she?

Pause.

Night school? What kind of night school?

MILLY She's studying foreign languages there. She's learning to speak two more languages.

ANNIE Yes, you can smell her up and down the house.

WALTER Smell her?

ANNIE Lovely perfumes she puts on.

MILLY Yes, I'll say that, it's a pleasure to smell her.

WALTER Is it?

ANNIE There's nothing wrong with a bit of perfume.

MILLY We're not narrow-minded over a bit of perfume.

ANNIE She's up to date, that's all.

MILLY Up to the latest fashion.

ANNIE I was, when I was a girl.

MILLY What about me?

ANNIE So were you. But you weren't as up to date as I was.

MILLY I was. I didn't have anything coming over me.

Pause.

WALTER Does she know where I've been?

ANNIE Oh, yes.

WALTER You told her I've been in the nick?

ANNIE Oh, we told her, yes.

WALTER Did you tell her why?

MILLY Oh, no. Oh no, we didn't tell her why.

ANNIE Oh, no, we didn't discuss that . . . But I mean it didn't worry her, did it, Milly? I mean she was very interested. Oh, she was terribly interested.

WALTER (*slowly*) She was, was she?

ANNIE Yes.

Walter stands abruptly, slamming the table.

WALTER Where am I going to put my case?

ANNIE You can put it in the hall.

WALTER The hall? That means I'll have to keep running out to the hall whenever I want anything.

Pause.

I can't live in these conditions for long. I'm used to something better. I'm used to privacy. I could have her walking in here any time of the day or night. This is the living room. I don't want to share my meals with a stranger.

ANNIE She only has bed and breakfast. I take it up to her room.

WALTER What does she have?

ANNIE She has a nice piece of bacon with a poached egg, and she enjoys every minute of it.

WALTER For thirty-five and six a week? They're charging three pounds ten everywhere up and down the country. She's doing you. She's got hot and cold running water, every comfort, breakfast in a first-class bed. She's taking you for a ride.

ANNIE No, she's not.

Pause.

WALTER I left something in my room. I'm going to get it.

He goes out and up the stairs. The bathroom door opens and SALLY comes out. She descends the stairs half-way down. They meet.

SALLY Mr Street?

WALTER Yes.

SALLY I'm so pleased to meet you. I've heard so much about you.

WALTER Oh yes.

Pause.

I . . . er . . .

SALLY Your aunts are charming people.

WALTER Mmmm.

Pause.

SALLY Are you glad to be back?

WALTER I've left something in my room. I've got to get it.

SALLY Oh, well, we'll meet again. Bye-bye.

She goes to her room. He follows.

The footsteps stop.

WALTER Could I just . . . ?

SALLY What?

WALTER Come in.

SALLY Come in? But . . . well, yes . . . do . . . if you want to.

They go in. WALTER *shuts the door, follows her.*

I'm sorry. Everything's all over the place. I'm at school all day. I don't have much time to tidy up.

Pause.

I believe I'm teaching at the school you went to. In the infants.

242

WALTER Round the corner? Yes, I went there.

SALLY You wouldn't believe all the things I've heard about you. You're the apple of your aunts' eyes.

WALTER So are you.

Pause.

SALLY I'm happy here. I get on very well with them.

WALTER Look . . . I've got to get something in here . . .

SALLY In here? I thought you said you'd left something in your room.

WALTER This is my room.

Pause.

SALLY This?

WALTER You've taken my room.

SALLY Have I? I never . . . realised that. Nobody ever told me that. I'm terribly sorry. Do you want it back?

WALTER I wouldn't mind.

SALLY Oh dear . . . this is very awkward . . . I must say I'm very comfortable here . . . I mean, where else could I sleep?

WALTER There's a put-u-up downstairs.

SALLY Oh, I don't trust those things, do you? I mean, this is such a lovely bed.

WALTER I know it is. It's mine.

SALLY You mean I'm sleeping in your bed?

WALTER Yes.

SALLY Oh.

Pause.

WALTER I've got something in here I want to get.

SALLY Well . . . carry on.

WALTER It's in a rather private place.

SALLY Do you want me to go out?

WALTER Yes, if you don't mind.

SALLY Go out of the room, you mean?

WALTER It won't take me a minute.

SALLY What are you looking for?

WALTER It's a private matter.

SALLY Is it a gun?

Pause.

Can't I turn my back?

WALTER Two minutes. That's all I want.

SALLY All right. Two minutes.

*She leaves the room and stands on the landing
outside the door.* WALTER *grunts and mutters to
himself.*

WALTER Look at those frills. Frills . . . all over the
place. Bloody dolls' house. My damn room.

SALLY's *voice is heard from the landing.*

SALLY Are you finished?

WALTER Just a minute.

He opens the cupboard and rummages.

(*Muttering.*) Where's that damn case? Wait a minute . . . what's this?

Sound of large envelope tearing.

(*Softly.*) Gaw . . . huuhh!

SALLY All right?

WALTER Yes. Thank you.

SALLY *enters the room.*

SALLY Find it?

WALTER Yes, thank you.

He goes to the door.

What do you teach – ballet?

SALLY Ballet? No. What a funny question.

WALTER Not funny. Lots of women teach ballet.

SALLY I don't dance.

Pause.

WALTER I'm sorry I disturbed your . . . evening.

SALLY That's all right.

WALTER Good night.

SALLY Good night.

Fade out.

Fade in.

ANNIE Have another piece of lemon meringue, Mr Solto.

SOLTO With pleasure.

ANNIE You'll like it.

SOLTO They wanted three hundred and fifty pounds income tax off me the other day. My word of honour. I said to them, you must be mad! What are you trying to do, bring me to an early death? Buy me a cheap spade I'll get up first thing in the morning before breakfast and dig my own grave. Three hundred and fifty-five nicker, eh? I said to them, I said, show me it, I said show me it down in black and white, show me where I've earned – must be round about a thousand pound, you ask me for all that. It's an estimate, they said, we've estimated your earnings. An estimate? Who did your estimate? A blind man with double vision? I'm an old-age pensioner. I'm in receipt of three pound a week, find me something to estimate! What do you say, Walter?

WALTER They're a lot of villains, the lot of them.

ANNIE They don't care for the old.

MILLY Still, you've still got plenty of energy left in you, Mr Solto.

SOLTO Plenty of what?

MILLY Energy.

SOLTO Energy? You should have seen me in the outback, in Australia. I was the man who opened up the Northern Territory for them out there.

MILLY It's a wonder you never got married, Mr Solto.

SOLTO I've always been a lone wolf. The first time I was seduced, I said to myself, Solto, watch your step, mind how you go, go so far but no further. If they want to seduce you, let them seduce you, but marry them? Out of the question.

WALTER Where was that, in Australia or Greece?

SOLTO Australia.

WALTER How did you get to Australia from Greece?

SOLTO By sea. How do you think? I worked my passage. And what a trip. I was only a pubescent. I killed a man with my own hands, a six-foot-ten Lascar from Madagascar.

ANNIE From Madagascar?

SOLTO Sure. A Lascar.

MILLY Alaska?

SOLTO Madagascar.

Pause.

WALTER It's happened before.

SOLTO And it'll happen again.

MILLY Have another piece of swiss roll, Mr Solto.

247

ANNIE I bet you some woman could have made you a good wife.

SOLTO If I wanted to get married, I could clinch it tomorrow – like that! But I'm like Wally; I'm a lone wolf.

WALTER How's the scrap business, Mr Solto?

SOLTO Ssshh! That's the same question the tax inspector asked me. I told him I retired years ago. He says to me, 'Why don't you fill out your income tax returns? Why don't you fill out all the forms we send you?' I said, I got no income tax to declare, that's why. 'You're the only man in the district who won't fill out his forms,' he says. 'You want to go to prison?' Prison, I said, a man like me, a clean-living old man like me, a man who discovered Don Bradman, it's a national disgrace! 'Fill out your forms,' he says. 'There'll be no trouble. Listen! I said if you want me to fill out these forms, if you want me to go through all that clerical work, all right, pay me a small sum, pay me for my trouble. Pay me to do it. Otherwise fill them out yourself, leave me alone. Three hundred and fifty-five nicker? They got a fat chance.

ANNIE A good wife wouldn't have done you no harm. She'd fill out your forms – for you.

SOLTO That's what I'm afraid of.

MILLY Have a custard tart, Mr Solto.

ANNIE He's still got a good appetite.

SOLTO I've been saving it up since I last come here.

WALTER Why, when were you last here, Mr Solto?

MILLY It was just after you went inside.

SOLTO I brought round some daffodils.

ANNIE Nine months ago, he remembers.

SOLTO How're they doing?

ANNIE What?

SOLTO The daffodils.

ANNIE Oh, they died.

SOLTO Go on. (*Eats.*)

WALTER So you don't know about the lodger?

SOLTO Lodger?

WALTER Yes, we've got a lodger now.

MILLY She's a school teacher.

SOLTO A school teacher, eh? Hmm. Where does she sleep? On the put-u-up?

WALTER My aunts gave her my room.

MILLY Come on. Annie, help me clear the table.

SOLTO The lady who first seduced me, in Australia – she kicked her own husband out and gave me his room. I bumped into him years later making a speech at Marble Arch. It wasn't a bad speech, it so happens.

MILLY (*stacking plates*) Why don't you lend Wally a few pound, Mr Solto?

SOLTO Me?

ANNIE Yes, why don't you?

MILLY You could help to set him up.

SOLTO Why don't you go to the Prisoners Help Society. They'll give you a loan. I mean, you've done two stretches, you must have a few good references.

WALTER You wouldn't miss two hundred quid.

SOLTO Two hundred here, three fifty-five there – what do you think I am, a bank manager?

MILLY You can't take it with you, Mr Solto.

WALTER He wants to be the richest man in the cemetery.

ANNIE It won't do you much good where you're going, Mr Solto.

SOLTO Who's going anywhere?

MILLY Come on, Annabel.

ANNIE There's one rock cake left, Mr Solto.

SOLTO I'll tell you what,

ANNIE Keep the rock cake.

MILLY Annabel.

ANNIE *and* MILLY *go out with plates.*

SOLTO I wish I could give you a helping hand, Wally. Honest. But things are very tight. I had six cross doubles the other day. Three came home. Number four developed rheumatism at the last hurdle. I went without food for two days.

WALTER I could do with a lift up. I'm thinking of going straight.

SOLTO Why? You getting tired of a life of crime?

WALTER I'm not good enough. I get caught too many times. I'm not clever enough.

SOLTO You're still on the post-office books?

WALTER Yes.

SOLTO It's a mug's game. I've told you before. If you want to be a forger you've got to have a gift. It's got to come from the heart.

WALTER I'm not a good enough forger.

SOLTO You're a terrible forger.

WALTER That's why I'm always getting caught.

SOLTO I'm a better forger than you any day. And I don't forge.

WALTER I haven't got the gift.

SOLTO A forger's got to love his work. You don't love your work, that's your trouble, Walter.

WALTER If you lent me two hundred quid I could go straight.

SOLTO I'm an old-age pensioner, Wally. What are you talking about?

WALTER If only I could get my room back! I could get settled in, I could think, about things!

SOLTO Why, who's this school teacher, then? What's the game?

WALTER (*casually*) Listen, I want to show you something.

SOLTO What?

WALTER This photo.

SOLTO Who's this?

WALTER A girl . . . I want to find.

SOLTO Who is she?

WALTER That's what I want to find out.

SOLTO We were just talking about forging, about your room, about the school teacher. What's this got to do with it?

WALTER This is a club, isn't it, in the photo?

SOLTO Sure.

WALTER And that girl's a hostess, isn't she?

SOLTO Sure.

WALTER Can you locate her?

SOLTO Me?

Pause.

WALTER Do you know any of these men – these men with her?

SOLTO O-oh, one of them . . . looks familiar.

WALTER Find that girl for me. It's important. As a favour. You're the only man I know who could find her. You know these clubs.

SOLTO Do you know the girl?

Pause.

WALTER No.

SOLTO Well, where'd you get hold of the photo?

WALTER I got hold of it.

SOLTO What have you done? Fallen in love with a photo?

WALTER Sure. That's right.

SOLTO Yes . . . A very attractive girl. A lovely girl. All right, Wally. I'll try to find her for you.

WALTER Thanks.

Front door slams.

Footsteps up the stairs.

SOLTO Who's that?

WALTER That's our lodger. The school teacher.

Fade out.

Fade in.

MILLY I don't want the milk hot, I want it cold.

ANNIE It is cold.

MILLY I thought you warmed it up.

ANNIE I did. The time I got up here it's gone cold.

MILLY You should have kept it in the pan. If you'd brought it up in the pan it would have still been hot.

ANNIE I thought you said you didn't want it hot.

MILLY I don't want it hot.

ANNIE Well, that's why I'm saying it's cold.

MILLY I know that. But if I had wanted it hot. That's all I'm saying. (*She sips the milk.*) It could be colder.

ANNIE Do you want a piece of anchovy or a doughnut.

MILLY I'll have the anchovy. What are you going to have?

ANNIE I'm going downstairs, to have a doughnut.

MILLY You can have this one.

ANNIE No, I've got one downstairs. You can have it after the anchovy.

MILLY Why don't you have the anchovy?

ANNIE You know what I wouldn't mind? I wouldn't mind a few pilchards.

MILLY Herring. A nice bit of herring, that's what I could do with.

ANNIE A few pilchards with a drop of vinegar. And a plate of chocolate mousse to go after it.

MILLY Chocolate mousse?

ANNIE Don't you remember when we had chocolate mousse at Clacton?

MILLY Chocolate mousse wouldn't go with herrings.

ANNIE I'm not having herrings. I'm having pilchards.

Noise of steps upstairs.

Listen.

ANNIE *turns the door-handle, listens.*

WALTER *knocks on* SALLY's *door.*

SALLY Yes?

WALTER It's me.

SALLY Just a moment. Come in.

Door opens.

WALTER How are you?

SALLY I'm fine.

Door closes.

ANNIE He's in.

MILLY What do you mean, he's in?

ANNIE He's gone in.

MILLY Gone in where, Annie?

ANNIE Into her room.

MILLY His room.

255

ANNIE His room.

MILLY He's gone in?

ANNIE Yes.

MILLY Is she in there?

ANNIE Yes.

MILLY So he's in there with her.

ANNIE Yes.

MILLY Go out and have a listen.

ANNIE *goes out of the door and down the landing to* SALLY's *door, where she stops.*

We hear the following dialogue from her point of view.

WALTER Let's have some of this. I've brought it for you.

SALLY What is it?

WALTER Brandy.

SALLY What is this in aid of?

WALTER Well, I thought we might as well get to know each other, both living in the same house.

SALLY Yes, why not?

WALTER Do you drink?

SALLY Oh, not really.

WALTER Just one or two now and again, eh?

SALLY Very occasionally.

WALTER But you'll have a drop of this?

SALLY Just a drop . . . Glasses . . .

WALTER I've got them.

SALLY All prepared, eh?

He opens the bottle and pours.

WALTER Cheers.

SALLY Good health.

WALTER I wanted to say . . . I was a bit rude
yesterday. I wanted to apologise.

SALLY You weren't rude.

WALTER It'll just take a bit of getting used to, that's
all, you having my room.

SALLY Well, look, I've been thinking . .. perhaps we
could share the room, in – in a kind of way.

WALTER Share it?

SALLY I mean, you could use it when I'm not here, or
something.

WALTER Oh, I don't know about that.

SALLY It'd be quite easy. I'm at school all day.

WALTER What about the evenings?

SALLY Well, I'm out three nights a week, you see.

WALTER Where do you go?

257

SALLY Oh, night school. I'm studying languages.
Then I usually go on with a girl friend of mine, a
history teacher, to listen to some music.

WALTER What kind of music?

SALLY Mozart, Brahms. That kind of stuff.

WALTER Oh, all that kind of stuff.

SALLY Yes.

   Pause.

WALTER Well, it's cosy in here. Have another one.

SALLY Oh, I . . .

WALTER (*pouring*) Just one.

SALLY Thanks. Cheers.

   Pause.

WALTER I've never been in this room with a lady
before.

SALLY Oh.

WALTER The boys used to come here, though. This is
where we used to plan our armed robberies.

SALLY Really?

WALTER My aunts never told you why I've been
inside, have they?

SALLY No.

WALTER Well, what it is, you see. I'm a gunman.

SALLY Oh.

WALTER Ever met a gunman before?

SALLY I don't think so.

WALTER It's not a bad life, all things considered.
Plenty of time off. You know, holidays with pay, you
could say. No, there's plenty of worse occupations.
You're not frightened of me now you know I'm a
gunman, are you?

SALLY No, I think you're charming.

WALTER Oh, you're right there. That's why I got on
so well in prison, you see. Charm. You know what I
was doing in there? I was running the prison library. I
was the best librarian they ever had. The day I left the
Governor gave me a personal send-off. Saw me all the
way to the gate. He told me business at the library
had shot up out of all recognition since I'd been in
charge.

SALLY What a wonderful compliment.

WALTER (*pouring more drink*) He told me that if I'd
consider giving up armed robbery he'd recommend me
for a job in the British Museum. Looking after rare
manuscripts. You know, writing my opinion of them.

SALLY I should think that's quite a skilled job.

WALTER Cheers. Skilled? Well, funny enough, I've
had a good bit to do with rare manuscripts in my
time. I used to know a bloke who ran a business
digging them up.

SALLY Digging what up?

WALTER Rare manuscripts. Out of tombs. I used to give him a helping hand when I was on the loose. Very well paid it was, too. You see, they were nearly always attached to a corpse, these manuscripts, you had to lift up the pelvis bone with a pair of tweezers. Big tweezers. Can't leave fingerprints on a corpse, you see. Canon law. The biggest shock I ever had was when a skeleton collapsed on top of me and nearly bit my ear off. I had a funny feeling at that moment. I thought I was the skeleton and he was my long-lost uncle come to kiss me good night. You've never been inside a grave, I suppose. I can recommend it, honest, I mean if you want to taste everything life has to offer.

SALLY Well, I'll be inside one, one day.

WALTER Oh, I don't know. You might be cremated, or drowned at sea, mightn't you?

> ANNIE *creeps back down the landing into the aunts' room and gets into bed.*

MILLY Did you listen?

ANNIE Yes.

MILLY Well?

ANNIE I heard them talking.

MILLY What were they saying?

ANNIE Don't ask me.

MILLY Go to the door again. Listen properly.

ANNIE Why don't you go.

MILLY I'm in bed.

ANNIE So am I.

MILLY But I've been in bed longer than you.

ANNIE *mutters and grumbles to herself, gets out of bed and goes back along the landing to the door. The dialogue heard is still from her point of view.*

WALTER You're a Northerner?

SALLY That's clever of you. I thought I'd . . .

WALTER I can tell the accent.

SALLY I thought I'd lost it . . .

WALTER There's something in your eyes too. You only find it in Lancashire girls.

SALLY Really? What?

WALTER (*moving closer*) You seem a bit uncomfortable with me. Why's that?

SALLY I'm not uncomfortable.

WALTER Why's that, then? You seem a bit uneasy.

SALLY I'm not.

WALTER Let's fill you up, eh? I mean you were different yesterday. You were on top of yourself yesterday.

SALLY It's you who were different. You're different today.

WALTER You don't want to worry about me being an armed robber. They call me the gentle gunman.

SALLY I'm not worried.

Pause.

WALTER My aunties think you're marvellous. I think they've got us in mind for the marriage stakes.

SALLY What?

WALTER Yes, I think they think they've found me a wife.

SALLY How funny.

WALTER They've roped you in to take part in a wedding. They've forgotten one thing, though.

SALLY What's that?

WALTER I'm married. As a matter of fact, I'm married to three women. I'm a triple bigamist. Do you believe me?

SALLY I think you're in a very strange mood.

WALTER It's the look in your eyes that's brought it on.

SALLY You haven't got such bad eyes yourself.

WALTER Your eyes, they're Northern eyes. They're full of soot.

SALLY Thank you.

WALTER (*pouring*) Top it up. Come on.

SALLY To our eyes.

WALTER I thought you didn't drink. You can knock it back all right. Keep in practice in school, I suppose. In the milk break. Keeps you in trim for netball. Or at that night school, eh? I bet you enjoy yourself there. Come on. Tell me what you get up to at that night school.

ANNIE *yawns slightly and pads back to her room. She closes door and gets into bed.*

ANNIE Still talking.

MILLY (*sleepily*) What are they talking about?

ANNIE I can't make it out.

MILLY I should have gone. You're as deaf as a post.

They settle in bed. Squeaks.

ANNIE The doughnut's given me heartburn. (*Faintly.*) Good night.

MILLY *snores briefly.*

Fade into SALLY's *room.*

SALLY I lead a quiet life, a very quiet life, I don't mix with people.

WALTER Except me. You're mixing with me.

SALLY I don't have any kind of social life.

WALTER I'll have to take you round a few of the clubs I know, show you the sights.

SALLY No, I don't like that.

WALTER What do you like?

Pause.

SALLY Lying here . . . by myself . . .

WALTER On my bed.

SALLY Yes.

WALTER Doing what?

SALLY Thinking.

WALTER Think about me last night?

SALLY You?

WALTER This offer to share your room, I might consider it.

Pause.

I bet you're thinking about me now.

Pause.

SALLY Why should I be?

WALTER I'm thinking about you. Pause. I don't know why I made such a fuss about this room. It's just an ordinary room, there's nothing to it. I mean if you weren't here. If you weren't in it, there'd be nothing to it.

Pause.

Why don't you stay in it? It's not true that I'm married. I just said that. I'm not attached. To tell you the truth . . . to tell you the truth, I'm still looking for Miss Right

SALLY I think I should move away from here.

WALTER Where would you go?

Pause.

SALLY Anywhere.

WALTER Would you go to the seaside? I could come
with you. We could do a bit of fishing . . . on the pier.
Yes, we could go together. Or, on the other hand, we
could stay here. We could stay where we are.

SALLY Could we?

WALTER Sit down.

SALLY What?

WALTER Sit down.

Pause.

Cross your legs.

SALLY Mmmmm?

WALTER Cross your legs.

Pause.

Uncross them.

Pause.

Stand up.

Pause.

Turn round.

Pause.

Stop.

Pause.

Sit down.

Pause.

Cross your legs.

Pause.

Uncross your legs.

Silence.

Night-club music.

TULLY No, I tell you, it must be . . . wait a minute, must be round about ten years. The last time was when I was down at Richmond.

SOLTO Yes, the Donkey Club.

TULLY The Donkey, sure. I left there three years ago.

SOLTO How long you been here, then? I haven't been down here for about three years.

TULLY You must have missed me. I come here three years ago, that's exacdy when I come here. (*Calls.*) Charlie!

TULLY *clicks his fingers for the* WAITER,

SOLTO It was a real dive before then, I can tell you.

WAITER.

Same again, Mr Tully?

TULLY Same again. Dive – course it was a dive. They asked me to come here and give it – you know – a bit of class, about three years ago. I gave the boot to about a dozen lowlives from the start, you know, I made my position clear.

SOLTO Didn't they give you no trouble?

TULLY With me? Listen, they know if they want to start making trouble they picked the right customer. Don't you remember me at Blackheath.

SOLTO You're going back a bit.

TULLY I'm going back a few years before the war.

SOLTO You're going back to when the game was good.

TULLY What about you at Blackheath?

SOLTO Blackheath. It's another story when you start talking about Blackheath.

TULLY Thanks, Charlie. Here you are, Ambrose. Cheers.

Pause.

No, you can see it's not a dive no more. I got the place moving, I mean, we got a band up there – well, I say a band – a piano and a double bass, but they're very good boys, they're good boys. We got a very nice clientele come in here. You know, you get a lot of musicians . . . er . . . musicians coming down here. They make up a very nice clientele. Of course, you get a certain amount of business executives. I mean, high-class people. I was talking to a few of them only the other night. They come over from Hampton Court, they come, from Twickenham, from Datchet.

SOLTO All the way from Datchet?

TULLY Sure, they get in the car, how long's it taken them? They come here for a bit of relaxation. I mean, we got a two-o'clock licence. We got three resident birds. What made you come down here all of a sudden?

SOLTO Ah, just one of them funny things, Cyril. I heard of a little bird.

TULLY What, one of the birds here?

SOLTO Still sharp, eh, Cyril?

TULLY You heard about the quality we got here, eh? We got some high-class dolls down here, don't worry. They come all the way from finishing school. Fade out.

Fade in: girls' dressing-room.

BARBARA What did he say then?

SALLY Come over with me one Sunday, he says, come over and have Sunday dinner, meet the wife. Why, I said, what are you going to introduce me as, your sister? No, he says; she's very broad-minded, my wife; she'll be delighted to meet you.

MAVIS Oh yes, I've heard of that kind of thing before.

SALLY Yes, that's what I said. Oh yes, I said, I've heard of that kind of thing before. Go on, get off out of it, I said, buzz off before I call a copper.

BARBARA Which was he, the one with the big nose?

SALLY Yes.

MANAGER Come on, girls, move yourselves, we're ready for the off.

BARBARA Who asked you to come into the ladies' room?

MANAGER Don't give me no lip. Get your skates on. (*To* SALLY.) Cyril wants you at his table right away.

SALLY I'll kick him in the middle of his paraphernalia one of these days.

BARBARA Go on, what happened then?

SALLY Why don't you come on the river with me one of these days? he says. I'll take you for a ride in a punt.

MAVIS In a what?

BARBARA A punt.

MAVIS What's a punt?

SALLY I said to him, In a punt, with you? You must be mad. You won't get me in no punt.

BARBARA I thought you said he attracted you.

SALLY Oh, he did to start off, that's all. I thought he wasn't bad. But, you know, he came from Australia. He'd got a lot of Australian habits, they didn't go down very well with me.

MANAGER Come on, come on, I don't want to tell you again. Where do you think you are, on Brighton front? (*To* SALLY.) Cyril wants you at his table.

SALLY I'll cut his ears off one of these days.

She goes into the dub.

SOLTO So I thought to myself Tully, Big Johnny Bolsom. She must be all right.

TULLY Sure she's all right.

SOLTO So I thought I'd follow it up.

TULLY You couldn't have done better. Here she is, here she is, come on, darling. This is an old friend of mine, Ambrose Solto.

SOLTO How do you do?

SALLY How do you do?

TULLY Sit down, Ambrose. I want you to meet this girl, Ambrose. This is the cleverest girl we got here. She speaks three languages.

SOLTO What languages?

TULLY Tell him.

SALLY Well, English for a start.

SOLTO She's witty, too eh?

TULLY Witty? She's my favourite girl.

SALLY Oh, I'm not.

SOLTO Aren't you going to tell me your name?

SALLY Katina.

SOLTO Katina. What a coincidence! My childhood sweetheart was called Katina.

TULLY No. Go on!

SALLY Really, Mr Solto?

SOLTO Yes, when I was a little boy, when I was a little boy in Athens. That's when it was.

Fade out.

Fade in.

WALTER I just took the train down to Southend, that's all.

ANNIE Southend? What for?

WALTER I felt like having a look at the seaside. It wasn't bad down there. I rolled around, that's all. Smelt the old sea, that's all.

Pause.

ANNIE You've got a secret.

WALTER Have I?

ANNIE Oh, come on, Wally, what do you think of her? She's nice, isn't she?

WALTER Who, the girl upstairs? Yes, she's a very nice girl.

ANNIE You like her, eh?

WALTER Who?

ANNIE Don't you?

WALTER What, the one that lives upstairs, eh?

ANNIE All larking aside.

WALTER Well . . . all larking aside . . . without any larking . . . I'd say she was all right.

ANNIE You didn't like her, though, the first going off, did you?

WALTER Ah well, the first going off . . . ain't anything like . . . the second going off, is it? What I mean to say . . . is that the second going off . . . often turns out to be very different . . . from what you thought it was going to be . . . on the first going off. If you see what I'm saying.

ANNIE Hasn't she made the room lovely, eh?

WALTER Very snazzy.

ANNIE She's made it really feminine, hasn't she?

WALTER Oh . . . without a shadow of doubt.

ANNIE She should be in soon. She should be due home from night school in about half an hour.

Fade out and in: night club.

SOLTO What do you think of that?

SALLY No, you've got real rhythm. Mr Solto, it's a pleasure.

SOLTO I've always had rhythm. Take it from me. I was born with rhythm. My big toe can dance a polka by himself. My word of honour. My sweetheart and me, we used to dance by the sea at night, with the waves coming in. You ever done that?

SALLY No. Never. Let's have a drink.

TULLY How you getting on, you two?

SOLTO Marvellous.

SALLY Lovely.

SOLTO See us on the floor?

TULLY What were you doing on the floor?

SALLY Dancing!

SOLTO You should have seen him at Blackheath. Go on, off you go, Cyril, we're talking about philosophy here.

TULLY Mind how you go.

He goes.

SOLTO *and* SALLY *go to the table and sit.*

SOLTO I was going to say something to you.

SALLY What?

SOLTO I own a private beach. On the South Coast. It's all my own. A little beach hut. Well, not so little. It's big. It's not a hut either. It's a bit bigger than a hut. It's got Indian carpets, it's got the front side full of windows looking out to the sea, it's got central heating, and the waves . . . the waves come right up to the front step. You can lie on a divan and watch them come closer and closer. How would you like to he there in the moonlight, eh, and watch the waves come closer and closer?

SALLY Sounds . . . very nice.

SOLTO Next week-end we'll go down, eh.

SALLY Well, I . . .

SOLTO No excuses! I'll barbecue a boar on the beach, my word of honour.

SALLY Where you going to get the boar?

SOLTO Specially from France – where else? Listen. You want to know a little secret? I came down here specifically to look for you.

SALLY What do you mean?

SOLTO I got hold of this photo of you, see? So I got hold of the photographer. He told me what club it was, and here I am.

SALLY Where'd you get the photo?

SOLTO That I'm not supposed to tell you. You see, what I was doing, I was looking for you for a pal of mine.

SALLY A pal? . . . Who?

SOLTO Don't worry about it. I'm not going to tell him where he can find you. No. I wouldn't let a man like that get hold of a lovely girl like you.

SALLY What's his name?

SOLTO He's a man called Wally. Wally Street. He's always in and out of the nick. He's a forger, a petty thief, does post-office books. You know him?

SALLY No.

SOLTO Funny . . . I don't know what he . . . anyway, forget all about it. But I'll give him his due. If it wasn't for him showing me this photo, where would I be, eh. And where would you be.

SALLY Yes. Where would I be?

Fade out and in.

A knock at the front door.

WALTER *goes through the hall door.*

SOLTO Hullo, Wally, I'll come in a minute. I've got a cab outside.

They go into the room.

WALTER What's up? Have you found the girl?

SOLTO The girl? What girl?

WALTER The girl. That photo I gave you. You know.

SOLTO Oh, the girl! You mean the girl I was trying to . . .

WALTER Yes, I thought that might be why you've come round.

SOLTO You're dead right. That's exacdy why I've come round.

WALTER That's what I thought.

SOLTO And you weren't wrong.

Pause.

WALTER Well. Where is she?

275

SOLTO That's what I wanted to tell you. I can't find her.

WALTER You can't find her?

SOLTO Not a smell. That's exactly what I came round to tell you.

WALTER Not a smell, eh.

SOLTO Not a whiff.

WALTER I thought you were on her track.

SOLTO There's no track. I been everywhere. The Madrigal. The Whip Room. The Gamut. Pedro's. Nobody knew the face. Wait a minute – Pedro said he might have seen her once round a few back doubles in Madrid. She been to Madrid?

WALTER How would I know? I've never met her.

SOLTO I thought you had.

WALTER Didn't you locate that club?

SOLTO What club?

WALTER In the photo.

SOLTO No. What I thought, the best thing to do would be to get hold of the photographer, you see. So I paid him a call.

WALTER What did he say?

SOLTO He wasn't there. He'd gone to Canada for a conference.

WALTER What kind of conference?

SOLTO A dental conference. He's going to be a dentist.

WALTER Why'd he give up photography?

SOLTO He had a change of heart. You know how it is. He gave me a cup of coffee, told me his life story.

WALTER Who did?

SOLTO His brother. The chiropodist. He's in dead trouble that boy, he can't meet his overheads.

WALTER Look here, Mr Solto, if I were you, I'd give up the whole thing.

SOLTO You want my opinion? I think the photo's a fake. There's no such club. There's no girl. They don't exist.

WALTER That's exactly what I think.

   Pause.

SOLTO You do?

WALTER Exactly.

SOLTO Who knows? You might be right.

WALTER That photo. It's a fake. You'll never find her.

SOLTO How can it be a fake? I thought you knew her.

WALTER I never said I knew her. I've never met her.

SOLTO But that's what I'm saying. There's no one to know. You've never seen her. I've never seen her. There's no one to see.

WALTER She doesn't exist.

Pause.

SOLTO All the same look, the girl's there. That's the photo of someone.

WALTER No one I know.

Pause.

SOLTO Take my tip, Wally, wipe the whole business from your head, wipe it clean out of your mind.

WALTER That's what I think you'd better do, Mr Solto.

Front door. Footsteps.

SOLTO What's that?

WALTER That's the school teacher.

SOLTO That's your mark. Someone with an education. She keeps nice hours for a school teacher. Where's she been, night school?

Fade out and in to footsteps on stairs.

Knock on the door.

WALTER Are you there?

He tries the door. It is locked.

Are you in there? I want to speak to you. Let me in a minute. Will you let me in a minute? What's up with you? What the hell's up with you? Let me in. I want to speak to you.

Silence.

ANNIE She's gone.

MILLY Gone?

ANNIE Here's a note.

MILLY Where's she gone?

ANNIE She left a note.

MILLY What does it say?

ANNIE 'Dear Misses Billet. I'm very sorry, but an urgent matter has called me away suddenly. I don't know when I'll be back, so I thought I better take everything. I didn't want to wake you up. Thank you. Good-bye.' I'm going to tell Wally.

ANNIE's *footsteps into the front room.*

Wally. Wake up.

Pause.

She's gone away.

WALTER Who?

ANNIE She left a note. Look.

Pause while he reads.

WALTER Yes, well . . . she . . . obviously had to go away.

Pause.

ANNIE You didn't have any arguments with her, did you, Wally?

WALTER No.

ANNIE You didn't see her last night after she came back from night school?

WALTER No.

MILLY *enters.*

MILLY I just found this photo in her room.

ANNIE Ah. Doesn't she look lovely holding that netball?

MILLY With all the schoolgirls.

ANNIE I never knew she was the games mistress. She never told us.

Pause.

MILLY It looks as though she's gone for good.

Pause.

WALTER Yes.

Pause.

That's what it looks like.

Fade.

THE DWARFS

The Dwarfs was first performed on the BBC Third Programme on 2 December 1960 with the following cast:-

LEN   Richard Pasco
PETE   Jon Rollason
MARK   Alex Scott

Produced by Barbara Bray

The play was first presented in a new version for the stage by Michael Codron and David Hall at the New Arts Theatre, London, on 18 September, 1963 with the following cast:

LEN   John Hurt
PETE   Philip Bond
MARK   Michael Forrest

Directed by Harold Pinter *assisted by* Guy Vaesen

Characters

LEN

PETE

MARK

all are in their late twenties

The two main areas are:

1. A room in LEN's *house. Solid middle-European furniture. Piles of books. A small carved table with a chenille cloth, a bowl of fruit, books. Two marquetry chairs. A hanging lamp with dark shade.*

2. The living room in MARK's *flat. Quite modern. Comfortable. Two armchairs and a coffee table.*

3. There is also a central downstage area of isolation and, for a short scene later in the play, a bed in a hospital, upstage on a higher level.

MARK's *room, midnight. Lamps are alight. Two cups and saucers, a sugar-bowl and a teapot are on a tray on the coffee table.*

PETE *is sitting, reading.*

LEN *is playing a recorder. The sound is fragmentary.*

LEN Pete.

PETE What?

LEN Come here.

PETE What?

LEN What's the matter with this recorder?

He pulls recorder in half, looks down, blows, taps.

There's something wrong with this recorder.

PETE Let's have some tea.

LEN I can't do a thing with it.

Re-assembles recorder. Another attempt to play.

Where's the milk?

He puts recorder on tray.

PETE You were going to bring it.

LEN That's right.

PETE Well, where is it?

LEN I forgot it. Why didn't you remind me?

PETE Give me the cup.

LEN What do we do now?

PETE Give me the tea.

LEN Without milk?

PETE There isn't any milk.

LEN What about sugar? (*Moving towards door.*) He must have a pint of milk somewhere.

He exits to kitchen. Noise of opening cupboards etc. He reappears with a couple of gherkins in a jar.

Here's a couple of gherkins. What about a gherkin? (*Takes jar to* PETE.) Fancy a gherkin.

PETE *sniffs, looks up in disgust,* LEN *sniffs and exits.*

Wait a minute.

Kitchen noises. LEN *reappears with a bottle of milk.*

Ah! Here we are. I knew he'd have a pint laid on. (*Pressing the top.*) Uuh! Uuuhh . . . It's stiff.

PETE I wouldn't open that.

LEN Uuuhh . . . why not? I can't drink tea without milk. Uuh! That's it. (*Picking up cup to pour.*) Give us your cup.

PETE Leave it alone.

Pause. LEN *shakes bottle over cup.*

LEN It won't come out.

Pause.

The milk won't come out of the bottle.

PETE It's been in there two weeks, why should it come out?

LEN Two weeks? He's been away longer than two weeks.

Slight pause.

It's stuck in the bottle.

Slight pause.

You'd think a man like him would have a maid, wouldn't you, to look after the place while he's away, to look after his milk? Or a gentleman. A gentleman's gentleman. Are you quite sure he hasn't got a gentleman's gentleman tucked away somewhere, to look after the place for him?

PETE (*rising to replace book on shelf*) Only you. You're the only gentleman's gentleman he's got.

Pause.

LEN Well, if I'm his gentleman's gentleman, I should have been looking after the place for him.

Pause. PETE *takes brass toasting fork off wall.*

PETE What's this?

LEN That? You've seen that before. It's a toasting fork.

PETE It's got a monkey's head.

LEN It's Portuguese. Everything in this house is Portuguese.

PETE Why's that?

LEN That's where he comes from.

PETE Does he?

LEN Or at least, his grandmother on his father's side. That's where the family comes from.

PETE Well, well.

He hangs up the toasting fork.

LEN What time's he coming?

PETE Soon.

He pours himself a cup of tea.

LEN You're drinking black tea.

PETE What about it?

LEN You're not in Poland.

He plays recorder. PETE *sits in armchair.*

PETE What's the matter with that thing?

LEN Nothing. There's nothing wrong with it. But it must be broken. It's a year since I played it. (*He sneezes.*) Aah! I've got the most shocking blasted cold I've ever had in all my life. (*He blows his nose.*) Still, it's not much of a nuisance really.

PETE Don't wear me out.

Slight pause.

Why don't you pull yourself together? You'll be ready for the loony bin next week if you go on like this.

LEN *uses recorder as a telescope to the back of* PETE's *head.*

Pause.

LEN Ten to one he'll be hungry.

PETE Who?

LEN Mark. When he comes. He can eat like a bullock, that bloke. Still, he won't find much to come home to, will he? There's nothing in the kitchen, there's not even a bit of lettuce. It's like the workhouse here.

Pause.

He can eat like a bullock, that bloke.

Pause.

I've seen him finish off a loaf of bread before I'd got my jacket off.

Pause.

He'd never leave a breadcrumb on a plate in the old days.

Pause.

Of course, he may have changed. Things do change. But I'm the same. Do you know, I had five solid square meals one day last week? At eleven o'clock, two o'clock, six o'clock, ten o'clock and one o'clock. Not bad going. Work makes me hungry. I was working that day.

Pause.

I'm always starving when I get up. Daylight has a funny effect on me. As for the night, that goes without saying. As far as I'm concerned the only thing you can do in the night is eat. It keeps me fit, especially if I'm at home. I have to run downstairs to put the kettle on, run upstairs to finish what I'm doing, run downstairs to cut a sandwich or arrange a salad, run upstairs to finish what I'm doing, run back downstairs to see to the sausages, if I'm having sausages, run back upstairs to finish what I'm doing, run back downstairs to lay the table, run back upstairs to finish what I'm doing, run back –

PETE Yes!

LEN Where did you get those shoes?

PETE What?

LEN Those shoes. How long have you had them?

PETE What's the matter with them?

LEN Have you been wearing them all night?

Pause.

PETE When did you last sleep?

His hand is lying open, palm upward.

LEN Sleep? Don't make me laugh. All I do is sleep.

PETE What about work? How's work?

LEN Paddington? It's a big railway station. An oven.
It's an oven. Still, bad air is better than no air. It's best
on night shift. The trains come in, I give a bloke half
a dollar, he does my job, I curl up in the corner and
read the timetables. But they tell me I might make a
first-class porter. I've been told I've got the makings
of a number one porter. What are you doing with your
hand?

PETE What are you talking about?

LEN What are you doing with your hand?

PETE (*coolly*) What do you think I'm doing with it?
Eh? What do you think?

LEN I don't know.

PETE I'll tell you, shall I? Nothing. I'm not doing
anything with it. It's not moving. I'm doing *nothing*
with it.

LEN You're holding it palm upwards.

PETE What about it?

LEN It's not normal. Let's have a look at that hand.
Let's have a look at it.

Pause. He gasps through his teeth.

You're a homicidal maniac.

PETE Is that a fact?

LEN Look. Look at that hand. Look, look at it. A straight line right across the middle. Right across the middle, see? Horizontal. That's all you've got. What else have you got? You're a nut.

PETE Oh yes?

LEN You couldn't find two men in a million with a hand like that. It sticks out a mile. A mile. That's what you are, that's exactly what you are, you're a homicidal maniac!

A knock on the outer door.

PETE (*rising to exit*) That's him.

He goes off. The lights begin to fade to blackout.

MARK (*off*) Anyone here?

PETE (*off*) Yes, how are you?

MARK (*off*) Any tea?

PETE (*off*) Polish tea.

Blackout. The lights come up in LEN's *room – overhead lamp.*

LEN *is sitting at the side of the table.*

LEN There is my table. That is a table. There is my chair. There is my table. That is a bowl of fruit. There is my chair. There are my curtains. There is no wind. It is past night and before morning. This is my room. This is a room. There is the wallpaper, on the walls.

There are six walls. Eight walls. An octagon. This room is an octagon.

There are my shoes, on my feet.

This is a journey and an ambush. This is the centre of the cold, a halt to the journey and no ambush. This is the deep grass I keep to. This is the thicket in the centre of the night and the morning. There is my hundred watt bulb like a dagger. This room moves. This room is moving. It has moved. It has reached . . . a dead halt. This is my fixture. There is no web. All's clear, and abundant. Perhaps a morning will arrive. If a morning arrives, it will not destroy my fixture, nor my luxury. If it is dark in the night or light, nothing obtrudes. I have my compartment. I am wedged. Here is my arrangement, and my kingdom. There are no voices. They make no hole in my side.

The doorbell rings. LEN *searches for his glasses on the table, rummaging among the books. Lifts tablecloth. Is still. Searches in armchair. Then on mantelpiece. Bell rings again. He searches under table. Bell rings again. He rises, looks down, sees glasses in top pocket of jacket. Smiles, puts them on. Exits to open front door.* MARK *enters to below table.* LEN *follows.*

LEN What's this, a suit? Where's your carnation?

MARK What do you think of it?

LEN It's not a schmutta.

MARK It's got a zip at the hips.

LEN A zip at the hips? What for?

MARK Instead of a buckle. It's neat.

LEN Neat? I should say it's neat.

MARK No turn-ups.

LEN I can see that. Why didn't you have turn-ups?

MARK It's smarter without turn-ups.

LEN Of course it's smarter without turn-ups.

MARK I didn't want it double-breasted.

LEN Double-breasted? Of course you couldn't have it double-breasted.

MARK What do you think of the cloth?

LEN The cloth?

He examines it, gasps and whistles through his teeth. At a great pace:

What a piece of cloth. What a piece of cloth. What a piece of cloth. What a piece of cloth. What a piece of *cloth*.

MARK You like the cloth?

LEN WHAT A PIECE OF CLOTH!

MARK What do you think of the cut?

LEN What do I think of the cut? The cut? The cut? What a cut! What a cut! I've never seen such a cut!

Pause. He sits and groans.

MARK (*combing his hair and sitting*) Do you know where I've just been?

LEN Where?

MARK Earl's Court.

LEN Uuuuhh! What were you doing there? That's beside the point.

MARK What's the matter with Earl's Court?

LEN It's a mortuary without a corpse.

Pause.

There's a time and place for everything . . .

MARK You're right there.

LEN What do you mean by that?

MARK There's a time and place for everything.

LEN You're right there.

Puts glasses on, rises to MARK.

Who have you been with? Actors and actresses? What's it like when you act? Does it please you? Does it please anyone else?

MARK What's wrong with acting?

LEN It's a time-honoured profession – it's time-honoured.

Pause.

But what does it do? Does it please you when you

walk on to a stage and everybody looks up and watches you? Maybe they don't want to watch you at all. Maybe they'd prefer to watch someone else. Have you ever asked them?

MARK *chuckles*.

You should follow my example and take up mathematics. (*Showing him open book.*) Look! All last night I was working at mechanics and determinants. There's nothing like a bit of calculus to cheer you up.

Pause.

MARK I'll think about it.

LEN Have you got a telephone here?

MARK It's your house.

LEN Yes. What are you doing here? What do you want here?

MARK I thought you might give me some bread and honey.

LEN I don't want you to become too curious in this room. There's no place for curiosities here. Keep a sense of proportion. That's all I ask.

MARK That's all.

LEN I've got enough on my plate with this room as it is.

MARK What's the matter with it?

LEN The rooms we live in . . . open and shut.

Pause.

Can't you see? They change shape at their own will. I wouldn't grumble if only they would keep to some consistency. But they don't. And I can't tell the limits, the boundaries, which I've been led to believe are natural. I'm all for the natural behaviour of rooms, doors, staircases, the lot. But I can't rely on them. When, for example, I look through a train window, at night, and see the yellow lights, very clearly, I can see what they are, and I see that they're still. But they're only still because I'm moving. I know that they do move along with me, and when we go round a bend, they bump off. But I know that they are still, just the same. They are, after all, stuck on poles which are rooted to the earth. So they must be still, in their own right, insofar as the earth itself is still, which of course it isn't. The point is, in a nutshell, that I can only appreciate such facts when I'm moving. When I'm still, nothing around me follows a natural course of conduct. I'm not saying I'm any criterion, I wouldn't say that. After all, when I'm on the train I'm not really moving at all. That's obvious. I'm in the corner seat. I'm still. I am perhaps being moved, but I do not move. Neither do the yellow lights. The train moves, granted, but what's a train got to do with it?

MARK Nothing.

LEN You're frightened.

MARK Am I?

LEN You're frightened that any moment I'm liable to put a red hot burning coal in your mouth.

MARK Am I?

LEN But when the time comes, you see, what I shall do is place the red hot burning coal in my own mouth.

Swift blackout. PETE *sits where* MARK *has been. Lights snap up.*

I've got some beigels.

PETE This is a very solid table, isn't it?

LEN I said I've got some beigels.

PETE No thanks. How long have you had this table?

LEN It's a family heirloom.

PETE Yes, I'd like a good table, and a good chair. Solid stuff. Made for the bearer. I'd put them in a boat. Sail it down the river. A houseboat. You could sit in the cabin and look out at the water.

LEN Who'd be steering?

PETE You could park it. Park it. There's not a soul in sight.

LEN *brings half-full bottle of wine and glass to table. Reads label. Sniffs at bottle. Pours some into glass, savours then gargles, walking about. Spits wine back into glass, returns bottle and glass at sideboard, after a defensive glance at* PETE. *Returns to above table.*

LEN (*muttering*) Impossible, impossible, impossible.

PETE (*briskly*) I've been thinking about you.

LEN Oh?

PETE Do you know what your trouble is? You're not elastic. There's no elasticity in you. You want to be more elastic.

LEN Elastic? Elastic. Yes, you're quite right. Elastic. What are you talking about?

PETE Giving up the ghost isn't so much a failure as a tactical error. By elastic I mean being prepared for your own deviations. You don't know where you're going to come out next at the moment. You're like a rotten old shirt. Buck your ideas up. They'll lock you up before you're much older.

LEN No. There is a different sky each time I look. The clouds run about in my eye. I can't do it.

PETE The apprehension of experience must obviously be dependent upon discrimination if it's to be considered valuable. That's what you lack. You've got no idea how to preserve a distance between what you smell and what you think about it. You haven't got the faculty for making a simple distinction between one thing and another. Every time you walk out of this door you go straight over a cliff. What you've got to do is nourish the power of assessment. How can you hope to assess and verify anything if you walk about with your nose stuck between your feet all day long? You knock around with Mark too much. He can't do you any good. I know how to handle him. But I don't think he's your sort. Between you and me, I sometimes think he's a man of weeds. Sometimes I think he's just

301

playing a game. But what game? I like him all right when you come down to it. We're old pals. But you look at him and what do you see? An attitude. Has it substance or is it barren? Sometimes I think it's as barren as a bombed site. He'll be a spent force in no time if he doesn't watch his step.

Pause.

I'll tell you a dream I had last night. I was with a girl in a tube station, on the platform. People were rushing about. There was some sort of panic. When I looked round I saw everyone's faces were peeling, blotched, blistered. People were screaming, booming down the tunnels. There was a fire bell clanging. When I looked at the girl I saw that her face was coming off in slabs too, like plaster. Black scabs and stains. The skin was dropping off like lumps of cat's meat. I could hear it sizzling on the electric rails. I pulled her by the arm to get her out of there. She wouldn't budge. Stood there, with half a face, staring at me. I screamed at her to come away. Then I thought, Christ, what's my face like? Is that why she's staring? Is that rotting too?

Lights change, LEN's *room,* PETE *and* MARK *looking at chess board.* LEN *watching them. Silence.*

LEN Eh . . .

They don't look up.

The dwarfs are back on the job.

Pause.

I said the dwarfs are back on the job.

MARK The what?

LEN The dwarfs.

MARK Oh yes?

LEN Oh yes. They've been waiting for a smoke signal you see. I've just sent up the smoke signal.

Pause.

MARK You've just sent it up, have you?

LEN Yes. I've called them in on the job. They've taken up their positions. Haven't you noticed?

PETE I haven't noticed. (*To* MARK.) Have you noticed?

MARK *chuckles.*

LEN But I'll tell you one thing. They don't stop work until the job in hand is finished, one way or another. They never run out on a job. Oh no. They're true professionals. Real professionals.

PETE Listen. Can't you see we're trying to play chess?

Pause.

LEN I've called them in to keep an eye on you two, you see. They're going to keep a very close eye on you. So am I. We're waiting for you to show your hand. We're all going to keep a very close eye on you two. Me and the dwarfs.

Pause.

MARK (*referring to chess*) I think I've got you knackered, Pete.

PETE *looks at him.*

PETE Do you?

Lights change and come up full in room. LEN *enters with old gilt mirror.* MARK *follows.*

MARK Put that mirror back.

LEN This is the best piece of furniture you've got in the house. It's Spanish. No, Portuguese. You're Portuguese, aren't you?

MARK Put it back.

LEN Look at your face in this mirror. Look. It's a farce. Where are your features? You haven't got any features. You couldn't call those features. What are you going to do about it, eh? What's the answer?

MARK Mind that mirror. It's not insured.

LEN I saw Pete the other day. In the evening. You didn't know that. I wonder about you. I often wonder about you. But I must keep pedalling. I must. There's a time limit. Who have you got hiding here? You're not alone here. What about your Esperanto? Don't forget, anything over two ounces goes up a penny.

MARK Thanks for the tip.

LEN Here's your mirror.

304

MARK *exits with mirror.* LEN *picks out apple from a fruit bowl, sits in armchair staring at it.* MARK *returns.*

This is a funny looking apple.

He tosses it back to MARK, *who replaces it.*

Pete asked me to lend him a shilling.

MARK Uh?

LEN I refused.

MARK What?

LEN I refused downright to lend him a shilling.

MARK What did he say to that?

LEN Plenty. Since I left him I've been thinking thoughts I've never thought before. I've been thinking thoughts I've never thought before.

MARK You spend too much time with Pete.

LEN What?

MARK Give it a rest. He doesn't do you any good. I'm the only one who knows how to get on with him. I can handle him. You can't. You take him too seriously. He doesn't worry me. I know how to handle him. He doesn't take any liberties with me.

LEN Who says he takes liberties with me? Nobody takes liberties with me. I'm not the sort of man you can take liberties with.

MARK You should drop it.

LEN *sees toasting fork, takes it to* MARK.

LEN This is a funny toasting fork. Do you ever make any toast?

He drops the fork on the floor.

Don't touch it! You don't know what will happen if you touch it! You mustn't touch it! You mustn't bend! Wait.

Pause.

I'll bend. I'll . . . pick it up. I'm going to touch it.

Pause . . . softly:

There. You see? Nothing happens when I touch it. Nothing. Nothing can happen. No one would bother.

A broken sigh.

You see, I can't see the broken glass. I can't see the mirror I have to look through. I see the other side. The other side. But I can't see the mirror side.

Pause.

I want to break it, all of it. But how can I break it? How can I break it when I can't see it?

Lights fade and come up again in MARK's *room.* LEN *is sitting in an armchair.* MARK *enters with whisky bottle and two glasses. He pours drinks for* PETE *and himself.* PETE, *who has followed him in, takes his glass,* MARK *sits in other armchair. Neither takes any notice of* LEN.

Silence.

PETE Thinking got me into this and thinking's got to get me out. You know what I want? An efficient idea. You know what I mean? An efficient idea. One that'll work. Something I can pin my money on. An each-way bet. Nothing's guaranteed, I know that. But I'm willing to gamble. I gambled when I went to work in the city. I want to fight them on their own ground, not moan about them from a distance. I did it and I'm still living. But I've had my fill of these city guttersnipes – all that scavenging scum! They're the sort of people, who, if the gates of heaven opened to them, all they'd feel would be a draught. I'm wasting away down there. The time has come to act. I'm after something truly workable, something deserving of the proper and active and voluntary application of my own powers. And I'll find it.

LEN I squashed a tiny insect on a plate the other day. And I brushed the remains off my finger with my thumb. Then I saw that the fragments were growing, like fluff. As they were falling, they were becoming larger, like fluff. I had put my hand into the body of a dead bird.

PETE The trouble is, you've got to be quite sure of what you mean by efficient. Look at a nutcracker. You press the cracker and the cracker cracks the nut. You might think that's an exact process. It's not. The nut cracks, but the hinge of the cracker gives out a friction which is completely incidental to the particular idea. It's unnecessary, an escape and wastage of energy to no purpose. So there's nothing efficient about a nutcracker.

He sits, drinks.

LEN They've gone on a picnic.

MARK Who?

LEN The dwarfs.

PETE Oh Christ.

Picks up paper.

LEN They've left me to sweep the yard, to keep the place in order. It's a bloody liberty. They're supposed to be keeping you under observation. What do they think I am, a bloody charlady? I can't look after the place by myself, it's not possible. Piles and piles and piles of muck and leavings all over the place, spewed up spewed up, I'm not a skivvy, they don't pay me, I pay them.

MARK Why don't you settle down?

LEN Oh don't worry, it's basically a happy relationship. I trust them. They're very efficient. They know what they're waiting for. But they've got a new game, did I tell you? It's to do with beetles and twigs. There's a rockery of red-hot cinder. I like watching them. Their hairs are curled and oily on their necks. Always squatting and bending, dipping their wicks in the custard. Now and again a lick of flame screws up their noses. Do you know what they do? They run wild. They yowl, they pinch, they dribble, they whimper, they gouge, and then they soothe each others' orifices with a local ointment, and then, all gone, all forgotten, they lark about, each with his buddy, get out the nose spray and the scented syringe, settle down for the night with a bun and a doughnut.

PETE See you Mark.

Exit.

MARK Why don't you put it on the table?

Pause.

Open it up, Len.

Pause.

I'm supposed to be a friend of yours.

LEN You're a snake in my house.

MARK Really?

LEN You're trying to buy and sell me. You think I'm a ventriloquist's dummy. You've got me pinned to the wall before I open my mouth. You've got a tab on me, you're buying me out of house and home, you're a calculating bastard.

Pause.

Answer me. Say something.

Pause.

Do you understand?

Pause.

You don't agree?

Pause.

You disagree?

Pause.

You think I'm mistaken?

Pause.

But am I?

Pause.

Both of you bastards, you've made a hole in my side, I can't plug it!

Pause.

I've lost a kingdom. I suppose you're taking good care of things. Did you know that you and Pete are a music hall act? What happens? What do you do when you're alone? Do you do a jig? I suppose you're taking good care of things. I've got my treasure too. It's in my corner. Everything's in my corner. Everything is from the corner's point of view. I don't hold the whip. I'm a labouring man. I do the corner's will. I slave my guts out. I thought, at one time, that I'd escaped it, but it never dies, it's never dead. I feed it, it's well fed. Things that at one time seem to me of value I have no resource but to give it to eat and what was of value turns into pus. I can hide nothing. I can't lay anything aside. Nothing can be put aside, nothing can be hidden, nothing can be saved, it waits, it eats, it's voracious, you're in it, Pete's in it, you're all in my corner. There must be somewhere else!

Swift cross fade of lights to down centre area.

PETE *is seen vaguely, standing downstage below* LEN's *room.* MARK *is seated in his room. Unlit,* LEN *crouches, watching* PETE.

Pete walks by the river. Under the woodyard wall stops. Stops. Hiss of the yellow grass. The wood battlements jaw over the wall. Dust in the fairground ticks. The night ticks. He hears the tick of the roundabout, up river with the sweat. Pete walks by the river. Under the woodyard wall stops. Stops. The wood hangs. Death mask on the water. Pete walks by the – gull. Slicing gull. Gull. Down. He stops. Rat corpse in the yellow grass. Gull pads. Gull probes. Gull stamps his feet. Gull whinnies up. Gull screams, tears, Pete, tears, digs, Pete cuts, breaks, Pete stretches the corpse, flaps his wings, Pete's beak grows, probes, digs, pulls, the river jolts, no moon, what can I see, the dwarfs collect, they slide down the bridge, they scutter by the shoreside, the dwarfs collect, capable, industrious, they wear raincoats, it is going to rain, Pete digs, he screws in to the head, the dwarfs watch, Pete tugs, he tugs, he's tugging, he kills, he's killing, the rat's head, with a snap the cloth of the rat's head tears. Pete walks by the . . .

Deep groan.

He sinks into chair left of his table. Lights in LEN's *room swiftly fade up.* PETE *turns to him.*

PETE You look the worse for wear. What's the matter with you?

LEN I've been ill.

PETE Ill? What's the matter?

LEN Cheese. Stale cheese. It got me in the end. I've been eating a lot of cheese.

PETE Yes, well, it's easy to eat too much cheese.

LEN It all came out, in about twenty-eight goes. I couldn't stop shivering and I couldn't stop squatting. It got me all right. I'm all right now. I only go three times a day now. I can more or less regulate it. Once in the morning. A quick dash before lunch. Another quick dash after tea, and then I'm free to do what I want. I don't think you understand. That cheese didn't die. It only began to live when you swallowed it, you see, after it had gone down. I bumped into a German one night, he came home with me and helped me finish it off. He took it to bed with him, he sat up in bed with it, in the guest's suite. I went in and had a gander. He had it taped. He was brutal with it. He would bite into it and then concentrate. I had to hand it to him. The sweat came out on his nose but he stayed on his feet. After he'd got out of bed, that was. Stood bolt upright, swallowed it, clicked his fingers, ordered another piece of blackcurrant pie. It's my pie-making season. His piss stank worse than the cheese. You look in the pink.

PETE You want to watch your step. You know that? You're going from bad to worse. Why don't you pull yourself together? Eh? Get a steady job. Cultivate a bit of go and guts for a change. Make yourself useful, mate, for Christ's sake. As you are, you're just a dead weight round everybody's neck. You want to listen to your friends, mate. Who else have you got?

> PETE *taps him on the shoulder and exits. A light comes up on* MARK. *The lights in* LEN's *room fade out.* LEN *rises to down centre.*

LEN Mark sits by the fireside. Crosses his legs. His fingers wear a ring. The finger poised. Mark regards his finger. He regards his legs. He regards the fireside. Outside the door is the black blossom. He combs his hair with an ebony comb, he sits, he lies, he lowers his eyelashes, raises them, sees no change in the posture of the room, lights a cigarette, watches his hand clasp the lighter, watches the flame, sees his mouth go forward, sees the consummation, is satisfied. Pleased, sees the smoke in the lamp, pleased with the lamp and the smoke and his bulk, pleased with his legs and his ring and his hand and his body in the lamp. Sees himself speaking, the words arranged on his lips, sees himself with pleasure silent.

Under the twigs they slide, by the lilac bush, break the stems, sit, scutter to the edge of the lawn and there wait, capable, industrious, put up their sunshades, watch. Mark lies, heavy, content, watches his smoke in the window, times his puff out, his hand fall, (*with growing disgust.*) smiles at absent guests, sucks in all comers, arranges his web, lies there a spider.

> LEN *moves to above armchair in* MARK's *room as lights fade up. Down centre area fades out.*

What did you say?

MARK I never said anything.

LEN What do you do when you're tired, go to bed?

MARK That's right.

LEN You sleep like a log.

MARK Yes.

LEN What do you do when you wake up?

MARK Wake up.

LEN I want to ask you a question.

MARK No doubt.

LEN Are you prepared to answer questions?

MARK No.

LEN What do you do in the day when you're not walking about?

MARK I rest.

LEN Where do you find a resting place?

MARK Here and there.

LEN By consent?

MARK Invariably.

LEN But you're not particular?

MARK Yes, I'm particular.

LEN You choose your resting place?

MARK Normally.

THE DWARFS

LEN That might be anywhere?

MARK Yes.

LEN Does that content you?

MARK Sure! I've got a home. I know where I live.

LEN You mean you've got roots. Why haven't I got
roots? My house is older than yours. My family lived
here. Why haven't I got a home?

MARK Move out.

LEN Do you believe in God?

MARK What?

LEN Do you believe in God?

MARK Who?

LEN God.

MARK God?

LEN Do you believe in God?

MARK Do I believe in God?

LEN Yes.

MARK Would you say that again?

> LEN *goes swiftly to shelf. Picks up biscuit jar.*
> *Offers to* MARK.

LEN Have a biscuit.

MARK Thanks.

LEN They're your biscuits.

MARK There's two left. Have one yourself.

LEN *puts biscuits away.*

LEN You don't understand. You'll never understand.

MARK Really?

LEN Do you know what the point is? Do you know what it is?

MARK No.

LEN The point is, who are you? Not why or how, not even what. I can see what, perhaps, clearly enough. But who are you? It's no use saying you know who you are just because you tell me you can fit your particular key into a particular slot, which will only receive your particular key because that's not foolproof and certainly not conclusive. Just because you're inclined to make these statements of faith has nothing to do with me. It's not my business. Occasionally I believe I perceive a little of what you are but that's pure accident. Pure accident on both our parts, the perceived and the perceiver. It's nothing like an accident, it's deliberate, it's a joint pretence. We depend on these accidents, on these contrived accidents, to continue. It's not important then that it's conspiracy or hallucination. What you are, or appear to be to me, or appear to be to you, changes so quickly, so horrifyingly, I certainly can't keep up with it and I'm damn sure you can't either. But who you are I can't even begin to recognise, and sometimes I recognise it so wholly, so forcibly, I

316

can't look, and how can I be certain of what I see? You have no number. Where am I to look, where am I to look, what is there to locate, so as to have some surety, to have some rest from this whole bloody racket? You're the sum of so many reflections. How many reflections? Whose reflections? Is that what you consist of? What scum does the tide leave? What happens to the scum? When does it happen? I've seen what happens. But I can't speak when I see it. I can only point a finger. I can't even do that. The scum is broken and sucked back. I don't see where it goes. I don't see when, what do I see, what have I seen? What have I seen, the scum or the essence? What about it? Does all this give you the right to stand there and tell me you know who you are? It's a bloody impertinence. There's a great desert and there's a wind stopping. Pete's been eating too much cheese, he's ill from it, it's eating his flesh away, but that doesn't matter, you're still both in the same boat, you're eating all my biscuits, but that doesn't matter, you're still both in the same boat, you're still standing behind the curtains together. He thinks you're a fool, Pete thinks you're a fool, but that doesn't matter, you're still both of you standing behind my curtains, moving my curtains in my room. He may be your Black Knight, you may be his Black Knight, but I'm cursed with the two of you, with two Black Knights, that's friendship, that's this that I know. That's what I know.

MARK Pete thinks I'm a fool? (*Pause.*) Pete . . . Pete thinks that I'm a *fool*?

LEN *exits. Lights in* MARK's *room fade out and then fade in again. Doorbell rings,* MARK *rises, goes off to front door.*

Silence.

PETE (*entering*) Hullo, Mark.

MARK (*re-enters and sits again*) Hullo.

PETE What are you doing?

MARK Nothing.

PETE Can I sit down?

MARK Sure.

PETE *sits right armchair. Pause.*

PETE Well, what are you doing with yourself?

MARK When's that?

PETE Now.

MARK Nothing.

MARK *files his nails. Pause.*

PETE Len's in hospital.

MARK Len? What's the matter with him?

PETE Kidney trouble. Not serious.

Pause.

Well, what have you been doing with yourself?

MARK When?

PETE Since I saw you.

MARK This and that.

PETE This and what?

MARK That.

Pause.

PETE Do you want to go and see Len?

MARK When? Now?

PETE Yes. It's visiting time.

Pause.

Are you busy?

MARK No.

Pause.

PETE What's up?

MARK What?

PETE What's up?

MARK What do you mean?

PETE You're wearing a gas mask.

MARK Not me.

Pause.

PETE (*rising*) Ready?

MARK Yes.

He rises and exits.

PETE (*as he follows* MARK *off*) Fine day.

Pause.

Bit chilly.

The door slams as they leave the house. Lights up on LEN *in hospital bed. Listening to wireless (earphones).*

PETE *and* MARK *enter.*

LEN You got here.

PETE (*sitting left of bed*) Yes.

LEN They can't do enough for me here.

PETE Why's that?

LEN Because I'm no trouble.

MARK *sits right of bed.*

They treat me like a king. These nurses, they treat me exactly like a king.

Pause.

Mark looks as though he's caught a crab.

MARK Do I?

PETE Airy, this ward.

LEN Best quality blankets, home cooking, everything you could wish for. Look at the ceiling. It's not too high and it's not too low.

Pause.

PETE By the way, Mark, what happened to your pipe?

MARK Nothing happened to it.

Pause.

LEN You smoking a pipe?

Pause.

What's it like out today?

PETE Bit chilly.

LEN Bound to be.

PETE The sun's come out.

LEN The sun's come out?

Pause.

Well, Mark, bring off the treble chance this week?

MARK Not me.

Pause.

LEN Who's driving the tank?

PETE What?

LEN Who's driving the tank?

PETE Don't ask me. We've been walking up the road back to back.

LEN You've what?

Pause.

You've been walking up the road back to back?

Pause.

What are you doing sitting on my bed? You're not supposed to sit on the bed, you're supposed to sit on the chairs!

PETE (*rising and moving off*) Well, give me a call when you get out.

He exits.

MARK (*rising and following him*) Yes, give me a call.

He exits.

LEN (*calling after them*) How do I know you'll be in?

Blackout. Lights come up on MARK's flat. MARK enters and sits. PETE enters, glances at MARK, sits.

PETE Horizontal personalities, those places. You're the only vertical. Makes you feel dizzy.

Pause.

You ever been inside one of those places?

MARK I can't remember.

PETE Right.

Stubs out cigarette, rises, goes to exit.

MARK All right. Why do you knock on my door?

PETE What?

MARK Come on. Why do you knock on my door?

PETE What are you talking about?

MARK Why?

PETE I call to see you.

MARK What do you want with me? Why come and see me?

PETE Why?

MARK You're playing a double game. You've been playing a double game. You've been using me. You've been leading me up the garden.

PETE Mind how you go.

MARK You've been wasting my time. For years.

PETE Don't push me, boy.

MARK You think I'm a fool.

PETE Is that what I think?

MARK That's what you think. You think I'm a fool.

PETE You are a fool.

MARK You've always thought that.

PETE From the beginning.

MARK You've been leading me up the garden.

PETE And you.

MARK You know what you are? You're an infection.

PETE Don't believe it. All I've got to do to destroy you is to leave you as you wish to be.

He walks out of the room. MARK *stares, slowly goes off as lights fade. Lights come up on the down centre area. Enter* LEN.

LEN They've stopped eating. It'll be a quick get out when the whistle blows. All their belongings are stacked in piles. They've doused the fire. But I've heard nothing. What is the cause for alarm? Why is everything packed? Why are they ready for the off? But they say nothing. They've cut me off without a penny. And now they've settled down to a wide-eyed kip, cross-legged by the fire. It's insupportable. I'm left in the lurch. Not even a stale frankfurter, a slice of bacon rind, a leaf of cabbage, not even a mouldy piece of salami, like they used to sling me in the days when we told old tales by suntime. They sit, chock-full. But I smell a rat. They seem to be anticipating a rarer dish, a choicer spread. And this change. All about me the change. The yard as I know it is littered with scraps of cat's meat, pig bollocks, tin cans, bird brains, spare parts of all the little animals, a squelching, squealing carpet, all the dwarfs' leavings spittled in the muck, worms stuck in the poisoned shit heaps, the alleys a whirlpool of piss, slime, blood, and fruit juice. Now all is bare. All is clean. All is scrubbed. There is a lawn. There is a shrub. There is a flower.

THE COLLECTION

The Collection first published
by Methuen & Co. 1963,
second edition 1964
© FPinter Limited, 1963, 1964

The Collection was first broadcast by Associated Rediffusion Television, London, on 11 May 1961, with the following cast:

HARRY	Griffith Jones
JAMES	Anthony Bate
STELLA	Vivien Merchant
BILL	John Ronane

Directed by Joan Kemp-Welch

The play was first presented on the stage at the Aldwych Theatre, Londn, on 18 June 1962, with the following cast:

HARRY	Michael Hordern
JAMES	Kenneth Haigh
STELLA	Barbara Murray
BILL	John Ronane

Directed by Peter Hall and Harold Pinter

Characters

HARRY
a man in his forties

JAMES
a man in his thirties

STELLA
a woman in her thirties

BILL
a man in his late twenties

Autumn

The stage is divided into three areas, two peninsulas and a promontory. Each area is distinct and separate from the other.

Stage left, HARRY's house in Belgravia. Elegant décor. Period furnishing. This set comprises the living room, hall, front door and staircase to first floor. Kitchen exit below staircase.

Stage right, JAMES's flat in Chelsea. Tasteful contemporary furnishing. This set comprises the living room only. Offstage right, other rooms and front door.

Upstage centre on promontory, telephone box.

The telephone box is lit in a half light. A figure can be dimly observed inside it, with his back to the audience. The rest of the stage is dark. In the house the telephone is ringing. It is late at night.

Night light in house fades up. Street fades up.

HARRY *approaches the house, opens the front door and goes in. He switches on a light in the hall, goes into the living room, walks to the telephone and lifts it.*

HARRY Hullo.

VOICE Is that you, Bill?

HARRY No, he's in bed. Who's this?

VOICE In bed?

HARRY Who is this?

VOICE What's he doing in bed?

   Pause.

HARRY Do you know it's four o'clock in the morning?

VOICE Well, give him a nudge. Tell him I want a word with him.

   Pause.

331

HARRY Who is this?

VOICE Go and wake him up, there's a good boy.

Pause.

HARRY Are you a friend of his?

VOICE He'll know me when he sees me.

HARRY Oh yes?

Pause

VOICE Aren't you going to wake him?

HARRY No, I'm not.

Pause.

VOICE Tell him I'll be in touch.

The telephone cuts off. HARRY *replaces the receiver and stands still. The figure leaves the telephone box.* HARRY *walks slowly into the hall and up the stairs.*

Fade to blackout.

Fade up on flat. It is morning.

JAMES, *smoking, enters and sits on the sofa.*

STELLA *enters from a bedroom fixing a bracelet on her wrist.*

She goes to the cabinet, takes a perfume atomiser from her handbag and uses it on her throat and hands. She puts the atomiser into her bag and begins to put her gloves on.

STELLA I'm going.

Pause.

Aren't you coming in today?

Pause.

JAMES No.

STELLA You had to meet those people from . . .

Pause. She slowly walks to an armchair, picks up her jacket and puts it on.

You had to meet those people about that order. Shall I phone them when I get to the shop?

JAMES You could do . . . yes.

STELLA What are you going to do?

He looks at her, with a brief smile, then away.

Jimmy . . .

Pause.

Are you going out?

Pause.

Will you . . . be in tonight?

JAMES reaches for a glass ashtray, flicks ash, and regards the ashtray. STELLA turns and leaves the room. The front door slams. JAMES continues regarding the ashtray.

Fade to half light.

Fade up on house. Morning.

BILL *brings on a tray from the kitchen and places it on the table, arranges it, pours tea, sits, picks up a newspaper, reads, drinks.* HARRY, *in a dressing-gown, descends the stairs, trips, stumbles.*

BILL (*turning*) What have you done?

HARRY I tripped on that stair rod!

He comes into the room.

BILL All right.

HARRY It's that stair rod. I thought you said you were going to fix it.

BILL I did fix it.

HARRY Well, you didn't fix it very well.

He sits, holding his head.

Ooh.

BILL *pours tea for him.*

In the flat, JAMES *stubs his cigarette and goes out. The lights in the flat fade out.*

HARRY *sips the tea, then puts the cup down.*

Where's my fruit juice? I haven't had my fruit juice.

BILL *regards the fruit juice on the tray.*

What's it doing over there?

BILL *gives it to him.* harry *sips it.*

What's this? Pineapple?

BILL Grapefruit.

334

Pause.

HARRY I'm sick and tired of that stair rod. Why don't you screw it in or something? You're supposed . . . you're supposed to be able to use your hands.

Pause.

BILL What time did you get in?

HARRY Four.

BILL Good party?

Pause.

HARRY You didn't make any toast this morning

BILL No. Do you want some?

HARRY No. I don't.

BILL I can if you like.

HARRY It's all right. Don't bother.

Pause.

How are you spending your day today?

BILL Go and see a film, I think.

HARRY Wonderful life you lead. (*Pause.*) Do you know some maniac telephoned you last night?

BILL *looks at him.*

Just as I got in. Four o'clock. Walked in the door and the telephone was ringing.

BILL Who was it?

HARRY I've no idea.

BILL What did he want?

HARRY You. He was shy, wouldn't tell me his name.

BILL Huh.

Pause.

HARRY Who could it have been?

BILL I've no idea.

HARRY He was very insistent. Said he was going to get in touch again. (*Pause.*) Who the hell was it?

BILL I've just said . . . I haven't the remotest idea.

Pause.

HARRY Did you meet anyone last week?

BILL Meet anyone? What do you mean?

HARRY I mean could it have been anyone you met? You must have met lots of people.

BILL I didn't speak to a soul.

HARRY Must have been miserable for you.

BILL I was only there one night, wasn't I? Some more?

HARRY No, thank you.

BILL *pours tea for himself.*

The telephone box fades up to half light, disclosing a figure entering it.

I must shave.

HARRY *sits, looking at* BILL, *who is reading the paper After a moment* BILL *looks up.*

BILL Mmnnn?

Silence, HARRY *stands, leaves the room and exits up the stairs, treading carefully over the stair rod.* BILL *reads the paper. The telephone rings.* BILL *lifts the receiver.*

Hullo.

VOICE Is that you, Bill?

BILL Yes?

VOICE Are you in?

BILL Who's this?

VOICE Don't move. I'll be straight round.

BILL What do you mean? Who is this?

VOICE About two minutes. All right?

BILL You can't do that. I've got some people here.

VOICE Never mind. We can go into another room.

BILL This is ridiculous. Do I know you?

VOICE You'll know me when you see me.

BILL Do you know me?

VOICE Just stay where you are. I'll be right round.

BILL But what do you want, who –? You can't do that. I'm going straight out. I won't be in.

VOICE See you.

The phone cuts off. BILL *replaces the receiver.*

The lights on the telephone box fade as the figure comes out and exits left.

BILL *puts on his jacket, goes into the hall, puts on his overcoat, swift but not hurried, opens the front door, and goes out. He exits up right,* HARRY's *voice from upstairs.*

HARRY Bill, was that you?

He appears at the head of the stairs.

Bill!

He goes downstairs, into the living room, stands, observes the tray, and takes the tray into the kitchen.

JAMES *comes from up left in the street and looks at the house.*

HARRY *comes out of the kitchen, goes into the hall and up the stairs.*

JAMES *rings the bell.*

HARRY *comes down the stairs and opens the door.*

Yes?

JAMES I'm looking for Bill Lloyd.

HARRY He's out. Can I help?

JAMES When will he be in?

HARRY I can't say. Does he know you?

JAMES I'll try some other time then.

HARRY Well, perhaps you'd like to leave your name. I can tell him when I see him.

JAMES No, that's all right. Just tell him I called.

HARRY Tell him who called?

JAMES Sorry to bother you.

HARRY Just a minute.

JAMES *turns back.*

You're not the man who telephoned last night, are you?

JAMES Last night?

HARRY You didn't telephone early this morning?

JAMES No . . . sorry . . .

HARRY Well, what do you want?

JAMES I'm looking for Bill.

HARRY You didn't by any chance telephone just now?

JAMES I think you've got the wrong man.

HARRY I think you have.

JAMES I don't think you know anything about it.

JAMES *turns and goes.* HARRY *stands watching him.*
Fade to blackout.
Fade up moonlight in flat.
The front door closes, in flat.

STELLA *comes in, stands, switches on a lamp. She turns in the direction of the other rooms.*

STELLA Jimmy?

Silence.

She takes her gloves off, puts her handbag dozen, and is still. She goes to the record player, and puts on a record. It is 'Charlie Parker'. She listens, then exists to the bedroom.

Fade up house. Night.

BILL *enters the living-room from the kitchen with magazines. He throws them in the hearth, goes to the drinks table and pours a drink, then lies on the floor with a drink by the hearth, flicking through a magazine.* STELLA *comes back into the room with a white Persian kitten. She lies back on the sofa, nuzzling it.* HARRY *comes downstairs, glances in at* BILL, *exits and walks down the street to up right,* JAMES *appears at the front door of the house from up left, looks after* HARRY, *and rings the bell,* bill *stands, and goes to the door.*

Fade flat to half light and music out.

BILL Yes?

JAMES Bill Lloyd?

BILL Yes?

JAMES Oh, I'd . . . I'd like to have a word with you.

Pause.

BILL I'm sorry, I don't think I know you?

JAMES Don't you?

BILL No.

JAMES Well, there's something I'd like to talk to you about

BILL I'm terribly sorry, I'm busy.

JAMES It won't take long.

BILL I'm awfully sorry. Perhaps you'd like to put it down on paper and send it to me.

JAMES That's not possible.

    Pause.

BILL (*closing door*) Do forgive me –

JAMES (*foot in door*) Look. I want to speak to you.

    Pause.

BILL Did you phone me today?

JAMES That's right. I called, but you'd gone out.

BILL You called here? I didn't know that.

JAMES I think I'd better come in, don't you?

BILL You can't just barge into someone's house like this, you know. What do you want?

JAMES Why don't you stop wasting your time and let me in?

BILL I could call the police.

JAMES Not worth it.

    They stare at each other.

341

BILL All right.

> JAMES *goes in.* BILL *closes the door,* JAMES *goes
> through the hall and into the living room.* BILL
> *follows.* JAMES *looks about the room.*

JAMES Got any olives?

BILL How did you know my name?

JAMES No olives?

BILL Olives? I'm afraid not.

JAMES You mean to say you don't keep olives for
your guests?

BILL You're not my guest, you're an intruder. What
can I do for you?

JAMES Do you mind if I sit down?

BILL Yes, I do.

JAMES You'll get over it.

> JAMES *sits.* BILL *stands.* JAMES *stands, takes off his
> overcoat, throws it on an armchair, and sits again.*

BILL What's your name, old boy?

> JAMES *reaches to a bowl of fruit and breaks off a
> grape, which he eats.*

JAMES Where shall I put the pips?

BILL In your wallet.

> JAMES *takes out his wallet and deposits the pips.
> He regards* BILL.

JAMES You're not a bad-looking bloke.

BILL Oh, thanks.

JAMES You're not a film star, but you're quite tolerable looking, I suppose.

BILL That's more than I can say for you.

JAMES I'm not interested in what you can say for me.

BILL To put it quite blundy, old chap, I'm even less interested than you are. Now look, come on please, what do you want?

> JAMES *stands, walks to the drinks table and stares at the bottles. In the flat,* STELLA *rises with the kitten and goes off slowly, nuzzling it. The flat fades to blackout.* JAMES *pours himself a whisky.*

Cheers.

JAMES Did you have a good time in Leeds last week?

BILL What?

JAMES Did you have a good time in Leeds last week?

BILL Leeds?

JAMES Did you enjoy yourself?

BILL What makes you think I was in Leeds.

JAMES Tell me all about it. See much of the town? Get out to the country at all?

BILL What are you talking about?

> *Pause.*

343

JAMES (*with fatigue*) Aaah. You were down there for the dress collection. You took some of your models.

BILL Did I?

JAMES You stayed at the Westbury Hotel.

BILL Oh?

JAMES Room 142.

BILL 142? Oh. Was it comfortable?

JAMES Comfortable enough.

BILL Oh, good.

JAMES Well, you had your yellow pyjamas with you.

BILL Did I really? What, the ones with the black initials?

JAMES Yes, you had them on you in 165.

BILL In what?

JAMES 165.

BILL 165? I thought I was in 142.

JAMES You booked into 142. But you didn't stay there.

BILL Well, that's a bit silly, isn't it? Booking a room and not staying in it?

JAMES 165 is just along the passage to 142; you're not far away.

BILL Oh well, that's a relief.

344

JAMES You could easily nip back to shave.

BILL From 165?

JAMES Yes.

BILL What was I doing there?

JAMES (*casually*) My wife was in there. That's where you slept with her.

  Silence.

BILL Well . . . who told you that?

JAMES She did.

BILL You should have her seen to.

JAMES Be careful.

BILL Mmmm? Who is your wife?

JAMES You know her.

BILL I don't think so.

JAMES No?

BILL No, I don't think so at all.

JAMES I see.

BILL I was nowhere near Leeds last week, old chap. Nowhere near your wife either, I'm quite sure of that. Apart from that, I . . . just don't do such things. Not in my book.

  Pause.

I wouldn't dream of it. Well, I think that closes that

subject, don't you?

JAMES Come here. I want to tell you something.

BILL I'm expecting guests in a minute, you know. Cocktails, I'm standing for Parliament next season.

JAMES Come here.

BILL I'm going to be Minister for Home Affairs.

JAMES *moves to him.*

JAMES (*confidentially*) When you treat my wife like a whore, then I think I'm entitled to know what you've got to say about it.

BILL But I don't know your wife.

JAMES You do. You met her at ten o'clock last Friday in the lounge. You fell into conversation, you bought her a couple of drinks, you went upstairs together in the lift. In the lift you never took your eyes from her, you found you were both on the same floor, you helped her out, by her arm. You stood with her in the corridor, looking at her. You touched her shoulder, said good night, went to your room, she went to hers, you changed into your yellow pyjamas and black dressing-gown, you went down the passage and knocked on her door, you'd left your toothpaste in town. She opened the door, you went in, she was still dressed. You admired the room, it was so feminine, you felt awake, didn't feel like sleeping, you sat down, on the bed. She wanted you to go, you wouldn't. She became upset, you sympathised, away from home, on a business trip, horrible life, especially for a woman, you comforted her, you gave her solace, you stayed.

Pause.

BILL Look, do you mind . . . just going off now. You're giving me a bit of a headache.

JAMES You knew she was married . . . why did you feel it necessary . . . to do that?

BILL She must have known she was married, too. Why did she feel it necessary . . . to do that?

Pause.

(*With a chuckle.*) That's got you, hasn't it?

Pause.

Well, look, it's really just a lot of rubbish. You know that

BILL *goes to the cigarette box and lights a cigarette.*

Is she supposed to have resisted me at all?

JAMES A little.

BILL Only a little?

JAMES Yes.

BILL Do you believe her?

JAMES Yes.

BILL Everything she says?

JAMES Sure.

BILL Did she bite at all?

JAMES No.

BILL Scratch?

JAMES A little.

BILL You've got a devoted wife, haven't you? Keeps you well informed, right up to the minutest detail. She scratched a little, did she? Where? (*Holds up a hand.*) On the hand? No scar. No scar anywhere. Absolutely unscarred. We can go before a commissioner of oaths, if you like. I'll strip, show you my unscarred body. Yes, what we need is an independent witness. You got any chambermaids on your side or anything?

JAMES *applauds briefly.*

JAMES You're a wag, aren't you? I never thought you'd be such a wag. You've really got a sense of fun. You know what I'd call you?

BILL What?

JAMES A wag.

BILL Oh, thanks very much.

JAMES No, I'm glad to pay a compliment when a compliment's due. What about a drink?

BILL That's good of you.

JAMES What will you have?

BILL Got any vodka?

JAMES Let's see. Yes, I think we can find you some vodka.

BILL Oh, scrumptious.

JAMES Say that again.

BILL What?

JAMES That word.

BILL What, scrumptious?

JAMES That's it.

BILL Scrumptious.

JAMES Marvellous. You probably remember that from school, don't you?

BILL Now that you mention it I think you might be right.

JAMES I thought I was. Here's your vodka.

BILL That's very generous of you.

JAMES Not at all. Cheers.

They drink.

BILL Cheers.

JAMES Eh, come here.

BILL What?

JAMES I bet you're a wow at parties.

BILL Well, it's nice of you to say so, but I wouldn't say I was all that much of a wow.

JAMES Go on, I bet you are.

Pause.

BILL You think I'm a wow, do you?

JAMES At parties I should think you are.

BILL No, I'm not much of a wow really. The bloke I share this house with is, though.

JAMES Oh, I met him. Looked a jolly kind of chap.

BILL Yes, he's very good at parties. Bit of a conjurer.

JAMES What, rabbits?

BILL Well, not so much rabbits, no.

JAMES No rabbits?

BILL No. He doesn't like rabbits, actually. They give him hay fever.

JAMES Poor chap.

BILL Yes, it's a pity.

JAMES Seen a doctor about it?

BILL Oh, he's had it since he was that high.

JAMES Brought up in the country, I suppose?

BILL In a manner of speaking, yes.

Pause.

Ah well, it's been very nice meeting you, old chap. You must come again when the weather's better.

JAMES *makes a sudden move forward.* BILL *starts back, and falls over a pouffe on to the floor.* JAMES *chuckles. Pause.*

You've made me spill my drink. You've made me spill it on my cardigan.

JAMES *stands over him.*

I could easily kick you from here.

Pause.

Are you going to let me get up?

Pause.

Are you going to let me get up?

Pause.

Now listen . . . I'll tell you what . . .

Pause.

If you let me get up ..

Pause.

I'm not very comfortable.

Pause.

If you let me get up . . . I'll . . . I'll tell you . . . the truth . . .

Pause.

JAMES Tell me the truth from there.

BILL No. No, when I'm up.

JAMES Tell me from there.

Pause.

BILL Oh well. I'm only telling you because I'm utterly bored . . . The truth . . . is that it never happened . . . what you said, anyway. I didn't know she was married. She never told me. Never said a word. But nothing of that . . . happened, I can assure you. All that happened was . . . you were right, actually, about going up in the lift . . . we . . . got out of the lift, and then suddenly she was in my arms. Really wasn't my fault, nothing was further from my mind, biggest surprise of my life, must have found me terribly attractive quite suddenly, I don't know . . . but I . . . I didn't refuse. Anyway, we just kissed a bit, only a few minutes, by the lift, no one about, and that was that – she went to her room.

He props himself up on the pouffe.

The rest of it just didn't happen. I mean, I wouldn't do that sort of thing. I mean, that sort of thing . . . it's just meaningless. I can understand that you're upset, of course, but honestly, there was nothing else to it. Just a few kisses.

BILL *rises, wiping his cardigan.*

I'm dreadfully sorry, really, I mean, I've no idea why she should make up all that. Pure fantasy. Really rather naughty of her. Rather alarming. (*Pause.*) Do you know her well?

JAMES And then about midnight you went into her private bathroom and had a bath. You sang 'Coming through the Rye'. You used her bath towel. Then you walked about the room with her bath towel, pretending you were a Roman.

BILL Did I?

JAMES Then I phoned.

Pause.

I spoke to her. Asked her how she was. She said she was all right. Her voice was a little low. I asked her to speak up. She didn't have much to say. You were sitting on the bed, next to her.

Silence.

BILL Not sitting. Lying.

Blackout.

Church bells.

Full light up on both the flat and the house.

Sunday morning.

JAMES *is sitting alone in the living room of the flat, reading the paper.* HARRY *and* BILL *are sitting in the living room of the house, coffee before them.* BILL *is reading the paper.*

HARRY *is watching him.*

Silence.

Church bells.

Silence.

HARRY Put that paper down.

BILL What?

HARRY Put it down.

BILL Why?

HARRY You've read it.

BILL No, I haven't. There's lots to read, you know.

HARRY I told you to put it down.

> BILL *looks at him, throws the paper at him coolly and rises.* HARRY *picks it up and reads.*

BILL Oh, you just wanted it yourself, did you?

HARRY Want it? I don't want it.

> HARRY *crumples the paper deliberately and drops it.*

I don't want it. Do you want it?

BILL You're being a little erratic this morning, aren't you?

HARRY Am I?

BILL I would say you were.

HARRY Well, you know what it is, don't you?

BILL No.

HARRY It's the church bells. You know how church bells always set me off. You know how they affect me.

BILL I never hear them.

HARRY You're not the sort of person who would, are you?

354

BILL I'm finding all this faintly idiotic.

BILL *bends to pick up the paper.*

HARRY Don't touch that paper.

BILL Why not?

HARRY Don't touch it.

BILL *stares at him and then slowly picks it up.*

Silence.

He tosses it to HARRY.

BILL You have it. I don't want it.

BILL *goes out and up the stairs.* HARRY *opens the paper and reads it.*

In the flat, STELLA *comes in with a tray of coffee and biscuits. She places the tray on the coffee table and passes a cup to* JAMES. *She sips.*

STELLA Would you like a biscuit?

JAMES No, thank you.

Pause.

STELLA I'm going to have one.

JAMES You'll get fat.

STELLA From biscuits?

JAMES You don't want to get fat, do you?

STELLA Why not?

JAMES Perhaps you do.

355

STELLA It's not one of my aims.

JAMES What is your aim?

Pause.

I'd like an olive.

STELLA Olive? We haven't got any.

JAMES How do you know?

STELLA I know.

JAMES Have you looked?

STELLA I don't need to look, do I? I know what I've got.

JAMES You know what you've got?

Pause.

Why haven't we got any olives?

STELLA I didn't know you liked them.

JAMES That must be the reason why we've never had them in the house. You've simply never been interested enough in olives to ask whether I liked them or not.

The telephone rings in the house. HARRY f puts the paper down and goes to it. BILL comes down the stairs. They stop, facing each other, momentarily. HARRY lifts the receiver. BILL walks into the room, picks up the paper and sits.

HARRY Hullo. What? No. Wrong number. (*Replaces receiver.*) Wrong number. Who do you think it was?

356

BILL I didn't think.

HARRY Oh, by the way, a chap called for you yesterday.

BILL Oh yes?

HARRY Just after you'd gone out.

BILL Oh yes?

HARRY Ah well, time for the joint. Roast or chips?

BILL I don't want any potatoes, thank you.

HARRY No potatoes? What an extraordinary thing. Yes, this chap, he was asking for you, he wanted you.

BILL What for?

HARRY He wanted to know if you ever cleaned your shoes with furniture polish.

BILL Really? How odd.

HARRY Not odd. Some kind of national survey.

BILL What did he look like?

HARRY Oh . . . lemon hair, nigger brown teeth, wooden leg, bottlegreen eyes and a toupee. Know him?

BILL Never met him.

HARRY You'd know him if you saw him.

BILL I doubt it.

HARRY What, a man who looked like that?

BILL Plenty of men look like that.

HARRY That's true. That's very true. The only thing is that this particular man was here last night.

BILL Was he? I didn't see him.

HARRY Oh yes, he was here, but I've got a funny feeling he wore a mask. It was the same man, but he wore a mask, that's all there is to it. He didn't dance here last night, did he, or do any gymnastics?

BILL No one danced here last night.

HARRY Aah. Well, that's why you didn't notice his wooden leg. I couldn't help seeing it myself when he came to the front door because he stood on the top step stark naked. Didn't seem very cold, though. He had a waterbottle under bis arm instead of a hat.

BILL Those church bells have certainly left their mark on you.

HARRY They haven't helped, but the fact of the matter is, old chap, that I don't like strangers coming into my house without an invitation. (*Pause.*) Who is this man and what does he want?

Pause. BILL *rises.*

BILL Will you excuse me? I really think it's about time I was dressed, don't you?

BILL *goes up the stairs.*

HARRY, *after a moment, turns and follows. He slowly ascends the stairs.*

Fade to blackout on house.

In the flat JAMES *is still reading the paper,* STELLA *is sitting silently.*

Silence.

STELLA What do you think about going for a run today . . . in the country?

Pause. JAMES *puts the paper down.*

JAMES I've come to a decision.

STELLA What?

JAMES I'm going to go and see him.

STELLA See him? Who? (*Pause.*) What for?

JAMES Oh . . . have a chat with him.

STELLA What's the point of doing that?

JAMES I feel I'd like to.

STELLA I just don't see . . . what there is to be gained. What's the point of it?

Pause.

What are you going to do, hit him?

JAMES No, no. I'd just like to hear what he's got to say.

STELLA Why?

JAMES I want to know what his attitude is.

Pause.

STELLA He doesn't matter.

JAMES What do you mean?

STELLA He's not important.

JAMES Do you mean anyone would have done? You mean it just happened to be him, but it might as well have been anyone?

STELLA No.

JAMES What then?

STELLA Of course it couldn't have been anyone. It was him. It was just . . . something . . .

JAMES That's what I mean. It was him. That's why I think he's worth having a look at. I want to see what he's like It'll be instructive, educational.

Pause.

STELLA Please don't go and see him. You don't know where he lives, anyway.

JAMES You don't think I should see him?

STELLA It won't. . . make you feel any better.

JAMES I want to see if he's changed.

STELLA What do you mean?

JAMES I want to see if he's changed from when I last saw him. He may have gone down the drain since I last saw him. I must say he looked in good shape, though.

STELLA You've never seen him.

Pause.

You don't know him.

Pause.

You don't know where he lives?

Pause.

When did you see him?

JAMES We had dinner together last night.

STELLA What?

JAMES Splendid host.

STELLA I don't believe it.

JAMES Ever been to his place?

Pause.

Rather nice. Ever been there?

STELLA I met him in Leeds, that's all.

JAMES Oh, is that all. Well, we'll have to go round there one night. The grub's good, I can't deny it. I found him quite charming.

Pause.

He remembered the occasion well. He was perfectly frank. You know, a man's man. Straight from the shoulder. He entirely confirmed your story.

STELLA Did he?

JAMES Mmm. Only thing . . . he rather implied that you led him on. Typical masculine thing to say, of course.

STELLA That's a lie.

JAMES You know what men are. I reminded him that you'd resisted, and you'd hated the whole thing, but that you'd been – how can we say – somehow hypnotised by him, it happens sometimes. He agreed it can happen sometimes. He told me he'd been hypnotised once by a cat. Wouldn't go into any more details, though. Still, I must admit we rather hit it off. We've got the same interests. He was most amusing over the brandy.

STELLA I'm not interested.

JAMES In fact, he was most amusing over the whole thing.

STELLA Was he?

JAMES But especially over the brandy. He's got the right attitude, you see. As a man, I can only admire it.

STELLA What is his attitude?

JAMES What's your attitude?

STELLA I don't know what you're . . . I just don't know what you're . . . I just . . . hoped you'd understand . . .

She covers her face, crying.

JAMES Well, I do understand, but only after meeting him. Now I'm perfecdy happy. I can see it both ways, three ways, all ways . . . every way. It's perfectly clear, there's nothing to it, everything's back to normal. The only difference is that I've come across a man I can respect. It isn't often you can do that, that that happens, and really I suppose I've got you to thank.

He bends forward and pats her arm.

Thanks.

Pause.

He reminds me of a bloke I went to school with. Hawkins. Honestly, he reminded me of Hawkins. Hawkins was an opera fan, too. So's what's-his-name. I'm a bit of an opera fan myself. Always kept it a dead secret. I might go along with your bloke to the opera one night. He says he can always get free seats. He knows quite a few of that crowd. Maybe I can track old Hawkins down and take him along, too. He's a very cultivated bloke, your bloke, quite a considerable intelligence at work there, I thought. He's got a collection of Chinese pots stuck on a wall, must have cost at least fifteen hundred a piece. Well, you can't help noticing that sort of thing. I mean, you couldn't say he wasn't a man of taste. He's brimming over with it. Well, I suppose he must have struck you the same way. No, really, I think I should thank you, rather than anything else. After two years of marriage it looks as though, by accident, you've opened up a whole new world for me.

Fade to blackout. Fade up house. Night.

BILL *comes in from the kitchen with a tray of olives, cheese, crisps, and a transistor radio, playing Vivaldi, very quietly. He puts the tray on the table, arranges the cushions and eats a crisp.* JAMES *appears at the front door and rings the bell.* BILL *goes to the door, opens it, and* JAMES *comes in. In the hall he helps* JAMES *off with his coat.*

JAMES *comes into the room.* BILL *follows.* JAMES *notices the tray with the olives, and smiles.* BILL *smiles.* JAMES *goes up to the Chinese vases and examines them.* BILL *pours drinks. In the flat the telephone rings.*

Fade up on flat. Night.

Fade up half light on telephone box.

A figure can be dimly seen in the telephone box. STELLA *enters from the bedroom, holding the kitten. She goes to the telephone.* BILL *gives* JAMES *a glass. They drink.*

STELLA Hullo.

HARRY Is that you, James?

STELLA What? No, it isn't. Who's this?

HARRY Where's James?

STELLA He's out.

HARRY Out? Oh, well, all right. I'll be straight round.

STELLA What are you talking about? Who are you?

HARRY Don't go out.

The telephone cuts off. STELLA *replaces the receiver and sits upright with the kitten on the chair. Fade to half light on flat. Fade telephone box.*

JAMES You know something? You remind me of a chap I knew once. Hawkins. Yes. He was quite a tall lad.

BILL Tall, was he?

JAMES Yes.

BILL Now why should I remind you of him?

JAMES He was quite a card.

Pause.

BILL Tall, was he?

JAMES That's . . . what he was.

BILL Well, you're not short.

JAMES I'm not tall.

BILL Quite broad.

JAMES That doesn't make me tall.

BILL I never said it did.

JAMES Well, what are you saying?

BILL Nothing.

Pause.

JAMES I wouldn't exactly say I was broad, either.

BILL Well, you only see yourself in the mirror, don't you?

JAMES That's good enough for me.

BILL They're deceptive.

JAMES Mirrors?

BILL Very.

JAMES Have you got one?

BILL What?

JAMES A mirror.

BILL There's one right in front of you.

JAMES So there is.

JAMES *looks into the mirror.*

Come here. You look in it, too.

BILL *stands by him and looks. They look together; and then* JAMES *goes to the left of the mirror, and looks again at* BILL's *reflection.*

I don't think mirrors are deceptive.

JAMES *sits.* BILL *smiles, and turns up the radio. They sit listening.*

Fade to half light on house and radio out.

Fade up full on flat.

Doorbell.

STELLA *rises and goes off to the front door. The voices are heard off.*

STELLA Yes?

HARRY How do you do. My name's Harry Kane. I wonder if I might have a word with you. There's no need to be alarmed. May I come in?

STELLA Yes.

HARRY (*entering*) In here?

STELLA Yes.

They come into the room.

HARRY What a beautiful lamp.

STELLA What can I do for you?

HARRY Do you know Bill Lloyd?

STELLA No.

HARRY Oh, you don't?

STELLA No.

HARRY You don't know him personally?

STELLA I don't, no.

HARRY I found him in a slum, you know, by accident. Just happened to be in a slum one day and there he was. I realised he had talent straight away. I gave him a roof, gave him a job, and he came up trumps. We've been close friends for years.

STELLA Oh yes?

HARRY You know of him, of course, don't you, by repute? He's a dress designer.

STELLA I know of him.

HARRY You're both dress designers.

STELLA Yes.

HARRY You don't belong to the Rags and Bags Club, do you?

STELLA The what?

HARRY The Rags and Bags Club. I thought I might have seen you down there.

STELLA No, I don't know it.

HARRY Shame. You'd like it.

Pause.

Yes.

Pause.

I've come about your husband.

STELLA Oh?

HARRY Yes. He's been bothering Bill recently, with some fantastic story.

STELLA I know about it. I'm very sorry.

HARRY Oh, you know? Well, it's really been rather disturbing. I mean, the boy has his work to get on with. This sort of thing spoils his concentration.

STELLA I'm sorry. It's . . . very unfortunate.

HARRY It is.

Pause.

STELLA I can't understand it . . . We've been happily married for two years, you see. I've . . . been away before, you know . . . showing dresses, here and there, my husband runs the business. But it's never happened before.

HARRY What hasn't?

STELLA Well, that my husband has suddenly dreamed up such a fantastic story, for no reason at all.

HARRY That's what I said it was. I said it was a fantastic story.

STELLA It is.

HARRY That's what I said and that's what Bill says. We both think it's a fantastic story.

STELLA I mean, Mr Lloyd was in Leeds, but I hardly saw him, even though we were staying in the same hotel. I never met him or spoke to him . . . and then my husband suddenly accused me of . . . it's really been very distressing.

HARRY Yes. What do you think the answer is? Do you think your husband . . . doesn't trust you, or something?

STELLA Of course he does – he's just not been very well lately, actually . . . overwork.

HARRY That's bad. Still, you know what it's like in our business. Why don't you take him on a long holiday? South of France.

STELLA Yes. I'm very sorry that Mr Lloyd has had to put up with all this, anyway.

HARRY Oh, what a beautiful kitten, what a really beautiful kitten. Kitty, kitty, kitty, what do you call her, come here, kitty, kitty.

> HARRY *sits next to* STELLA *and proceeds to pet and nuzzle the kitten.*
>
> *Fade flat to half light.*
>
> *Fade up full on house.*
>
> BILL *and* JAMES, *with drinks in the same position.*
>
> *Music comes up.* BILL *turns off the radio.*
>
> *Music out.*

BILL Hungry?

JAMES No.

BILL Biscuit?

JAMES I'm not hungry.

BILL I've got some olives.

JAMES Really?

BILL Like one?

JAMES No, thanks.

BILL Why not?

JAMES I don't like them.

> *Pause.*

BILL Don't like olives?

Pause.

What on earth have you got against olives?

Pause.

JAMES I detest them.

BILL Really?

JAMES It's the smell I hate.

Pause.

BILL Cheese? I've got a splendid cheese knife.

He picks up a cheese knife.

Look. Don't you think it's splendid?

JAMES Is it sharp?

BILL Try it. Hold the blade. It won't cut you. Not if you handle it properly. Not if you grasp it firmly up to the hilt.

JAMES does not touch the knife.

BILL stands holding it.

Lights in house remain.

Fade up flat to full.

HARRY (*standing*) Well, goodbye, I'm glad we've had our little chat.

STELLA Yes.

HARRY It's all quite clear now.

371

STELLA I'm glad.

They move to the door.

HARRY Oh, Mr Lloyd asked me if I would give you his best wishes . . . and sympathies.

He goes out. She stands still.

Goodbye.

The front door closes. STELLA *lies on the sofa with the kitten. She rests her head, is still. Fade flat to half light.*

BILL What are you frightened of?

JAMES (*moving away*) What's that?

BILL What?

JAMES I thought it was thunder.

BILL (*to him*) Why are you frightened of holding this blade?

JAMES I'm not frightened. I was just thinking of the thunder last week, when you and my wife were in Leeds.

BILL Oh, not again, surely? I thought we'd left all that behind. Surely we have? You're not still worried about that, are you?

JAMES Oh no. Just nostalgia, that's all.

BILL Surely the wound heals when you know the truth, doesn't it? I mean, when the truth is verified? I would have thought it did.

JAMES Of course.

BILL What's there left to think about? It's a thing regretted, never to be repeated. No past, no future. Do you see what I mean? You're a chap who's been married for two years, aren't you happily? There's a bond of iron between you and your wife. It can't be corroded by a trivial thing like this. I've apologised, she's apologised. Honestly, what more can you want?

Pause. JAMES *looks at him.* BILL *smiles.* HARRY *appears at the front door, opens and closes it quietly, and remains in the hall, unnoticed by the others.*

JAMES Nothing.

BILL Every woman is bound to have an outburst of . . . wild sensuality at one time or another. That's the way I look at it, anyway. It's part of their nature. Even though it may be the kind of sensuality of which you yourself have never been the fortunate recipient. What? (*He laughs.*) That is a husband's fate, I suppose. Mind you, I think it's the system that's at fault, not you. Perhaps she'll never need to do it again, who knows.

JAMES *stands, goes to the fruit bowl, and picks up the fruit knife. He runs his finger along the blade.*

JAMES This is fairly sharp.

BILL What do you mean?

JAMES Come on.

BILL I beg your pardon?

JAMES Come on. You've got that one. I've got this one.

BILL What about it?

JAMES I get a bit tired of words sometimes, don't you? Let's have a game. For fun.

BILL What sort of game?

JAMES Let's have a mock duel.

BILL I don't want a mock duel, thank you.

JAMES Of course you do. Come on. First one who's touched is a sissy.

BILL This is all rather unsubtle, don't you think?

JAMES Not in the least. Come on, into first position.

BILL I thought we were friends.

JAMES Of course we're friends. What on earth's the matter with you? I'm not going to kill you. It's just a game, that's all. We're playing a game. You're not windy, are you?

BILL I think it's silly.

JAMES I say, you're a bit of a spoilsport, aren't you?

BILL I'm putting my knife down anyway.

JAMES Well, I'll pick it up.

JAMES *does so and faces him with two knives.*

BILL Now you've got two.

JAMES I've got another one in my hip pocket.

Pause.

BILL What do you do, swallow them?

JAMES Do you?

Pause. They stare at each other.

(*Suddenly.*) Go on! Swallow it!

JAMES *throws a knife at* BILL'*s face.* BILL *throws up a hand to protect his face and catches the knife by the blade It cuts his hand.*

BILL Ow!

JAMES Well caught! What's the matter?

He examines BILL'*s hand.*

Let's have a look. Ah yes. Now you've got a scar on your hand. You didn't have one before, did you?

HARRY *comes into the room.*

HARRY (*entering*) What have you done, nipped your hand? Let's have a look. (*To* JAMES.) Only a little nip, isn't it? It's his own fault for not ducking. I must have told him dozens of times, you know, that if someone throws a knife at you the silliest thing you can do is to catch it. You're bound to hurt yourself, unless it's made of rubber. The safest thing to do is duck. You're Mr Home?

JAMES That's right.

HARRY I'm so glad to meet you. My name's Harry Kane. Bill been looking after you all right? I asked him to see that you stayed until I got back. So glad

375

you could spare the time. What are we drinking?
Whisky? Let's fill you up. You and your wife run that
little boutique down the road, don't you? Funny we've
never met, living so close, all in the same trade, eh?
Here you are. Got one, Bill? Where's your glass? This
one? Here . . . you are. Oh, stop rubbing your hand,
for goodness' sake. It's only a cheese knife. Well, Mr
Home, all the very best. Here's wishing us all health,
happiness and prosperity in the time to come, not
forgetting your wife, of course. Healthy minds in
healthy bodies. Cheers.

They drink.

By the way, I've just seen your wife. What a beautiful
kitten she has. You should see it, Bill; it's all white. We
had a very pleasant chat, your wife and I. Listen . . .
old chap . . . can I be quite blunt with you?

JAMES Of course.

HARRY Your wife . . . you see . . . made a little tiny
confession to me. I think I can use that word.

Pause.

BILL *is sucking his hand.*

What she confessed was . . . that she'd made the whole
thing up. She'd made the whole damn thing up. For
some odd reason of her own. They never met, you see,
Bill and your wife; they never even spoke. This is what
Bill says, and this is now what your wife admits. They
had nothing whatever to do with each other; they
don't know each other. Women are very strange. But

I suppose you know more about that than I do; she's your wife. If I were you I'd go home and knock her over the head with a saucepan and tell her not to make up such stories again.

Pause.

JAMES She made the whole thing up, eh?

HARRY I'm afraid she did.

JAMES I see. Well, thanks very much for telling me.

HARRY I thought it would be clearer for you, coming from someone completely outside the whole matter.

JAMES Yes. Thank you.

HARRY Isn't that so, Bill?

BILL Oh, quite so. I don't even know the woman. Wouldn't know her if I saw her. Pure fantasy.

JAMES How's your hand?

BILL Not bad.

JAMES Isn't it strange that you confirmed the whole of her story?

BILL It amused me to do so.

JAMES Oh?

BILL Yes. You amused me. You wanted me to confirm it. It amused me to do so.

Pause.

HARRY Bill's a slum boy, you see, he's got a slum
sense of humour. That's why I never take him along
with me to parties. Because he's got a slum mind. I
have nothing against slum minds per se, you
understand, nothing at all. There's a certain kind of
slum mind which is perfectly all right in a slum, but
when this kind of slum mind gets out of the slum it
sometimes persists, you see, it rots everything. That's
what Bill is. There's something faintly putrid about
him, don't you find? Like a slug. There's nothing
wrong with slugs in their place, but he's a slum slug;
there's nothing wrong with slum slugs in their place,
but this one won't keep his place – he crawls all over
the walls of nice houses, leaving slime, don't you,
boy? He confirms stupid sordid little stories just to
amuse himself, while everyone else has to run round
in circles to get to the root of the matter and smooth
the whole thing out. All he can do is sit and suck his
bloody hand and decompose like the filthy putrid
slum slug he is. What about another whisky, Home?

JAMES No, I think I must be off now. Well, I'm glad
to hear that nothing did happen. Great relief to me.

HARRY It must be.

JAMES My wife's not been very well lately, actually.
Overwork.

HARRY That's bad. Still, you know what it's like in
our business.

JAMES Best thing to do is take her on a long holiday,
I think.

HARRY South of France.

JAMES The Isles of Greece.

HARRY Sun's essential, of course.

JAMES I know. Bermuda.

HARRY Perfect.

JAMES Well, thanks very much, Mr Kane, for clearing my mind. I don't think I'll mention it when I get home. Take her out for a drink or something. Forget all about it.

HARRY Better hurry up. It's nearly closing time.

JAMES *moves to* BILL, *who is sitting.*

JAMES I'm very sorry I cut your hand. You're lucky you caught it, of course. Otherwise it might have cut your mouth. Still, it's not too bad, is it?

Pause.

Look . . . I really think I ought to apologise for this silly story my wife made up. The fault is really all hers, and mine, for believing her. You're not to blame for taking it as you did. The whole thing must have been an impossible burden for you. What do you say we shake hands, as a testimony of my goodwill?

JAMES *extends his hand.* BILL *rubs his hand but does not extend it.*

HARRY Come on, Billy, I think we've had enough of this stupidity, don't you?

Pause.

BILL I'll. . . tell you . . . the truth.

HARRY Oh, for God's sake, don't be ridiculous. Come on, Mr Home, off you go now, back to your wife, old boy, leave this . . . tyke to me.

JAMES *does not move. He looks down at* BILL.

Come on, Jimmy, I think we've had enough of this stupidity, don't you?

JAMES *looks at him sharply.* HARRY *stops still.*

BILL I never touched her . . . we sat . . . in the lounge, on a sofa . . . for two hours . . . talked . . . we talked about it . . . we didn't . . . move from the lounge. . . never went to her room . . . just talked . . . about what we would do . . . if we did get to hei room . . . two hours . . . we never touched . . . we just talked about it . . .

Long silence.

JAMES *leaves the house.*

HARRY *sits.* BILL *remains sitting sucking his hand.*

Silence.

Fade house to half light.

Fade up full on flat.

STELLA *is lying with the kitten.*

The flat door closes. JAMES *comes in. He stands looking at her.*

JAMES You didn't do anything, did you?

Pause.

He wasn't in your room. You just talked about it, in the lounge.

Pause.

That's the truth, isn't it?

Pause.

You just sat and talked about what you would do if you went to your room. That's what you did.

Pause.

Didn't you?

Pause.

That's the truth . . . isn't it?

STELLA *looks at him, neither confirming nor denying. Her face is friendly, sympathetic.*

Fade flat to half light.

The four figures are still, in the half light.

Fade to blackout.

Curtain.

THE LOVER

The Lover first published by
Methuen & Co. 1963,
second edition 1964
© FPinter Limited, 1963, 1964

The Lover was first broadcast by Associated-Rediffusion Television, London, on 28 March 1963, with the following cast:

RICHARD   Alan Badel
SARAH   Vivien Merchant
JOHN   Michael Forest

Directed by Joan Kemp-Welch

The play was first presented on stage by Michael Codron and David Hall at the Arts Theatre, London, on 18 September 1963, with the following cast:

RICHARD   Scott Forbes
SARAH   Vivien Merchant
JOHN   Michael Forest

Directed by Harold Pinter *assisted by* Guy Vaesen

It was produced at the Young Vic in June 1987 with the following cast:

RICHARD   Simon Williams
SARAH   Judy Buxton
JOHN   Malcolm Ward

Directed by Kevin Billington

Characters

RICHARD

SARAH

JOHN

Summer.

A detached house near Windsor.

The stage consists of two areas. Living room right, with small hall and front door up centre. Bedroom and balcony, on a level, left. There is a short flight of stairs to bedroom door. Kitchen off right. A table with a long velvet cover stands against the left wall of the living room, centre stage. In the small hall there is a cupboard. The furnishings are tasteful, comfortable.

SARAH *is emptying and dusting ashtrays in the living room. It is morning. She wears a crisp, demure dress.* RICHARD *comes into the bedroom from bathroom, off left, collects his briefcase from hall cupboard, goes to* SARAH, *kisses her on the cheek. He looks at her for a moment smiling. She smiles.*

RICHARD (*amiably*) Is your lover coming today?

SARAH Mmnn.

RICHARD What time?

SARAH Three.

RICHARD Will you be going out . . . or staying in?

SARAH Oh . . . I think we'll stay in.

RICHARD I thought you wanted to go to that exhibition.

SARAH I did, yes . . . but I think I'd prefer to stay in with him today.

RICHARD Mmn-hmmn. Well, I must be off.

He goes to the hall and puts on his bowler hat.

RICHARD Will he be staying long do you think?

SARAH Mmmnnn . . .

RICHARD About . . . six, then.

SARAH Yes.

RICHARD Have a pleasant afternoon.

SARAH Mmnn.

RICHARD Bye-bye.

SARAH Bye.

He opens the front door and goes out. She continues dusting. The lights fade.

Fade up. Early evening. SARAH *comes into room from kitchen. She wears the same dress, but is now wearing a pair of very high-heeled shoes. She pours a drink and sits on chaise longue with magazine. There are six chimes of the clock. Richard comes in the front door. He wears a sober suit, as in the morning. He puts his briefcase down in the hall and goes into the room. She smiles at him and pours him a whisky.*

Hullo.

RICHARD Hullo.

He kisses her on the cheek. Takes glass, hands her the evening paper and sits down left. She sits on chaise longue with paper.

Thanks.

He drinks, sits back and sighs with contentment.

Aah.

SARAH Tired?

RICHARD Just a little.

SARAH Bad traffic?

RICHARD No. Quite good traffic, actually.

SARAH Oh, good.

RICHARD Very smooth.

Pause.

SARAH It seemed to me you were just a little late.

RICHARD Am I?

SARAH Just a little.

RICHARD There was a bit of a jam on the bridge.

SARAH *gets up, goes to drinks table to collect her glass, sits again on the chaise longue.*

Pleasant day?

SARAH Mmn. I was in the village this morning.

RICHARD Oh yes? See anyone?

SARAH Not really, no. Had lunch.

RICHARD In the village?

SARAH Yes.

RICHARD Any good?

SARAH Quite fair. (*She sits.*)

RICHARD What about this afternoon? Pleasant afternoon?

SARAH Oh yes. Quite marvellous.

RICHARD Your lover came, did he?

SARAH Mmnn. Oh yes.

RICHARD Did you show him the hollyhocks?

Slight pause.

SARAH The hollyhocks?

RICHARD Yes.

SARAH No, I didn't.

RICHARD Oh.

SARAH Should I have done?

RICHARD No, no. It's simply that I seem to remember your saying he was interested in gardening.

SARAH Mmnn, yes, he is.

Pause.

Not all that interested, actually.

RICHARD Ah.

Pause.

Did you go out at all, or did you stay in?

SARAH We stayed in.

RICHARD Ah. (*He looks up at the Venetian blinds.*)
That blind hasn't been put up properly.

SARAH Yes, it is a bit crooked, isn't it?
  Pause.

RICHARD Very sunny on the road. Of course, by the
time I got on to it the sun was beginning to sink. But I
imagine it was quite warm here this afternoon. It was
warm in the City.

SARAH Was it?

RICHARD Pretty stifling. I imagine it was quite warm
everywhere.

SARAH Quite a high temperature, I believe.

RICHARD Did it say so on the wireless?

SARAH I think it did, yes.
  Slight pause.

RICHARD One more before dinner?

SARAH Mmn.
  He pours drinks.

RICHARD I see you had the Venetian blinds down.

SARAH We did, yes.

RICHARD The light was terribly strong.

SARAH It was. Awfully strong.

RICHARD The trouble with this room is that it catches the sun so directly, when it's shining. You didn't move to another room?

SARAH No. We stayed here.

RICHARD Must have been blinding.

SARAH It was. That's why we put the blinds down.

Pause.

RICHARD The thing is it gets so awfully hot in here with the blinds down.

SARAH Would you say so?

RICHARD Perhaps not. Perhaps it's just that you feel hotter.

SARAH Yes. That's probably it.

Pause.

What did you do this afternoon?

RICHARD Long meeting. Rather inconclusive.

SARAH It's a cold supper. Do you mind?

RICHARD Not in the least.

SARAH I didn't seem to have time to cook anything today.

She moves towards the kitchen.

RICHARD Oh, by the way . . . I rather wanted to ask you something.

SARAH What?

RICHARD Does it ever occur to you that while you're spending the afternoon being unfaithful to me I'm sitting at a desk going through balance sheets and graphs?

SARAH What a funny question.

RICHARD No, I'm curious.

SARAH You've never asked me that before.

RICHARD I've always wanted to know.

Slight pause.

SARAH Well, of course it occurs to me.

RICHARD Oh, it does?

SARAH Mmnn.

Slight pause.

RICHARD What's your attitude to that, then?

SARAH It makes it all the more piquant.

RICHARD Does it really?

SARAH Of course.

RICHARD You mean while you're with him . . . you actually have a picture of me, sitting at my desk going through balance sheets?

SARAH Only at. . . certain times.

RICHARD Of course.

SARAH Not all the time.

RICHARD Well, naturally.

SARAH At particular moments.

RICHARD Mmnn. But, in fact, I'm not completely forgotten?

SARAH Not by any means.

RICHARD That's rather touching, I must admit.

Pause.

SARAH How could I forget you?

RICHARD Quite easily, I should think.

SARAH But I'm in your house.

RICHARD With another.

SARAH But it's you I love.

RICHARD I beg your pardon?

SARAH But it's you I love.

Pause. He looks at her, proffers his glass.

RICHARD Let's have another drink.

She moves forward. He withdraws his glass, looks at her shoes.

What shoes are they?

SARAH Mmnn?

RICHARD Those shoes. They're unfamiliar. Very high-heeled, aren't they?

SARAH (*muttering*) Mistake. Sorry.

RICHARD (*not hearing*) Sorry? I beg your pardon?

SARAH I'll . . . take them off.

RICHARD Not quite the most comfortable shoes for an evening at home, I would have thought.

She goes into hall, opens cupboard, puts high-heeled shoes into cupboard, puts on low-heeled shoes. He moves to drinks table, pours himself a drink. She moves to centre table, lights a cigarette.

So you had a picture of me this afternoon, did you, sitting in my office?

SARAH I did, yes. It wasn't a terribly convincing one, though.

RICHARD Oh, why not?

SARAH Because I knew you weren't there. I knew you were with your mistress.

Pause.

RICHARD Was I?

Short pause.

SARAH Aren't you hungry?

RICHARD I had a heavy lunch.

SARAH How heavy?

He stands at the window.

RICHARD What a beautiful sunset.

SARAH Weren't you?

He turns and laughs.

RICHARD What mistress?

SARAH Oh, Richard . . .

RICHARD No, no, it's simply the word that's so odd.

SARAH Is it? Why?

Slight pause.

I'm honest with you, aren't I? Why can't you be honest with me?

RICHARD But I haven't got a mistress. I'm very well acquainted with a whore, but I haven't got a mistress. There's a world of difference.

SARAH A whore?

RICHARD (*taking an olive*) Yes. Just a common or garden slut. Not worth talking about. Handy between trains, nothing more.

SARAH You don't travel by train. You travel by car.

RICHARD Quite. A quick cup of while cocoa they're checking the oil and water.

Pause.

SARAH Sounds utterly sterile

RICHARD No.

Pause.

SARAH I must say I never expected you to admit it so readily.

RICHARD Oh, why not? You've never put it to me so bluntly before, have you? Frankness at all costs. Essential to a healthy marriage. Don't you agree?

SARAH Of course.

RICHARD You agree.

SARAH Entirely.

RICHARD I mean, you're utterly frank with me, aren't you?

SARAH Utterly.

RICHARD About your lover. I must follow your example.

SARAH Thank you.

Pause.

Yes, I have suspected it for some time.

RICHARD Have you really?

SARAH Mmnn.

RICHARD Perceptive.

SARAH But, quite honesdy, I can't really believe she's just. . . what you say.

399

RICHARD Why not?

SARAH It's just not possible. You have such taste. You care so much for grace and elegance in women.

RICHARD And wit.

SARAH And wit, yes.

RICHARD Wit, yes. Terribly important, wit, for a man.

SARAH Is she witty?

RICHARD (*laughing*) These terms just don't apply. You can't sensibly inquire whether a whore is witty. It's of no significance whether she is or she isn't. She's simply a whore, a functionary who either pleases or displeases.

SARAH And she pleases you?

RICHARD Today she is pleasing. Tomorrow . . .? One can't say.

He moves towards the bedroom door taking off his jacket.

SARAH I must say I find your attitude to women rather alarming.

RICHARD Why? I wasn't looking for your double, was I? I wasn't looking for a woman I could respect, as you, whom I could admire and love, as I do you. Was I? All I wanted was . . . how shall I put it . . . someone who could express and engender lust with all lust's cunning. Nothing more.

He goes into the bedroom, hangs his jacket up in the wardrobe, and changes into his slippers.

In the living room SARAH *puts her drink down, hesitates and then follows into the bedroom.*

SARAH I'm sorry your affair possesses so little dignity.

RICHARD The dignity is in my marriage.

SARAH Or sensibility.

RICHARD The sensibility likewise. I wasn't looking for such attributes. I find them in you.

SARAH Why did you look at all?

Slight pause.

RICHARD What did you say?

SARAH Why look . . . elsewhere . . . at all?

RICHARD But my dear, you looked. Why shouldn't I look?

Pause.

SARAH Who looked first?

RICHARD You.

SARAH I don't think that's true.

RICHARD Who, then?

She looks at him with a slight smile.

Fade up. Night. Moonlight on balcony. The lights fade. RICHARD *comes in bedroom door in his pyjamas. He picks up a book and looks at it.*

SARAH *comes from bathroom in her nightdress. There is a double bed.* SARAH *sits at the dressing table. Combs her hair.*

SARAH Richard?

RICHARD Mnn?

SARAH Do you ever think about me at all . . . when you're with her?

RICHARD Oh, a little. Not much.

Pause.

We talk about you.

SARAH You talk about me with her?

RICHARD Occasionally. It amuses her.

SARAH Amuses her?

RICHARD

RICHARD (*choosing a book*) Mmnn.

SARAH How . . . do you talk about me?

RICHARD Delicately. We discuss you as we would play an antique music box. We play it for our titillation, whenever desired.

Pause.

SARAH I can't pretend the picture gives me great pleasure.

RICHARD It wasn't intended to. The pleasure is mine.

SARAH Yes, I see that, of course.

RICHARD (*sitting on the bed*) Surely your own afternoon pleasures are sufficient for you, aren't they? You don't expect extra pleasure from my pastimes, do you?

SARAH No, not at all.

RICHARD Then why all the questions?

SARAH Well, it was you who started it. Asking me so many questions about . . . my side of it. You don't normally do that.

RICHARD Objective curiosity, that's all.

He touches her shoulders.

You're not suggesting I'm jealous, surely?

She smiles, stroking his hand.

SARAH Darling. I know you'd never stoop to that.

RICHARD Good God, no.

He squeezes her shoulder.

What about you? You're not jealous, are you?

SARAH No. From what you tell me about your lady I seem to have a far richer time than you do.

RICHARD Possibly.

He opens the windows fully and stands by them, looking out.

What peace. Come and look.

She joins him at the window. They stand silently.

403

What would happen if I came home early one day, I wonder?

Pause.

SARAH   What would happen if I followed you one day, I wonder?

Pause.

RICHARD   Perhaps we could all meet for tea in the village.

SARAH   Why the village? Why not here?

RICHARD   Here? What an extraordinary remark.

Pause.

Your poor lover has never seen the night from this window, has he?

SARAH   No. He's obliged to leave before sunset, unfortunately.

RICHARD   Doesn't he get a bit bored with these damn afternoons? This eternal teatime? I would. To have as the constant image of your lust a milk jug and teapot. Must be terribly dampening.

SARAH   He's very adaptable. And, of course, when one puts the blinds down it does become a kind of evening.

RICHARD   Yes, I suppose it would.

Pause.

What does he think of your husband?

Slight pause.

SARAH He respects you.

Pause.

RICHARD I'm rather moved by that remark, in a strange kind of way. I think I can understand why you like him so much.

SARAH He's terribly sweet.

RICHARD Mmn-hmmnn.

SARAH Has his moods, of course.

RICHARD Who doesn't?

SARAH But I must say he's very loving. His whole body emanates love.

RICHARD How nauseating.

SARAH No.

RICHARD Manly with it, I hope?

SARAH Entirely.

RICHARD Sounds tedious.

SARAH Not at all.

Pause.

He has a wonderful sense of humour.

RICHARD Oh, jolly good. Makes you laugh, does he? Well, mind the neighbours don't hear you. The last thing we want is gossip.

Pause.

SARAH It's wonderful to live out here, so far away from the main road, so secluded.

RICHARD Yes, I do agree.

They go back into the room. They get into the bed. He picks up his book and looks at it. He closes it and puts it down.

This isn't much good.

He switches off his bedside lamp. She does the same. Moonlight.

He's married, isn't he?

SARAH Mmmmn.

RICHARD Happily?

SARAH Mmmmn.

Pause.

And you're happy, aren't you? You're not in any way jealous?

RICHARD No.

SARAH Good. Because I think things are beautifully balanced, Richard.

Fade.

Fade up. Morning. SARAH *putting on her negligee in the bedroom. She begins to make the bed.*

SARAH Darling.

Pause.

Will the shears be ready this morning?

RICHARD *(in bathroom, off)* The what?

SARAH The shears.

RICHARD No, not this morning.

He enters, fully dressed in his suit. Kisses her on the cheek.

Not till Friday. Bye-bye.

He leaves the bedroom, collects hat and briefcase from hall.

SARAH Richard.

He turns.

You won't be home too early today, will you?

RICHARD Do you mean he's coming again today? Good gracious. He was here yesterday. Coming again today?

SARAH Yes.

RICHARD Oh. No, well, I won't be home early. I'll go to the National Gallery.

SARAH Right.

RICHARD Bye-bye.

SARAH Bye.

The lights fade.

Fade up. Afternoon. SARAH *comes downstairs into living room. She wears a very tight, low-cut black dress. She hastily looks at herself in the mirror. Suddenly notices she is wearing low-heeled shoes. She goes quickly to cupboard changes them for her high-heeled shoes. Looks again in mirror, smoothes her hips. Goes to window, pulls Venetian blinds down, opens them, and closes them until there is a slight slit of light. There are three chimes of a clock. She looks at her watch, goes towards the flowers on the table. Door bell. She goes to door. It is the milkman, John.*

JOHN Cream?

SARAH You're very late.

JOHN Cream?

SARAH No, thank you.

JOHN Why not?

SARAH I have some. Do I owe you anything?

JOHN Mrs Owen just had three jars. Clotted.

SARAH What do I owe you?

JOHN It's not Saturday yet.

SARAH *(taking the milk)* Thank you.

JOHN Don't you fancy any cream? Mrs Owen had three jars.

SARAH Thank you.

She closes the door. Goes into the kitchen with

*milk. Comes back with a tea-tray, holding teapot
and cups, sets it on small table above chaise longue.
She briefly attends to the flowers, sits on the chaise
longue, crosses her legs, uncrosses them, puts her
legs up on chaise longue, smoothes her stockings
under her skirt. The doorbell rings. Pulling her
dress down she moves to the door, opens it.*

Hallo, Max.

RICHARD *comes in. He is wearing a suede jacket,
and no tie.*

He walks into the room and stands.

*She closes the door behind him. Walks slowly down
past him, and sits on the chaise longue, crossing her
legs.*

Pause.

*He moves slowly to chaise longue and stands very
close to her at her back. She arches her back,
uncrosses her legs, moves away to low chair down
left.*

Pause.

*He looks at her, then moves towards the hall
cupboard, brings out a bongo drum. He places the
drum on the chaise longue, stands.*

Pause.

*She rises, moves past him towards the hall, turns,
looks at him.*

*He moves below chaise. They sit at either end. He
begins to tap the drum. Her forefinger moves along*

drum towards his hand. She scratches the back of his hand sharply. Her hand retreats. Her fingers tap one after the other towards him, and rest. Her forefinger scratches between his fingers. Her other fingers do the same. His legs tauten. His hand clasps hers. Her hand tries to escape. Wild beats of their fingers tangling.

Stillness.

She gets up, goes to drinks table, lights a cigarette, moves to window. He puts drum down on chair down right, picks up cigarette, moves to her.

MAX Excuse me.

She glances at him and away.

Excuse me, have you got a light?

She does not respond.

Do you happen to have a light?

SARAH Do you mind leaving me alone?

MAX Why?

Pause.

I'm merely asking if you can give me a light.

She moves from him and looks up and down the room. He follows to her shoulder. She turns back.

SARAH Excuse me.

She moves past him. Close, his body follows. She stops.

I don't like being followed.

MAX Just give me a light and I won't bother you. That's all I want.

SARAH (*through her teeth*) Please go away. I'm waiting for someone.

MAX Who?

SARAH My husband.

MAX Why are you so shy? Eh? Where's your lighter?

He touches her body. An indrawn breath from her.

Here?

Pause.

Where is it?

He touches her body. A gasp from her.

Here?

She wrenches herself away. He traps her in the corner.

SARAH (*hissing*) What do you think you're doing?

MAX I'm dying for a puff.

SARAH I'm waiting for my husband!

MAX Let me get a light from yours.

They struggle silently.

She breaks away to wall.

Silence.

He approaches.

Are you all right, miss? I've just got rid of that . . .
gentleman. Did he hurt you in any way?

SARAH Oh, how wonderful of you. No, no, I'm all
right. Thank you.

MAX Very lucky I happened to be passing. You
wouldn't believe that could happen in such a beautiful
park.

SARAH No, you wouldn't.

MAX Still, you've come to no harm.

SARAH I can never thank you enough. I'm terribly
grateful, I really am.

MAX Why don't you sit down a second and calm
yourself.

SARAH Oh, I'm quite calm – but . . . yes, thank you.
You're so kind. Where shall we sit.

MAX Well, we can't sit out. It's raining. What about
that park-keeper's hut?

SARAH Do you think we should? I mean, what about
the park-keeper?

MAX I am the park-keeper.

They sit on the chaise tongue.

SARAH I never imagined I could meet anyone so kind.

MAX To treat a lovely young woman like you like
that, it's unpardonable.

SARAH (*gazing at him*) You seem so mature, so . . . appreciative.

MAX Of course.

SARAH So gentle. So. . . Perhaps it was all for the best.

MAX What do you mean?

SARAH So that we could meet. So that we could meet. You and I.

Her fingers trace his thigh. He stares at them, lifts them off.

MAX I don't quite follow you.

SARAH Don't you?

Her fingers trace his thigh. He stares at them, lifts them off.

MAX Now look, I'm sorry. I'm married.

She takes his hand and puts it on her knee.

SARAH You're so sweet, you mustn't worry.

MAX (*snatching his hand away*) No, I really am. My wife's waiting for me.

SARAH Can't you speak to strange girls?

MAX No.

SARAH Oh, how sickening you are. How tepid.

MAX I'm sorry.

SARAH You men are all alike. Give me a cigarette.

MAX I bloody well won't.

SARAH I beg your pardon?

MAX Come here, Dolores.

SARAH Oh no, not me. Once bitten twice shy, thanks. (*She stands.*) Bye-bye.

MAX You can't get out, darling. The hut's locked. We're alone. You're trapped.

SARAH Trapped! I'm a married woman. You can't treat me like this

MAX (*moving to her*) It's teatime, Mary.

She moves swiftly behind the table and stands there with her back to the wall. He moves to the opposite end of the table, hitches his trousers, bends and begins to crawl under the table towards her.

He disappears under the velvet cloth. Silence. She stares down at the table. Her legs are hidden from view. His hand is on her leg. She looks about, grimaces, grits her teeth, gasps, gradually sinks under the table, and disappears. Long silence.

HER VOICE

Max!

Lights fade.

Fade up.

MAX *sitting on chair down left.*

SARAH *pouring tea.*

SARAH Max.

MAX What?

SARAH (*fondly*) Darling.

Slight pause.

What is it? You're very thoughtful.

MAX No.

SARAH You are. I know it.

Pause.

MAX Where's your husband?

Pause.

SARAH My husband? You know where he is.

MAX Where?

SARAH He's at work.

MAX Poor fellow. Working away, all day.

Pause.

I wonder what he's like.

SARAH (*chuckling*) Oh, Max.

MAX I wonder if we'd get on. I wonder if we'd . . .
you know . . . hit it off.

SARAH I shouldn't think so.

MAX Why not?

SARAH You've got very little in common.

MAX Have we? He's certainly very accommodating. I mean, he knows perfectly well about these afternoons of ours, doesn't he?

SARAH Of course.

MAX He's known for years.

Slight pause.

Why does he put up with it?

SARAH Why are you suddenly talking about him? I mean what's the point of it? It isn't a subject you normally elaborate on.

MAX Why does he put up with it?

SARAH Oh, shut up.

MAX I asked you a question.

Pause.

SARAH He doesn't mind.

MAX Doesn't he?

Slight pause.

Well, I'm beginning to mind.

Pause.

SARAH What did you say.

MAX I'm beginning to mind.

Slight pause.

It's got to stop. It can't go on.

SARAH Are you serious?

416

Silence.

MAX It can't go on.

SARAH You're joking.

MAX No, I'm not.

SARAH Why? Because of my husband? Not because of my husband, I hope. That's going a little far, I think.

MAX No, nothing to do with your husband. It's because of my wife.

Pause.

SARAH Your wife?

MAX I can't deceive her any longer.

SARAH Max . . .

MAX I've been deceiving her for years. I can't go on with it. It's killing me.

SARAH But darling, look –

MAX Don't touch me.

Pause.

SARAH What did you say?

MAX You heard.

Pause.

SARAH But your wife . . . knows. Doesn't she? You've told her . . . all about us. She's known all the time.

417

MAX No, she doesn't know. She thinks I know a whore, that's all. Some spare-time whore, that's all. That's what she thinks.

SARAH Yes, but be sensible . . . my love . . . she doesn't mind, does she?

MAX She'd mind if she knew the truth, wouldn't she?

SARAH What truth? What are you talking about?

MAX She'd mind if she knew that, in fact . . . I've got a full-time mistress, two or three times a week, a woman of grace, elegance, wit, imagination –

SARAH Yes, yes, you have –

MAX In an affair that's been going on for years.

SARAH She doesn't mind, she wouldn't mind – she's happy, she's happy.

Pause.

I wish you'd stop this rubbish, anyway.

She picks up the tea-tray and moves towards the kitchen.

You're doing your best to ruin the whole afternoon.

She takes the tray out. She then returns, looks at MAX *and goes to him.*

Darling. You don't really think you could have what we have with your wife, do you? I mean, my husband, for instance, completely appreciates that I –

MAX How does he bear it, your husband? How does he bear it? Doesn't he smell me when he comes back

in the evenings? What does he say? He must be mad.
Now – what's the time – half-past four – now when
he's sitting in his office, knowing what's going on
here, what does he feel, how does he bear it?

SARAH Max –

MAX How?

SARAH He's happy for me. He appreciates the way I
am. He understands.

MAX Perhaps I should meet him and have a word
with him.

SARAH Are you drunk?

MAX Perhaps I should do that. After all, he's a man,
like me. We're both men. You're just a bloody
woman.

She slams the table.

SARAH Stop it! What's the matter with you? What's
happened to you? (*Quietly.*) Please, please, stop it.
What are you doing, playing a game?

MAX A game? I don't play games.

SARAH Don't you? You do. Oh, you do. You do.
Usually I like them.

MAX I've played my last game.

SARAH Why?

Slight pause.

MAX The children.

Pause.

SARAH What?

MAX The children. I've got to think of the children.

SARAH What children?

MAX My children. My wife's children. Any minute now they'll be out of boarding school. I've got to think of them.

She sits close to him.

SARAH I want to whisper something to you. Listen. Let me whisper to you. Mmmm? Can I? Please? It's whispering time. Earlier it was teatime, wasn't it? Wasn't it? Now it's whispering time.

Pause.

You like me to whisper to you. You like me to love you, whispering. Listen. You mustn't worry about . . . wives, husbands, things like that. It's silly. It's really silly. It's you, you now, here, here with me, here together, that's what it is, isn't it? You whisper to me, you take tea with me, you do that, don't you, that's what we are, that's us, love me.

He stands up.

MAX You're too bony.

He walks away.

That's what it is, you see. I could put up with everything if it wasn't for that. You're too bony.

SARAH Me? Bony? Don't be ridiculous.

MAX I'm not.

SARAH How can you say I'm bony?

MAX Every move I make, your bones stick into me. I'm sick and tired of your bones.

SARAH What are you talking about?

MAX I'm telling you you're too bony.

SARAH But I'm fat! Look at me. I'm plump anyway. You always told me I was plump.

MAX You were plump once. You're not plump any more.

SARAH Look at me.

  He looks.

MAX You're not plump enough. You're nowhere near plump enough. You know what I like. I like enormous women. Like bullocks with udders. Vast great uddered bullocks.

SARAH You mean cows.

MAX I don't mean cows. I mean voluminous great uddered feminine bullocks. Once, years ago, you vaguely resembled one.

SARAH Oh, thanks.

MAX But now, quite honestly, compared to my ideal . . .

  He stares at her.

 . . . you're skin and bone.

They stare at each other. He puts on his jacket.

SARAH You're having a lovely joke.

MAX It's no joke.

He goes out. She looks after him. She turns, goes slowly towards the bongo drum, picks it up, puts it in the cupboard. She turns, looks at chaise a moment, walks slowly into the bedroom, sits on the end of the bed. The lights fade.

Fade up. Early evening. Six chimes of the clock, RICHARD *comes in the front door. He is wearing his sober suit. He puts his briefcase in cupboard, hat on hook, looks about the room, pours a drink,* SARAH *comes into the bedroom from bathroom, wearing a sober dress. They both stand quite still in the two rooms for a few moments,* SARAH *moves to the balcony, looks out,* RICHARD *comes into the bedroom.*

RICHARD Hello.

Pause.

SARAH Hello.

RICHARD Watching the sunset?

He picks up a bottle.

Drink?

SARAH Not at the moment, thank you.

RICHARD Oh, what a dreary conference. Went on all day. Terribly fatiguing. Still, good work done, I think.

Something achieved. Sorry I'm rather late. Had to have a drink with one or two of the overseas people. Good chaps.

He sits.

How are you?

SARAH Fine.

RICHARD Good.

Silence.

You seem a little depressed. Anything the matter?

SARAH No.

RICHARD What sort of day have you had?

SARAH Not bad.

RICHARD Not good?

Pause.

SARAH Fair.

RICHARD Oh, I'm sorry.

Pause.

Good to be home, I must say. You can't imagine what a comfort it is.

Pause.

Lover come?

She does not reply.

Sarah?

SARAH What? Sorry. I was thinking of something.

RICHARD Did your lover come?

SARAH Oh yes. He came.

RICHARD In good shape?

SARAH I have a headache actually.

RICHARD Wasn't he in good shape?

Pause.

SARAH We all have our off days.

RICHARD He, too? I thought the whole point of being a lover is that one didn't. I mean if I, for instance, were called upon to fulfil the function of a lover and felt disposed, shall we say, to accept the job, well, I'd as soon give it up as be found incapable of executing its proper and consistent obligation.

SARAH You do use long words.

RICHARD Would you prefer me to use short ones?

SARAH No, thank you.

Pause.

RICHARD But I am sorry you had a bad day.

SARAH It's quite all right.

RICHARD Perhaps things will improve.

SARAH Perhaps.

Pause.

I hope so.

She leaves the bedroom, goes into the living room, lights a cigarette and sits. He follows.

RICHARD Nevertheless, I find you very beautiful.

SARAH Thank you.

RICHARD Yes, I find you very beautiful. I have great pride in being seen with you. When we're out to dinner, or at the theatre.

SARAH I'm so glad.

RICHARD Or at the Hunt Ball.

SARAH Yes, the Hunt Ball.

RICHARD Great pride, to walk with you as my wife on my arm. To see you smile, laugh, walk, talk, bend, be still. To hear your command of contemporary phraseology, your delicate use of the very latest idiomatic expression, so subtly employed. Yes. To feel the envy of others, their attempts to gain favour with you, by fair means or foul, your austere grace confounding them. And to know you are my wife. It's a source of a profound satisfaction to me.

Pause.

What's for dinner.

SARAH I haven't thought.

RICHARD Oh, why not?

SARAH I find the thought of dinner fatiguing. I prefer not to think about it.

RICHARD That's rather unfortunate. I'm hungry.

Slight pause.

You hardly expect me to embark on dinner after a day spent sifting matters of high finance in the City.

She laughs.

One could even suggest you were falling down on your wifely duties.

SARAH Oh dear.

RICHARD I must say I rather suspected this would happen, sooner or later.

Pause.

SARAH How's your whore?

RICHARD Splendid.

SARAH Fatter or thinner?

RICHARD I beg your pardon?

SARAH Is she fatter or thinner?

RICHARD She gets thinner every day.

SARAH That must displease you.

RICHARD Not at all. I'm fond of thin ladies.

SARAH I thought the contrary.

RICHARD Really? Why would you have thought that?

Pause.

THE LOVER

Of course, your failure to have dinner on the table is quite consistent with the life you've been leading for some time, isn't it?

SARAH Is it?

RICHARD Entirely.

Slight pause.

Perhaps I'm being unkind. Am I being unkind?

SARAH (*looks at him*) I don't know.

RICHARD Yes, I am. In the traffic jam on the bridge just now, you see, I came to a decision.

Pause.

SARAH Oh? What?

RICHARD That it has to stop.

SARAH What?

RICHARD Your debauchery.

Pause.

Your life of depravity. Your path of illegitimate lust.

SARAH Really?

RICHARD Yes, I've come to an irrevocable decision on that point.

She stands.

SARAH Would you like some cold ham?

RICHARD Do you understand me?

SARAH Not at all. I have something cold in the fridge.

RICHARD Too cold, I'm sure. The fact is this is my house. From today, I forbid you to entertain your lover on these premises. This applies to any time of the day. Is that understood.

SARAH I've made a salad for you.

RICHARD Are you drinking?

SARAH Yes, I'll have one.

RICHARD What are you drinking?

SARAH You know what I drink. We've been married ten years.

RICHARD So we have.

He pours.

It's strange, of course, that it's taken me so long to appreciate the humiliating ignominy of my position.

SARAH I didn't take my lover ten years ago. Not quite. Not on the honeymoon.

RICHARD That's irrelevant. The fact is I am a husband who has extended to his wife's lover open house on any afternoon of her desire. I've been too kind. Haven't I been too kind?

SARAH But of course. You're terribly kind.

RICHARD Perhaps you would give him my compliments, by letter if you like, and ask him to cease his visits from – *(He consults calendar.)* the twelfth inst.

Long silence.

SARAH How can you talk like this?

Pause.

Why today . . . so suddenly?

Pause.

Mmmm?

She is close to him.

You've had a hard day . . . at the office. All those overseas people. It's so tiring. But it's silly, it's so silly, to talk like this. I'm here. For you. And you've always appreciated . . . how much these afternoons . . . mean. You've always understood.

She presses her cheek to his.

Understanding is so rare, so dear.

RICHARD Do you think it's pleasant to know that your wife is unfaithful to you two or three times a week, with great regularity?

SARAH Richard –

RICHARD It's insupportable. It has become insupportable. I'm no longer disposed to put up with it.

SARAH (*to him*) Sweet. . . Richard . . . please.

RICHARD Please what?

She stops.

Can I tell you what I suggest you do?

SARAH What?

RICHARD Take him out into the fields. Find a ditch. Or a slag heap. Find a rubbish dump. Mmmm? What about that?

She stands still.

Buy a canoe and find a stagnant pond. Anything. Anywhere. But not my living-room.

SARAH I'm afraid that's not possible.

RICHARD Why not?

SARAH I said it's not possible.

RICHARD But if you want your lover so much, surely that's the obvious thing to do, since his entry to this house is now barred. I'm trying to be helpful, darling, because of my love for you. You can see that. If I find him on these premises I'll kick his teeth out.

SARAH You're mad.

He stares at her.

RICHARD I'll kick his head in.

Pause.

SARAH What about your own bloody whore?

RICHARD I've paid her off.

SARAH Have you? Why?

RICHARD She was too bony.

Slight pause.

SARAH But you liked . . . you said you liked . . .
Richard . . . but you love me . . .

RICHARD Of course.

SARAH Yes . . . you love me . . . you don't mind him .
. . you understand him. . . don't you? . . . I mean, you
know better than I do . . . darling . . . all's well . . .
all's well . . . the evenings . . . and the afternoons . . .
do you see? Listen, I do have dinner for you. It's
ready. I wasn't serious. It's Boeuf Bourgignon. And
tomorrow I'll have Chicken Chasseur. Would you like
it? They look at each other.

RICHARD (*softly*) Adulteress.

SARAH You can't talk like this, it's impossible, you
know you can't. What do you think you're doing?

*He remains looking at her for a second, then moves
into the hall.*

*He opens the hall cupboard and takes out the
bongo drum.*

She watches him.

He returns.

RICHARD What's this? I found it some time ago.
What is it?

Pause.

What is it?

SARAH You shouldn't touch that.

RICHARD But it's in my house. It belongs either to me, or to you, or to another.

SARAH It's nothing. I bought it in a jumble sale. It's nothing. What do you think it is? Put it back.

RICHARD Nothing? This? A drum in my cupboard?

SARAH Put it back!

RICHARD It isn't by any chance anything to do with your illicit afternoons?

SARAH Not at all. Why should it?

RICHARD It is used. This is used, isn't it? I can guess.

SARAH You guess nothing. Give it to me.

RICHARD How does he use it? How do you use it? Do you play it while I'm at the office?

She tries to take the drum. He holds on to it. They are still, hands on the drum.

What function does this fulfil? It's not just an ornament, I take it? What do you do with it?

SARAH (*with quiet anguish*) You've no right to question me. No right at all. It was our arrangement. No questions of this kind. Please. Don't, don't. It was our arrangement.

RICHARD I want to know.

She closes her eyes.

SARAH Don't . . .

RICHARD Do you both play it? Mmmmnn? Do you both play it? Together?

She moves away swiftly, then turns, hissing.

SARAH You stupid . . .! (*She looks at him coolly.*) Do you think he's the only one who comes! Do you? Do you think he's the only one I entertain? Mmmnn? Don't be silly. I have other visitors, other visitors, all the time, I receive all the time. Other afternoons, all the time. When neither of you know, neither of you. I give them strawberries in season. With cream. Strangers, total strangers. But not to me, not while they're here. They come to see the hollyhocks. And then they stay for tea. Always. Always.

RICHARD Is that so?

He moves towards her, tapping the drum gently.

He faces her, tapping, then grasps her hand and scratches it across the drum.

SARAH What are you doing?

RICHARD Is that what you do?

She jerks away, to behind the table. He moves towards her, tapping.

Like that?

Pause.

What fun.

He scratches the drum sharply and then places it on the chair.

433

Got a light?

Pause.

Got a light?

She retreats towards the table, eventually ending behind it.

Come on, don't be a spoilsport. Your husband won't mind, if you give me a light. You look a little pale. Why are you so pale? A lovely girl like you.

SARAH Don't, don't say that!

RICHARD You're trapped. We're alone. I've locked up.

SARAH You mustn't do this, you mustn't do it, you mustn't!

RICHARD He won't mind.

He begins to move slowly closer to the table.

No one else knows.

Pause.

No one else can hear us. No one knows we're here.

Pause.

Come on. Give us a light.

Pause.

You can't get out, darling. You're trapped.

They face each other from opposite ends of the table.

434

She suddenly giggles.

Silence.

SARAH I'm trapped.

Pause.

What will my husband say?

Pause.

He expects me. He's waiting. I can't get out. I'm trapped. You've no right to treat a married woman like this. Have you? Think, think, think of what you're doing.

She looks at him, bends and begins to crawl under the table towards him. She emerges from under the table and kneels at his feet, looking up. Her hand goes up his leg. He is looking down at her.

You're very forward. You really are. Oh, you really are. But my husband will understand. My husband does understand. Come here. Come down here. I'll explain. After all, think of my marriage. He adores me. Come here and I'll whisper to you. I'll whisper it. It's whispering time. Isn't it?

She takes his hands. He sinks to his knees, with her. They are kneeling together, close. She strokes his face.

It's a very late tea. Isn't it? But I think I like it. Aren't you sweet? I've never seen you before after sunset. My husband's at a late-night conference. Yes, you look different. Why are you wearing this strange suit, and

this tie? You usually wear something else, don't you?
Take off your jacket. Mmmnn? Would you like me to
change? Would you like me to change my clothes? I'll
change for you, darling. Shall I? Would you like that?

Silence. She is very close to him.

RICHARD Yes.

Pause.

Change.

Pause.

Change.

Pause.

Change your clothes.

Pause.

You lovely whore.

They are still, kneeling, she leaning over him.

The End.

TEA PARTY

Tea Party first published by
Methuen & Co. 1967
© H. Pinter Ltd, 1967

'Tea Party' (short story)
© FPinter Limited, 1965

Tea Party was commissioned by sixteen member countries of the European Broadcasting Union, to be transmitted by all of them under the title *The Largest Theatre in the World.* It was first presented by BBC Television on 25 March 1965 with the following cast:

DISSON	Leo McKern
WENDY	Vivien Merchant
DIANA	Jennifer Wright
WILLY	Charles Gray
DISLEY	John Le Mesurier
LOIS	Margaret Denyer
FATHER	Frederick Piper
MOTHER	Hilda Barry
TOM	Peter Bartlett
JOHN	Robert Bartlett

Directed by Charles Jarrott

Tea Party, in a double bill with *The Basement*, opened at the Duchess Theatre, London, on 17 September 1970, and produced by Eddie Kulukundis for Knightsbridge Theatrical Productions Ltd, with the following cast:

DISSON	Donald Pleasence
WENDY	Vivien Merchant
DIANA	Gabrielle Drake
WILLY	Barry Foster
TOM	Robin Angell
JOHN	Kevin Chippendale
DISLEY	Derek Aylward
LOIS	Jill Johnson
FATHER	Arthur Hewlett
MOTHER	Hilda Barry

Directed by James Hammerstein

Characters

DISSON

WENDY

DIANA

WILLY

TOM

JOHN

DISLEY

LOIS

FATHER

MOTHER

An electric lift rising to the top floor of an office block,
WENDY *stands in it.*

Corridor.

*The lift comes to rest in a broad carpeted corridor, the
interior of an office suite. It is well appointed, silent.
The walls are papered with Japanese silk. Along the
walk in alcoves are set, at various intervals, a selection
of individually designed wash basins, water closets and
bidets, all lit by hooded spotlights.*

WENDY *steps out of the lift and walks down the
corridor towards a door. She knocks. It opens.*

DISSON's *office. Morning.*

 DISSON *rising from a large desk. He goes round the
 desk to meet* WENDY *and shakes her hand.*

DISSON How do you do, Miss Dodd? Nice of you to
come. Please sit down.

 DISSON *goes back to his seat behind the desk,*
 WENDY *sits in a chair at the corner of the desk.*

That's right.

 He refers to papers on the desk.

Well now, I've had a look at your references. They seem to be excellent. You've had quite a bit of experience.

WENDY Yes, sir.

DISSON Not in my line, of course. We manufacture sanitary ware . . . but I suppose you know that?

WENDY Yes, of course I do, Mr Disson

DISSON You've heard of us, have you?

WENDY Oh yes.

WENDY *crosses her left leg over her right.*

DISSON Well, do you think you'd be interested in . . . in this area of work?

WENDY Oh, certainly, sir, yes, I think I would.

DISSON We're the most advanced sanitary engineers in the country. I think I can say that quite confidently.

WENDY Yes, I believe so.

DISSON Oh yes. We manufacture more bidets than anyone else in England. (*He laughs.*) It's almost by way of being a mission. Cantilever units, hidden cisterns, footpedals, you know, things like that.

WENDY Footpedals?

DISSON Instead of a chain or plug. A footpedal.

WENDY Oh. How marvellous.

DISSON They're growing more popular every day and rightly so.

WENDY *crosses her right leg over her left.*

Well now, this . . . post is, in fact, that of my personal
assistant. Did you understand that? A very private
secretary, in fact. And a good deal of responsibility
would undoubtedly devolve upon you. Would you . . .
feel yourself capable of discharging it?

WENDY Once I'd correlated all the fundamental
features of the work, sir, I think so, yes.

DISSON All the fundamental features, yes. Good.

WENDY *crosses her left leg over her right.*

I see you left your last job quite suddenly.

Pause.

May I ask the reason?

WENDY Well, it's . . . a litde embarrassing, sir.

DISSON Really?

Pause.

Well, I think I should know, don't you? Come on, you
can tell me. What was it?

WENDY *straightens her skirt over her knees.*

WENDY Well, it is rather personal, Mr Disson.

DISSON Yes, but I think I should know, don't you?

Pause.

WENDY Well, it's simply that I couldn't persuade-my
chief . . . to call a halt to his attentions.

DISSON *What?* (*He consults the papers on the desk.*) A firm of this repute? It's unbelievable.

WENDY I'm afraid it's true, sir.

Pause.

DISSON What sort of attentions?

WENDY Oh, I don't . . .

DISSON What sort?

Pause.

WENDY He never stopped touching me, Mr Disson, that's all.

DISSON Touching you?

WENDY Yes.

DISSON Where? (*Quickly.*) That must have been very disturbing for you.

WENDY Well, quite frankly, it is disturbing, to be touched all the time.

DISSON Do you mean at every opportunity?

WENDY Yes, sir.

Slight pause.

DISSON Did you cry?

WENDY Cry?

DISSON Did he make you cry?

WENDY Oh just a little, occasionally, sir.

DISSON What a monster.

Slight pause.

Well, I do sympathise.

WENDY Thank you, sir.

DISSON One would have thought this . . . tampering, this . . . interfering . . . with secretaries was something of the past, a myth, in fact, something that only took place in paperback books. Tch. Tch.

WENDY *crosses her right leg over her left.*

Anyway, be that as it may, your credentials are excellent and I would say you possessed an active and inquiring intelligence and a pleasing demeanour, two attributes I consider necessary for this post. I'd like you to start immediately.

WENDY Oh, that's wonderful. Thank you so much, Mr Disson.

DISSON Not at all.

They stand. He walks across the room to another desk.

This'll be your desk.

WENDY Ah.

DISSON There are certain personal arrangements I'd like you to check after lunch. I'm . . . getting married tomorrow.

WENDY Oh, congratulations.

DISSON Thanks. Yes, this is quite a good week for me, what with one thing and another.

The telephone rings on his desk. He crosses and picks it up.

Hullo, Disley How are you? . . . What? Oh my goodness, don't say that.

DISSON's *house. Sitting room. Evening.*

DIANA This is my brother Willy,

DISSON I'm very glad to meet you.

WILLY And I you. Congratulations.

DISSON Thank you.

DIANA (*giving him a drink*) Here you are, Robert.

DISSON Thanks. Cheers.

DIANA Cheers.

WILLY To tomorrow.

DISSON Yes.

They drink.

I'm afraid we've run into a bit of trouble.

DIANA Why?

DISSON I've lost my best man.

DIANA Oh no.

DISSON (*to* WILLY) My oldest friend. Man called

Disley. Gastric flu. Can't make it tomorrow.

WILLY Oh dear.

DISSON He was going to make a speech at the reception – in my honour. A superb speech. I read it. Now he can't make it.

Pause.

WILLY Isn't there anyone else you know?

DISSON Yes, of course. But not like him . . . you see. I mean, he was the natural choice.

DIANA How infuriating.

Pause.

WILLY Well, look, I can be your best man, if you like.

DIANA How can you, Willy? You're giving me away.

WILLY Oh yes.

DISSON Oh, the best man's not important; you can always get a best man – all he's got to do is stand there; it's the speech that's important, the speech in honour of the groom. Who's going to make the speech?

Pause.

WILLY Well, I can make the speech, if you like.

DISSON But how can you make a speech in honour of the groom when you're making one in honour of the bride?

WILLY Does that matter?

DIANA No. Why does it?

DISSON Yes, but look . . . I mean, thanks very much
. . . but the fact is . . . that you don't know me, do
you? I mean we've only just met. Disley knows me
well, that's the thing, you see. His speech centred
around our long-standing friendship. I mean, what he
knew of my character . . .

WILLY Yes, of course, of course. No, look, all I'm
saving is that I'm willing to have a crack at it if there's
no other solution. Willing to come to the aid of the
party, as it were.

DIANA He is a wonderful speaker, Robert.

Wedding reception. Private room. Exclusive restaurant.

DISSON, DIANA, WILLY, DISSON'S PARENTS,
DISSON'S SONS. WILLY *is speaking.*

WILLY I remember the days my sister and I used to
swim together in the lake at Sunderley. The grace of
her crawl, even then, as a young girl. I can remember
those long summer evenings at Sunderley, my mother
and I crossing the lawn towards the terrace and
through the great windows hearing my sister play
Brahms. The delicacy of her touch. My mother and I
would, upon entering the music room, gaze in silence
at Diana's long fingers moving in exquisite motion on
the keys. As for our father, our father knew no
pleasure keener than watching his daughter at her

needlework. A man whose business was the State's, a man eternally active, his one great solace from the busy world would be to sit for hours on end at a time watching his beloved daughter ply her needle. Diana – my sister – was the dear grace of our household, the flower, the blossom, and the bloom. One can only say to the groom: Groom, your fortune is immeasurable.

Applause. DIANA *kisses him.* DISSON *shakes his hand warmly.*

TOASTMASTER My lords, reverend gentlemen, ladies and gentlemen, pray silence for Mr William Pierrepoint Torrance, who will propose the toast in honour of the groom.

WILLY *turns. Applause.*

WILLY I have not known Robert for a long time, in fact I have known him only for a very short time. But in that short time I have found him to be a man of integrity, honesty and humility. After a modest beginning, he has built his business up into one of the proudest and most vigorous in the land. And this – almost alone. Now he has married a girl who equals, if not surpasses, his own austere standards of integrity. He has married my sister, who possesses within her that rare and uncommon attribute known as inner beauty, not to mention the loveliness of her exterior. Par excellence as a woman with a needle, beyond excellence as a woman of taste, discernment, sensibility and imagination. An excellent swimmer who, in all probability, has the beating of her husband in the two

451

hundred metres breast stroke.

Laughter and applause. WILLY *waits for silence.*

It is to our parents that she owes her candour, her elegance of mind, her *sensibility*. Our parents, who, though gone, have not passed from us, but who are here now on this majestic day, and offer you their welcome, the bride their love, and the groom their congratulations.

Applause. DIANA *kisses him.* DISSON *shakes his hand warmly.*

DISSON Marvellous.

WILLY Diana, I want to tell you something.

DIANA What?

WILLY You have married a good man. He will make you happy.

DIANA I know.

DISSON Wonderful speeches. Wonderful. Listen. What are you doing these days?

WILLY Nothing much.

TOASTMASTER My lords . . .

DISSON (*whispering*) How would you like to come in with me for a bit? See how you like it, how you get on. Be my second in command. Office of your own. Plenty of room for initiative.

TOASTMASTER My lords, reverend gentlemen, ladies

and gentlemen –

WILLY Marvellous idea. I'll say yes at once.

DISSON Good.

DIANA *kisses* DISSON.

DIANA Darling.

TOASTMASTER Pray silence for the groom.

DISSON *moves forward.*

Applause. Silence.

DISSON This is the happiest day of my life.

Sumptuous hotel room. Italy.

The light is on. The camera rests at the foot of the bed. The characters are not seen. Their voices heard only.

DISSON Are you happy?

DIANA Yes.

DISSON Very happy?

DIANA Yes.

DISSON Have you ever been happier? With any other man?

DIANA Never.

Pause.

DISSON I make you happy, don't I? Happier than you've ever been . . . with any other man.

DIANA Yes. You do.

Pause.

Yes.

Silence.

DISSON's *house. Workroom.*

DISSON *at his workbench. With sandpaper and file he is putting the finishing touches to a home-made model yacht. He completes the job, dusts the yacht, sets it on a shelf and looks at it with satisfaction.*

DISSON's *house. Breakfast room. Morning.* DISSON *and* DIANA *at the table.*

DISSON Your eyes are shining.

Pause.

They're shining.

DIANA Mmmnnn.

DISSON They've been shining for months.

DIANA (*smiling*). My eyes? Have they?

DISSON Every morning.

Pause.

I'm glad you didn't marry that . . . Jerry . . . whatever-his-name-was . . .

DIANA Oh, him . . .

DISSON Why didn't you?

DIANA He was weak.

Pause.

DISSON I'm not weak.

DIANA No.

DISSON Am I?

He takes her hand.

DIANA You're strong.

THE TWINS *enter the room.*

THE TWINS *mutter, 'Morning'.*

DIANA *and* DISSON *say 'Good morning'.*

Silence. THE TWINS *sit.* DIANA *pours tea for them.
They butter toast, take marmalade, begin to eat.*

Silence.

Would you like eggs?

TOM No, thanks.

DIANA John?

Silence.

DISSON John!

JOHN What?

DISSON Don't say what!

JOHN What shall I say?

DIANA Would you like eggs?

Pause.

JOHN Oh.

Pause.

No, thanks.

The boys giggle and eat. Silence. JOHN *whispers to* TOM.

DISSON What are you saying? Speak up.

JOHN Nothing.

DISSON Do you think I'm deaf?

TOM I've never thought about it.

DISSON I wasn't talking to you. I was talking to John.

JOHN Me? Sorry, sir.

DISSON Now don't be silly. You've never called me sir before. That's rather a daft way to address your father.

JOHN Uncle Willy called his father sir. He told me.

DISSON Yes, but you don't call me sir! Do you understand?

WILLY'*s office. Morning.*

DISSON *leads* WILLY *in.*

DISSON Here you are, Willy This'll be your office. How'd you like it?

WILLY First rate.

DISSON These two offices are completely cut off from the rest of the staff. They're all on the lower floor. Our only contact is by intercom, unless I need to see someone personally, which is rare. Equally, I dislike fraternisation between the two offices. We shall meet only by strict arrangement, otherwise we'll never get any work done. That suit you?

WILLY Perfecdy.

DISSON There was a man in here, but I got rid of him.

DISSON *leads* WILLY *through a communicating door into his own office.*

DISSON's *office.*

On a side table coffee is set for two. DISSON *goes to the table and pours.*

DISSON I think I should explain to you the sort of man I am. I'm a thorough man. I like things to be done and done well. I don't like dithering. I don't like indulgence. I don't like self-doubt. I don't like fuzziness. I like clarity. Clear intention. Precise execution. Black or white?

WILLY White, please.

DISSON But I've no patience with conceit and self-regard. A man's job is to assess his powers coolly and correctly and equally the powers of others. Having done this, he can proceed to establish a balanced and reasonable relationship with his fellows. In my view, living is a matter of active and willing participation. So is work. Sugar?

WILLY Two, please.

DISSON Now, dependence isn't a word I would use lightly, but I will use it and I don't regard it as a weakness. To understand the meaning of the term dependence is to understand that one's powers are limited and that to live with others is not only sensible but the only way work can be done and dignity achieved. Nothing is more sterile or lamentable than the man content to live within himself. I've always made it my business to be on the most direct possible terms with the members of my staff and the body of my business associates. And by my example opinions are declared freely, without shame or deception. It seems to me essential that we cultivate the ability to operate lucidly upon our problems and therefore be in a position to solve them. That's why your sister loves me. I don't play about at the periphery of matters. I go right to the centre. I believe life can be conducted efficiently. I never waste my energies in any kind of timorous expectation. Neither do I ask to be loved. I expect to be given only what I've worked for. If you make a plum pudding, what do you do with it? You don't shove it up on a shelf. You stick a knife into it and eat it. Everything has a function. In other words, if we're to work together we must appreciate that interdependence is the key word, that it's your job to understand me and mine to understand you. Agreed?

WILLY Absolutely.

DISSON Now, the first thing you need is a secretary. We'll get on to it at once.

WILLY Can I suggest someone? I know she's very keen and, I'd say, very competent.

DISSON Who?

WILLY My sister.

Pause.

DISSON Your sister? You mean my wife?

WILLY She told me she'd love to do it.

DISSON She hasn't told me.

WILLY She's shy.

DISSON But she doesn't need to work. Why should she want to work?

WILLY To be closer to you.

WILLY's *office.*

WILLY *and* DIANA *at their desks, both examining folders intently. Silence.*

DISSON's *office.*

DISSON *and* WENDY *at their desks,* WENDY *typing on an electric typewriter,* DISSON *looking out of the window.* DISSON *turns from the window, glances at the door leading to* WILLY's *office. The intercom buzzes on* WENDY's *desk. She switches through.*

WENDY Mr Disson does not want to be disturbed until 3.30.

DISSON *glances again at* WILLY's *door.*

Silence.

DISSON's *house. Sitting room. Early evening.* DIANA *and* THE TWINS *are sitting about, reading.*

DIANA Do you miss your mother?

JOHN We didn't know her very well. We were very young when she died.

DIANA Your father has looked after you and brought you up very well.

JOHN Oh, thank you. He'll be pleased to hear that.

DIANA I've told him.

JOHN What did he say?

DIANA He was pleased I thought so. You mean a great deal to him.

JOHN Children seem to mean a great deal to their parents, I've noticed. Though I've often wondered what 'a great deal' means.

TOM I've often wondered what 'mean' means.

DIANA Aren't you proud of your father's achievements?

JOHN We are. I should say we are.

Pause.

DIANA And now that your father has married again
. . . has the change in your life affected you very much?

JOHN What change?

DIANA Living with me.

JOHN Ah. Well, I think there definitely is an
adjustment to be made. Wouldn't you say that, Tom?

DIANA Of course there is. But would you say it's an
easy adjustment to make, or difficult?

JOHN Well, it really all depends on how good you are
at making adjustments. We're very good at making
adjustments, aren't we, Tom?

The front door slams, DIANA *and* THE TWINS *look
down at their books,* DISSON *comes in. They all
look up, smile.*

DISSON Hullo.

They all smile genially at him.

DISSON *looks quickly from one to the other.*

DISSON'*s office. Morning.*

Sun shining in the window. DISSON *at his desk.*
WENDY *at the cabinet. He watches her. She turns.*

WENDY Isn't it a beautiful day, Mr Disson?

DISSON Close the curtains.

WENDY *closes the curtains.*

461

Got your pad?

WENDY Yes, sir.

DISSON Sit down.

WENDY *sits in a chair by the corner of his desk.*

Warwick and Sons. We duly acknowledge receipt of your letter of the twenty-first inst. There should be no difficulty in meeting your requirements. What's the matter?

WENDY Sir?

DISSON You're wriggling.

WENDY I'm sorry, sir.

DISSON Is it the chair?

WENDY Mmn . . . it might be.

DISSON Too hard, I expect. A little hard for you.

Pause.

Is that it?

WENDY A little.

DISSON Sit on the desk.

WENDY The desk?

DISSON Yes, on the leather.

Slight pause.

It'll be softer . . . for you.

WENDY Well, that'll be nice.

Pause, WENDY *eventually uncrosses her legs and stands. She looks at the desk.*

I think it's a little high . . . to get up on.

DISSON Of course it isn't.

WENDY (*looking at the desk*). Hmmmn-mmmn . . .

DISSON Go on, get up. You couldn't call that high.

WENDY *places her back to the desk and slowly attempts to raise herself up on to it. She stops.*

WENDY I think I'll have to put my feet on the chair, really, to hoist myself up.

DISSON You can hoist yourself up without using your feet.

WENDY (*dubiously*) Well . . .

DISSON Look, get up or stay down. Make up your mind. One thing or the other. I want to get on with my letter to Birmingham.

WENDY I was just wondering if you'd mind if I put my high-heeled shoes on your chair . . . to help me get up.

Pause.

DISSON I don't mind.

WENDY But I'm worried in case my heels might chip the wood. They're rather sharp, these heels.

DISSON Are they?

Pause.

463

Well, try it, anyway. You won't chip the wood.

> WENDY *puts her feet on the chair and hoists herself up on to the desk.*

> *He watches.*

> WENDY *settles herself on the desk and picks up her pen and pad. She reads from the pad.*

WENDY There should be no difficulty in meeting your requirements.

DISSON's *house. Games room. Day.*

DISSON *and* WILLY *are playing ping-pong,* THE TWINS *watch.*

A long rally. DISSON *backhand flips to win the point.*

JOHN Good shot, Dad.

TOM Thirteen-eighteen.

WILLY Your backhand's in form, Robert.

JOHN Attack his forehand.

> WILLY *serves. A rally.* WILLY *attacks* DISSON's *forehand.*

> DISSON *moves over to his right and then flips backhand to win the point, the twins applaud.*

TOM Thirteen-nineteen.

WILLY Backhand nip on the forehand, eh?

> WILLY *serves.*

From DISSON's *point of view, see two balls bounce
and leap past both ears.*

TWINS Shot!

TOM Fourteen-nineteen.

DISSON *puts down his bat and walks slowly to*
WILLY,

DISSON You served two balls, old chap.

WILLY Two balls?

DISSON You sent me two balls.

WILLY No, no. Only one.

DISSON Two.

Pause.

JOHN One, Dad.

DISSON What?

TOM One.

Pause.

WILLY *walks to* DISSON's *end, bends.*

WILLY Look.

WILLY *picks up one ball.*

One ball. Catch!

He throws the ball, DISSON *gropes, loses sight of
the ball. It bounces under the table. He crouches,
leans under the table for it. Gets it, withdraws,
looks up.* WILLY *and the twins look down at him.*

DISLEY's *surgery.*

Room darkened.

A torch shining in DISSON's *eyes. First the left eye, then the right eye. Torch out. Light on.*

DISLEY There's nothing wrong with your eyes, old boy.

DISSON Nothing?

DISLEY They're in first-rate condition. Truly.

DISSON That's funny.

DISLEY I'd go as far as to say your sight was perfect.

DISSON Huh.

DISLEY Check the bottom line.

> DISLEY *switches off the light, puts on the light on the letter board.*

What is it?

DISSON EXJLNVCGTY.

DISLEY Perfect.

> *Board light off. Room light on.*

DISSON Yes, I know. I know that . . .

DISLEY Well, what are you worried about?

DISSON It's not that . . .

DISLEY Colour? Do you confuse colours? Look at me. What colour am I?

DISSON Colourless.

DISLEY (*laughs, stops*). Very funny. What distinguishing marks can you see about me?

DISSON Two.

DISLEY What?

DISSON You have one grey strip in your hair, quite faint.

DISLEY Good. What's the other?

DISSON You have a brown stain on your left cheek.

DISLEY A brown stain? Can you see that? (*He looks in the mirror.*) I didn't know it was so evident.

DISSON Of course it's evident. It stains your face.

DISLEY Don't . . . go on about it, old boy. I didn't realise it was so evident. No one's ever noticed it before.

DISSON Not even your wife?

DISLEY Yes, she has. Anyway, I'd say your eyes are sharp enough. What colour are those lampshades?

DISSON They're dark blue drums. Each has a golden rim. The carpet is Indian.

DISLEY That's not a colour.

DISSON It's white. Over there, by that cabinet, I can see a deep black burn.

DISLEY A burn? Where? Do you mean that shadow?

467

DISSON That's not a shadow. It's a burn.

DISLEY (*looking*) So it is. How the hell did that happen?

DISSON Listen . . . I never said I couldn't see. You don't understand. Most of the time . . . my eyesight is excellent. It always has been. But . . . it's become unreliable. It's become . . . erratic. Sometimes, quite suddenly, very occasionally, something happens . . . something . . . goes wrong . . . with my eyes.

  Pause.

DISLEY I can find no evidence that your sight is in any way deficient.

DISSON You don't understand.

  A knock at the door. LOIS *appears.*

LOIS I'm just going out. Wanted to say hullo to you before I go.

DISSON Hullo, Lois.

  He kisses her cheek.

LOIS You've been in here for ages. Don't tell me you need glasses?

DISLEY His eyes are perfect.

LOIS They look it.

DISSON What a lovely dress you're wearing.

LOIS Do you like it? Really?

DISSON Of course I like it.

LOIS You must see if the birds are still there.

She lifts the blind.

Yes, they are. They're all at the bird bath.

They all look into the garden.

Look at them. They're so happy. They love my bath.
They do, really. They love it. They make me so happy,
my birds. And they seem to know, instinctively, that
I adore them. They do, really.

DISSON's *house. Bedroom. Night.*

DISSON *alone, in front of a mirror.*

*He is tying his tie. He ties it. The front end hangs only
half-way down his chest. He unties it, ties it again. The
front end, this time, is even shorter.*

He unties it, holds the tie and looks at it.

*He then ties the tie again. This time the two ends are
of equal length.*

He breathes deeply, relaxes, goes out of the room.

DISSON's *house. Dining room. Night.*

DIANA, WILLY, DISSON *at dinner.*

DIANA I'd say she was a real find.

WILLY Oh, she's of inestimable value to the firm,
wouldn't you say, Robert?

DISSON Oh yes.

DIANA I mean for someone who's not . . . actually . . . part of us . . . I mean, an outsider . . . to give such devotion and willingness to the job, as she does . . . well, it's remarkable. We were very lucky to find her.

DISSON I found her, actually.

WILLY You found me, too, old boy.

DIANA (*laughing*). And me.

  Pause.

She's of course so completely trustworthy, and so very persuasive, on the telephone. I've heard her . . . when the door's been open . . . once or twice.

WILLY Oh, splendid girl, all round.

DISSON She's not so bloody marvellous.

  Pause. They look at him.

She's all right, she's all right. But she's not so bloody marvellous.

DIANA Well, perhaps not quite as accomplished as I am, no. Do you think I'm a good private secretary, Willy?

WILLY First rate.

  Pause. They eat and drink.

DISSON I don't think it's a good idea for you to work.

DIANA Me? Why not? I love it.

DISSON I never see you. If you were at home I could take the occasional afternoon off . . . to see you. As it is I never see you. In daytime.

DIANA You mean I'm so near and yet so far?

Pause.

DISSON Yes.

DIANA Would you prefer me to be your secretary?

DISSON No, no, of course not. That wouldn't work at all.

Pause.

WILLY But we do all meet at lunchtime. We meet in the evening.

DISSON *looks at him.*

DIANA But I like working. You wouldn't want me to work for someone else, would you, somewhere else?

DISSON I certainly wouldn't. You know what Wendy told me, don't you?

DIANA What?

DISSON She told me her last employer was always touching her.

WILLY No?

DISSON Always. Touching her.

DIANA Her body, you mean?

DISSON What else?

471

Pause.

DIANA Well, if we're to take it that that's general practice, I think it's safer to stay in the family, don't you? Mind you, they might not want to touch me in the way they wanted to touch her.

Pause.

But, Robert, you must understand that I not only want to be your wife, but also your employee. I'm not embarrassing you, am I, Willy?

WILLY No, of course you're not.

DIANA Because by being your employee I can help to further your interests, our interests. That's what I want to do. And so does Willy, don't you?

DISSON's *office. Morning.*

DISSON *alone. He stands in the centre of the room. He looks at the door, walks over to* WENDY's *desk. He looks down at her desk-chair. He touches it. Slowly, he sits in it. He sits still. The door opens,* WENDY *comes in. He stands.*

DISSON You're late.

WENDY You were sitting in my chair, Mr Disson.

DISSON I said you're late.

WENDY I'm not at all.

WENDY *walks to her desk.*

DISSON *makes way for her. He moves across the room.*

I'm hurt.

DISSON Why?

WENDY I've put on my new dress.

He turns, looks at her.

DISSON When did you put it on?

WENDY This morning.

Pause.

DISSON Where?

WENDY In my flat.

DISSON Which room?

WENDY In the hall, actually. I have a long mirror in the hall.

He stands looking at her.

Do you like it?

DISSON'*s house. Workroom.*

DISSON Hold it firmly. You're not holding it firmly.

TOM *holds a length of wood on the table.* DISSON *chips at its base.*

Use pressure. Grip it.

JOHN A clamp would be better.

473

DISSON A clamp? I want you boys to learn how to concentrate your physical energies, to do something useful.

JOHN What's it going to be, Dad?

DISSON You'll find out.

DISSON *chips. He straightens.*

Give me the saw.

JOHN Me?

DISSON The saw! Give me it! (*To* TOM.) What are you doing?

TOM I'm holding this piece of wood.

DISSON Well, stop it. I've finished chipping. Look at the point now.

JOHN If you put some lead in there you could make a pencil out of it.

DISSON They think you're very witty at your school, do they?

JOHN Well, some do and some don't, actually, Dad.

DISSON You. Take the saw.

TOM Me?

DISSON I want you to saw it off . . . from here.

DISSON *makes a line with his finger on the wood.*

TOM But I can't saw.

JOHN What about our homework, Dad? We've got to write an essay about the Middle Ages.

DISSON Never mind the Middle Ages.

JOHN Never mind the *Middle Ages*?

TOM Can't you demonstrate how to do it, Dad? Then we could watch.

DISSON Oh, give me it.

> DISSON *takes the saw and points to a mark on the wood.*

Now . . . from here.

TOM (*pointing*) You said from here.

DISSON No, no, from here.

JOHN (*pointing to the other end*). I could have sworn you said from there.

> *Pause.*

DISSON Go to your room.

> *Pause.*

Get out.

> JOHN *goes out.* DISSON *looks at* TOM.

Do you want to learn anything?

TOM Yes.

DISSON Where did I say I was going to saw it?

> *He stares at the wood,* TOM *holds it still.*

Hold it still. Hold it. Don't let it move.

> DISSON *saws. The saw is very near* TOM's *fingers.*
> TOM *looks down tensely.* DISSON *saws through.*

TOM You nearly cut my fingers off.

DISSON No, I didn't . . . I didn't . . .

> *He glares suddenly at* TOM.

You didn't hold the wood still!

DISSON's *office.*

The curtains are drawn.

DISSON Come here. Put your chiffon round my eyes.
My eyes hurt.

> WENDY *ties a chiffon scarf round his eyes.*

I want you to make a call to Newcastle, to Mr
Martin. We're still waiting for delivery of goods on
Invoice No. 634729. What is the cause for delay?

> WENDY *picks up the telephone, dials, waits.*

WENDY Could I have Newcastle 77254, please.
Thank you.

> *She waits. He touches her body.*

Yes, I'm holding.

> *He touches her. She moves under his touch.*

Hullo, Mr Martin, please. Mr Disson's office.

> *Camera on him. His arm stretching.*

Mr Martin? Mr Disson's office. Mr Disson . . . Ah, you know what it's about (*She laughs.*) Yes . . . Yes.

Camera on him. He leans forward, his arm stretching.

Oh, it's been dispatched? Oh good. Mr Disson will be glad.

She moves under his touch.

Oh, I will. Of course I will.

She puts the phone down. He withdraws his hand.

Mr Martin sends his apologies. The order has been dispatched.

The intercom buzzes. She switches through. WILLY's *voice.*

Yes?

WILLY Oh, Wendy, is Mr Disson there?

WENDY Did you want to speak to him, Mr Torrance?

WILLY No. Just ask him if I might borrow your services for five minutes.

WENDY Mr Torrance wants to know if he might borrow my services for five minutes.

DISSON What's happened to his own secretary?

WENDY Mr Disson would like to know what has happened to your own secretary.

WILLY She's unwell. Gone home. Just five minutes, that's all.

477

DISSON *gestures towards the door.*

WENDY Be with you in a minute, Mr Torrance.

WILLY Please thank Mr Disson for me.

The intercom switches off.

WENDY Mr Torrance would like me to thank you for him.

DISSON I heard.

WENDY *goes through the inner door into* WILLY's *office, shuts it.*

Silence.

DISSON *sits still, the chiffon round his eyes. He looks towards the door.*

He hears giggles, hissing, gurgles, squeals.

He goes to the door, squats by the handle, raises the chiffon, tries to look through the keyhole. Can see nothing through the keyhole. He drops the chiffon, puts his ear to the door.

The handle presses into his skull. The sounds continue.

Sudden silence.

The door has opened.

A pair of woman's legs stand by his squatting body.

He freezes, slowly puts forward a hand, touches a leg. He tears the chiffon from his eyes. It hangs from his neck. He looks up.

478

DIANA *looks down at him.*

Behind her, in the other room, WENDY *is sitting, taking dictation from* WILLY, *who is standing.*

DIANA What game is this?

He remains.

Get up. What are you doing? What are you doing with that scarf? Get up from the floor. What are you doing?

DISSON Looking for something.

DIANA What?

WILLY *walks to the door, smiles, closes the door.*

What were you looking for? Get up.

DISSON (*standing*). Don't speak to me like that. How dare you speak to me like that? I'll knock your teeth out.

She covers her face.

What were you doing in there? I thought you'd gone home. What were you doing in there?

DIANA I came back.

DISSON You mean you were in there with both of them? In there with both of them?

DIANA Yes! So what?

Pause.

DISSON (*calmly*). I was looking for my pencil, which had rolled off my desk. Here it is. I found it, just

479

before you came in, and put it in my pocket. My eyes hurt. I borrowed Wendy's scarf, to calm my eyes. Why are you getting so excited?

DISSON's *office. Day.*

DISSON *at his desk, writing,* WENDY *walks to the cabinet, examines a file. Silence.*

DISSON What kind of flat do you have, Wendy?

WENDY Quite a small one, Mr Disson. Quite pleasant.

DISSON Not too big for you, then? Too lonely?

WENDY Oh no, it's quite small. Quite cosy.

DISSON Bathroom fittings any good?

WENDY Adequate, Mr Disson Not up to our standard.

  Pause.

DISSON Live there alone, do you?

WENDY No, I share it with a girl friend. But she's away quite a lot of the time. She's an air hostess. She wants me to become one, as a matter of fact.

DISSON Listen to me, Wendy Don't ever . . . dream of becoming an air hostess. Never. The glamour may dazzle from afar, but, believe you me, it's a mess of a life . . . a mess of a life . . .

  He watches WENDY *walk to her desk with a file and then back to the cabinet.*

Were you lonely as a child?

WENDY No.

DISSON Nor was I. I had quite a lot of friends. True friends. Most of them live abroad now, of course – banana planters, oil engineers, Jamaica, the Persian Gulf. . . but if I were to meet them tomorrow, you know . . . just like that . . . there'd be no strangeness, no awkwardness at all. We'd continue where we left off, quite naturally.

WENDY bends low at the cabinet.

He stares at her buttocks.

It's a matter of a core of affection, you see . . . a core of undying affection . . .

Suddenly WENDY's body appears in enormous close-up. Her buttocks fill the screen.

His hands go up to keep them at bay.

His elbow knocks a round table lighter from his desk.

Picture normal.

WENDY turns from the cabinet, stands upright.

WENDY What was that?

DISSON My lighter.

She goes to his desk.

WENDY Where is it?

She kneels, looks under the desk. The lighter is at his feet.

She reaches for it. He kicks it across the room.

(*Laughing.*) Oh, Mr Disson, why did you do that?

She stands. He stands. She goes towards the lighter. He gets to it before her, stands with it at his feet. He looks at her.

She stops.

What's this?

DISSON *feints his body, left to right*

DISSON Come on.

WENDY What?

DISSON Tackle me. Get the ball.

WENDY What do I tackle with?

DISSON Your feet.

She moves forward deliberately.

He dribbles away, turns, kicks the lighter along the carpet towards her. Her foot stops the lighter. She turns with it at her foot.

Ah!

She stands, legs apart, the lighter between them, staring at him.

She taps her foot.

WENDY Come on, then!

He goes towards her. She eludes him. He grasps her arm.

482

That's a foul!

He drops her arm.

DISSON Sorry.

She stands with the lighter between her feet.

WENDY Come on, come on. Tackle me, tackle me. Come on, tackle me! Get the ball! Fight for the ball!

He begins to move, stops, sinks to the floor. She goes to him.

What's the matter?

DISSON Nothing. All right. Nothing.

WENDY Let me help you up.

DISSON No. Stay. You're very valuable in this office. Good worker. Excellent. If you have any complaints, just tell me. I'll soon put them right. You're a very efficient secretary. Something I've always needed. Have you everything you want? Are your working conditions satisfactory?

WENDY Perfecdy.

DISSON Oh good. Good . . . Good.

DISSON's *house. Bedroom. Night*

DISSON *and* DIANA *in bed, reading. She looks at him.*

DIANA You seem a little subdued . . . lately.

DISSON Me? Not at all. I'm reading the life of Napoleon, that's all.

483

DIANA No, I don't mean now, I mean generally. Is there –?

DISSON I'm not at all subdued. Really.

Pause.

DIANA It's our first anniversary next Wednesday, did you know that?

DISSON Of course I did. How could I forget? We'll go out together in the evening. Just you and I. Alone.

DIANA Oh. Good.

DISSON I'm also giving a little tea party in the office, in the afternoon. My mother and father'll be up.

DIANA Oh good.

Pause.

DISSON How have you enjoyed our first year?

DIANA It's been wonderful. It's been a very exciting year.

Pause.

DISSON You've been marvellous with the boys.

DIANA They like me.

DISSON Yes, they do. They do.

Pause.

It's been a great boon, to have you work for the firm.

DIANA Oh, I'm glad. I am glad.

484

Pause.

Be nice to get away to Spain.

Pause.

DISSON You've got enough money, haven't you? I mean, you have sufficient money to see you through, for all you want?

DIANA Oh yes. I have, thank you.

Pause.

DISSON I'm very proud of you, you know.

DIANA I'm proud of you.

Silence.

DISSON's *office.*

DISSON Have you written to Corley?

WENDY Yes,

DISSON And Turnbull?

WENDY Yes, Mr Disson.

DISSON And Erverley?

WENDY Yes, Mr Disson.

DISSON Carbon of the Erverley letter, please.

WENDY Here you are, Mr Disson.

DISSON Ah. I see you've spelt Erverley right.

WENDY Right?

485

DISSON People tend, very easily, to leave out the first
'r' and call him Everley. You haven't done that.

WENDY No. (*She turns.*)

DISSON Just a minute. How did you spell Tumbull?
You needn't show me. Tell me.

WENDY T-U-R-N-B-U-L-L.

DISSON Quite correct.

   Pause.

Quite correct. Now what about –?

   The screen goes black.

Where are you?

   Pause.

I can't see you.

WENDY I'm here, Mr Disson.

DISSON Where?

WENDY You're looking at me, Mr Disson.

DISSON You mean my eyes are open?

   Pause.

WENDY I'm where I was. I haven't moved.

DISSON Are my eyes open?

WENDY Mr Disson, really . . .

DISSON Is this you? This I feel?

WENDY Yes.

DISSON What, all this I can feel?

WENDY You're playing one of your games, Mr Disson. You're being naughty again.

Vision back.

DISSON *looks at her.*

You sly old thing.

Disley's surgery.

A torch shines in DISSON's *eyes, first right, then left. Torch out.*

Light on.

DISLEY There's nothing wrong with them.

DISSON What then?

DISLEY I only deal with eyes, old chap. Why do you come to me? Why don't you go to someone else?

DISSON Because it's my eyes that are affected.

DISLEY Look. Why don't you go to someone else?

DISLEY *begins to clear away his instruments.*

Nothing worrying you, is there?

DISSON Of course not. I've got everything I want.

DISLEY Getting a holiday soon?

DISSON Going to Spain.

DISLEY Lucky man.

Pause.

DISSON Look. Listen. You're my oldest friend. You were going to be the best man at my wedding.

DISLEY That's right.

DISSON You wrote a wonderful speech in my honour.

DISLEY Yes.

DISSON But you were ill. You had to opt out.

DISLEY That's right.

Pause.

DISSON Help me.

Pause.

DISLEY Who made the speech? Your brother-in-law, wasn't it?

DISSON I don't want you to think I'm not a happy man. I am.

DISLEY What sort of speech did he make?

DISSON's *house. Sitting room. Evening.*

DISSON Tell me about Sunderley.

WILLY Sunderley?

DISSON Tell me about the place where you two were born. Where you played at being brother and sister.

488

WILLY We didn't have to play at being brother and sister. We were brother and sister.

DIANA Stop drinking.

DISSON Drinking? You call this drinking? This? I used to down eleven or nine pints a night! Eleven or nine pints! Every night of the stinking week! Me and the boys! The boys! And me! I'd break any man's hand for . . . for playing me false. That was before I became a skilled craftsman. That was before . . .

He folk silent, sits.

WILLY Sunderley was beautiful.

DISSON I know.

WILLY And now it's gone, for ever.

DISSON I never got there.

DISSON stands, goes to get a drink. He turns from drinks table.

What are you whispering about? Do you think I don't hear? Think I don't see? I've got my memories, too. Long before this.

WILLY Yes, Sunderley was beautiful.

DISSON The lake.

WILLY The lake.

DISSON The long windows.

WILLY From the withdrawing room.

DISSON On to the terrace.

WILLY Music playing.

DISSON On the piano.

WILLY The summer nights. The wild swans.

DISSON What swans? What bloody swans?

WILLY The owls.

DISSON Negroes at the gate, under the trees.

WILLY No Negroes.

DISSON Why not?

WILLY We had no Negroes.

DISSON Why in God's name not?

WILLY Just one of those family quirks, Robert.

DIANA (*standing*). Robert.

  Pause.

Come to bed.

DISSON You can say that, in front of him?

DIANA Please.

DISSON In front of *him*?

  He goes to her.

Why did you marry me?

DIANA I admired you. You were so positive.

DISSON You loved me.

490

DIANA You were kind.

DISSON You loved me for that?

DIANA I found you admirable in your clarity of mind, your surety of purpose, your will, the strength your achievements had given you –

DISSON And you *adored* me for it?

WILLY (*to* DISSON). Can I have a private word with you?

DISSON You *adored* me for it?

   Pause.

DIANA You know I did.

WILLY Can I have a private word with you, old chap? (*To* DIANA.) Please.

DIANA *goes out of the room.* DISSON *looks at* WILLY,

DISSON Mind how you tread, Bill. Mind . . . how you tread, old Bill, old boy, old Bill.

WILLY Listen. I've been wondering. Is there anything on your mind?

DISSON My mind? No, of course not.

WILLY You're not dissatisfied with my work, or anything?

DISSON Quite the contrary. Absolutely the contrary.

WILLY Oh good. I like the work very much. Try to do my best.

DISSON Listen. I want you to be my partner. Hear me? I want you to share full responsibility . . . with me.

WILLY Do you really?

DISSON Certainly.

WILLY Well, thank you very much. I don't know what to say.

DISSON Don't say anything.

DISSON's *office.* WILLY *at the door.*

WILLY Coming, old chap?

DISSON Yes.

WILLY (*to* WENDY) Important lunch, this. But I think we'll swing it, don't you, Robert? (*To* WENDY.) Great prospects in store.

> DISSON *and* WILLY *go out.* WENDY *clips some papers together.*
>
> DIANA *comes in through the inner door.*

WENDY Oh, hullo, Mrs Disson.

DIANA Hullo, Wendy.

> *Pause.*
>
> DIANA *watches* WENDY *clip the papers.*

Do you like being a secretary?

WENDY I do, yes. Do you?

DIANA I do, yes.

Pause.

I understand your last employer touched your body . . .
rather too much.

WENDY It wasn't a question of too much, Mrs
Disson. One touch was enough for me.

DIANA Oh, you left after the first touch?

WENDY Well, not quite the first, no.

  Pause.

DIANA Have you ever asked yourself why men will
persist in touching women?

WENDY No, I've never asked myself that, Mrs Disson.

DIANA Few women do ask themselves that question.

WENDY Don't they? I don't know. I've never spoken
to any other women on the subject.

DIANA You're speaking to me.

WENDY Yes. Well, have you ever asked yourself that
question, Mrs Disson?

DIANA Never. No.

  Pause.

Have lunch with me today. Tell me about yourself.

WENDY I'll have lunch with you with pleasure.

  DISSON *comes in. They look at him. He at them.
  Silence.*

DISSON Forgotten . . . one of the designs.

DIANA *smiles at him.* WENDY *clips her papers. He goes to his desk, collects a folder, stands upright.*

DIANA *looks out of the window.* WENDY *clips papers. He looks at them, goes out.* DIANA *and* WENDY *remain silent.*

DISSON's *house. Games room.*

DISSON *and* WILLY *playing ping-pong. They are in the middle of a long rally.* THE TWINS *watch.* WILLY *is on the attack,* DISSON *playing desperately, retrieving from positions of great difficulty. He cuts, chops, pushes.*

TWINS (*variously*) Well done, Dad. Good shot, Dad. Good one, Dad.

WILLY *forces* DISSON *on to the forehand. He slams viciously.*

DISSON *skids.*

The screen goes black.

Good shot!

DISSON Aaah!

Vision back.

DISSON *is clutching the table, bent over it.* WILLY *throws the ball on to the table.*

It bounces gently across it.

DISSON's *house. Sitting room. Evening.* DISSON's *parents.*

MOTHER Have I seen that mirror before?

DISSON No. It's new.

MOTHER I knew I hadn't seen it. Look at it, John. What a beautiful mirror.

FATHER Must have cost you a few bob.

MOTHER Can you see the work on it, John? I bet it must be a few years old, that mirror.

DISSON It's a few hundred years old.

FATHER I bet it must have cost you a few bob.

DISSON It wasn't cheap.

FATHER Cheap?

MOTHER What a beautiful mirror.

FATHER Cheap? Did you hear what he said, Dora? He said it wasn't cheap!

MOTHER No, I bet it wasn't.

FATHER (*laughing*). Cheap!

  Pause.

MOTHER Mrs Tidy sends you her love.

DISSON Who?

FATHER Mrs Tidy. The Tidys.

DISSON Oh yes. How are they?

FATHER Still very tidy. (*Laughs.*) Aren't they, Dora?

MOTHER You remember the Tidys.

DISSON Of course I remember them.

  Pause.

How have you been keeping, then?

FATHER Oh, your mother's had a few pains. You know, just a few.

MOTHER Only a few, John I haven't had many pains.

FATHER I only said you'd had a few. Not many.

  Pause.

MOTHER Are the boys looking forward to their holiday?

DISSON Yes, they are.

FATHER When are you going?

DISSON I'm not.

DISSON's *office.*

DISSON Tighter.

  WENDY *ties the chiffon round his eyes.*

WENDY There. You look nice.

DISSON This chiffon stinks.

WENDY Oh, I do apologise. What of?

  Pause.

You're very rude to me. But you do look nice. You really do.

DISSON *tears the chiffon off.*

DISSON It's useless. Ring Disley. Tell him to come here.

WENDY But he'll be here at four o'clock, for your tea party.

DISSON I want him now! I want him . . . now.

WENDY Don't you like my chiffon any more, to put round your eyes? My lovely chiffon?

Pause.

He sits still.

I always feel like kissing you when you've got that on round your eyes. Do you know that? Because you're all in the dark.

Pause.

Put it on.

She picks up the chiffon and folds it.

I'll put it on . . . for you. Very gently.

She leans forward. He touches her.

No – you mustn't touch me, if you're not wearing your chiffon.

She places the chiffon on his eyes. He trembles, puts his hand to the chiffon, slowly lowers it, lets it fall.

497

It flutters to the floor. As she looks at him, he reaches for the telephone.

DISSON's *office.*

DISSON *in the same position.*

DISSON I need a tight bandage. Very tight.

DISLEY Anyone could do that for you.

DISSON No. You're my eye consultant. You must do it for me.

DISLEY All right

He takes a bandage from his case and ties it round DISSON's *eyes.*

Just for half an hour. You don't want it on when your guests arrive, do you?

DISLEY *ties the knots.*

This'll keep you in the dark, all right. Also lend pressure to your temples. Is that what you want?

DISSON That's it That's what I want.

DISLEY *cuts the strands.*

There. How's that?

Pause.

See anything?

DISSON's *office. Afternoon.*

DISSON *sits alone, the bandage round his eyes. Silence.*

WILLY *enters from his office. He sees* DISSON *and goes to him.*

WILLY How are you, old chap? Bandage on straight? Knots tight?

> *He pats him on the back and goes out through the front office door.*
>
> *The door slams.*
>
> DISSON *sits still.*

Corridor.

MR *and* MRS DISLEY *approaching the office.*

LOIS Why didn't he make it a cocktail party? Why a tea party, of all things?

DISLEY I couldn't say.

Office.

DISSON's *head.*

Soft clicks of door opening and closing, muffled steps, an odd cough, slight rattle of teacups.

Corridor.

DISSON's *parents approaching the office.*

MOTHER I could do with a cup of tea, couldn't you, John?

Office.

DISSON's *head.*

Soft clicks of door opening and closing, muffled steps, an odd cough, slight rattle of teacups.

Corridor.

THE TWINS *approach, silent.*

Office.

DISSON's *head.*

Soft clicks of door opening and closing, muffled steps, an odd cough, slight rattle of teacups, a short whisper.

Corridor.

DIANA *and* WILLY *approach.*

DIANA Why *don't* you come to Spain with us?

WILLY I think I will.

Office.

DISSON's *head.*

Soft clicks of door opening and closing, muffled steps, an odd cough, slight rattle of teacups, whispers.

TEA PARTY

Corridor.

WENDY *approaches.*

Office.

DISSON's *head.*

Soft clicks of door opening and closing, muffled steps, an odd cough, slight rattle of teacups, whispers.

Office.

A buffet table has been set out. Two elderly ladies serve tea, sandwiches, bridge rolls, buns and cakes. The gathering is grouped around the table in silence, DISLEY *whispers to them.*

DISLEY His eyes are a little strained, that's all. Just resting them. Don't mention it. It'll embarrass him. It's quite all right.

They all take their tea, choose edibles, and relax.

JOHN (*choosing a cake*) These are good.

TOM What are they?

DIANA (*choosing a bridge roll*) These look nice.

LOIS You look wonderful, Mrs Disson. Absolutely wonderful. Doesn't she, Peter?

DISLEY Marvellous.

LOIS What do you think of your grandsons?

FATHER They've grown up now, haven't they?

LOIS Of course, we knew them when they were that high, didn't we, Tom?

FATHER So did we.

TOM Yes.

WILLY Big lads now, aren't they, these two?

JOHN Cake, Granny?

MOTHER No, I've had one.

JOHN Have two.

FATHER I'll have one.

MOTHER He's had one.

FATHER I'll have two.

> WENDY *takes a cup of tea to* DISSON *and puts it into his hands.*

WENDY Here's a cup of tea, Mr Disson. Drink it. It's warm.

LOIS (*to* DIANA). You're off to Spain quite soon, aren't you, Diana?

DIANA Yes, quite soon.

DISLEY (*calling*). We'll take off those bandages in a minute, old chap!

LOIS Spain is wonderful at this time of the year.

WILLY Any time of the year, really.

LOIS But I think it's best at this time of the year, don't you?

DIANA What sun lotion do you use, Lois?

DISSON's *point of view.*

No dialogue is heard in all shots from DISSON's *point of view.*

Silence.

Figures mouthing silently, in conspiratorial postures, seemingly whispering together.

Shot including DISSON.

TOM I went into goal yesterday.

WILLY How did you do?

LOIS You can get it anywhere. It's perfect.

JOHN He made two terrific saves.

TOM The first was a fluke.

LOIS How do you sun, then?

DIANA I have to be rather carefuL

TOM Second save wasn't a bad save.

LOIS How do you sun, Wendy?

WENDY Oh not too bad, really.

LOIS (*to* MRS DISSON). We go to our little island every year and when we go we have to leave our poor little Siamese with my mother.

MOTHER Do you really?

LOIS They're almost human, aren't they, Siamese?

DIANA I'm sure my Siamese was.

LOIS Aren't they, Peter, almost human?

DIANA Wasn't Tiger a human cat, Willy, at Sunderley?

WILLY He adored you.

DISLEY They really are almost human, aren't they, Siamese?

DISSON's *point of view.*

Silence.

The party splits into groups. Each group whispering.

The two ELDERLY LADIES *at the buffet table.*

DISSON's *parents, sitting together.*

THE TWINS *and the* DISLEYS.

WILLY, WENDY *and* DIANA *in a corner.*

Shot including DISSON.

The gathering in a close group, the parents sitting.

LOIS I'd go like a shot.

WENDY What, me? Come to Spain?

DIANA Yes, why not?

WILLY *leans across* DISLEY.

WILLY Yes, of course you must come. Of course you must come.

WENDY How wonderful.

DISSON's *point of view.*

WILLY *approaches* DISSON. *With a smile, he takes a ping-pong ball from his pocket, and puts it into* DISSON's *hand.* DISSON *clutches it.*

Disson's point of view.

WILLY *returns to* WENDY *and diana, whispers to them.*

DIANA *laughs (silently), head thrown back, gasps with laughter.*

WENDY *smiles.*

WILLY *puts one arm round* WENDY, *the other round* DIANA.

He leads them to WENDY's *desk.*

WILLY *places cushions on the desk.*

DIANA *and* WENDY, *giggling silently, hoist themselves up on to the desk. They lie head to toe.*

DISSON's *point of view. Close-up.*

WENDY's *face.* WILLY's *fingers caressing it.* DIANA's *shoes in background.*

DISSON's *point of view. Close-up.*

DIANA's *face.* WILLY's *fingers caressing it.* WENDY's *shoes in background.*

DISSON's *point of view.*

LOIS *powdering her nose.*

DISSON's *point of view.*

The ELDERLY LADIES *drinking tea, at the table.*

DISSON's *point of view.*

DISLEY *talking to the boys by the window,* THE TWINS *listening intently.*

DISSON's *point of view.*

DISSON's *parents sitting, dozing.*

DISSON's *point of view.*

The base of WENDY's *desk.*

A shoe drops to the floor.

Shot including DISSON.

DISSON *falls to the floor in his chair with a crack. His teacup drops and spills.*

The gathering is grouped by the table, turns.

DISLEY *and* WILLY *go to him.*

They try to lift him from the chair, are unable to do so.

DISLEY *cuts the bandage and takes it off.*

DISSON's *eyes are open.*

DISLEY *feels his pulse.*

DISLEY He's all right. Get him up.

> DISLEY *and* WILLY *try to pull him up from the chair, are unable to do so.*

> JOHN *and* TOM *join them.*

Get it up.

> *The four of them, with great effort, manage to set the chair on its feet.*

> DISSON *is still seated.*

He must lie down. Now, two hold the chair, and two pull him.

> JOHN *and* WILLY *hold the chair.* DISLEY *and* TOM *pull.*

The chair.

The chair scrapes, moves no farther.

The group around the chair.

They pull, with great effort.

The chair.

The chair scrapes, moves no farther.

The room.

WILLY Anyone would think he was chained to it!

DISLEY (*pulling*) Come out!

MOTHER Bobbie!

They stop pulling.

DISSON *in the chair, still, his eyes open.*

DIANA *comes to him.*

She kneels by him.

DIANA This is . . . Diana.

Pause.

Can you hear me?

Pause.

Can he see me?

Pause.

Robert

Pause.

Can you hear me?

Pause.

Robert, can you see me?

Pause.

It's me. It's me, darling.

Slight pause.

It's your wife.

DISSON's *face in close-up.*

DISSON's *eyes. Open.*

THE BASEMENT

The Basement first published
by Methuen & Co. 1967
© FPinter Limited, 1967

The Basement was first presented by BBC Television
on 20 February 1967 with the following cast:

STOTT	Harold Pinter
JANE	Kika Markham
LAW	Derek Godfrey

Directed by Charles Jarrott

Characters

STOTT

JANE

LAW

Exterior. Front area of a basement flat.

Winter. Night.

Rain falling.

Short stone flight of steps from street.

Light shining through the basement door.

The upper part of the house is dark.

The back of a man, STOTT. *He stands in the centre of the area, looking towards the door.*

He wears a raincoat, his head is bare.

Exterior. Front area.

STOTT'*s face. Behind him, by the wall, a girl,* JANE. *She is huddled by the wall. She wears a rain hat, clasps her raincoat to her.*

Interior. Room.

The room is large and long. A window at one end looks out to a small concrete yard. There are doors to bathroom and kitchen. The room is comfortable, relaxed, heavily furnished. Numerous side tables,

*plants, armchairs, book cabinets, bookshelves, velvet
cloths, a desk, paintings, a large double bed. There is a
large fire in the grate.*

*The room is lit by a number of table and standard
lamps.* LAW *is lying low in an armchair, reading, by
the fireside.*

Silence.

Exterior. Front area.

STOTT *still.*

Interior. Room.

LAW *in arm-chair. He is smiling at his book.*

*He giggles. He is reading a Persian love manual, with
illustrations.*

Exterior. Front area.

JANE *huddled by the wall.*

STOTT *moves to the door.*

Interior. Room,

Doorbell. LAW *looks up from his book. He closes it,
puts it on a side table, goes into the hall.*

Interior. Small hall.

LAW *approaches the front door. He opens it.*

Silence.

He stares at STOTT. *From his position in the doorway*
LAW *cannot see the girl.*

LAW (*with great pleasure*) Stott! s

STOTT (*smiling*) Hullo, Tim.

LAW Good God. Come in!

   LAW *laughs.*

Come in!

   STOTT *enters.*

I can't believe it!

Interior. Room.

LAW *and* STOTT *enter.*

LAW Give me your coat. You're soaking. Come on.
That's it. I'm absolutely flabbergasted. You must be
freezing.

STOTT I am a bit.

LAW Go on, warm yourself. Warm yourself by the fire.

STOTT Thanks.

LAW Sit down by the fire. Go on.

   STOTT *moves to the fire.*

   LAW *takes the coat into hall.*

Interior. Hall.

LAW *comes into the hall, shaking the raincoat. He looks inside it, at the label, smiles. He hangs it on a hook.*

Interior. Room.

STOTT *warming his hands at the fire,* LAW *comes in.*

LAW You haven't changed at all. You haven't changed . . . at all!

STOTT *laughs.*

You've got a new raincoat though. Oh yes, I noticed. Hold on, I'll get you a towel.

LAW *goes to the bathroom.*

STOTT, *alone, looks up and about him at the room.*

Interior. Room.
The room.

Interior. Bathroom.

LAW *in bathroom, at the airing cupboard. He swiftly throws aside a number of towels, chooses a soft one with a floral pattern.*

Interior. Room.

LAW *comes in with a towel.*

LAW Here's a towel. Go on, give it a good wipe.
That's it. You didn't walk here, did you? You're
soaking. What happened to your car? You could have
driven here. Why didn't you give me a ring? But how
did you know my address? My God, it's years. If
you'd have rung I would have picked you up. I would
have picked you up in my car. What happened to your
car?

STOTT *finishes drying his hair, puts the towel on
the arm of a chair.*

STOTT I got rid of it.

LAW But how are you? Are you well? You look well.

STOTT How are you?

LAW Oh, I'm well. Just a minute, I'll get you some
slippers.

LAW *goes to the cupboard, bends.*

You're going to stay the night, aren't you? You'll have
to, look at the time. I wondered if you'd ever turn up
again. Really. For years. Here you are. Here's some
slippers.

STOTT Thanks.

STOTT *takes the slippers, changes his shoes.*

LAW I'll find some pyjamas in a minute. Still, we'll
have a cup of coffee first, or some . . . Or a drink?
What about a drink?

STOTT Ah.

LAW *pours drinks, brings the drinks to the sofa and sits down by* STOTT.

LAW You're not living at Chatsworth Road any more, are you? I know that. I've passed by there, numbers of times. You've moved. Where are you living now?

STOTT I'm looking for a place.

LAW Stay here! Stay here as long as you like. I've got another bed I can fit up. I've got a camp bed I can fit up.

STOTT I don't want to impose upon you.

LAW Not a bit, not a bit.

Pause.

STOTT Oh, by the way, I've got a friend outside. Can she come in?

LAW A friend?

STOTT Outside.

LAW A friend? Outside?

STOTT Can she come in?

LAW Come in? Yes . . . yes . . . of course . . .

STOTT *goes towards the door.*

What's she doing outside?

Exerior. Front door.

JANE *is standing in the narrow porch outside the door. The door opens.*

Interior. Room.

STOTT *brings the girl in.*

STOTT This is Jane. This is Tim Law.

She smiles.

JANE It's kind of you.

LAW How do you do? I . . . must get you a towel.

JANE No, thank you. My hair was covered.

LAW But your face?

STOTT *comes forward.*

STOTT It's very kind of you, Tim. It really is. Here's a towel. (*He gives it to her.*) Here.

LAW But that's your towel.

JANE I don't mind, really.

LAW I have clean ones, dry ones.

JANE (*patting her face*) This is clean.

LAW But it's not dry.

JANE It's very soft.

LAW I have others.

JANE There. I'm dry.

LAW You can't be.

JANE What a splendid room.

STOTT Isn't it? A little bright, perhaps.

LAW Too much light?

STOTT *turns a lamp off.*

STOTT Do you mind?

LAW No.

JANE *begins to take her clothes off.*

In the background STOTT *moves about the room, turning off the lamps.*

LAW *stands still.*

STOTT *turns off all the lamps but one, by the fireside.*

JANE, *naked, gets into the bed.*

Can I get you some cocoa? Some hot chocolate?

STOTT *takes his clothes off and, naked, gets into the bed.*

I was feeling quite lonely, actually. It is lonely sitting here, night after night. Mind you, I'm very happy here. Remember that place we shared? That awful place in Chatsworth Road? I've come a long way since then. I bought this flat cash down. It's mine. I don't suppose you've noticed the hi-fi stereo? There's all sorts of things I can show you.

LAW *unbuttons his cardigan.*

He places it over the one lit lamp, so shading the light. He sits by the fire.

The lamp covered by the cardigan.

Patch of light on the ceiling.

Patch of light at LAW's *feet.*

LAW's *hands on the chair arms. A gasp from* JANE, LAW's *hands do not move.*

LAW's *legs. Beyond them, the fire almost dead.*

LAW *puts on his glasses.*

LAW *reaches for* The Persian Manual of Love.

LAW *peers to read.*
A long sigh from JANE.
LAW *reads.*

Exterior. Cliff-top. Day. Summer.
Long-shot of STOTT *standing on a cliff-top.*

Exterior. Beach.
The beach is long and deserted. LAW *and* JANE, *in swimming costumes.* JANE *building a sandcastle.* LAW *watches her.*

LAW How old are you?

JANE I'm very young.

LAW You are young.

He watches her work.

You're a child.

He watches her.

Have you known him long?

JANE No.

LAW I have. Charming man. Man of great gifts. Very old friend of mine, as a matter of fact. Has he told you?

JANE No.

LAW You don't know him very well?

JANE No.

LAW He has a connection with the French aristocracy. He was educated in France. Speaks French fluently, of course. Have you read his French translations?

JANE No.

LAW Ah. They're immaculate. Great distinction. Formidable scholar, Stott Do you know what he got at Oxford? He got a First in Sanskrit at Oxford. A First in Sanskrit!

JANE How wonderful.

LAW You never knew?

JANE Never.

LAW I know for a fact he owns three chateaux. Three superb chateaux. Have you ever ridden in his Alvis? His Facel Vega? What an immaculate driver. Have you seen his yachts? Huh! What yachts. What yachts.

JANE *completes her sandcastle.*

How pleased I was to see him. After so long. One loses touch . . . so easily.

Interior. Cave. Day.

STOTT's *body lying in the sand, asleep.*

LAW *and* JANE *appear at the mouth of the cave. They arrive at the body, look down.*

LAW What repose he has.

STOTT's *body in the sand.*

Their shadows across him.

Interior. Room. Night.

LAW *lying on the floor, a cushion at his head, covered by a blanket.*

His eyes are closed.

Silence.

A long gasp from JANE.

LAW's *eyes open.*

STOTT *and* JANE *in bed.*

527

STOTT *turning to wall.*

JANE *turns to the edge of the bed.*

She leans over the edge of the bed and smiles at LAW.

LAW *looks at her.*

JANE *smiles.*

Interior. Room. Day.

STOTT *lifts a painting from the wall, looks at it.*

STOTT No.

LAW No, you're quite right. I've never liked it.

STOTT *walks across room to a second picture, looks at it. He turns to look at* LAW.

No.

STOTT *takes it down and turns to look at the other paintings.*

All of them. All of them. You're right. They're terrible. Take them down.

The paintings are all similar watercolours. STOTT *begins to take them from the walls.*

Interior. Kitchen. Day.

JANE *in the kitchen, cooking at the stove, humming.*

Exerior. Backyard. Winter. Day.

The yard is surrounded by high blank walls.

STOTT *and* LAW *sitting at an iron table, with a pole for an umbrella.*

They are drinking lager.

LAW Who is she? Where did you meet her?

STOTT She's charming, isn't she?

LAW Charming. A little young.

STOTT She comes from a rather splendid family, actually.

LAW Really?

STOTT Rather splendid.

  Pause.

LAW Very helpful, of course, around the house.

STOTT Plays the harp, you know.

LAW Well?

STOTT Remarkably well.

LAW What a pity I don't possess one. You don't possess a harp, do you?

STOTT Of course I possess a harp.

LAW A recent acquisition?

STOTT No, I've had it for years.

Pause.

LAW You don't find she's lacking in maturity?

Exterior. Beach. Summer. Day.

LAW *and* JANE *lying in the sand.* JANE *caressing him.*

JANB (*whispering*) Yes, yes, yes, oh you are, oh you are, oh you are . . .

LAW We can be seen.

JANE Why do you resist? How can you resist?

LAW We can be seen! Damn youl

Exterior. Backyard. Winter. Day.

STOTT *and* LAW *at the table with lager.* JANE *comes to the back door.*

IANE *Lunch is upl*

Interior. Hall. Day.

LAW *and* JANE *come in at the front door with towels over their shoulders.*

Interior. Room. Day. Summer.

LAW *and* JANE *at the entrance of the room, towels over their shoulders, staring at the room.*

The room is unrecognisable. The furnishing has changed. There are Scandinavian tables and desks.

*Large bowls of Swedish glass. Tubular chairs. An
Indian rug. Parquet floors, shining. A new hi-fi
cabinet, etc. Fireplace blocked. The bed is the same.*

STOTT *is at the window, closing the curtains. He turns.*

STOTT Have a good swim?

Interior. Room. Night. Winter. (Second furnishing.)

STOTT *and* JANE *in bed, smoking,* LAW *sitting.*

STOTT Let's have some music. We haven't heard your
hi-fi for ages. Let's hear your stereo. What are you
going to play?

Interior. Bar. Evening.

Large empty bar. All the tables unoccupied.

STOTT, LAW *and* JANE *at one table.*

STOTT This was one of our old haunts, wasn't it,
Tim? This was one of our haunts. Tim was always my
greatest friend, you know. Always. It's marvellous. I've
found my old friend again-

    Looking at JANE.

And discovered a new. And you like each other so much.

It's really very warming.

LAW Same again? (*To* WAITER.) Same again. (*To*
JANE.) Same again? (*To* WAITER.) Same again. The
same again, all round. Exactly the same.

STOTT I'll change to Campari.

LAW (*clicking fas fingers at the* WAITER). One Campari here. Otherwise the same again.

STOTT Remember those nights reading Proust? Remember them?

LAW (*to* JANE). In the original.

STOTT The bouts with Laforgue? What bouts.

LAW I remember.

STOTT The great elms they had then. The great elm trees.

LAW And the poplars.

STOTT The cricket. The squash courts. You were pretty hot stuff at squash, you know.

LAW You were unbeatable.

STOTT Your style was deceptive.

LAW It still is.

　LAW *laughs.*

It still is!

STOTT Not any longer.

　The WAITER *serves the drinks.*

　Silence, STOTT *lifts his glass.*

Yes, I really am a happy man.

Exerior. Field. Evening. Winter.

STOTT *and* LAW. JANE *one hundred yards across the field.*

She holds a scarf.

LAW (*shouting*) Hold the scarf up. When you drop it, we run.

   She holds the scarf up.

   LAW *rubs his hands.* STOTT *looks at him.*

STOTT Are you quite sure you want to do this?

LAW Of course I'm sure.

JANE On your marks!

   STOTT *and* LAW *get on their marks.*

Get set!

   They get set.

   JANE *drops scarf.*

Go!

   LAW *runs,* STOTT *stays still.*

   LAW, *going fast, turns to look for* STOTT; *off balance, stumbles, falls, hits his chin on the ground.*

   Lying flat, he looks back at STOTT.

LAW Why didn't you run?

Exterior. Field.

JANE *stands, scarf in her hand. Downfield,* STOTT *stands.*

LAW *lies on the grass.* LAW's *voice:*

LAW Why didn't you run?

Interior. Room. Night. Winter. (Second furnishing.)

STOTT Let's have some music. We haven't heard your hi-fi for ages.

STOTT *opens the curtains and the window.*

Moonlight, LAW *and* JANE *sit in chairs, clench their bodies with cold.*

Exterior. Backyard. Day. Winter.

STOTT *walking,* LAW, *wearing a heavy overcoat, collar turned up, watching him.* LAW *approaches him.*

LAW Listen. Listen. I must speak to you. I must speak frankly. Listen. Don't you think it's a bit crowded in that flat, for the three of us?

STOTT No, no. Not at all.

LAW Listen, listen. Stop walking. Stop walking. Please. Wait.

STOTT *stops.*

Listen. Wouldn't you say that the flat is a little small, for three people?

STOTT (*patting his shoulder*) No, no. Not at all.

STOTT *continues walking.*

LAW (*following him*) To look at it another way, to look at it another way, I can assure you that the

Council would object strenuously to three people living in these conditions. The Town Council, I know for a fact, would feel it incumbent upon itself to register the strongest possible objections. And so would the Church.

STOTT *stops walking, looks at him.*

STOTT Not at all. Not at all.

Interior. Room. Day. Summer.

The curtains are closed. The three at lunch, at the table. STOTT *and* JANE *ore wearing tropical clothes.* JANE *is sitting on* STOTT'*s lap.*

LAW Why don't we open the curtains?

STOTT *eats a grape.*

It's terribly close. Shall I open the window?

STOTT What are you going to play? Debussy, I hope.

LAW *goes to the record cabinet. He examines record after record, feverishly, flings them one after the other at the wall.*

STOTT Where's Debussy?

STOTT *kisses* JANE.

Another record hits the wall.

Where's Debussy? That's what we want. That's what we need. That's what we need at the moment.

JANE *breaks away from* STOTT *and goes out into the yard.*

STOTT *sits still.*

LAW I've found it!

Interior. Room. Night. Winter.

LAW *turns with the record.*

The room is furnished as at the beginning.

STOTT *and* JANE, *naked, climb into bed.*

LAW *puts the record down and places his cardigan over the one lit lamp.*

He sits, picks up the poker and pokes the dying fire.

Exterior. Backyard. Day. Summer.

JANE *sitting at the iron table.*

STOTT *approaches her with a glass and bottle.*

He pours wine into the glass.

He bends over her, attempts to touch her breast.

She moves her body away from him.

STOTT *remains still.*

LAW *watches from the open windows.*

He moves to the table with the record and smiles at STOTT.

LAW I've found the record. The music you wanted.

STOTT *slams his glass on the table and goes into the room.*

LAW *sits at the table, drinks from the bottle, regards* JANE.

JANE *plays with a curl in her hair.*

Interior. Cave by the sea. Evening. Summer.

LAW *and* JANE *He lying, she sitting, by him.*

She bends and whispers to him.

JANE Why don't you tell him to go? We had such a lovely home. We had such a cosy home. It was so warm. Tell him to go. It's your place. Then we could be happy again. Like we used to. Like we used to. In our first blush of love. Then we could be happy again, like we used to. We could be happy again. Like we used to.

Exterior. Backyard. Night. Winter. (Second furnishing.) The yard is icy. The window is open. The room is lit. LAW *is whispering to* STOTT *at the window. In the background* JANE *sits sewing.*

Exterior. Backyard. Window.

LAW *and* STOTT *at the open window,* STOTT's *body hunched.*

LAW (*whispering very deliberately*) She betrays you. She betrays you. She has no loyalty. After all you've done for her. Shown her the world. Given her faith. You've been deluded. She's a savage. A viper. She sullies this room. She dirties this room. All this beautiful furniture. This beautiful Scandinavian furniture. She dirties it. She sullies the room.

STOTT *turns slowly to regard* JANE.

Interior. Room. Day. (Second furnishing.)

The curtains are closed.

STOTT *in bed.* JANE *bending over him, touching his head. She looks across at* LAW.

Silence.

LAW Is he breathing?

JANE Just.

LAW His last, do you think?

Pause.

Do you think it could be his last?

JANE It could be.

LAW How could it have happened? He seemed so fit. He was fit. As fit as a fiddle. Perhaps we should have called a doctor. And now he's dying. Are you heartbroken?

JANE Yes.

LAW So am I.

Pause.

538

JANE What shall we do with the body?

LAW Body? He's not dead yet. Perhaps he'll recover.

They stare at each other.

Interior. Room. Night.

LAW *and* JANE *in a corner, snuffling each other like animals.*

Interior. Room. Night.

STOTT *at the window. He opens the curtains. Moonlight pierces the room. He looks round.*

Interior. Room. Night.

LAW *and* JANE *in a corner, looking up at the window, blinking.*

Interior. Room. Day.

STOTT *at the window, closing the curtains. He turns into the room.*

The room is unrecognisable. The walls are hung with tapestries, an oval Florentine mirror, an oblong Italian Master. The floor is marble tiles. There are marble pillars with hanging plants, carved golden chairs, a rich carpet along the room's centre.

STOTT *sits in a chair,* JANE *comes forward with a bowl of fruit.*

539

STOTT *chooses a grape. In the background* LAW, *in a corner, playing the flute.* STOTT *bites into the grape, tosses the bowl of fruit across the room. The fruit scatters.* JANE *rushes to collect it.*

STOTT *picks up a tray containing large marbles.*

He rolls the tray. The marbles knock against each other.

He selects a marble. He looks across the room at LAW *playing the flute.*

LAW *with flute.*

At the other end of the room STOTT *prepares to bowl.*

STOTT Play!

STOTT *bowls.*

The marble crashes into the wall behind LAW.

LAW *stands, takes guard with his flute.*

STOTT Play!
   STOTT *bowls.*

The marble crashes into the window behind LAW.

LAW *takes guard.*

STOTT Play!

STOTT *bowls. The marble hits* LAW *on the knee.*

LAW *hops.*

LAW *takes guard.*

STOTT Play!

STOTT *bowls.*

LAW *brilliantly cuts marble straight into golden fish tank. The tank smashes. Dozens of fish swim across the marble tiles.*

JANE, *in the corner, applauds.*

LAW *waves his flute in acknowledgement.*

STOTT Play!

STOTT *bowls.*

Marble crashes into LAW's *forehead. He drops.*

Interior. Kitchen. Night.

JANE *in the kitchen, putting spoonfuls of instant coffee into two cups.*

Interior. Room. Night.

The room is completely bare.

Bare walls. Bare floorboards. No furniture. One hanging bulb.

STOTT *and* LAW *at opposite ends of the room.*

They face each other. They are barefooted. They each hold a broken milk bottle. They are crouched, still.

LAW's *face, sweating.*

STOTT's *face, sweating.*

LAW *from* STOTT's *viewpoint.*

STOTT *from* LAW's *viewpoint.*

JANE *pouring sugar from a packet into the bowl.*

LAW *pointing his bottle before him, his arm taut.*

STOTT *pointing his bottle before him, his arm taut.*

JANE *pouring milk from a bottle into a jug.*

STOTT *slowly advancing along bare boards.*

LAW *slowly advancing.*

JANE *pouring a small measure of milk into the cups.*

LAW *and* STOTT *drawing closer.*

JANE *putting sugar into the cups.*

The broken milk bottles, in shaking hands, almost touching.

The broken milk bottles fencing, not touching.

JANE *stirring milk, sugar and coffee in the cups.*

The broken milk bottles, in a sudden thrust, smashing together.

Record turning on a turntable. Sudden music. Debussy's 'Girl with the Flaxen Hair'.

Exterior. Front area. Night.

LAW *standing centre, looking at the basement door.*

JANE *crouched by the wall. Rainhat. Raincoat,* LAW *wearing* STOTT's *raincoat.*

Interior. Room.

Furnished as at the beginning.

STOTT *sitting by the fire, reading. He is smiling at his book.*

Exterior. Front area.

LAW *still.*

Interior. Room.

STOTT *turns a page.*

Doorbell.

STOTT *looks up, puts his book down, stands, goes into the hall.*

Interior. Room.

The room still. The fire burning.

Interior. Hall.

STOTT *approaches the front door. He opens it.*

Silence.

He stares at LAW. *From his position in the doorway* STOTT *cannot see* JANE.

STOTT (*with great pleasure*) Law!

LAW (*smiling*) Hullo, Charles.

STOTT Good God. Come in!

   STOTT *laughs.*

Come in!

   LAW *enters.*

I can't believe it!

LANDSCAPE

Landscape first published with *Silence* and *Night* by
Methuen & Co. 1969
© FPinter Limited, 1968

Landscape was first presented on BBC Radio on
25 April 1968, with the following cast:

BETH   Peggy Ashcroft
DUFF   Eric Porter

Directed by Guy Vaesen

The play was first presented on stage by the Royal
Shakespeare Company at the Aldwych Theatre,
London, on 2 July 1969, with the following cast:

BETH   Peggy Ashcroft
DUFF   David Waller

Directed by Peter Hall

Characters

DUFF
a man in his early fifties

BETH
a woman in her late forties

The kitchen of a country house.

A long kitchen table.

Beth sits in an armchair, which stands away
from the table, to its left.

Duff sits in a chair at the right corner
of the table. The background, of a sink,
stove, etc., and a window, is dim.

Evening.

Note

Duff refers normally to Beth,
but does not appear to hear her voice.

Beth never looks at Duff,
and does not appear to hear his voice.

Both characters are relaxed, in no sense rigid.

BETH I would like to stand by the sea. It is there.

Pause.

I have. Many times. It's something I cared for. I've done it.

Pause.

I'll stand on the beach. On the beach. Well it was very fresh. But it was hot, in the dunes. But it was so fresh, on the shore. I loved it very much.

Pause.

Lots of people . . .

Pause.

People move so easily. Men. Men move.

Pause.

I walked from the dune to the shore. My man slept in the dune. He turned over as I stood. His eyelids. Belly button. Snoozing how lovely.

Pause.

Would you like a baby? I said. Children? Babies? Of our own? Would be nice.

Pause.

Women turn, look at me.

Pause.

Our own child? Would you like that?

Pause.

Two women looked at me, turned and stared. No. I was walking, they were still. I turned.

Pause.

Why do you look?

Pause.

I didn't say that, I stared. Then I was looking at them.

Pause.

I am beautiful.

Pause.

I walked back over the sand. He had turned. Toes under sand, head buried in his arms.

DUFF The dog's gone. I didn't tell you.

Pause.

I had to shelter under a tree for twenty minutes yesterday. Because of the rain. I meant to tell you. With some youngsters. I didn't know them.

Pause.

Then it eased. A downfall. I walked up as far as the pond. Then I felt a couple of big drops. Luckily I was only a few yards from the shelter. I sat down in there. I meant to tell you.

Pause.

Do you remember the weather yesterday? That downfall.?

BETH He felt my shadow. He looked up at me standing above him.

DUFF I should have had some bread with me. I could have fed the birds.

BETH Sand on his arms.

DUFF They were hopping about. Making a racket.

BETH I lay down by him, not touching.

DUFF There wasn't anyone else in the shelter. There was a man and woman, under the trees, on the other side of the pond. I didn't feel like getting wet. I stayed where I was.

Pause.

Yes, I've forgotten something. The dog was with me.

Pause

BETH Did those women know me? I didn't remember their faces. I'd never seen their faces before. I'd never seen those women before. I'm certain of it. Why were they looking at me? There's nothing strange about me. There's nothing strange about the way I look. I look like anyone.

DUFF The dog wouldn't have minded me feeding the birds. Anyway, as soon as we got in the shelter he fell asleep. But even if he'd been awake . . .

Pause

BETH They all held my arm lightly, as I stepped out of the car, or out of the door, or down the steps. Without exception. If they touched the back of my neck, or my hand, it was done so lightly. Without exception. With one exception.

DUFF Mind you, there was a lot of shit all over the place, all along the paths, by the pond. Dogshit, duckshit . . . all kinds of shit . . . all over the paths. The rain didn't clean it up. It made it even more treacherous.

Pause.

The ducks were well away, right over on their island. But I wouldn't have fed them, anyway. I would have fed the sparrows.

BETH I could stand now. I could be the same. I dress differently, but I am beautiful.

Silence.

DUFF You should have a walk with me one day down to the pond, bring some bread. There's nothing to stop you.

Pause.

I sometimes run into one or two people I know. You might remember them.

Pause

BETH When I watered the flowers he stood, watching me, and watched me arrange them. My gravity, he

554

said. I was so grave, attending to the flowers, I'm going to water and arrange the flowers, I said. He followed me and watched, standing at a distance from me. When the arrangement was done I stayed still. I heard him moving. He didn't touch me. I listened. I looked at the flowers, blue and white, in the bowl.

Pause.

Then he touched me.

Pause.

He touched the back of my neck. His fingers, lightly, touching, lightly, touching, the back, of my neck.

DUFF The funny thing was, when I looked, when the shower was over, the man and woman under the trees on the other side of the pond had gone. There wasn't a soul in the park.

BETH I wore a white beach robe. Underneath I was naked.

Pause.

There wasn't a soul on the beach. Very far away a man was sitting, on a breakwater. But even so he was only a pinpoint, in the sun. And even so I could only see him when I was standing, or on my way from the shore to the dune. When I lay down I could no longer see him, therefore he couldn't see me.

Pause.

I may have been mistaken. Perhaps the beach was empty. Perhaps there was no one there.

Pause.

He couldn't see . . . my man . . . anyway. He never stood up.

Pause.

Snoozing how lovely I said to him. But I wasn't a fool, on that occasion. I lay quiet, by bis side.

Silence.

DUFF Anyway . . .

BETH My skin . . .

DUFF I'm sleeping all right these days.

BETH Was stinging.

DUFF Right thtough the night, every night.

BETH I'd been in the sea.

DUFF Maybe it's something to do with the fishing. Getting to learn more about fish.

BETH Stinging in the sea by myself.

DUFF They're very shy creatures. You've got to woo them. You must never get excited with them. Or flurried. Never.

BETH I knew there must be a hotel near, where we could get some tea.

Silence.

DUFF Anyway . . . luck was on my side for a change. By the time I got out of the park the pubs were open.

Pause.

So I thought I might as well pop in and have a pint. I wanted to tell you. I met some nut in there. First of all I had a word with the landlord. He knows me. Then this nut came in. He ordered a pint and he made a criticism of the beer. I had no patience with it.

BETH But then I thought perhaps the hotel bar will be open. We'll sit in the bar. He'll buy me a drink. What will I order? But what will he order? What will he want? I shall hear him say it. I shall hear his voice. He will ask me what I would like first. Then he'll order the two drinks. I shall hear him do it.

DUFF This beer is piss, he said. Undrinkable. There's nothing wrong with the beer, I said. Yes there is, he said, I just told you what was wrong with it. It's the best beer in the area, I said. No it isn't, this chap said, it's piss. The landlord picked up the mug and had a sip. Good beer, he said. Someone's made a mistake, this fellow said, someone's used this pintpot instead of the boghole.

Pause.

The landlord threw a half a crown on the bar and told him to take it. The pint's only two and three, the man said, I owe you threepence, but I haven't got any change. Give the threepence to your son, the landlord said, with my compliments. I haven't got a son, the man said, I've never had any children. I bet you're not even married, the landlord said. This man said: 'I'm not married. No one'll marry me.'

Pause.

557

Then the man asked the landlord and me if we would have a drink with him. The landlord said he'd have a pint. I didn't answer at first, but the man came over to me and said: 'Have one with *me*. Have one with *me*.'

Pause.

He put down a ten bob note and said he'd have a pint as well.

Silence.

BETH Suddenly I stood. I walked to the shore and into the water. I didn't swim. I don't swim. I let the water billow me. I rested in the water. The waves were very light, delicate. They touched the back of my neck

Silence.

DUFF One day when the weather's good you could go out into the garden and sit down. You'd like that. The open air. I'm often out there. The dog liked it.

Pause.

I've put in some flowers. You'd find it pleasant. Looking at the flowers. You could cut a few if you liked. Bring them in. No one would see you. There's no one there.

Pause.

That's where we're lucky, in my opinion. To live in Mr Sykes' house in peace, no one to bother us. I've thought of inviting one or two people I know from the village in here for a bit of a drink once or twice but I decided against it. It's not necessary.

Pause.

You know what you get quite a lot of out in the garden? Butterflies.

BETH I slipped out of my costume and put on my beachrobe. Underneath I was naked. There wasn't a soul on the beach. Except for an elderly man, far away on a breakwater. I lay down beside him and whispered. Would you like a baby? A child? Of our own? Would be nice.

Pause

DUFF What did you think of that downfall?

Pause.

Of course the youngsters I met under the first tree, during the first shower, they were larking about and laughing. I tried to listen, to find out what they were laughing about, but I couldn't work it out. They were whispering. I tried to listen, to find out what the joke was.

Pause.

Anyway I didn't find out.

Pause.

I was thinking . . . when you were young . . . you didn't laugh much. You were . . . grave.

Silence.

BETH That's why he'd picked such a desolate place. So that I could draw in peace. I had my sketch book

with me. I took it out. I took my drawing pencil out.
But there was nothing to draw. Only the beach, the sea.

Pause.

Could have drawn him. He didn't want it. He laughed.

Pause.

I laughed, with him.

Pause.

I waited for him to laugh, then I would smile, turn
away, he would touch my back, turn me, to him. My
nose . . . creased. I would laugh with him, a little.

Pause.

He laughed. I'm sure of it. So I didn't draw him.

Silence.

DUFF You were a first-rate housekeeper when you
were young. Weren't you? I was very proud. You
never made a fuss, you never got into a state, you
went about your work. He could rely on you. He did.
He trusted you, to run his house, to keep the house
up to the mark, no panic.

Pause.

Do you remember when I took him on that trip to the
north? That long trip. When we got back he thanked
you for looking after the place so well, everything
running like clockwork.

Pause.

You'd missed me. When I came into this room you stopped still. I had to walk all the way over the floor towards you.

Pause.

I touched you.

Pause.

But I had something to say to you, didn't I? I waited, I didn't say it then, but I'd made up my mind to say it, I'd decided I would say it, and I did say it, the next morning. Didn't I?

Pause.

I told you that I'd let you down. I'd been unfaithful to you.

Pause.

You didn't cry. We had a few hours off. We walked up to the pond, with the dog. We stood under the trees for a bit. I didn't know why you'd brought that carrier bag with you. I asked you. I said what's in that bag? It turned out to be bread. You fed the ducks. Then we stood under the trees and looked across the pond.

Pause.

When we got back into this room you put your hands on my face and you kissed me.

BETH But I didn't really want a drink.

Pause.

561

I drew a face in the sand, then a body. The body of a woman. Then the body of a man, close to her, not touching. But they didn't look like anything. They didn't look like human figures. The sand kept on slipping, mixing the contours. I crept close to him and put my head on his arm, and closed my eyes. All those darting red and black flecks, under my eyelid. I moved my cheek on his skin. And all those darting red and black flecks, moving about under my eyelid. I buried my face in his side and shut the light out.

Silence.

DUFF Mr Sykes took to us from the very first interview, didn't he?

Pause.

He said I've got the feeling you'll make a very good team. Do you remember? And that's what we proved to be. No question. I could drive well, I could polish his shoes well, I earned my keep. Turn my hand to anything. He never lacked for anything, in the way of being looked after. Mind you, he was a gloomy bugger.

Pause.

I was never sorry for him, at any time, for his lonely life.

Pause.

That nice blue dress he chose for you, for the house, that was very nice of him. Of course it was in his own interests for you to look good about the house, for guests.

BETH He moved in the sand and put his arm around me.

Silence.

DUFF Do you like me to talk to you?

Pause.

Do you like me to tell you about all the things I've been doing?

Pause.

About all the things I've been thinking?

Pause.

Mmmnn?

Pause.

I think you do.

BETH And cuddled me.

Silence.

DUFF Of course it was in his own interests to see that you were attractively dressed about the house, to give a good impression to his guests.

BETH I caught a bus to the crossroads and then walked down the lane by the old church. It was very quiet, except for birds. There was an old man fiddling about on the cricket pitch, bending. I stood out of the sun, under a tree.

Pause.

I heard the car. He saw me and stopped me. I stayed still. Then the car moved again, came towards me slowly. I moved round the front of it, in the dust. I couldn't see him for the sun, but he was watching me. When I got to the door it was locked. I looked through at him. He leaned over and opened the door. I got in and sat beside him. He smiled at me. Then he reversed, all in one movement, very quickly, quite straight, up the lane to the crossroads, and we drove to the sea.

Pause

DUFF We're the envy of a lot of people, you know, living in this house, having this house all to ourselves. It's too big for two people.

BETH He said he knew a very desolate beach, that no one else in the world knew, and that's where we are going.

DUFF I was very gentle to you. I was kind to you, that day. I knew you'd had a shock, so I was gentle with you. I held your arm on the way back from the pond. You put your hands on my face and kissed me.

BETH All the food I had in my bag I had cooked myself, or prepared myself. I had baked the bread myself.

DUFF The girl herself I considered unimportant. I didn't think it necessary to go into details. I decided against it.

BETH The windows were open but we kept the hood up.

Pause.

DUFF Mr Sykes gave a little dinner party that Friday. He complimented you on your cooking and the service.

Pause.

Two women. That was all. Never seen them before. Probably his mother and sister.

Pause.

They wanted coffee late. I was in bed. I fell asleep. I would have come down to the kitchen to give you a hand but I was too tired.

Pause.

But I woke up when you got into bed. You were out on your feet. You were asleep as soon as you hit the pillow. Your body . . . just fell back.

BETH He was right. It was desolate. There wasn't a soul on the beach.

Silence.

DUFF I had a look over the house the other day. I meant to tell you. The dust is bad. We'll have to polish it up.

Pause.

We could go up to the drawing room, open the windows. I could wash the old decanters. We could have a drink up there one evening, if it's a pleasant evening.

Pause.

I think there's moths. I moved the curtain and they flew out.

Pause.

BETH Of course when I'm older I won't be the same as I am, I won't be what I am, my skirts, my long legs, I'll be older, I won't be the same.

DUFF At least now . . . at least now, I can walk down to the pub in peace and up to the pond in peace, with no one to nag the shit out of me.

Silence.

BETH All it is, you see . . . I said . . . is the lightness of your touch, the lightness of your look, my neck, your eyes, the silence, that is my meaning, the loveliness of my flowers, my hands touching my flowers, that is my meaning.

Pause.

I've watched other people. I've seen them.

Pause.

All the cars zooming by. Men with girls at their sides. Bouncing up and down. They're dolls. They squeak.

Pause.

All the people were squeaking in the hotel bar. The girls had long hair. They were smiling.

DUFF That's what matters, anyway. We're together. That's what matters.

Silence.

BETH But I was up early. There was still plenty to be done and cleared up. I had put the plates in the sink to soak. They had soaked overnight. They were easy to wash. The dog was up. He followed me. Misty morning. Comes from the river.

DUFF This fellow knew bugger all about beer. He didn't know I'd been trained as a cellarman. That's why I could speak with authority.

BETH I opened the door and went out. There was no one about. The sun was shining. Wet, I mean wetness, all over the ground.

DUFF A cellarman is the man responsible. He's the earliest up in the morning. Give the drayman a hand with the barrels. Down the slide through the cellarflaps. Lower them by rope to the racks. Rock them on the belly, put a rim up them, use balance and leverage, hike them up on to the racks.

BETH Still misty, but thinner, thinning.

DUFF The bung is on the vertical, in the bunghole. Spile the bung. Hammer the spile through the centre of the bung. That lets the air through the bung, down the bunghole, lets the beer breathe.

BETH Wetness all over the air. Sunny. Trees like feathers.

DUFF Then you hammer the tap in.

BETH I wore my blue dress.

DUFF Let it stand for three days. Keep wet sacks over the barrels. Hose the cellar floor daily. Hose the barrels daily.

BETH It was a beautiful autumn morning.

DUFF Run water through the pipes to the bar pumps daily.

BETH I stood in the mist.

DUFF Pull off. Pull off. Stop pulling just before you get to the dregs. The dregs'll give you the shits. You've got an ullage barrel. Feed the slops back to the ullage barrel, send them back to the brewery.

BETH In the sun.

DUFF Dip the barrels daily with a brass rod. Know your gallonage. Chalk it up. Then you're tidy. Then you never get caught short.

BETH Then I went back to the kitchen and sat down.

  Pause.

DUFF This chap in the pub said he was surprised to hear it. He said he was surprised to hear about hosing the cellar floor. He said he thought most cellars had a thermostatically controlled cooling system. He said he thought keg beer was fed with oxygen through a cylinder. I said I wasn't talking about keg beer, I was talking about normal draught beer. He said he thought they piped the beer from a tanker into metal containers. I said they may do, but he wasn't talking about the quality of beer I was. He accepted that point.

Pause

BETH The dog sat down by me. I stroked him.
Through the window I could see down into the valley.
I saw children in the valley. They were running through
the grass. They ran up the hill.

Long silence.

DUFF I never saw your face. You were standing by
the windows. One of those black nights. A downfall.
All I could hear was the rain on the glass, smacking
on the glass. You knew I'd come in but you didn't
move. I stood close to you. What were you looking
at? It was black outside. I could just see your shape
in the window, your reflection. There must have been
some kind of light somewhere. Perhaps just your face
reflected, lighter than all the rest. I stood close to you.
Perhaps you were just thinking, in a dream. Without
touching you, I could feel your bottom.

Silence.

BETH I remembered always, in drawing, the basic
principles of shadow and light. Objects intercepting
the light cast shadows. Shadow is deprivation of light.
The shape of the shadow is determined by that of the
object. But not always. Not always directly. Sometimes
it is only indirectly affected by it. Sometimes the cause
of the shadow cannot be found.

Pause.

But I always bore in mind the basic principles of
drawing.

Pause.

So that I never lost track. Or heart.

Pause

DUFF You used to wear a chain round your waist.
On the chain you carried your keys, your thimble,
your notebook, your pencil, your scissors.

Pause.

You stood in the hall and banged the gong.

Pause.

What the bloody hell are you doing banging that
bloody gong?

Pause.

It's bullshit. Standing in an empty hall banging a
bloody gong. There's no one to listen. No one'll hear.
There's not a soul in the house. Except me. There's
nothing for lunch. There's nothing cooked. No stew.
No pie. No greens. No joint. Fuck all.

Pause

BETH So that I never lost track. Even though, even
when, I asked him to turn, to look at me, but he
turned to look at me but I couldn't see his look.

Pause.

I couldn't see whether he was looking at me.

Pause.

Although he had turned. And appeared to be looking at me.

DUFF I took the chain off and the thimble, the keys, the scissors slid off it and clattered down. I booted the gong down the hall. The dog came in. I thought you would come to me, I thought you would come into my arms and kiss me, even . . . offer yourself to me. I would have had you in front of the dog, like a man, in the hall, on the stone, banging the gong, mind you don't get the scissors up your arse, or the thimble, don't worry, I'll throw them for the dog to chase, the thimble will keep the dog happy, he'll play with it with his paws, you'll plead with me like a woman, I'll bang the gong on the floor, if the sound is too flat, lacks resonance, I'll hang it back on its hook, bang you against it swinging, gonging, waking the place up, calling them all for dinner, lunch is up, bring out the bacon, bang your lovely head, mind the dog doesn't swallow the thimble, slam –

   Silence.

BETH He lay above me and looked down at me. He supported my shoulder.

   Pause.

So tender his touch on my neck. So softly his kiss on my cheek.

   Pause.

My hand on his rib.

   Pause.

So sweetly the sand over me. Tiny the sand on my skin.

Pause.

So silent the sky in my eyes. Gently the sound of the tide.

Pause.

Oh my true love I said.

SILENCE

Silence was first presented by the Royal Shakespeare
Company at the Aldwych Theatre, London, on 2 July
1969, with the following cast:

ELLEN	Frances Cuka
RUMSEY	Anthony Bate
BATES	Norman Rodway

Directed by Peter Hall

Characters

ELLEN
a girl in her twenties

RUMSEY
a man of forty

BATES
a man in his middle thirties

Three areas.
A chair in each area.

RUMSEY I walk with my girl who wears a grey blouse when she walks and grey shoes and walks with me readily wearing her clothes considered for me. Her grey clothes.

She holds my arm.

On good evenings we walk through the hills to the top of the hill past the dogs the clouds racing just before dark or as dark is falling when the moon

When it's chilly I stop her and slip her raincoat over her shoulders or rainy slip arms into the arms, she twisting her arms. And talk to her and tell her everything.

She dresses for my eyes.

I tell her my thoughts. Now I am ready to walk, her arm in me her hand in me.

I tell her my life's thoughts, clouds racing. She looks up at me or listens looking down. She stops in mid-sentence, my sentence, to look up at me. Sometimes her hand has slipped from mine, her arm loosened, she walks slightly apart, dog barks.

ELLEN There are two. One who is with me sometimes, and another. He listens to me. I tell him what I know. We walk by the dogs.

Sometimes the wind is so high he does not hear me.
I lead him to a tree, clasp closely to him and whisper
to him, wind going, dogs stop, and he hears me.

But the other hears me.

BATES Caught a bus to the town. Crowds. Lights
round the market, rain and stinking. Showed her the
bumping lights. Took her down around the dumps.
Black roads and girders. She clutching me. This way
the way I bring you. Pubs throw the doors smack into
the night. Cars barking and the lights. She with me,
clutching.

Brought her into this place, my cousin runs it. Undressed
her, placed my hand.

ELLEN I go by myself with the milk to the top, the
clouds racing, all the blue changes, I'm dizzy
sometimes, meet with him under some place.

One time visited his house. He put a light on, it
reflected the window, it reflected in the window.

RUMSEY She walks from the door to the window to
see the way she has come, to confirm that the house
which grew nearer is the same one she stands in, that
the path and the bushes are the same, that the gate is
the same. When I stand beside her and smile at her, she
looks at me and smiles.

BATES How many times standing clenched in the
pissing dark waiting ?

The mud, the cows, the river.

You cross the field out of darkness. You arrive.

You stand breathing before me. You smile.

I put my hands on your shoulders and press. Press the smile off your face.

ELLEN There are two. I turn to them and speak. I look them in their eyes. I kiss them there and say, I look away to smile, and touch them as I turn.

Silence.

RUMSEY I watch the clouds. Pleasant the ribs and tendons of cloud.

I've lost nothing.

Pleasant alone and watch the folding light. My animals are quiet. My heart never bangs. I read in the evenings. There is no one to tell me what is expected or not expected of me. There is nothing required of me.

BATES I'm at my last gasp with this unendurable racket. I kicked open the door and stood before them. Someone called me Grandad and told me to button it. It's they should button it. Were I young . . .

One of them told me I was lucky to be alive, that I would have to bear it in order to pay for being alive, in order to give thanks for being alive.

It's a question of sleep. I need something of it, or how can I remain alive, without any true rest, having no solace, no constant solace, not even any damn inconstant solace.

I am strong, but not as strong as the bastards in the other room, and their tittering bitches, and their music, and their love.

If I changed my life, perhaps, and lived deliberately at night, and slept in the day. But what exactly would I do? What can be meant by living in the dark?

ELLEN Now and again I meet my drinking companion and have a drink with her. She is a friendly woman, quite elderly, quite friendly. But she knows little of me, she could never know much of me, not really, not now. She's funny. She starts talking sexily to me, in the corner, with our drinks. I laugh.

She asks me about my early life, when I was young, never departing from her chosen subject, but I have nothing to tell her about the sexual part of my youth. I'm old, I tell her, my youth was somewhere else, anyway I don't remember. She does the talking anyway.

I like to get back to my room. It has a pleasant view. I have one or two friends, ladies. They ask me where I come from. I say of course from the country. I don't see much of them.

I sometimes wonder if I think. I heard somewhere about how many thoughts go through the brain of a person. But I couldn't remember anything I'd actually thought, for some time.

It isn't something that anyone could ever tell me, could ever reassure me about, nobody could tell, from looking at me, what was happening.

But I'm still quite pretty really, quite nice eyes, nice skin.

BATES *moves to* ELLEN.

BATES Will we meet tonight ?

ELLEN I don't know.

Pause.

BATES Come with me tonight.

ELLEN Where?

BATES Anywhere. For a walk.

Pause.

ELLEN I don't want to walk.

BATES Why not?

Pause.

ELLEN I want to go somewhere else

Pause.

BATES Where?

ELLEN I don't know.

Pause.

BATES What's wrong with a walk ?

ELLEN I don't want to walk.

Pause.

BATES What do you want to do ?

ELLEN I don't know.

Pause.

BATES Do you want to go anywhere else?

ELLEN Yes.

BATES Where?

ELLEN I don't know.

  Pause.

BATES Do you want me to buy you a drink?

ELLEN No.

  Pause.

BATES Come for a walk.

ELLEN No.

  Pause.

BATES All right. I'll take you on a bus to the town.
I know a place. My cousin runs it.

ELLEN No.

  Silence.

RUMSEY It is curiously hot. Sitting weather, I call it.
The weather sits, does not move. Unusual. I shall walk
down to my horse and see how my horse is. He'll
come towards me.

Perhaps he doesn't need me. My visit, my care, will be
like any other visit, any other care. I can't believe it.

BATES I walk in my mind. But can't get out of the
walls, into a wind.

Meadows are walled, and lakes. The sky's a wall.

Once I had a little girl. I took it for walks. I held it by its hand. It looked up at me and said, I see something in a tree, a shape, a shadow. It is leaning down. It is looking at us.

Maybe it's a bird, I said, a big bird, resting. Birds grow tired, after they've flown over the country, up and down in the wind, looking down on all the sights, so sometimes, when they reach a tree, with good solid branches, they rest.

Silence.

ELLEN When I run . . . when I run . . . when I run . . . over the grass

RUMSEY She floats . . . under me. Floating . . . under me.

ELLEN I turn. I turn. I wheel. I glide. I wheel. In stunning light. The horizon moves from the sun. I am crushed by the light.

Silence.

RUMSEY Sometimes I see people. They walk towards me, no, not so, walk in my direction, but never reaching me, turning left, or disappearing, and then reappearing, to disappear into the wood.

So many ways to lose sight of them, then to recapture sight of them. They are sharp at first sight . . . then smudged . . . then lost . . . then glimpsed again . . . then gone.

BATES Funny. Sometimes I press my hand on my forehead, calmingly, feel all the dust drain out, let it go, feel the grit slip away. Funny moment. That calm moment.

ELLEN *moves to* RUMSEY.

ELLEN It's changed. You've painted it. You've made shelves. Everything. It's beautiful.

RUMSEY Can you remember . . . when you were here last?

ELLEN Oh yes.

RUMSEY You were a little girl.

ELLEN I was.
   Pause.

RUMSEY Can you cook now?

ELLEN Shall I cook for you?

RUMSEY Yes.

ELLEN Next time I come. I will.
   Pause.

RUMSEY Do you like music?

ELLEN Yes.

RUMSEY I'll play you music.
   Pause.

Look at your reflection.

ELLEN Where?

RUMSEY In the window.

ELLEN It's very dark outside.

RUMSEY It's high up.

ELLEN Does it get darker the higher you get ?

RUMSEY No.

Silence.

ELLEN Around me sits the night. Such a silence. I can hear myself. Cup my ear. My heart beats in my ear. Such a silence. Is it me? Am I silent or speaking? How can I know? Can I know such things? No one has ever told me. I need to be told things. I seem to be old. Am I old now? No one will tell me. I must find a person to tell me these things.

BATES My landlady asks me in for a drink. Stupid conversation. What are you doing here? Why do you live alone? Where do you come from? What do you do with yourself? What kind of life have you had? You seem fit. A bit grumpy. You can smile, surely, at something? Surely you have smiled, at a thing in your life? At something? Has there been no pleasantness in your life? No kind of loveliness in your life? Are you nothing but a childish old man, suffocating himself?

I've had all that. I've got all that. I said.

ELLEN He sat me on his knee, by the window, and asked if he could kiss my right cheek. I nodded he could. He did. Then he asked, if, having kissed my right, he could do the same with my left. I said yes. He did.

Silence.

RUMSEY She was looking down. I couldn't hear what she said.

BATES I can't hear you. Yes you can, I said.

RUMSEY What are you saying? Look at me, she said.

BATES I didn't. I didn't hear you, she said. I didn't hear what you said.

RUMSEY But I am looking at you. It's your head that's bent.

Silence.

BATES The little girl looked up at me. I said: at night horses are quite happy. They stand about, then after a bit of a time they go to sleep. In the morning they wake up, snort a bit, canter, sometimes, and eat. You've no cause to worry about them.

ELLEN *moves to* RUMSEY.

RUMSEY Find a young man.

ELLEN There aren't any.

RUMSEY Don't be stupid.

ELLEN I don't like them.

RUMSEY You're stupid.

ELLEN I hate them.

Pause.

RUMSEY Find one.

Silence.

BATES For instance, I said, those shapes in the trees, you'll find they're just birds, resting after a long journey.

ELLEN I go up with the milk. The sky hits me. I walk in this wind to collide with them waiting.

There are two. They halt to laugh and bellow in the yard. They dig and punch and cackle where they stand. They turn to move, look round at me to grin. I turn my eyes from one, and from the other to him.

Silence.

BATES From the young people's room – silence. Sleep? Tender love?

It's of no importance.

Silence.

RUMSEY I walk with my girl who wears –

BATES Caught a bus to the town. Crowds. Lights round.

Silence.

ELLEN After my work each day I walk back through people but I don't notice them. I'm not in a dream or anything of that sort. On the contrary. I'm quite wide awake to the world around me. But not to the people. There must be something in them to notice, to pay attention to, something of interest in them. In fact I know there is. I'm certain of it. But I pass through them noticing nothing. It is only later, in my room, that I remember. Yes, I remember. But I'm never sure that what I remember is of today or of yesterday or of a long time ago.

And then often it is only half things I remember, half things, beginnings of things.

My drinking companion for the hundredth time asked me if I'd ever been married. This time I told her I had. Yes, I told her I had. Certainly. I can remember the wedding.

Silence,

RUMSEY On good evenings we walk through the hills to the top of the hill past the dogs the clouds racing

ELLEN Sometimes the wind is so high he does not hear me.

BATES Brought her into this place, my cousin runs it.

ELLEN all the blue changes, I'm dizzy sometimes

Silence.

RUMSEY that the path and the bushes are the same, that the gate is the same

BATES You cross the field out of darkness.
You arrive.

ELLEN I turn to them and speak.

Silence,

RUMSEY and watch the folding light.

BATES and their tittering bitches, and their music, and their love.

ELLEN They ask me where I come from. I say of course from the country.

Silence.

BATES Come with me tonight.

ELLEN Where?

BATES Anywhere. For a walk.

Silence.

RUMSEY My visit, my care, will be like any other visit, any other care.

BATES I see something in a tree, a shape, a shadow.

Silence.

ELLEN When I run . . .

RUMSEY Floating . . . under me.

ELLEN The horizon moves from the sun.

Silence.

RUMSEY They are sharp at first sight . . . then smudged . . . then lost . . . then glimpsed again . . . then gone.

BATES feel all the dust drain out, let it go, feel the grit slip away.

ELLEN I look them in their eyes.

Silence.

RUMSEY It's high up.

ELLEN Does it get darker the higher you get?

RUMSEY No.

Silence.

ELLEN Around me sits the night. Such a silence.

BATES I've had all that. I've got all that. I said.

ELLEN I nodded he could.

Silence.

RUMSEY She was looking down.

BATES Yes you can, I said.

RUMSEY What are you saying ?

BATES I didn't hear you, she said.

RUMSEY But I am looking at you. It's your head that's bent.

Silence.

BATES In the morning they wake up, snort a bit, canter, sometimes, and eat.

Silence.

ELLEN There aren't any.

RUMSEY Don't be stupid.

ELLEN I don't like them.

RUMSEY You're stupid.

Silence.

BATES For instance, I said, those shapes in the trees.

ELLEN I walk in this wind to collide with them waiting.

Silence.

BATES Sleep? Tender love? It's of no importance.

ELLEN I kiss them there and say

Silence.

RUMSEY I walk

Silence.

BATES Caught a bus

Silence.

ELLEN Certainly. I can remember the wedding.

Silence.

RUMSEY I walk with my girl who wears a grey blouse

BATES Caught a bus to the town. Crowds. Lights round the market

Long silence.

Fade lights.

MONOLOGUE

Monologue was first transmitted on on BBC Television on 13 April 1973.

MAN   Henry Woolf

Directed by Christopher Morahan

MAN *alone in a chair.*

He refers to another chair, which is empty.

MAN I think I'll nip down to the games room. Stretch my legs. Have a game of ping pong. What about you? Fancy a game? How would you like a categorical thrashing? I'm willing to accept any challenge, any stakes, any gauntlet you'd care to fling down. What have you done with your gauntlets, by the way? In fact, *while we're at it*, what happened to your motorbike?

    Pause.

You looked bold in black. The only thing I didn't like was your face, too white, the face, stuck between your black helmet and your black hair and your black motoring jacket, kind of aghast, blatantly vulnerable, veering towards pitiful. Of course, you weren't cut out to be a motorbikist, it went against your nature, I never understood what you were getting at. What is certain is that it didn't work, it never convinced me, it never got you on to any top shelf with me. You should have been black, you should have had a black face, then you'd be getting somewhere, really making a go of it.

Pause.

I often had the impression . . . often . . . that you two were actually brother and sister, some kind of link-up, some kind of identical shimmer, deep down in your characters, an inkling, no more, that at one time you had shared the same pot. But of course she was black. Black as the Ace of Spades. And a life-lover, to boot.

Pause.

All the same, you and I, even then, never mind the weather, weren't we, we were always available for net practice, at the drop of a hat, or a game of fives, or a walk and talk through the park, or a couple of rounds of putting before lunch, given fair to moderate conditions, and no burdensome commitments.

Pause.

The thing I like, I mean quite immeasurably, is this kind of conversation, this kind of exchange, this class of mutual reminiscence.

Pause.

Sometimes I think you've forgotten the black girl, the ebony one. Sometimes I think you've forgotten me.

Pause.

You haven't forgotten *me*. Who was your best mate, who was your truest mate? You introduced me to Webster and Tourneur, admitted, but who got you going on Tristan Tzara, Breton, Giacometti and all that lot? Not to mention Louis-Ferdinand Celine, now out of favour. And John Dos. Who bought you both all those custard tins cut price? I say both. I was the best friend either of you ever had and I'm still prepared to prove it, I'm still prepared to wrap my braces round anyone's neck, in your defence.

Pause.

Now you're going to say you loved her soul and I loved her body. You're going to trot that old one out. I know you were much more beautiful than me, much more *aquiline*, I know *that*, that I'll give you, more *ethereal*, more thoughtful, *slyer*, while I had both feet firmly planted on the deck. But I'll tell you one thing you don't know. She loved my soul. It was my soul she loved.

Pause.

You never say what you're ready for now. You're not even ready for a game of ping pong. You're incapable of saying of what it is you're capable, where your relish lies, where you're sharp, excited, why you never are capable . . . never are . . . capable of exercising a crisp and full-bodied appraisal of the buzzing possibilities of your buzzing brain cells. You often, I'll be frank, act as if you're dead, as if the Balls Pond Road and the lovely ebony lady never existed, as if the rain in the light on the pavements in the twilight never existed, as if our sporting and intellectual life never was.

Pause.

She was tired. She sat down. She was tired. The journey. The rush hour. The weather, so unpredictable. She'd put on a woollen dress because the morning was chilly, but the day had changed, totally, totally changed. She cried. You jumped up like a . . . those things, forgot the name, monkey on a box, *jack in a box*, held her hand, made her tea, a rare burst. Perhaps the change in the weather had gone to your head.

Pause.

I loved her body. Not that, between ourselves, it's one way or another a thing of any importance. My spasms could be your spasms. Who's to tell or care?

Pause.

Well. . . she did . . . can . . . could . . .

Pause.

We all walked, arm in arm, through the long grass, over the bridge, sat outside the pub in the sun by the river, the pub was shut.

Pause.

Did anyone notice us? Did you see anyone looking at us?

Pause.

Touch my body, she said to you. You did. Of course you did. You'd be a bloody fool if you didn't. You'd have been a bloody fool if you hadn't. It was perfectly *normal*.

Pause.

That was behind the partition.

Pause.

I brought her to see you, after you'd pissed off to live in Notting Hill Gate. Naturally. They all end up there. I'll never end up there. I'll never end up on that side of the Park.

Pause.

Sitting there with your record player, growing bald, Beethoven, cocoa, cats. That really dates it. The cocoa dates it. It was your detachment was dangerous. I knew it of course like the back of my hand. That was the web my darling black darling hovered in, wavered in, my black *moth*. She stuttered in that light, your slightly sullen, non-committal, deadly dangerous light. But it's a fact of life. The ones that keep silent are the best off.

Pause.

As for me, I've always liked simple love scenes, the classic set-ups, the sweet. . . the sweet. . . the sweet farewell at Paddington Station. My collar turned up. Her soft cheeks. Standing close to me, legs under her raincoat, the platform, her cheeks, her hands, nothing like the sound of steam to keep love warm, to keep it moist, to bring it to the throat, my ebony love, she smiles at me, I touched her.

Pause.

I feel for you. Even if you feel nothing . . . for me. I feel for you, old chap.

Pause.

I keep busy in the *mind*, and that's why I'm still sparking, get it? I've got a hundred per cent more energy in me now than when I was twenty-two. When I was twenty-two I slept twenty-four hours a day. And twenty-two hours a day at twenty-four. Work it out for yourself. But now I'm sparking, at my peak, *up here*, two thousand revolutions a second, every living hour of the day and night. I'm a front runner. My watchword is vigilance. I'm way past mythologies, left them all behind, cocoa, sleep, Beethoven, cats, rain, black girls, bosom pals, literature, custard. You'll say I've been talking about nothing else all night, but can't you see, you bloody fool, that I can *afford* to do it, can't you appreciate the irony? Even if you're too dim to catch the irony in the words themselves, the words I have chosen myself, quite scrupulously, and with intent, you can't miss the irony in the tone of *voice*!

Pause.

What you are in fact witnessing is freedom. I no longer participate in holy ceremony. The crap is cut.

Silence.

You should have had a black face, that was your mistake. You could have made a going concern out of it, you could have chalked it up in the book, you could have had two black kids.

Pause.

I'd have died for them.

Pause.

I'd have been their uncle.

Pause.

I am their uncle.

Pause.

I'm your children's uncle.

Pause.

I'll take them out, tell them jokes.

Pause.

I love your children.

FAMILY VOICES

Family Voices first published by
Next Editions 1981
© Fraser52 Limited, 1981

Family Voices was first broadcast on BBC Radio 3 on 22 January 1981. The cast was as follows:

VOICE 1	Michael Kitchen
VOICE 2	Peggy Ashcroft
VOICE 3	Mark Dignam

Directed by Peter Hall

The play was presented in a 'platform performance' by the National Theatre, London, on 13 February 1981, with the same cast and director. The decor was by John Bury.

Family Voices was subsequently presented with *A Kind of Alaska* and *Victoria Station* as part of the triple bill *Other Places,* first performed at the National Theatre, London, on 14 October 1982. The cast was as follows:

VOICE 1	Nigel Havers
VOICE 2	Anna Massey
VOICE 3	Paul Rogers

Directed by Peter Hall

VOICE 1 I am having a very nice time.

The weather is up and down, but surprisingly warm, on the whole, more often than not.

I hope you're feeling well, and not as peaky as you did, the last time I saw you.

No, you didn't feel peaky, you felt perfectly well, you simply looked peaky.

Do you miss me?

I am having a very nice time and I hope you are glad of that.

At the moment I am dead drunk.

I had five pints in The Fishmongers Arms tonight, followed by three double Scotches, and literally rolled home.

When I say home I can assure you that my room is extremely pleasant. So is the bathroom. Extremely pleasant. I have some very pleasant baths indeed in the bathroom. So does everybody else in the house. They all lie quite naked in the bath and have very pleasant baths indeed. All the people in the house go about saying what a superb bath and bathroom the one we share is, they go about telling literally everyone they meet what lovely baths you can get in this place, more or less unparalleled, to put it bluntly.

It's got a lot to do with the landlady, who is a Mrs Withers, a person who turns out be an utterly charming person, of impeccable credentials.

When I said I was drunk I was of course making a joke.

I bet you laughed.

Mother?

Did you get the joke? You know I never touch alcohol.

I like being in this enormous city, all by myself. I expect to make friends in the not too distant future.

I expect to make girlfriends too.

I expect to meet a very nice girl. Having met her, I shall bring her home to meet my mother.

I like walking in this enormous city, all by myself. It's fun to know no one at all. When I pass people in the street they don't realise that I don't know them from Adam. They know other people and even more other people know them, so they naturally think that even if I don't know them I know the other people. So they look at me, they try to catch my eye, they expect me to speak. But as I do not know them I do not speak. Nor do I ever feel the slightest temptation to do so.

You see, Mother, I am not lonely, because all that has ever happened to me is with me, keeps me company;

my childhood, for example, through which you, my mother, and he, my father, guided me.

I get on very well with my landlady, Mrs Withers. She tells me I am her solace. I have a drink with her at lunchtime and another one at teatime and then take her for a couple in the evening at The Fishmongers Arms.

She was in the Women's Air Force in the Second World War. Don't drop a bollock, Charlie, she's fond of saying, call him Flight Sergeant and he'll be happy as a pig in shit.

You'd really like her, Mother.

I think it's dawn. I can see it coming up. Another day. A day I warmly welcome. And so I shall end this letter to you, my dear Mother, with my love.

VOICE 2 Darling. Where are you? The flowers are wonderful here. The blooms. You so loved them. Why do you never write?

I think of you and wonder how you are. Do you ever think of me? Your mother? Ever? At all?

Have you changed your address?

Have you made friends with anyone? A nice boy? Or a nice girl?

There are so many nice boys and nice girls about. But please don't get mixed up with the other sort. They can land you in such terrible trouble. And you'd hate it so. You're so scrupulous, so particular.

I often think that I would love to live happily ever after with you and your young wife. And she would be such a lovely wife to you and I would have the occasional dinner with you both. A dinner I would be quite happy to cook myself, should you both be tired after your long day, as I'm sure you will be.

I sometimes walk the cliff path and think of you. I think of the times you walked the cliff path, with your father, with cheese sandwiches. Didn't you? You both sat on the clifftop and ate my cheese sandwiches together. Do you remember our little joke? Munch, munch. We had a damn good walk, your father would say. You mean you had a good munch munch, I would say. And you would both laugh.

Darling. I miss you. I gave birth to you. Where are you?

I wrote to you three months ago, telling you of your father's death. Did you receive my letter?

VOICE 1 I'm not at all sure that I like the people in this house, apart from Mrs Withers and her daughter, Jane. Jane is a schoolgirl who works hard at her homework.

She keeps her nose to the grindstone. This I find impressive. There's not too much of that about these days. But I'm not so sure about the other people in this house.

One is an old man.

The one who is an old man retires early. He is bald.

The other is a woman who wears red dresses.

The other one is another man.

He is big. He is much bigger than the other man. His hair is black. He has black eyebrows and black hair on the back of his hands.

I ask Mrs Withers about them but she will talk of nothing but her days in the Women's Air Force in the Second World War.

I have decided that Jane is not Mrs Withers' daughter but her grand-daughter. Mrs Withers is seventy. Jane is fifteen. That I am convinced is the truth.

At night I hear whispering from the other rooms and do not understand it. I hear steps on the stairs but do not dare go out to investigate.

VOICE 2 As your father grew closer to his death he spoke more and more of you, with tenderness and bewilderment. I consoled him with the idea that you had left home to make him proud of you. I think I succeeded in this. One of his last sentences was: 'Give him a slap on the back from me. Give him a slap on the back from me.'

VOICE 1 I have made a remarkable discovery. The old man who is bald and who retires early is named Withers. Benjamin Withers. Unless it is simply a coincidence it must mean that he is a relation.

I asked Mrs Withers what the truth of this was. She poured herself a gin and looked at it before she drank it. Then she looked at me and said: 'You are my little pet.

615

I've always wanted a little pet but I've never had one and now I've got one.'

Sometimes she gives me a cuddle, as if she were my mother.

But I haven't forgotten that I have a mother and that you are my mother.

VOICE 2 Sometimes I wonder if you remember that you have a mother.

VOICE 1 Something has happened. The woman who wears red dresses stopped me and asked me into her room for a cup of tea. I went into her room. It was far bigger than I had expected, with sofas and curtains and veils and shrouds and rugs and soft material all over the walls, dark blue. Jane was sitting on a sofa doing her homework, by the look of it. I was invited to sit on the same sofa. Tea had already been made and stood ready, in a china teaset, of a most elegant design. I was given a cup. So was Jane, who smiled at me. I haven't introduced myself, the woman said, my name is Lady Withers. Jane sipped her tea with her legs up on the sofa. Her stockinged toes came to rest on my thigh. It wasn't the biggest sofa in the world. Lady Withers sat opposite us on a substantially bigger sofa. Her dress, I decided, wasn't red but pink. Jane was in green, apart from her toes, which were clad in black. Lady Withers asked me about you, Mother. She asked me about my mother. I said, with absolute conviction, that you were the best mother in the world. She asked me to call her Lally. And to call Jane Jane. I said I did

call Jane Jane. Jane gave me a bun. I think it was a
bun. Lady Withers bit into her bun. Jane bit into her
bun, her toes now resting on my lap. Lady Withers
seemed to be enjoying her bun, on her sofa. She
finished it and picked up another. I had never seen so
many buns. One quick glance told me they were perched
on cakestands, all over the room. Lady Withers went
through her second bun with no trouble at all and was
at once on to another. Jane, on the other hand, chewed
almost dreamily at her bun and when a currant was
left stranded on her upper lip she licked it off, without
haste. I could not reconcile this with the fact that her
toes were quite restless, even agitated. Her mouth,
eating, was measured, serene; her toes, not eating,
were agitated, highly strung, some would say
hysterical. My bun turned out to be rock solid. I bit
into it, it jumped out of my mouth and bounced into
my lap. Jane's feet caught it. It calmed her toes down.
She juggled the bun, with some expertise, along them.
I recalled that, in an early exchange between us, she
had told me she wanted to be an acrobat.

VOICE 2 Darling. Where are you? Why do you never
write? Nobody knows your whereabouts. Nobody
knows if you are alive or dead. Nobody can find you.
Have you changed your name?

If you are alive you are a monster. On his deathbed
your father cursed you. He cursed me too, to tell the
truth. He cursed everyone in sight. Except that you
were not in sight. I do not blame you entirely for your
father's ill humour, but your absence and silence were

a great burden on him, a weariness to him. He died in lamentation and oath. Was that your wish? Now I am alone, apart from Millie, who sometimes comes over from Dover. She is some consolation. Her eyes well with tears when she speaks of you, your dear sister's eyes well with tears. She has made a truly happy marriage and has a lovely little boy. When he is older he will want to know where his uncle is. What shall we say?

Or perhaps you will arrive here in a handsome new car, one day, in the not too distant future, in a nice new suit, quite out of the blue, and hold me in your arms.

VOICE 1 Lady Withers stood up. As Jane is doing her homework, she said, perhaps you would care to leave and come again another day. Jane withdrew her feet, my bun clasped between her two big toes. Yes of course, I said, unless Jane would like me to help her with her homework. No thank you, said Lady Withers, I shall help her with her homework.

What I didn't say is that I am thinking of offering myself out as a tutor. I consider that I would make an excellent tutor, to the young, in any one of a number of subjects. Jane would be an ideal pupil. She possesses a true love of learning. That is the sense of her one takes from her every breath, her every sigh and exhalation. When she turns her eyes upon you you see within her eyes, raw, untutored, unexercised but willing, a deep love of learning.

These are midnight thoughts, Mother, although the time is ten twenty-three, precisely.

VOICE 2 Darling?

VOICE 1 While I was lying in my bath this afternoon, thinking on these things, there was apparently a knock on the front door. The man with black hair apparently opened the door. Two women stood on the doorstep. They said they were my mother and my sister, and asked for me. He denied knowledge of me. No, he had not heard of me. No, there was no one of that name resident. This was a family house, no strangers admitted. No, they got on very well, thank you very much, without intruders. I suggest, he said, that you both go back to where you come from, and stop bothering innocent hardworking people with your slanders and your libels, these all too predictable excrescences of the depraved mind at the end of its tether. I can smell your sort a mile off and I am quite prepared to put you both on a charge of malicious mischief, insulting behaviour and vagabondage, in other words wandering around on doorsteps knowingly, without any visible means of support. So piss off out of it before I call a copper.

I was lying in my bath when the door opened. I thought I had locked it. My name's Riley, he said, How's the bath? Very nice, I said. You've got a well-knit yet slender frame, he said, I thought you only a snip, I never imagined you would be as well-knit and slender as I now see you are. Oh thank you, I said. Don't thank me, he said, it's God you have to thank.

Or your mother. I've just dismissed a couple of imposters at the front door. We'll get no more shit from that quarter. He then sat on the edge of the bath and recounted to me what I've just recounted to you.

It interests me that my father wasn't bothered to make the trip.

VOICE 2 I hear your father's step on the stair. I hear his cough. But his step and his cough fade. He does not open the door.

Sometimes I think I have always been sitting like this. I sometimes think I have always been sitting like this, alone by an indifferent fire, curtains closed, night, winter.

You see, I have my thoughts too. Thoughts no one else knows I have, thoughts none of my family ever knew I had. But I write of them to you now, wherever you are.

What I mean is that when, for example, I was washing your hair, with the most delicate shampoo, and rinsing, and then drying your hair so gently with my soft towel, so that no murmur came from you, of discomfort or unease, and then looked into your eyes, and saw you look into mine, knowing that you wanted no one else, no one at all, knowing that you were entirely happy in my arms, I knew also, for example, that I was at the same time silting by an indifferent fire, alone in winter, in eternal night without you.

VOICE 1 Lady Withers plays the piano. They were sitting, the three women, about the room. About the room were bottles of a vin rosé, of a pink I shall never

620

forget. They sipped their wine from such lovely glass, an elegance of gesture and grace I thought long dead. Lady Withers wore a necklace around her alabaster neck, a neck amazingly young. She played Schumann. She smiled at me. Mrs Withers and Jane smiled at me. I took a seat. I took it and sat in it. I am in it. I will never leave it.

Oh Mother, I have found my home, my family. Little did I ever dream I could know such happiness.

VOICE 2 Perhaps I should forget all about you. Perhaps I should curse you as your father cursed you. Oh I pray, I pray your life is a torment to you. I wait for your letter begging me to come to you. I'll spit on it.

VOICE 1 Mother, Mother, I've had the most unpleasant, the most mystifying encounter, with the man who calls himself Mr Withers. Will you give me your advice?

Come in here, son, he called. Look sharp. Don't mess about. I haven't got all night. I went in. A jug. A basin. A bicycle.

You know where you are? he said. You're in my room. It's not Euston Station. Get me? It's a true oasis.

This is the only room in this house where you can pick up a caravanserai to all points West. Compris? Comprende? Get me? Are you prepared to follow me down the mountain? Look at me. My name's Withers. I'm there or thereabouts. Follow? Embargo on all duff terminology. With me? Embargo on all things redundant. All areas in that connection verboten. You're in a disease-ridden land, boxer. Keep your weight on all the left feet you can lay your hands on. Keep dancing. The old foxtrot is the classical response but that's not the response I'm talking about. Nor am I talking about the other response. Up the slaves. Get me? This is a place of creatures, up and down stairs. Creatures of the rhythmic splits, the rhythmic sideswipes, the rums and roulettes, the macaroni tatters, the dumplings in jam mayonnaise, a catapulting ordure of gross and ramshackle shenanigans, open-ended paraphernalia. Follow me? It all adds up. It's before you and behind you. I'm the only saviour of the grace you find yourself wanting in. Mind how you go. Look sharp. Get my drift? Don't let it get too mouldy. Watch the mould. Get the feel of it, sonny, get the density. Look at me.

And I did.

VOICE 2 I am ill.

VOICE 1 It was like looking into a pit of molten lava, Mother. One look was enough for me.

VOICE 2 Come to me.

VOICE 1 I joined Mrs Withers for a Campari and soda in the kitchen. She spoke of her youth. I was a right titbit, she said. I was like a piece of plum duff. They used to come from miles to try their luck. I fell head over heels with a man in the Fleet Air Arm. He adored me. They had him murdered because they didn't want us to know happiness. I could have married him and had tons of sons. But oh no. He went down with his ship. I heard it on the wireless.

VOICE 2 I wait for you.

VOICE I Later that night Riley and I shared a cup of
cocoa in his quarters. I like slender lads, Riley said.
Slender but strong. I've never made any secret of it.
But I've had to restrain myself, I've had to keep a tight
rein on my inclinations. That's because my deepest
disposition is towards religion. I've always been a
deeply religious man. You can imagine the tension this
creates in my soul. I walk about in a constant state of
spiritual, emotional, psychological and physical tension.
It's breathtaking, the discipline I'm called upon to exert.
My lust is unimaginably violent but it goes against my
best interests,which are to keep on the right side of
God. I'm a big man, as you see, I could crush a slip
of a lad such as you to death, I mean the death that is
love, the death I understand love to be. But meet it is
that I keep those desires shackled in handcuffs and
leg-irons. I'm good at that sort of thing because I'm a
policeman by trade. And I'm highly respected. I'm
highly respected both in the force and in church. The
only place where I'm not highly respected is in this
house. They don't give a shit for me here. Although
I've always been a close relation. Of a sort. I'm a fine
tenor but they never invite me to sing. I might as well
be living in the middle of the Sahara Desert. There are
too many women here, that's the trouble. And it's no
use talking to Baldy. He's well away. He lives in another
area, best known to himself. I like health and strength
and intelligent conversation. That's why I took a fancy
to you, chum, apart from the fact that I fancy you. I've
got no one to talk to. These women treat me like a
leper. Even though I am a relation. Of a sort.

623

What relation?

Is Lady Withers Jane's mother or sister?

If either is the case why isn't Jane called Lady Jane Withers? Or perhaps she is. Or perhaps neither is the case? Or perhaps Mrs Withers is actually the Honourable Mrs Withers? But if that is the case what does that make Mr Withers? And which Withers is he anyway? I mean what relation is he to the rest of the Witherses? And who is Riley?

But if you find me bewildered, anxious, confused, uncertain and afraid, you also find me content. My life possesses shape. The house has a very warm atmosphere, as you have no doubt gleaned. And as you have no doubt noted from my account I talk freely to all its inhabitants, with the exception of Mr Withers, to whom no one talks, to whom no one refers, with evidently good reason. But I rarely leave the house. No one seems to leave the house. Riley leaves the house but rarely. He must be a secret policeman. Jane continues to do a great deal of homework while not apparently attending any school. Lady Withers never leaves the house. She has guests. She receives guests. Those are the steps I hear on the stairs at night.

VOICE 3 I know your mother has written to you to tell you that I am dead. I am not dead. I am very far from being dead, although lots of people have wished me dead, from time immemorial, you especially. It is you who have prayed for my death, from time immemorial. I have heard your prayers. They ring in my ears.

Prayers yearning for my death. But I am not dead.

Well, that is not entirely true, not entirely the case. I'm lying. I'm leading you up the garden path, I'm playing about, I'm having my bit of fun, that's what. Because I am dead. As dead as a doornail. I'm writing to you from my grave. A quick word for old time's sake. Just to keep in touch. An old hullo out of the dark. A last kiss from Dad.

I'll probably call it a day after this canter. Not much more to say. All a bit of a sweat. Why am I taking the trouble? Because of you, I suppose, because you were such a loving son. I'm smiling, as I lie in this glassy grave.

Do you know why I use the word glassy? Because I can see out of it.

Lots of love, son. Keep up the good work.

There's only one thing bothers me, to be quite frank. While there is, generally, absolute silence everywhere, absolute silence throughout all the hours, I still hear, occasionally, a dog barking. I hear this dog. Oh, it frightens me.

VOICE 1 They have decided on a name for me. They call me Bobo. Good morning, Bobo, they say, or, See you in the morning, Bobo, or, Don't drop a goolie, Bobo, or, Don't forget the diver, Bobo, or, Keep your eye on the ball, Bobo, or, Keep this side of the tramlines, Bobo, or, How's the lead in your pencil, Bobo, or, How's tricks in the sticks, Bobo, or, Don't get too much gum in your gumboots, Bobo.

The only person who does not call me Bobo is the old man. He calls me nothing. I call him nothing. I don't see him. He keeps to his room. I don't go near it. He is old and will die soon.

VOICE 2 The police are looking for you. You may remember that you are still under twenty-one. They have issued your precise description to all the organs. They will not rest, they assure me, until you are found. I have stated my belief that you are in the hands of underworld figures who are using you as a male prostitute. I have declared in my affidavit that you have never possessed any strength of character whatsoever and that you are palpably susceptible to even the most blatant form of flattery and blandishment. Women were your downfall, even as a nipper. I haven't forgotten Françoise the French maid or the woman who masqueraded under the title of governess, the infamous Miss Carmichael. You will be found, my boy, and no mercy will be shown to you.

VOICE 1 I'm coming back to you, Mother, to hold you in my arms.

I am coming home.

I am coming also to clasp my father's shoulder. Where is the old boy? I'm longing to have a word with him. Where is he? I've looked in all the usual places, including the old summerhouse, but I can't find him. Don't tell me he's left home at his age? That would be inexpressibly skittish a gesture, on his part. What have you done with him, Mother?

VOICE 2 I'll tell you what, my darling. I've given you up as a very bad job. Tell me one last thing. Do you think the word love means anything?

VOICE 1 I am on my way back to you. I am about to make the journey back to you. What will you say to me?

VOICE 3 I have so much to say to you. But I am quite dead. What I have to say to you will never be said.

A KIND OF ALASKA

A Kind of Alaska was first published in
Other Places in 1982.
It was first performed in
a triple bill, Other Places, by the National
Theatre on 14 October 1982,
and was subsequently published on its
own, published in 1983.
A Kind of Alaska, pp. 5-9

A Kind of Alaska was presented with *Victoria Station* and *Family Voices* as part of the triple bill *Other Places,* first performed at the National Theatre, London, on 14 October 1982 with the following cast:

DEBORAH   Judi Dench
HORNBY   Paul Rogers
PAULINE   Anna Massey

Directed by Peter Hall

It was subsequently presented with *Victoria Station* and *One for the Road* at the Duchess Theatre, London, on 7 March 1985 with the following cast:

DEBORAH   Dorothy Tutin
HORNBY   Colin Blakely
PAULINE   Susan Engel

Directed by Kenneth Ives

It was produced by Central Television in December 1984 with the following cast:

DEBORAH   Dorothy Tutin
HORNBY   Paul Scofield
PAULINE   Susan Engel

Directed by Kenneth Ives

Note

In the winter of 1916–17, there spread over Europe, and subsequently over the rest of the world, an extraordinary epidemic illness which presented itself in innumerable forms – as delirium, mania, trances, coma, sleep, insomnia, restlessness, and states of Parkinsonism. It was eventually identified by the great physician Constantin von Economo and named by him *encephalitis lethargica,* or sleeping sickness.

Over the next ten years almost five million people fell victim to the disease of whom more than a third died. Of the survivors some escaped almost unscathed, but the majority moved into states of deepening illness. The worst affected sank into singular states of 'sleep' – conscious of their surroundings but motionless, speechless, and without hope or will, confined to asylums or other institutions.

Fifty years later, with the development of the remarkable drug L-DOPA, they erupted into life once more.

Characters

DEBORAH

HORNBY

PAULINE

*A woman in a white bed. Mid-forties. She sits up
against high-banked pillows, stares ahead.*

A table and two chairs. A window.

A man in a dark suit sits at the table. Early sixties.

The woman's eyes move. She slowly looks about her.

Her gaze passes over the man and on. He watches her.

She stares ahead, still.

She whispers.

DEBORAH Something is happening.

   Silence.

HORNBY Do you recognise me?

   Silence.

Do you know me?

   Silence.

Can you hear me?

   She does not look at him.

DEBORAH Are you speaking?

HORNBY Yes.

Pause.

Do you know who I am?

Pause.

Who am I?

DEBORAH No one hears what I say. No one is listening to me.

Pause.

HORNBY Do you know who I am?

Pause.

Who am I?

DEBORAH You are no one.

Pause.

Who is it? It is miles away. The rain is falling. I will get wet.

Pause.

I can't get to sleep. The dog keeps turning about. I think he's dreaming. He wakes me up, but not himself up. He's my best dog though. I talk French.

Pause.

HORNBY I would like you to listen to me.

Pause.

You have been asleep for a very long time. You have now woken up. We are here to care for you.

Pause.

You have been asleep for a very long time. You are older, although you do not know that. You are still young, but older.

Pause.

DEBORAH Something is happening.

HORNBY You have been asleep. You have awoken. Can you hear me? Do you understand me?

She looks at him for the first time.

DEBORAH Asleep?

Pause.

I do not remember that.

Pause.

People have been looking at me. They have been touching me. I spoke, but I don't think they heard what I said.

Pause.

What language am I speaking? I speak French, I know that. Is this French?

Pause.

I've not seen Daddy today. He's funny. He makes me laugh. He runs with me. We play with balloons.

Pause.

Where is he?

Pause.

I think it's my birthday soon.

Pause.

No, no. No, no. I sleep like other people. No more no less. Why should I? If I sleep late my mother wakes me up. There are things to do.

Pause.

If I have been asleep, why hasn't Mummy woken me up?

HORNBY I have woken you up.

DEBORAH But I don't know you.

Pause.

Where is everyone? Where is my dog? Where are my sisters? Last night Estelle was wearing my dress. But I said she could.

Pause.

I am cold.

HORNBY How old are you?

DEBORAH I am twelve. No. I am sixteen. I am seven.

Pause.

I don't know. Yes. I know. I am fourteen. I am fifteen. I'm lovely fifteen.

Pause.

A KIND OF ALASKA

You shouldn't have brought me here. My mother will ask me where I've been.

Pause.

You shouldn't have touched me like that. I shan't tell my mother. I shouldn't have touched you like that.

Pause.

Oh Jack.

Pause.

It's time I was up and about. All those dogs are making such a racket. I suppose Daddy's feeding them. Is Estelle going to marry that boy from Townley Street? The ginger boy? Pauline says he's got nothing between his ears. Thick as two planks. I've given it a good deal of rather more mature thought and I've decided she should not marry him. Tell her not to marry him. She'll listen to you.

Pause.

Daddy?

HORNBY She didn't marry him.

DEBORAH Didn't?

Pause.

It would be a great mistake. It would ruin her life.

HORNBY She didn't marry him.

Silence.

641

DEBORAH I've seen this room before. What room is this? It's not my bedroom. My bedroom has blue lilac on the walls. The sheets are soft, pretty. Mummy kisses me.

Pause.

This is not my bedroom.

HORNBY You have been in this room for a long time. You have been asleep. You have now woken up.

DEBORAH You shouldn't have brought me here. What are you saying? Did I ask you to bring me here? Did I make eyes at you? Did I show desire for you? Did I let you peep up my skirt? Did I flash my teeth? Was I as bold as brass? Perhaps I've forgotten.

HORNBY I didn't bring you here. Your mother and father brought you here.

DEBORAH My father? My mother?

Pause.

Did they bring me to you as a sacrifice? Did they sacrifice me to you?

Pause.

No, no. You stole me . . . in the night.

Pause.

Have you had your way with me?

HORNBY I am here to take care of you.

DEBORAH They all say that.

Pause.

You've had your way with me. You made me touch you. You stripped me. I cried . . . but . . . but it was my lust made me cry. You are a devil. My lust was my own. I kept it by me. You took it from me. Once open never closed. Never closed again. Never closed always open. For eternity. Terrible. You have ruined me.

Pause.

I sound childish. Out of . . . tune.

Pause.

How old am I?

Pause.

Eighteen?

HORNBY No.

DEBORAH Well then, I've no idea how old I am. Do you know?

HORNBY Not exactly.

DEBORAH Why not?

Pause.

My sisters would know. We're very close. We love each other. We're known as the three bluebells.

Pause.

Why is everything so quiet? So still? I'm in a sandbag. The sea. Is that what I hear? A long way away. Gulls.

643

Haven't heard a gull for ages. God what a racket. Where's Pauline? She's such a mischief. I have to keep telling her not to be so witty. That's what I say. You're too witty for your own good. You're so sharp you'll cut yourself. You're too witty for your own tongue. You'll bite your own tongue off one of these days and I'll keep your tongue in a closed jar and you'll never ever ever ever be witty again.

Pause.

She's all right, really. She just talks too much. Whereas Estelle is as deep as a pond. She's marvellous at crossing her legs. Sen-su-al.

Pause.

This is a hotel. A hotel near the sea. Hastings? Torquay? There's more to this than meets the eye. I'm coming to that conclusion. There's something very shady about you. Pauline always says I'll end up as part of the White Slave Traffic.

Pause.

Yes. This is a white tent. When I open the flap I'll step out into the Sahara Desert.

HORNBY You've been asleep.

DEBORAH Oh, you keep saying that! What's wrong with that? Why shouldn't I have a long sleep for a change? I need it. My body demands it. It's quite natural. I may have overslept but I didn't do it deliberately. If I had any choice in the matter I'd much prefer to be up

644

and about. I love the morning. Why do you blame me? I was simply obeying the law of the body.

HORNBY I know that. I'm not blaming you.

DEBORAH Well, how long have I been asleep?

Pause.

HORNBY You have been asleep for twenty-nine years.

Silence.

DEBORAH You mean I'm dead?

HORNBY No.

DEBORAH I don't feel dead.

HORNBY You're not.

DEBORAH But you mean I've been dead?

HORNBY If you had been dead you wouldn't be alive now.

DEBORAH Are you sure?

HORNBY No one wakes from the dead.

DEBORAH No, I shouldn't think so.

Pause.

Well, what was I doing if I wasn't dead?

HORNBY We don't know . . . what you were doing.

DEBORAH We?

Pause.

Where's my mother? My father? Estelle? Pauline?

645

HORNBY Pauline is here. She's waiting to see you.

DEBORAH She shouldn't be out at this time of night. I'm always telling her. She needs her beauty sleep. Like I do, by the way. But of course I'm her elder sister so she doesn't listen to me. And Estelle doesn't listen to me because she's my elder sister. That's family life. And Jack? Where's Jack? Where's my boyfriend? He's my boyfriend. He loves me. He loves me. I once saw him cry. For love. Don't make him cry again. What have you done to him? What have you done with him? What? What? What?

HORNBY Be calm. Don't agitate yourself.

DEBORAH Agitate myself?

HORNBY There's no hurry about any of this.

DEBORAH Any of what?

HORNBY Be calm.

DEBORAH I am calm.

Pause.

I've obviously committed a criminal offence and am now in prison. I'm quite prepared to face up to the facts. But what offence? I can't imagine what offence it could be. I mean one that would bring . . . such a terrible sentence.

HORNBY This is not a prison. You have committed no offence.

DEBORAH But what have I done? What have I been doing? Where have I been?

HORNBY Do you remember nothing of where you've been? Do you remember nothing . . . of all that has happened to you?

DEBORAH Nothing has happened to me. I've been nowhere.

Silence.

HORNBY I think we should –

DEBORAH I certainly don't want to see Pauline. People don't want to see their sisters. They're only their sisters. They're so witty. All I hear is chump chump. The side teeth. Eating everything in sight. Gold chocolate. So greedy eat it with the paper on. Munch all the ratshit on the sideboard. Someone has to polish it off. Been there for years. Statues of excrement. Wrapped in gold. I've never got used to it. Sisters are diabolical. Brothers are worse. One day I prayed I would see no one ever again, none of them ever again. All that eating, all that wit.

Pause.

HORNBY I didn't know you had any brothers.

DEBORAH What?

Pause.

HORNBY Come. Rest. Tomorrow . . . is another day.

DEBORAH No it isn't. No it isn't. It is not!

She smiles.

Yes, of course it is. Of course it is. Tomorrow is another day. I'd love to ask you a question.

HORNBY Are you not tired?

DEBORAH Tired? Not at all. I'm wide awake. Don't you think so?

HORNBY What is the question?

DEBORAH How did you wake me up?

Pause.

Or did you not wake me up? Did I just wake up myself? All by myself? Or did you wake me with a magic wand?

HORNBY I woke you with an injection.

DEBORAH Lovely injection. Oh how I love it. And am I beautiful?

HORNBY Certainly.

DEBORAH And you are my Prince Charming. Aren't you?

Pause.

Oh speak up.

Pause.

Silly shit. All men are alike.

Pause.

I think I love you.

HORNBY No, you don't.

DEBORAH Well, I'm not spoilt for choice here, am I? There's not another man in sight. What have you done

648

with all the others? There's a boy called Peter. We play
with his trains, we play. . . Cowboys and Indians . . .
I'm a tomboy. I knock him about. But that was . . .

Pause.

But now I've got all the world before me. All life
before me. All my life before me.

Pause.

I've had enough of this. Find Jack. I'll say yes. We'll
have kids. I'll bake apples. I'm ready for it. No point
in hanging about. Best foot forward. Mummy's motto.
Bit of a cheek, I think, Mummy not coming in to say
hullo, to say goodnight, to tuck me up, to sing me a
song, to warn me about going too far with boys.
Daddy I love but he is a bit absent-minded. Thinking
of other things. That's what Pauline says. She says he
has a mistress in Fulham. The bitch. I mean Pauline.
And she's only . . . thirteen. I keep telling her I'm not
prepared to tolerate her risible, her tendentious, her
eclectic, her ornate, her rococo insinuations and
garbled inventions. I tell her that every day of the week.

Pause.

Daddy is kind and so is Mummy. We all have breakfast
together every morning in the kitchen. What's
happening?

Pause.

HORNBY One day suddenly you stopped.

DEBORAH Stopped?

HORNBY Yes.

Pause.

You fell asleep and no one could wake you. But although I use the word sleep, it was not strictly sleep.

DEBORAH Oh, make up your mind!

Pause.

You mean you thought I was asleep but I was actually awake?

HORNBY Neither asleep nor awake.

DEBORAH Was I dreaming?

HORNBY Were you?

DEBORAH Well was I? I don't know.

Pause.

I'm not terribly pleased about all this. I'm going to ask a few questions in a few minutes. One of them might be: What did I look like while I was asleep, or while I was awake, or whatever it was I was? Bet you can't tell me.

HORNBY You were quite still. Fixed. Most of the time.

DEBORAH Show me.

Pause.

Show me what I looked like.

He demonstrates a still, fixed position. She studies him. She laughs, stops abruptly.

Most of the time? What about the rest of the time?

HORNBY You were taken for walks twice a week. We encouraged your legs to move.

Pause.

At other times you would suddenly move of your own volition very quickly, very quickly indeed, spasmodically, for short periods, and as suddenly as you began you would stop.

Pause.

DEBORAH Did you ever see . . . tears . . . well in my eyes?

HORNBY No.

DEBORAH And when I laughed . . . did you laugh with me?

HORNBY You never laughed.

DEBORAH Of course I laughed. I have a laughing nature.

Pause.

Right. I'll get up now.

He moves to her.

No! Don't! Don't be ridiculous.

She eases herself out of the bed, stands, falls. He moves to her.

No! Don't! Don't! Don't! Don't! touch me.

She stands, very slowly. He retreats, watching.

She stands still, begins to walk, in slow motion, towards him.

Let us dance.

She dances, by herself, in slow motion.

I dance.

She dances.

I've kept in practice, you know. I've been dancing in very narrow spaces. Kept stubbing my toes and bumping my head. Like Alice. Shall I sit here? I shall sit here.

She sits at the table. He joins her.

She touches the arms of her chair, touches the table, examines the table.

I like tables, don't you? This is a rather beautiful table. Any chance of a dry sherry?

HORNBY Not yet. Soon we'll have a party for you.

DEBORAH A party? For me? How nice. Lots of cakes and lots of booze?

HORNBY That's right.

DEBORAH How nice.

Pause.

Well, it's nice at this table. What's the news? I suppose the war's still over?

HORNBY It's over, yes.

DEBORAH Oh good. They haven't started another one?

HORNBY No.

DEBORAH Oh good.

Pause.

HORNBY You danced in narrow spaces?

DEBORAH Oh yes. The most crushing spaces. The most punishing spaces. That was tough going. Very difficult. Like dancing with someone dancing on your foot all the time, I mean *all* the time, on the same spot, just slam, slam, a big boot on your foot, not the most ideal kind of dancing, not by a long chalk. But sometimes the space opened and became light, sometimes it opened and I was so light, and when you feel so light you can dance till dawn and I danced till dawn night after night, night after night . . . for a time . . . I think . . . until . . .

She has become aware of the figure o/ PAULINE, standing in the room. She stares at her. PAULINE is a woman in her early forties.

PAULINE Deborah.

DEBORAH *stares at her.*

Deborah. It's Pauline.

PAULINE *turns to* HORNBY.

She's looking at me.

She turns back to DEBORAH.

653

You're looking at me. Oh Deborah . . . you haven't looked at me . . . for such a long time.

Pause.

I'm your sister. Do you know me?

DEBORAH *laughs shortly and turns away.* HORNBY *stands and goes to* PAULINE.

HORNBY I didn't call you.

PAULINE *regards him.*

Well, all right. Speak to her.

PAULINE What shall I say?

HORNBY Just talk to her.

PAULINE Doesn't it matter what I say?

HORNBY No.

PAULINE I can't do her harm?

HORNBY No.

PAULINE Shall I tell her lies or the truth?

HORNBY Both.

Pause.

PAULINE You're trembling.

HORNBY Am I?

PAULINE Your hand.

HORNBY Is it?

He looks at his hand.

Trembling? Is it? Yes.

PAULINE *goes to* DEBORAH, *sits with her at the table.*

PAULINE Debby. I've spoken to the family. Everyone was so happy. I spoke to them all, in turn. They're away, you see. They're on a world cruise. They deserve it. It's been so hard for them. And Daddy's not too well, although in many respects he's as fit as a fiddle, and Mummy . . . It's a wonderful trip. They passed through the Indian Ocean. And the Bay of Bosphorus. Can you imagine? Estelle also . . . needed a total break. It's a wonderful trip. Quite honestly, it's the trip of a lifetime. They've stopped off in Bangkok. That's where I found them. I spoke to them all, in turn. And they all send so much love to you. Especially Mummy.

Pause.

I spoke by radio telephone. Shore to ship. The captain's cabin. Such excitement.

Pause.

Tell me. Do you . . . remember me?

DEBORAH *stands and walks to her bed, in slow motion.*

Very slowly she gets into the bed.

She lies against the pillow, closes her eyes.

She opens her eyes, looks at PAULINE, *beckons to her.*

PAULINE *goes to the bed.*

DEBORAH Let me look into your eyes.

She looks deeply into PAULINE'*s eyes.*

So you say you're my sister?

PAULINE I am.

DEBORAH Well, you've changed. A great deal. You've aged . . . substantially. What happened to you?

DEBORAH *turns to* HORNBY.

What happened to her? Was it a sudden shock? I know shocks can age people overnight. Someone told me.

She turns to PAULINE.

Is that what happened to you? Did a sudden shock age you overnight?

PAULINE No it was you –

PAULINE *looks at* HORNBY. *He looks back at her, impassive,* PAULINE *turns back to* DEBORAH.

It was you. You were standing with a vase of flowers in your hands. You were about to put it down on the table. But you didn't put it down. You stood still, with the vase in your hands, as if you were . . . fixed. I was with you, in the room. I looked into your eyes.

Pause.

I said: 'Debby?'

Pause.

But you remained . . . quite . . . still. I touched you. I said: 'Debby?' Your eyes were open. You were looking nowhere. Then you suddenly looked at me and saw me and smiled at me and put the vase down on the table.

Pause.

But at the end of dinner, we were all laughing and talking, and Daddy was making jokes and making us laugh, and you said you couldn't see him properly because of the flowers in the middle of the table, where you had put them, and you stood and picked up the vase and you took it towards that little side table by the window, walnut, and Mummy was laughing and even Estelle was laughing and then we suddenly looked at you and you had stopped. You were standing with the vase by the side table, you were about to put it down, your arm was stretched towards it but you had stopped.

Pause.

We went to you. We spoke to you. Mummy touched you. She spoke to you.

Pause.

Then Daddy tried to take the vase from you. He could not . . . wrench it from your hands. He could not . . . move you from the spot. Like . . . marble.

Pause.

You were sixteen.

DEBORAH *turns to* HORNBY.

DEBORAH She must be an aunt I never met. One of those distant cousins.

(*To* PAULINE.) Have you left me money in your will? Well, I could do with it.

PAULINE I'm Pauline.

DEBORAH Well, if you're Pauline you've put on a remarkable amount of weight in a very short space of time. I can see you're not keeping up with your ballet classes. My God! You've grown breasts!

> DEBORAH *stares at* PAULINE's *breasts and suddenly looks down at herself.*

PAULINE We're women.

DEBORAH Women?

HORNBY You're a grown woman, Deborah.

DEBORAH (*to* PAULINE) Is Estelle going to marry that ginger boy from Townley Street?

HORNBY Deborah. Listen. You're not listening.

DEBORAH To what?

HORNBY To what your sister has been saying.

DEBORAH (*to* PAULINE) Are you my sister?

PAULINE Yes. Yes.

DEBORAH But where did you get those breasts?

PAULINE They came about.

DEBORAH *looks down at herself.*

DEBORAH I'm slimmer. Aren't I?

PAULINE Yes.

DEBORAH Yes. I'm slimmer.

Pause.

I'm going to run into the sea and fall into the waves.
I'm going to rummage about in all the water.

Pause.

Are we going out to dinner tonight?

Pause.

Where's Jack? Tongue-tied as usual. He's too shy for
his own good, and Pauline's so sharp she'll cut herself.
And Estelle's such a flibbertigibbet. I think she should
marry that ginger boy from Townley Street and settle
down before it's too late.

Pause.

PAULINE I am a widow.

DEBORAH This woman is mad.

HORNBY No. She's not.

Pause.

She has been coming to see you regularly . . . for a
long time. She has suffered for you. She has never
forsaken you. Nor have I.

Pause.

659

I have been your doctor for many years. This is your sister. Your father is blind. Estelle looks after him. She never married. Your mother is dead.

Pause.

It was I who took the vase from your hands. I lifted you on to this bed, like a corpse. Some wanted to bury you. I forbade it. I have nourished you, watched over you, for all this time.

Pause.

I injected you and woke you up. You will ask why I did not inject you twenty-nine years ago. I'll tell you. I did not possess the appropriate fluid.

Pause.

You see, you have been nowhere, absent, indifferent. It is we who have suffered.

Pause.

You do see that, I'm sure. You were an extremely intelligent young girl. All opinions confirm this. Your mind has not been damaged. It was merely suspended, it took up a temporary habitation . . . in a kind of Alaska. But it was not entirely static, was it? You ventured into quite remote . . . utterly foreign . . . territories. You kept on the move. And I charted your itinerary. Or did my best to do so. I have never let you go –

Silence.

I have never let you go.

Silence.

I have lived with you.

Pause.

Your sister Pauline was twelve when you were left for dead. When she was twenty I married her. She is a widow. I have lived with you.

Silence.

DEBORAH I want to go home.

Pause.

I'm cold.

She takes PAULINE's *hand.*

Is it my birthday soon? Will I have a birthday party? Will everyone be there? Will they all come? All our friends? How old will I be?

PAULINE You will. You will have a birthday party. And everyone will be there. All your family will be there. All your old friends. And we'll have presents for you. All wrapped up . . . wrapped up in such beautiful paper.

DEBORAH What presents?

PAULINE Ah, we're not going to tell you. We're not going to tell you that. Because they're a secret.

Pause.

Think of it. Think of the thrill . . . of opening them, of unwrapping them, of taking out your presents and looking at them.

DEBORAH Can I keep them?

PAULINE Of course you can keep them. They're your presents. They're for you . . . only.

DEBORAH I might lose them.

PAULINE No, no. We'll put them all around you in your bedroom. We'll see that nobody else touches them. Nobody will touch them. And we'll kiss you goodnight. And when you wake up in the morning your presents . . .

Pause.

DEBORAH I don't want to lose them.

PAULINE They'll never be lost. Ever.

Pause.

And we'll sing to you. What will we sing?

DEBORAH What?

PAULINE We'll sing 'Happy Birthday' to you.

Pause.

DEBORAH Now what was I going to say?

She begins to flick her cheek, as if brushing something from it.

Now what –? Oh dear, oh no. Oh dear.

Pause.

Oh dear.

The flicking of her cheek grows faster.

Yes, I think they're closing in. They're closing in.
They're closing the walls in. Yes.

*She bows her head, flicking faster, her fingers now
moving about over her face.*

Oh . . . well . . . oooohhhhh . . . oh no . . . oh no . . .

*During the course of this speech her body becomes
hunchbacked.*

Let me out. Stop it. Let me out. Stop it. Stop it. Stop it.
Shutting the walls on me. Shutting them down on me.
So tight, so tight. Something panting, something
panting. Can't see. Oh, the light is going. The light is
going. They're shutting up shop. They're closing my
face. Chains and padlocks. Bolting me up. Stinking.
The smell. Oh my goodness, oh dear, oh my goodness,
oh dear, I'm so young. It's a vice. I'm in a vice. It's at
the back of my neck. Ah. Eyes stuck. Only see the
shadow of the tip of my nose. Shadow of the tip of my
nose. Eyes stuck.

*She stops flicking abruptly, sits still. Her body
straightens. She looks up. She looks at her fingers,
examines them.*

Nothing.

Silence.

She speaks calmly, is quite still.

Do you hear a drip?

Pause.

I hear a drip. Someone's left the tap on.

663

Pause.

I'll tell you what it is. It's a vast series of halls. With enormous interior windows masquerading as walls. The windows are mirrors, you see. And so glass reflects glass. For ever and ever.

Pause.

You can't imagine how still it is. So silent I hear my eyes move.

Silence.

I'm lying in bed. People bend over me, speak to me. I want to say hullo, to have a chat, to make some inquiries. But you can't do that if you're in a vast hall of glass with a tap dripping.

Silence.

She looks at PAULINE.

I must be quite old. I wonder what I look like. But it's of no consequence. I certainly have no intention of looking into a mirror.

Pause.

No.

She looks at HORNBY.

You say I have been asleep. You say I am now awake. You say I have not awoken from the dead. You say I was not dreaming then and am not dreaming now. You say I have always been alive and am alive now. You say I am a woman.

664

She looks at PAULINE, *then back at* HORNBY.

She is a widow. She doesn't go to her ballet classes any more. Mummy and Daddy and Estelle are on a world cruise. They've stopped off in Bangkok. It'll be my birthday soon. I think I have the matter in proportion.

Pause.

Thank you.

VICTORIA STATION

Victoria Station first published by
Methuen London Ltd 1982
© Fraser52 Limited, 1982

Victoria Station was presented as part of the triple bill *Other Places,* first performed at the National Theatre, London, on 14 October 1982 with the following cast:

CONTROLLER   Paul Rogers
DRIVER   Martin Jarvis

Directed by Peter Hall

It was subsequently presented with *A Kind of Alaska* and *One for the Road* at the Duchess Theatre, London, on 7 March 1985 with the following cast:

CONTROLLER   Colin Blakely
DRIVER   Roger Davidson

Directed by Kenneth Ives

Characters

CONTROLLER

DRIVER

Lights up on office, CONTROLLER *sitting at microphone.*

CONTROLLER 274? Where are you?

   Lights up on DRIVER *in car.*

CONTROLLER 274? Where are you? *Pause.*

DRIVER Hullo?

CONTROLLER 274?

DRIVER Hullo?

CONTROLLER Is that 274?

DRIVER That's me.

CONTROLLER Where are you?

DRIVER What?

   Pause.

CONTROLLER I'm talking to 274? Right?

DRIVER Yes. That's me. I'm 274. Who are you?

   Pause.

CONTROLLER Who am I?

DRIVER Yes.

CONTROLLER Who do you think I am? I'm your office.

DRIVER Oh yes.

CONTROLLER Where are you?

DRIVER I'm cruising.

CONTROLLER What do you mean?

Pause.

Listen son. I've got a job for you. If you're in the area I think you're in. Where are you?

DRIVER I'm just cruising about.

CONTROLLER Don't cruise. Stop cruising. Nobody's asking you to cruise about. What the fuck are you cruising about for?

Pause.

274?

DRIVER Hullo. Yes. That's me.

CONTROLLER I want you to go to Victoria Station. I want you to pick up a customer coming from Boulogne. That is what I want you to do. Do you follow me? Now the question I want to ask you is this. Where are you? And don't say you're just cruising about. Just tell me if you're anywhere near Victoria Station.

DRIVER Victoria what?

Pause.

CONTROLLER Station.

Pause.

Can you help me on this?

DRIVER Sorry?

CONTROLLER Can you help me on this? Can you
come to my aid on this?

   Pause.

You see, 274, I've got no one else in the area, you see.
I've only got you in the area. I think. Do you follow
me?

DRIVER I follow you, yes.

CONTROLLER And this is a good job, 274. He wants
you to take him to Cuckfield.

DRIVER Eh?

CONTROLLER He wants you to take him to Cuckfield.
You're meeting the 10.22 from Boulogne. The
European Special. His name's MacRooney. He's a little
bloke with a limp. I've known him for years. You pick
him up under the clock. You'll know him by his hat.
He'll have a hat on with a feather in it. He'll be
carrying fishing tackle. 274?

DRIVER Hullo?

CONTROLLER Are you hearing me?

DRIVER Yes.

Pause.

CONTROLLER What are you doing?

DRIVER I'm not doing anything.

CONTROLLER How's your motor? Is your motor working?

DRIVER Oh yes.

CONTROLLER Your ignition's not on the blink?

DRIVER No.

CONTROLLER So you're sitting in a capable car?

DRIVER I'm sitting in it, yes.

CONTROLLER Are you in the driving seat?

Pause.

Do you understand what I mean?

Pause.

Do you have a driving wheel in front of you?

Pause.

Because I haven't, 274. I'm just talking into this machine, trying to make some sense out of our lives. That's my function. God gave me this job. He asked me to do this job, personally. I'm your local monk, 274. I'm a monk. You follow? I lead a restricted life. I haven't got a choke and a gear lever in front of me. I haven't got a cooling system and four wheels. I'm not sitting here with wing mirrors and a jack in the boot.

676

And if I did have a jack in the boot I'd stick it right up your arse.

Pause.

Listen, 274. I've got every reason to believe that you're driving a Ford Cortina. I would very much like you to go to Victoria Station. *In* it. That means I don't want you to walk down there. I want you to drive down there. Right?

DRIVER Everything you say is correct. This is a Ford Cortina.

CONTROLLER Good. That's right. And you're sitting in it while we're having this conversation, aren't you?

DRIVER That's right.

CONTROLLER Where?

DRIVER By the side of a park.

CONTROLLER By the side of a park?

DRIVER Yes.

CONTROLLER What park?

DRIVER A dark park.

CONTROLLER Why is it dark?

Pause.

DRIVER That's not an easy question.

Pause.

CONTROLLER Isn't it?

DRIVER No.

Pause.

CONTROLLER You remember this customer I was talking to you about? The one who's coming in to Victoria Station? Well, he's very keen for you to take him down to Cuckfield. He's got an old aunt down there. I've got a funny feeling she's going to leave him all her plunder. He's going down to pay his respects. He'll be in a good mood. If you play your cards right you might come out in front. Get me?

Pause.

274?

DRIVER Yes? I'm here.

CONTROLLER Go to Victoria Station.

DRIVER I don't know it.

CONTROLLER You don't know it?

DRIVER No. What is it?

Silence.

CONTROLLER It's a station, 274.

Pause.

Haven't you heard of it?

DRIVER No. Never. What kind of place is it?

Pause.

CONTROLLER You've never heard of Victoria Station?

DRIVER Never. No.

CONTROLLER It's a famous station.

DRIVER Well, I honestly don't know what I've been doing all these years.

CONTROLLER What have you been doing all these years?

DRIVER Well, I honestly don't know.

Pause.

CONTROLLER All right 274. Report to the office in the morning. 135? Where are you? 135? Where are you?

DRIVER Don't leave me.

CONTROLLER What? Who's that?

DRIVER It's me. 274. Please. Don't leave me.

CONTROLLER 135? Where are you?

DRIVER Don't have anything to do with 135. He's not your man. He'll lead you into blind alleys by the dozen. They all will. Don't leave me. I'm your man. I'm the only one you can trust.

Pause.

CONTROLLER Do I know you, 274? Have we met?

Pause.

Well, it'll be nice to meet you in the morning. I'm really looking forward to it. I'll be sitting here with my cat o'nine tails, son. And you know what I'm going to do with it? I'm going to tie you up bollock naked to a butcher's table and I'm going to flog you to death all the way to Crystal Palace.

DRIVER   That's where I am! I knew I knew the place.

   Pause.

I'm sitting by a little dark park underneath Crystal Palace. I can see the Palace. It's silhouetted against the sky. It's a wonderful edifice, isn't it?

   Pause.

My wife's in bed. Probably asleep. And I've got a little daughter.

CONTROLLER   Oh, you've got a little daughter?

   Pause.

DRIVER   Yes, I think that's what she is.

CONTROLLER   Report to the office at 9 a.m. 135? Where are you? Where the fuck is 135? 246? 178? 101? Will somebody help me? Where's everyone gone? I've got a good job going down to Cuckfield. Can anyone hear me?

DRIVER   I can hear you.

CONTROLLER   Who's that?

DRIVER   274. Here. Waiting. What do you want me to do?

CONTROLLER   You want to know what I want you to do?

DRIVER   Oh by the way, there's something I forgot to tell you.

CONTROLLER   What is it?

DRIVER   I've got a P.O.B.

CONTROLLER   You've got a P.O.B.?

DRIVER   Yes. That means passenger on board.

CONTROLLER   I know what it means, 274. It means you've got a passenger on board.

DRIVER   That's right.

CONTROLLER   You've got a passenger on board sitting by the side of a park?

DRIVER   That's right.

CONTROLLER   Did I book this job?

DRIVER   No, I don't think you came into it.

CONTROLLER   Well, where does he want to go?

DRIVER   He doesn't want to go anywhere. We just cruised about for a bit and then we came to rest.

CONTROLLER   In Crystal Palace?

DRIVER   Not *in* the Palace.

CONTROLLER   Oh, you're not *in* the Palace?

DRIVER   No. I'm not right inside it.

CONTROLLER   I think you'll find the Crystal Palace burnt down years ago, old son. It burnt down in the Great Fire of London.

Pause.

DRIVER Did it?

CONTROLLER 274?

DRIVER Yes. I'm here.

CONTROLLER Drop your passenger. Drop your
passenger at his chosen destination and proceed to
Victoria Station. Otherwise I'll destroy you bone by
bone. I'll suck you in and blow you out in little
bubbles. I'll chew your stomach out with my own
teeth. I'll eat all the hair off your body. You'll end up
looking like a pipe cleaner. Get me?

Pause.

274?

Pause.

You're beginning to obsess me. I think I'm going to
die. I'm alone in this miserable freezing fucking office
and nobody loves me. Listen, pukeface –

DRIVER Yes?

Pause.

CONTROLLER 135? 135? Where are you?

DRIVER Don't have anything to do with 135. They're
all bloodsuckers. I'm the only one you can trust.

Pause.

CONTROLLER You know what I've always dreamed of
doing? I've always had this dream of having a holiday

in sunny Barbados. I'm thinking of taking this holiday at the end of this year, 274. I'd like you to come with me. To Barbados. Just the two of us. I'll take you snorkelling. We can swim together in the blue Caribbean.

Pause.

In the meantime, though, why don't you just pop back to the office now and I'll make you a nice cup of tea? You can tell me something about your background, about your ambitions and aspirations. You can tell me all about your little hobbies and pastimes. Come over and have a nice cup of tea, 274.

DRIVER I'd love to but I've got a passenger on board.

CONTROLLER Put your passenger on to me. Let me have a word with him.

DRIVER I can't. She's asleep on the back seat.

CONTROLLER She?

DRIVER Can I tell you a secret?

CONTROLLER Please do.

DRIVER I think I've fallen in love. For the first time in my life.

CONTROLLER Who have you fallen in love with?

DRIVER With this girl on the back seat. I think I'm going to keep her for the rest of my life. I'm going to stay in this car with her for the rest of my life. I'm going to marry her in this car. We'll die together in this car.

Pause.

CONTROLLER So you've found true love at last, eh, 274?

DRIVER Yes. I've found true love at last.

CONTROLLER So you're a happy man now then, are you?

DRIVER I'm very happy. I've never known such happiness.

CONTROLLER Well, I'd like to be the first to congratulate you, 274. I'd like to extend my sincere felicitations to you.

DRIVER Thank you very much.

CONTROLLER Don't mention it. I'll have to make a note in my diary not to forget your Golden Wedding, won't I? I'll bring along some of the boys to drink your health. Yes, I'll bring along some of the boys. We'll all have a few jars and a bit of a sing-song.

Pause.

274?

Pause.

DRIVER Hullo. Yes. It's me.

CONTROLLER Listen. I've been thinking. I've decided that what I'd like to do now is to come down there and shake you by the hand straightaway. I'm going to shut this little office and I'm going to jump into my old car and I'm going to pop down to see you, to shake you by the hand. All right?

DRIVER Fine. But what about this man coming off the train at Victoria Station – the 10.22 from Boulogne?

CONTROLLER He can go and fuck himself.

DRIVER I see.

CONTROLLER No, I'd like to meet your lady friend, you see. And we can have a nice celebration. Can't we? So just stay where you are. Right?

Pause.

Right?

Pause.

274?

DRIVER Yes?

CONTROLLER Don't move. Stay exactly where you are. I'll be right with you.

DRIVER No, I won't move.

Silence.

I'll be here.

Light out in office. The DRIVER *sits still. Light out in car.*

ONE FOR THE ROAD

One for the Road first published by
Methuen London Ltd in 1984
© Fraser52 Limited, 1984

One for the Road was first performed at the Lyric
Theatre Studio, Hammersmith, in March 1984, with
the following cast:

NICOLAS	Alan Bates
VICTOR	Roger Lloyd Pack
GILA	Jenny Quayle
NICKY	Stephen Kember and Felix Yates

Directed by Harold Pinter

It was subsequently presented as part of the triple bill
Other Places, at the Duchess Theatre, London, on 7
March 1985, with the following cast:

NICOLAS	Colin Blakely
VICTOR	Roger Davidson
GILA	Rosie Kerslake
NICKY	Daniel Kipling and Simon Vyvyan

Directed by Kenneth Ives

Characters

NICOLAS
mid-forties

VICTOR
thirty

GILA
thirty

NICKY
seven

NICOLAS *at his desk. He leans forward and speaks into a machine.*

NICOLAS Bring him in.

He sits back. The door opens, VICTOR *walks in, slowly. His clothes are torn. He is bruised. The door closes behind him.*

Hello! Good morning. How are you? Let's not beat about the bush. Anything but that. *D'accord?* You're a civilised man, So am I. Sit down.

VICTOR *slowly sits.,* NICOLAS *stands, walks over to him.*

What do you think this is? It's my finger. And this is my little finger. This is my big finger and this is my little finger. I wave my big finger in front of your eyes. Like this. And now I do the same with my little finger. I can also use both . . . at the same time. Like this. I can do absolutely anything I like. Do you think I'm mad? My mother did.

He laughs.

Do you think waving fingers in front of people's eyes is silly? I can see your point. You're a man of the highest intelligence. But would you take the same view if it was my boot – or my penis? Why am I so obsessed with eyes? Am I obsessed with eyes? Possibly. Not my eyes. Other people's eyes. The eyes of people who are brought to me here. They're so vulnerable. The soul shines through them. Are you a religious man? I am. Which side do you think God is on? I'm going to have a drink.

He goes to sideboard, pours whisky.

You're probably wondering where your wife is. She's in another room.

He drinks.

Good-looking woman.

He drinks.

God, that was good.

He pours another.

Don't worry, I can hold my booze.

He drinks.

You may have noticed I'm the chatty type. You probably think I'm part of a predictable, formal, long-established pattern; i.e. I chat away, friendly, insouciant, I open the batting, as it were, in a light-hearted, even carefree manner, while another waits in the wings, silent, introspective, coiled like a puma. No, no. It's not quite like that. I run the place. God speaks through me. I'm referring to the Old Testament God, by the way, although I'm a long way from being Jewish.

Everyone respects me here. Including you, I take it?
I think that is the correct stance.

Pause.

Stand up.

VICTOR *stands.*

Sit down.

VICTOR *sits.*

Thank you so much.

Pause.

Tell me something . . .

Silence.

What a good-looking woman your wife is. You're a
very lucky man. Tell me . . . one for the road, I think . . .

He pours whisky.

You do respect me, I take it?

He stands in front of VICTOR *and looks down at
him.* VICTOR *looks up.*

I would be right in assuming that?

Silence.

VICTOR (*quietly*) I don't know you.

NICOLAS But you respect me.

VICTOR I don't know you.

NICOLAS Are you saying you don't respect me?

695

Pause.

Are you saying you would respect me if you knew me better? Would you like to know me better?

Pause.

Would you like to know me better?

VICTOR What I would like . . . has no bearing on the matter.

NICOLAS Oh yes it has.

Pause.

I've heard so much about you. I'm terribly pleased to meet you. Well, I'm not sure that pleased is the right word. One has to be so scrupulous about language. Intrigued. I'm intrigued. Firstly because I've heard so much about you. Secondly because if you don't respect me you're unique. Everyone else knows the voice of God speaks through me. You're not a religious man, I take it?

Pause.

You don't believe in a guiding light?

Pause.

What then?

Pause.

So . . . morally. . . you flounder in wet shit. You know . . . like when you've eaten a rancid omelette.

Pause.

I think I deserve one for the road.

He pours, drinks.

Do you drink whisky?

Pause.

I hear you have a lovely house. Lots of books. Someone told me some of my boys kicked it around a bit. Pissed on the rugs, that sort of thing. I wish they wouldn't do that. I do really. But you know what it's like – they have such responsibilities – and they feel them – they are constantly present – day and night – these responsibilities – and so, sometimes, they piss on a few rugs. You understand. You're not a fool.

Pause.

Is your son all right?

VICTOR I don't know.

NICOLAS Oh, I'm sure he's all right. What age is he . . . seven . . . or thereabouts? Big lad, I'm told. Nevertheless, silly of him to behave as he did. But is he all right?

VICTOR I don't know.

NICOLAS Oh, I'm sure he's all right. Anyway, I'll have a word with him later and find out. He's somewhere on the second floor, I believe.

Pause.

Well now . . .

Pause.

What do you say? Are we friends?

697

Pause.

I'm prepared to be frank, as a true friend should. I love death. What about you?

Pause.

What about you? Do you love death? Not necessarily your own. Others'. The death of others. Do you love the death of others, or at any rate, do you love the death of others as much as I do?

Pause.

Are you always so dull? I understood you enjoyed the cut and thrust of debate.

Pause.

Death. Death. Death. Death. As has been noted by the most respected authorities, it is beautiful. The purest, most harmonious thing there is. Sexual intercourse is nothing compared to it.

He drinks.

Talking about sexual intercourse . . .

He laughs wildly, stops.

Does she . . . fuck? Or does she . . .? Or does she . . . like . . . you know. . . what? What does she like? I'm talking about your wife. Your *wife*.

Pause.

You know the old joke? Does she fuck?

Heavily, in another voice:

698

Does she fuck!

He laughs.

It's ambiguous, of course. It could mean she fucks like a rabbit or she fucks not at all.

Pause.

Well, we're all God's creatures. Even your wife.

Pause.

There is only one obligation. *To be honest.* You have no other obligation. Weigh that. In your mind. Do you know the man who runs this country? No? Well, he's a very nice chap. He took me aside the other day, last Wednesday, I think it was, he took me aside, at a reception, visiting dignitaries, he took *me* aside, *me*, and he said to me, he said, in what I can only describe as a hoarse whisper, Nic, he said, Nic (that's my name), Nic, if you ever come across anyone whom you have good reason to believe is getting on my tits, tell them one thing, tell them honesty is the best policy. The cheese was superb. Goat. One for the road.

He pours.

Your wife and I had a very nice chat but I couldn't help noticing she didn't look her best. She's probably menstruating. Women do that.

Pause.

You know, old chap, I do love other things, apart from death. So many things. Nature. Trees, things like that. A nice blue sky. Blossom.

Pause.

Tell me . . . truly . . . are you beginning to love me?

Pause.

I think your wife is. Beginning. She is beginning to fall in love with me. On the brink . . . of doing so. The trouble is, I have rivals. Because everyone here has fallen in love with your wife. It's her eyes have beguiled them. What's her name? Gila . . . or something?

Pause.

Who would you prefer to be? You or me?

Pause.

I'd go for me if I were you. The trouble about you, although I grant your merits, is that you're on a losing wicket, while I can't put a foot wrong. Do you take my point? Ah God, let me confess, let me make a confession to you. I have never been more moved, in the whole of my life, as when – only the other day, last Friday, I believe – the man who runs this country announced to the country: We are all patriots, we are as one, we all share a common heritage. Except you, apparently.

Pause.

I feel a link, you see, a bond. I share a commonwealth of interest. I am not alone. I am not alone!

Silence.

VICTOR Kill me.

NICOLAS What?

VICTOR Kill me.

NICOLAS *goes to him, puts his arm around him.*

NICOLAS What's the matter?

Pause.

What in heaven's name is the matter?

Pause.

Mmmnnn?

Pause.

You're probably just hungry. Or thirsty. Let me tell you something. I hate despair. I find it intolerable. The stink of it gets up my nose. It's a blemish. Despair, old fruit, is a cancer. It should be castrated. Indeed I've often found that that works. Chop the balls off and despair goes out the window. You're left with a happy man. Or a happy woman. Look at me.

VICTOR *does so.*

Your soul shines out of your eyes.

Blackout.

Lights up. Afternoon.

NICOLAS *standing with a small boy.*

NICOLAS What is your name?

NICKY Nicky.

NICOLAS Really? How odd.

Pause.

Do you like cowboys and Indians?

NICKY Yes. A bit.

NICOLAS What do you really like?

NICKY I like aeroplanes.

NICOLAS Real ones or toy ones?

NICKY I like both kinds of ones.

NICOLAS Do you?

Pause.

Why do you like aeroplanes?

Pause.

NICKY Well. . . because they go so fast. Through the air. The real ones do.

NICOLAS And the toy ones?

NICKY I pretend they go as fast as the real ones do.

Pause.

NICOLAS Do you like your mummy and daddy?

Pause.

Do you like your mummy and daddy?

NICKY Yes.

NICOLAS Why?

Pause.

Why?

Pause.

Do you find that a hard question to answer?

Pause.

NICKY Where's Mummy?

NICOLAS You don't like your mummy and daddy?

NICKY Yes, I do.

NICOLAS Why?

Pause.

Would you like to be a soldier when you grow up?

NICKY I don't mind.

NICOLAS You don't? Good. You like soldiers. Good. But you spat at my soldiers and you kicked them. You attacked them.

NICKY Were they your soldiers?

NICOLAS They are your country's soldiers.

NICKY I didn't like those soldiers.

NICOLAS They don't like you either, my darling.

Blackout.

Lights up. Night.

NICOLAS *sitting,* GILA *standing. Her clothes are torn. She is bruised.*

NICOLAS When did you meet your husband?

703

GILA When I was eighteen.

NICOLAS Why?

GILA Why?

NICOLAS Why?

GILA I just met him.

NICOLAS Why?

GILA I didn't plan it.

NICOLAS Why not?

GILA I didn't know him.

NICOLAS Why not?

Pause.

Why not?

GILA I didn't know him.

NICOLAS Why not?

GILA I met him.

NICOLAS When?

GILA When I was eighteen.

NICOLAS Why?

GILA He was in the room.

NICOLAS Room?

Pause.

Room?

GILA   The same room.

NICOLAS   As what?

GILA   As I was.

NICOLAS   As I was?

   Pause.

GILA   (*screaming*) As I was!

NICOLAS   Room? What room?

GILA   A room.

NICOLAS   What room?

GILA   My father's room.

NICOLAS   Your father? What's your father got to do with it?

   Pause.

Your *father?* How dare you? Fuckpig.

   Pause.

Your father was a wonderful man. His country is proud of him. He's dead. He was a man of honour. He's dead. Are you prepared to insult the memory of your father?

   Pause.

Are you prepared to defame, to debase, the memory of your father? Your father fought for his country. I knew him. I revered him. Everyone did. He believed in God. He didn't *think*, like you shitbags. He *lived*. He lived.

He was iron and gold. He would die, he would die, he would die, for his country, for his God. And he did die, he died, he died, for his God. You turd. To spawn such a daughter. What a fate. Oh, poor, perturbed spirit, to be haunted for ever by such scum and spittle. How do you dare speak of your father to me? I loved him, as if he were my own father.

Silence.

Where did you meet your husband?

GILA In a street.

NICOLAS What were you doing there?

GILA Walking.

NICOLAS What was he doing?

GILA Walking.

Pause.

I dropped something. He picked it up.

NICOLAS What did you drop?

GILA The evening paper.

NICOLAS You were drunk.

Pause.

You were drugged.

Pause.

You had absconded from your hospital.

GILA I was not in a hospital.

NICOLAS Where are you now?

Pause.

Where are you now? Do you think you are in a hospital?

Pause.

Do you think we have nuns upstairs?

Pause.

What do we have upstairs?

GILA No nuns.

NICOLAS What do we have?

GILA Men.

NICOLAS Have they been raping you?

She stares at him.

How many times?

Pause.

How many times have you been raped?

Pause.

How many times?

He stands, goes to her, lifts his finger.

This is my big finger. And this is my little finger. Look. I wave them in front of your eyes. Like this. How many times have you been raped?

707

GILA I don't know.

NICOLAS And you consider yourself a reliable witness?

He goes to sideboard, pours drink, sits, drinks.

You're a lovely woman. Well, you were.

He leans back, drinks, sighs.

Your son is . . . seven. He's a little prick. You made him so. You have taught him to be so. You had a choice. You could have encouraged him to be a good person. Instead, you encouraged him to be a little prick. You encouraged him to spit, to strike at soldiers of honour, soldiers of God.

Pause.

Oh well . . . in one way I suppose it's academic.

Pause.

You're of no interest to me. I might even let you out of here, in due course. But I should think you might entertain us all a little more before you go.

Blackout.

Lights up. Night.

NICOLAS *standing*, VICTOR *sitting*, VICTOR *is tidily dressed.*

NICOLAS How have you been? Surviving?

VICTOR Yes.

NICOLAS Yes?

VICTOR Yes. Yes.

NICOLAS Really? How?

VICTOR Oh...

Pause.

NICOLAS I can't hear you.

VICTOR It's my mouth.

NICOLAS Mouth?

VICTOR Tongue.

NICOLAS What's the matter with it?

Pause.

What about a drink? One for the road. What do you
say to a drink?

*He goes to bottle, pours two glasses, gives a glass
to* VICTOR.

Drink up. It'll put lead in your pencil. And then we'll
find someone to take it out.

He laughs.

We can do that, you know. We have a first-class
brothel upstairs, on the sixth floor, chandeliers, the lot.
They'll suck you in and blow you out in little bubbles.
All volunteers. Their daddies are in our business.
Which is, I remind you, to keep the world clean for
God. Get me? Drink up. Drink up. Are you refusing to
drink with me?

VICTOR *drinks. His head falls back.*

Cheers.

NICOLAS *drinks.*

You can go.

Pause.

You can leave. We'll meet again, I hope. I trust we will always remain friends. Go out. Enjoy life. Be good. Love your wife. She'll be joining you in about a week, by the way. If she feels up to it. Yes. I feel we've both benefited from our discussions.

VICTOR *mutters.*

What?

VICTOR *mutters.*

What?

VICTOR My son.

NICOLAS Your son? Oh, don't worry about him. He was a little prick.

VICTOR *straightens and stares at* NICOLAS.

Silence.

Blackout.

MOUNTAIN LANGUAGE

Mountain Language first published by
Faber and Faber Ltd 1988
© Fraser52 Limited, 1988

Mountain Language was first performed at the
National Theatre, London, on 20 October 1988.
The cast was as follows:

YOUNG WOMAN	Miranda Richardson
ELDERLY WOMAN	Eileen Atkins
SERGEANT	Michael Gambon
OFFICER	Julian Wadham
GUARD	George Harris
PRISONER	Tony Haygarth
HOODED MAN	Alex Hardy
SECOND GUARD	Douglas McFerran

Directed by Harold Pinter
Designed by Michael Taylor

Moutain Language was revived in a double bill with
Ashes to Ashes at the Royal Court Theatre, London,
in June 2001 with the following cast:

YOUNG WOMAN	Anastasia Hille
ELDERLY WOMAN	Gabrielle Hamilton
SERGEANT	Neil Dudgeon
OFFICER	Geoffrey Streatfeild
GUARD	Daniel Cerqueira
PRISONER	Paul Hilton
SECOND GUARD	Tim Treloar

Directed by Katie Mitchell
Designed by Vicki Mortimer

Characters

YOUNG WOMAN

ELDERLY WOMAN

SERGEANT

OFFICER

GUARD

PRISONER

HOODED MAN

SECOND GUARD

One

A PRISON WALL

A line of women. An ELDERLY WOMAN, *cradling her hand. A basket at her feet. A* YOUNG WOMAN *with her arm around the* WOMAN'S *shoulders.*

A SERGEANT *enters, followed by an* OFFICER. *The* SERGEANT *points to the* YOUNG WOMAN.

SERGEANT Name!

YOUNG WOMAN We've given our names.

SERGEANT Name?

YOUNG WOMAN We've given our names.

SERGEANT Name?

OFFICER (*to* SERGEANT) Stop this shit. (*To* YOUNG WOMAN.) Any complaints?

YOUNG WOMAN She's been bitten.

OFFICER Who?

   Pause.

Who? Who's been bitten?

YOUNG WOMAN She has. She has a torn hand. Look. Her hand has been bitten. This is blood.

SERGEANT (*to* YOUNG WOMAN) What is your name?

717

OFFICER Shut up.

He walks over to ELDERLY WOMAN.

What's happened to your hand? Has someone bitten your hand?

The WOMAN *slowly lifts her hand. He peers at it.*

Who did this? Who bit you?

YOUNG WOMAN A Doberman Pinscher.

OFFICER Which one?

Pause.

Which one?

Pause.

Sergeant!

SERGEANT *steps forward.*

SERGEANT Sir!

OFFICER Look at this woman's hand. I think the thumb is going to come off. (*To* ELDERLY WOMAN.) Who did this?

She stares at him.

Who did this?

YOUNG WOMAN A big dog.

OFFICER What was his name?

Pause.

What was his *name*?

Pause.

Every dog has a *name*! They answer to their name.
They are given a name by their parents and that is
their name, that is their *name*! Before they bite, they
state their name. It's a formal procedure. They state
their name and then they bite. What was his name?
If you tell me one of our dogs bit this woman without
giving his name I will have that dog shot!

Silence.

Now – attention! Silence and attention! Sergeant!

SERGEANT Sir?

OFFICER Take any complaints.

SERGEANT Any complaints? Has anyone got any
complaints?

YOUNG WOMAN We were told to be here at nine
o'clock this morning.

SERGEANT Right. Quite right. Nine o'clock this
morning. Absolutely right. What's your complaint?

YOUNG WOMAN We were here at nine o'clock this
morning. It's now five o'clock. We have been standing
here for eight hours. In the snow. Your men let
Dobermann pinschers frighten us. One bit this
woman's hand.

OFFICER What was the name of this dog?

She looks at him.

YOUNG WOMAN I don't know his name.

SERGEANT With permission sir?

OFFICER Go ahead.

SERGEANT Your husbands, your sons, your fathers, these men you have been waiting to see, are shithouses. They are enemies of the State. They are shithouses.

The OFFICER *steps towards the* WOMEN.

OFFICER Now hear this. You are mountain people. You hear me? Your language is dead. It is forbidden. It is not permitted to speak your mountain language in this place. You cannot speak your language to your men. It is not permitted. Do you understand? You may not speak it. It is outlawed. You may only speak the language of the capital. That is the only language permitted in this place. You will be badly punished if you attempt to speak your mountain language in this place. This is a military decree. It is the law. Your language is forbidden. It is dead. No one is allowed to speak your language. Your language no longer exists. Any questions?

YOUNG WOMAN I do not speak the mountain language.

Silence. The OFFICER *and* SERGEANT *slowly circle her. The* SERGEANT *puts his hand on her bottom.*

SERGEANT What language do you speak? What language do you speak with your arse?

OFFICER These women, Sergeant, have as yet committed no crime. Remember that.

SERGEANT Sir! But you're not saying they're without sin?

OFFICER Oh, no. Oh, no, I'm not saying that.

SERGEANT This one's full of it. She bounces with it.

OFFICER She doesn't speak the mountain language.

The WOMAN *moves away from the* SERGEANT's *hand and turns to face the two men.*

YOUNG WOMAN My name is Sara Johnson. I have come to see my husband. It is my right. Where is he?

OFFICER Show me your papers.

She gives him a piece of paper. He examines it, turns to SERGEANT.

He doesn't come from the mountains. He's in the wrong batch.

SERGEANT So is she. She looks like a fucking intellectual to me.

OFFICER But you said her arse wobbled.

SERGEANT Intellectual arses wobble the best.

Blackout.

Two

VISITORS' ROOM

A PRISONER *sitting. The* ELDERLY WOMAN *sitting, with basket. A* GUARD *standing behind her.*

The PRISONER *and the* WOMAN *speak in a strong rural accent.*

Silence.

ELDERLY WOMAN I have bread –

The GUARD *jabs her with a stick.*

GUARD Forbidden. Language forbidden.

She looks at him. He jabs her.

It's forbidden. (*To* PRISONER.) Tell her to speak the language of the capital.

PRISONER She can't speak it.

Silence.

She doesn't speak it.

Silence.

ELDERLY WOMAN I have apples –

The GUARD *jabs her and shouts.*

GUARD Forbidden! Forbidden forbidden forbidden!

Jesus Christ! (*To* PRISONER) Does she understand
what I'm saying?

PRISONER No.

GUARD Doesn't she?

He bends over her.

Don't you?

She stares up at him.

PRISONER She's old. She doesn't understand.

GUARD Whose fault is that?

He laughs.

Not mine, I can tell you. And I'll tell you another
thing. I've got a wife and three kids. And you're all
a pile of shit.

Silence.

PRISONER I've got a wife and three kids.

GUARD You've what?

Silence.

You've got what?

Silence.

What did you say to me? You've got what?

Silence.

You've got *what?*

He picks up the telephone and dials one digit.

Sergeant? I'm in the Blue Room . . . yes . . . I thought I should report, Sergeant . . . I think I've got a joker in here.

Lights to half. The figures are still.

Voices over:

ELDERLY WOMAN'S VOICE The baby is waiting for you.

PRISONER'S VOICE Your hand has been bitten.

ELDERLY WOMAN'S VOICE They are all waiting for you.

PRISONER'S VOICE They have bitten my mother's hand.

ELDERLY WOMAN'S VOICE When you come home there will be such a welcome for you. Everyone is waiting for you. They're all waiting for you. They're all waiting to see you.

Lights up. The SERGEANT *comes in.*

SERGEANT What joker?

Blackout.

Three

VOICE IN THE DARKNESS

SERGEANT'S VOICE Who's that fucking woman?
What's that fucking woman doing here? Who let that
fucking woman through that fucking door?

SECOND GUARD'S VOICE She's his wife.

Lights up.

A corridor.

A HOODED MAN *held up by the* GUARD *and the*
SERGEANT. *The* YOUNG WOMAN *at a distance from
them, staring at them.*

SERGEANT What is this, a reception for Lady Duck
Muck? Where's the bloody Babycham? Who's got the
bloody Babycham for Lady Duck Muck?

He goes to the YOUNG WOMAN.

Hello, Miss. Sorry. A bit of a breakdown in
administration, I'm afraid. They've sent you through
the wrong door. Unbelievable. Someone'll be done for
this. Anyway, in the meantime, what can I do for you,
dear lady, as they used to say in the movies?

Lights to half. The figures are still.

Voices over:

MAN'S VOICE I watch you sleep. And then your eyes
open. You look up at me above you and smile.

725

YOUNG WOMAN'S VOICE You smile. When my eyes open I see you above me and smile.

MAN'S VOICE We are out on a lake.

YOUNG WOMAN'S VOICE It is spring.

MAN'S VOICE I hold you. I warm you.

YOUNG WOMAN'S VOICE When my eyes open I see you above me and smile.

Lights up. The HOODED MAN *collapses. The* YOUNG WOMAN *screams.*

YOUNG WOMAN Charley!

The SERGEANT *clicks his fingers. The* GUARD *drags the* MAN *off.*

SERGEANT Yes, you've come in the wrong door. It must be the computer. The computer's got a double hernia. But I'll tell you what – if you want any information on any aspect of life in this place we've got a bloke comes into the office every Tuesday week, except when it rains. He's right on top of his chosen subject. Give him a tinkle one of these days and he'll see you all right. His name is Dokes. Joseph Dokes.

YOUNG WOMAN Can I fuck him? If I fuck him, will everything be all right?

SERGEANT Sure. No problem.

YOUNG WOMAN Thank you.

Blackout.

Four

VISITORS ROOM

GUARD, ELDERLY WOMAN, PRISONER.

Silence.

The PRISONER *has blood on his face. He sits trembling. The* WOMAN *is still. The* GUARD *is looking out of a window. He turns to look at them both.*

GUARD Oh, I forgot to tell you. They've changed the rules. She can speak. She can speak in her own language. Until further notice.

PRISONER She can speak?

GUARD Yes. Until further notice. New rules.

    Pause.

PRISONER Mother, you can speak.

    Pause.

Mother, I'm speaking to you. You see? We can speak. You can speak to me in our own language.

    She is still.

You can speak.

    Pause.

Mother. Can you hear me? I am speaking to you in our own language.

Pause.

Do you hear me?

Pause.

It's our language.

Pause.

Can't you hear me? Do you hear me?

She does not respond.

Mother?

GUARD Tell her she can speak in her own language. New rules. Until further notice.

PRISONER Mother?

She does not respond. She sits still.

The PRISONER's *trembling grows. He falls from the chair on to his knees, begins to gasp and shake violently.*

The SERGEANT *walks into the room and studies the* PRISONER *shaking on the floor.*

SERGEANT (*to* GUARD) Look at this. You go out of your way to give them a helping hand and they fuck it up.

Blackout.

THE NEW WORLD ORDER

The New World Order was first performed on 19 July
1991 at the Royal Court Theatre Upstairs, London.
The cast was as follows:

DES   Bill Paterson
LIONEL   Michael Byrne
BLINDFOLDED MAN   Douglas McFerran

Directed by Harold Pinter
Designed by Ian MacNeil
Lighting by Kevin Sleep

Characters

DES

LIONEL

BLINDFOLDED MAN

A BLINDFOLDED MAN *sitting on a chair.*

Two men (DES *and* LIONEL) *looking at him.*

DES Do you want to know something about this man?

LIONEL What?

DES He hasn't got any idea at all of what we're going to do to him.

LIONEL He hasn't, no.

DES He hasn't, no. He hasn't got any idea at all about any one of the number of things that we might do to him.

LIONEL That we will do to him.

DES That we will.

   Pause.

Well, some of them. We'll do some of them.

LIONEL Sometimes we do all of them.

DES That can be counterproductive.

LIONEL Bollocks.

   They study the man. He is still.

735

DES But anyway here he is, here he is sitting here, and he hasn't the faintest idea of what we might do to him.

LIONEL Well, he probably has the *faintest* idea.

DES A faint idea, yes. Possibly.

   DES *bends over the man.*

Have you? What do you say?

   He straightens.

Let's put it this way. He has *little* idea of what we might do to him, of what in fact we are about to do to him.

LIONEL Or his wife. Don't forget his wife. He has little idea of what we're about to do to his wife.

DES Well, he probably has *some* idea, he's probably got *some* idea. After all, he's read the papers.

LIONEL What papers?

   Pause.

DES You're right there.

LIONEL Who is this cunt anyway? What is he, some kind of peasant – or a lecturer in theology?

DES He's a lecturer in fucking peasant theology.

LIONEL Is he? What about his wife?

DES Women don't have theological inclinations.

LIONEL Oh, I don't know. I used to discuss that question with my mother – quite often.

736

DES What question?

LIONEL Oh you know, the theological aspirations of the female.

Pause.

DES What did she say?

LIONEL She said . . .

DES What?

Pause.

LIONEL I can't remember.

He turns to the man in the chair.

Motherfucker.

DES Fuckpig.

They walk round the chair.

LIONEL You know what I find really disappointing?

DES What?

LIONEL The level of ignorance that surrounds us. I mean, this prick here –

DES You called him a cunt last time.

LIONEL What?

DES You called him a cunt last time. Now you call him a prick. How many times do I have to tell you? You've got to learn to define your terms and stick to them. You can't call him a cunt in one breath and a

737

prick in the next. The terms are mutually contradictory. You'd lose face in any linguistic discussion group, take my tip.

LIONEL Christ. Would I?

DES Definitely. And you know what it means to you. You know what language means to you.

LIONEL Yes, I do know.

DES Yes, you do know. Look at this man here, for example. He's a first-class example. See what I mean? Before he came in here he was a big shot, he never stopped shooting his mouth off, he never stopped questioning received ideas. Now – because he's apprehensive about what's about to happen to him – he's stopped all that, he's got nothing more to say, he's more or less called it a day. I mean once – not too long ago – this man was a man of conviction, wasn't he, a man of principle. Now he's just a prick.

LIONEL Or a cunt.

DES And we haven't even finished with him. We haven't begun.

LIONEL No, we haven't even finished with him. We haven't even finished with him! Well, we haven't begun.

DES And there's still his wife to come.

LIONEL That's right. We haven't finished with him. We haven't even begun. And we haven't finished with his wife either.

THE NEW WORLD ORDER

DES We haven't even begun.

LIONEL *puts his hand over his face and sobs.*

DES What are you crying about?

LIONEL I love it. I love it. I love it.

He grasps DES*'s shoulder.*

Look. I have to tell you. I've got to tell you. There's no one else I can tell.

DES All right. Fine. Go on. What is it? Tell me.

Pause.

LIONEL I feel so pure.

Pause.

DES Well, you're right. You're right to feel pure. You know why?

LIONEL Why?

DES Because you're keeping the world clean for democracy.

They look into each other's eyes.

I'm going to shake you by the hand.

DES *shakes* LIONEL*'s hand. He then gestures to the man in the chair with his thumb.*

And so will he . . . (*He looks at his watch.*) in about thirty-five minutes.

PARTY TIME

Party Time first published
by Faber and Faber Ltd 1991
© Fraser52 Limited, 1991

Party Time was first performed by the Almeida
Theatre Company at the Almeida Theatre, London,
on 31 October 1991. The cast was as follows:

TERRY	Peter Howitt
GAVIN	Barry Foster
DUSTY	Cordelia Roche
MELISSA	Dorothy Tutin
LIZ	Tacye Nichols
CHARLOTTE	Nicola Pagett
FRED	Roger Lloyd Pack
DOUGLAS	Gawn Grainger
JIMMY	Harry Burton

Directed by Harold Pinter
Designed by Mark Thompson

Characters

TERRY
a man of forty

GAVIN
a man in his fifties

DUSTY
a woman in her twenties

MELISSA
a woman of seventy

LIZ
a woman in her thirties

CHARLOTTE
a woman in her thirties

FRED
a man in his forties

DOUGLAS
a man of fifty

JIMMY
a young man

GAVIN's *flat.*

*A large room. Sofas, armchairs, etc. People sitting,
standing. A* WAITER *with a drinks tray.*

*Two doors. One door, which is never used, is half
open, in a dim light.*

GAVIN *and* TERRY *stand in foreground. The others sit
in half-light, drinking.*

Spasmodic party music throughout the play.

TERRY I tell you, it's got everything.

GAVIN Has it?

TERRY Oh, yes. Real class.

GAVIN Really?

TERRY Real class. I mean, what I mean to say, you
play a game of tennis, you have a beautiful swim,
they've got a bar right there –

GAVIN Where?

TERRY By the pool. You can have a fruit juice on the
spot, no extra charge, then they give you this fantastic
hot towel –

GAVIN Hot?

TERRY Wonderful. And I mean hot. I'm not joking.

GAVIN Like the barber.

TERRY Barber?

GAVIN In the barber shop. When I was a boy.

TERRY Oh yes?

Pause.

What do you mean?

GAVIN They used to put a hot towel over your face, you see, over your nose and eyes. I had it done thousands of times. It got rid of all the blackheads, all the blackheads on your face.

TERRY Blackheads?

GAVIN It burnt them out. The towels, you see, were as hot as you could stand. That's what the barber used to say: 'Hot enough for you, sir?' It burnt all the blackheads out of your skin.

Pause.

I was born in the West Country, of course. So I could be talking only of West Country barber shops. But on the other hand I'm pretty sure that hot towels for blackheads were used in barber shops throughout the land in those days. Yes, I believe it was common practice in those days.

TERRY Well, I'm sure it was. I'm sure it was. But no, these towels I'm talking about are big bath towels, towels for the body, I'm just talking about pure comfort, that's why I'm telling you, the place has got real class, it's got everything. Mind you, there's a waiting list as long as – I mean you've got to be proposed and seconded, and then they've got to check you out, they don't let any old spare bugger in there, why should they?

GAVIN Quite right.

TERRY But of course it goes without saying that someone like yourself would be warmly welcome – as an honorary member.

GAVIN How kind.

DUSTY *walks through the door and joins them.*

DUSTY Did you hear what's happened to Jimmy? What's happened to Jimmy?

TERRY Nothing's happened.

DUSTY Nothing?

GAVIN Nobody is discussing this. Nobody's discussing it, sweetie. Do you follow me? Nothing's happened to Jimmy. And if you're not a good girl I'll spank you.

DUSTY What's going on?

TERRY Tell him about the new club. I've just been telling him about the club. She's a member.

GAVIN What's it like?

DUSTY Oh, it's beautiful. It's got everything. It's beautiful. The lighting's wonderful. Isn't it? Did you tell him about the alcoves?

TERRY Well, there's a bar, you see, with glass alcoves, looking out to under the water.

DUSTY People swim at you, you see, while you're having a drink.

TERRY Lovely girls.

DUSTY And men.

TERRY Mostly girls.

DUSTY Did you tell him about the food?

TERRY The cannelloni is brilliant.

DUSTY It's first class. The food is really first class.

TERRY They even do chopped liver.

GAVIN You couldn't describe that as a local dish.

MELISSA *comes through the door and joins them.*

MELISSA What on earth's going on out there? It's like the Black Death.

TERRY What is?

MELISSA The town's dead. There's nobody on the streets, there's not a soul in sight, apart from some . . . soldiers. My driver had to stop at a . . . you know . . . what do you call it? . . . a road block. We had to say who we were . . . it really was a trifle . . .

GAVIN Oh, there's just been a little . . . you know. . .

TERRY Nothing in it. Can I introduce you? Gavin White – our host. Dame Melissa.

GAVIN So glad you could come.

TERRY What are you drinking?

The WAITER *approaches.*

Have a glass of wine.

He hands MELISSA *a glass.*

DUSTY I keep hearing all these things. I don't know what to believe.

MELISSA (*to* GAVIN) What a lovely party.

TERRY (*to* DUSTY) What did you say?

DUSTY I said I don't know what to believe.

TERRY You don't have to believe anything. You just have to shut up and mind your own business, how many times do I have to tell you? You come to a lovely party like this, all you have to do is shut up and enjoy the hospitality and mind your own fucking business. How many more times do I have to tell you? You keep hearing all these things. You keep hearing all these things spread by pricks about pricks. What's it got to do with you?

Lights up on LIZ *and* CHARLOTTE, *sitting on a sofa.*

LIZ So beautiful. The mouth, really. And of course the eyes.

CHARLOTTE Yes.

LIZ Not to mention his hands. I'll tell you, I would have killed –

CHARLOTTE I could see –

LIZ But that bitch had her legs all over him.

CHARLOTTE I know.

LIZ I thought she was going to crush him to death.

CHARLOTTE Unbelievable.

LIZ Her skirt was right up to her neck – did you see?

CHARLOTTE So barefaced –

LIZ Next minute she's lugging him up the stairs.

CHARLOTTE I saw.

LIZ But as he was going, do you know what he did?

CHARLOTTE What?

LIZ He looked at me.

CHARLOTTE Did he?

LIZ I swear it. As he was being lugged out he looked back, he looked back, I swear, at me, like a wounded deer, I shall never, as long as I live, forget it, I shall never forget that look.

CHARLOTTE How beautiful.

LIZ I could have cut her throat, that nymphomaniac slut.

CHARLOTTE Yes, but think what happened. Think of the wonderful side of it. Because for you it was love, it was falling in love. That's what it was, wasn't it? You fell in love.

LIZ I did. You're right. I fell in love. I am in love. I haven't slept all night, I'm in love.

CHARLOTTE How many times does that happen? That's the point. How often does it really happen? How often does anyone experience such a thing?

LIZ Yes, you're right. That's what happened to me. That is what has happened – to me.

CHARLOTTE That's why you're in such pain.

LIZ Yes, because that big-titted tart –

CHARLOTTE Raped the man you love.

LIZ Yes she did. That's what she did. She raped my beloved.

Lights up on FRED *and* DOUGLAS, *drinking.*

FRED We've got to make it work.

DOUGLAS What?

FRED The country.

Pause.

DOUGLAS You've brought the house down with that one, Fred.

FRED But that's what matters. That's what matters. Doesn't it?

DOUGLAS Oh, it matters. It matters. I should say it matters. All this fucking-about has to stop.

FRED You mean it?

DOUGLAS I mean it all right.

FRED I admire people like you.

DOUGLAS So do I.

FRED *clenches his fist.*

FRED A bit of that.

DOUGLAS *clenches his fist.*

DOUGLAS A bit of that.

Pause.

FRED How's it going tonight?

DOUGLAS Like clockwork. Look. Let me tell you something. We want peace. We want peace and we're going to get it.

FRED Quite right.

DOUGLAS We want peace and we're going to get it. But we want that peace to be cast iron. No leaks. No draughts. Cast iron. Tight as a drum. That's the kind of peace we want and that's the kind of peace we're going to get. A cast-iron peace.

He clenches his fist.

Like this.

FRED You know, I really admire people like you.

DOUGLAS So do I.

Lights up on MELISSA, DUSTY, TERRY *and* GAVIN.

MELISSA (*to* DUSTY) How sweet of you to say so.

DUSTY But you do have a really wonderful figure. Honestly. Doesn't she?

TERRY I've known this lady for years. Haven't I? How many years have I known you? Years. And she's always looked the same. Haven't you? She's always looked the same. Hasn't she?

GAVIN Has she?

DUSTY Always. Haven't you?

TERRY She has. Isn't that right?

MELISSA Oh, you're joking.

TERRY Not me. I never joke. Have you ever heard me crack a joke?

MELISSA No, if I still look all right, it's probably because I've just joined this new club – (*To* GAVIN.) Do you know it?

TERRY We were just telling him. We were just telling him all about it.

MELISSA Oh, were you?

GAVIN Just now, yes. Sounds delightful. You're a member, are you?

MELISSA Oh yes. I think it's saved my life. The swimming. Why don't you join? Do you play tennis?

GAVIN I'm a golfer. I play golf.

MELISSA What else do you do?

GAVIN (*smiling*) I don't understand what you mean.

TERRY What else does he do? He doesn't do anything else. He plays golf. That's what he does. That's all he does. He plays golf.

GAVIN Well . . . I do sail. I do own a boat.

DUSTY I love boats.

TERRY What?

DUSTY I love boats. I love boating.

TERRY Boating. Did you hear that?

DUSTY I love cooking on boats.

TERRY The only thing she doesn't like on boats is being fucked on boats. That's what she doesn't like.

MELISSA That's funny. I thought everyone liked that.

Silence.

DUSTY Does anyone know what's happened to my brother Jimmy?

TERRY I don't know what it is. Perhaps she's deaf or perhaps my voice isn't strong enough or distinct enough. What do you think, folks? Perhaps there's something faulty with my diction. I'm forced to float all these possibilities because I thought I had said that we don't discuss this question of what has happened to Jimmy, that it's not up for discussion, that it's not on anyone's agenda. I thought I had already made that point quite clearly. But perhaps my voice isn't strong enough or perhaps my articulation isn't good enough or perhaps she's deaf.

DUSTY It's on my agenda.

TERRY What did you say?

DUSTY I said it's on my agenda.

TERRY No no, you've got it wrong there, old darling. What you've got wrong there, old darling, what you've got totally wrong, is that you don't have any agenda. Got it? You have no agenda. Absolutely the opposite is the case. (*To the others.*) I'm going to have to give her a real talking to when I get her home, I can see that.

GAVIN So odd, the number of men who can't control their wives.

TERRY What?

GAVIN (*to* MELISSA) It's the root of so many ills, you know. Uncontrollable wives.

MELISSA Yes, I know what you mean.

TERRY What are you saying to me?

GAVIN (*to* MELISSA) I went for a walk in the woods the other day. I had no idea how many squirrels were still left in this country. I find them such vivacious creatures, quite enchanting.

757

MELISSA I used to love them as a girl.

GAVIN Did you really? What about hawks?

MELISSA Oh I loved hawks too. And eagles. But certainly hawks. The kestrel. The way it flew, and hovered, over my valley. It made me cry. I still cry.

> *The lights in the room dim.*
>
> *The light beyond the open door gradually intensifies. It burns into the room.*
>
> *The door light fades down. The room lights come up on* DOUGLAS, FRED, LIZ *and* CHARLOTTE.

DOUGLAS Oh, have you met my wife?

FRED (*to* LIZ) How do you do?

LIZ This is Charlotte.

FRED We've met before.

LIZ You've met before?

CHARLOTTE Oh yes. We've met. He gave me a leg up in life.

DOUGLAS Did you really? How exciting.

FRED It was.

DOUGLAS Was it exciting for you too? To be given a leg up?

CHARLOTTE Mmmmnnn. Yes. Oh, yes. I'm still trembling.

DOUGLAS How exciting.

LIZ I think this is such a gorgeous party. Don't you?
I mean I just think it's such a gorgeous party. Don't
you? I think it's such fun. I love the fact that people are
so well dressed. Casual but good. Do you know what
I mean? Is it silly to say I feel proud? I mean to be part
of the society of beautifully dressed people? Oh God
I don't know, elegance, style, grace, taste, don't these
words, these concepts, mean anything any more? I'm
not alone, am I, in thinking them incredibly important?
Anyway I love everything that flows. I can't tell you
how happy I feel.

FRED (*to* CHARLOTTE) You married someone. I've
forgotten who it was.

Silence.

CHARLOTTE He died.

Silence.

DOUGLAS If you're free this summer do come to our
island. We take an island for the summer. Do come.
There's more or less nobody there. Just a few local
people who do us proud. Terribly civil. Everything
works. I have my own generator. But the storms are
wild, aren't they, darling? If you like storms. Siroccos.
Makes you feel alive. Truly alive. Makes the old pulse
go rat-a-tat-tat. God it can be wild, can't it, darling?
Makes the old pulse go rat-a-tat-tat. Raises the ante.
You know. Gets the blood up. Actually, when I'm out
there on the island I feel ten years younger. I could
take anyone on. Man, woman or child, what?

He laughs.

I could take a wild animal on. But then when the storm is over and night falls and the moon is out in all its glory and all you're left with is the rhythm of the sea, of the waves, you know what God intended for the human race, you know what paradise is.

Lights up on TERRY *and* DUSTY, *in a corner of the room.*

TERRY Are you mad? Do you know what that man is?

DUSTY Yes, I think I know what that man is.

TERRY You don't know what he is. You have no idea. You don't know what his position is. You have simply no idea. You simply have no idea.

DUSTY He has lovely manners. He seems to come from another world. A courteous, caring world. He'll send me flowers in the morning.

TERRY No he bloody won't. Oh no he bloody won't.

DUSTY Poor darling, are you upset? Have I let you down? I've let you down. And I've always tried to be such a good wife. Such a good wife.

They stare at each other.

Perhaps you'll kill me when we get home? Do you think you will? Do you think you'll put an end to it? Do you think there is an end to it? What do you think? Do you think that if you put an end to me that would be the end of everything for everyone? Will everything and everyone die with me?

TERRY Yes, you're all going to die together, you and all your lot.

DUSTY How are you going to do it? Tell me.

TERRY Easy. We've got dozens of options. We could suffocate every single one of you at a given signal or we could shove a broomstick up each individual arse at another given signal or we could poison all the mother's milk in the world so that every baby would drop dead before it opened its perverted bloody mouth.

DUSTY But will it be fun for me? Will it be fun?

TERRY You'll love it. But I'm not going to tell you which method we'll use. I just want you to have a lot of sexual anticipation. I want you to look forward to whatever the means employed with a lot of sexual anticipation.

DUSTY But you still love me?

TERRY Of course I love you. You're the mother of my children.

DUSTY Oh incidentally, what's happened to Jimmy?

Lights up on FRED *and* CHARLOTTE.

FRED Such a long time.

CHARLOTTE Such a long time.

FRED Isn't it?

CHARLOTTE Oh, yes. Ages.

FRED You're looking as beautiful as ever.

CHARLOTTE So are you.

FRED Me? Not me.

CHARLOTTE Oh, you are. Well, in a manner of speaking.

FRED What do you mean, in a manner of speaking?

CHARLOTTE Oh, I meant you look as beautiful as ever.

FRED But I never was beautiful. In any way.

CHARLOTTE No, that's true. You weren't. In any way at all. I've been talking shit. In a manner of speaking.

FRED Your language was always deplorable.

CHARLOTTE Yes. Appalling.

FRED Are you enjoying the party?

CHARLOTTE Best party I've been to in years.

Pause.

FRED You said your husband died.

CHARLOTTE My what?

FRED Your husband.

CHARLOTTE Oh my husband. Oh yes. That's right. He died.

FRED Was it a long illness?

CHARLOTTE Short.

FRED Ah.

    Pause.

Quick then.

CHARLOTTE Quick, yes. Short and quick.

    Pause.

FRED Better that way.

CHARLOTTE Really?

FRED I would have thought.

CHARLOTTE Ah. I see. Yes.

    Pause.

Better for who?

FRED What?

CHARLOTTE You said it would be better. Better for who?

FRED For you.

    CHARLOTTE *laughs.*

CHARLOTTE Yes! I'm glad you didn't say him.

FRED Well, I could say him. A quick death must be better than a slow one. It stands to reason.

CHARLOTTE No it doesn't.

    Pause.

Anyway, I'll bet it can be quick and slow at the same time. I bet it can. I bet death can be both things at the same time. Oh by the way, he wasn't ill.

Pause.

FRED You're still very beautiful.

CHARLOTTE I think there's something going on in the street.

FRED What?

CHARLOTTE I think there's something going on in the street.

FRED Leave the street to us.

CHARLOTTE Who's us?

FRED Oh, just us . . . you know.

She stares at him.

CHARLOTTE God, your looks! No, seriously. You're still so handsome! How do you do it? What's your diet? What's your regime? What *is* your regime by the way? What do you do to keep yourself so . . . I don't know . . . so . . . oh, I don't know . . . so trim, so fit?

FRED I lead a clean life.

DOUGLAS *and* LIZ *join them.*

CHARLOTTE (*to* DOUGLAS) Do you too?

DOUGLAS Do I what?

CHARLOTTE Fred says he looks so fit and so . . . handsome . . . because he leads a clean life. What about you?

DOUGLAS I lead an incredibly clean life. It doesn't make me handsome but it makes me happy.

LIZ And it makes me happy too. So happy.

DOUGLAS Even though I'm not handsome?

LIZ But you are. You are. Isn't he? He is. You are. Isn't he?

DOUGLAS *puts his arm around her.*

DOUGLAS When we were first married we lived in a two-roomed flat. I was – I'll be frank – I was a traveller, a commercial traveller, a salesman – it's true, that's what I was and I don't deny it – and travel I did. Didn't I? Travel I did. Because my little girl here had given birth to twins.

He laughs.

Can you believe it? Twins. I had to slave my guts out, I can tell you. But this girl here, this little girl here, do you know what she did? She looked after those twins all by herself! No maid, no help, nothing. She did it herself – all by herself. And when I got back from my travelling I would find the flat immaculate, the twins bathed and in bed, tucked up in bed, fast asleep, my wife looking beautiful and my dinner in the oven.

FRED *applauds.*

And that's why we're still together.

He kisses LIZ *on the cheek.*

That's why we're still together.

The lights in the room dim.

The light beyond the open door gradually intensifies. It burns into the room.

The door light fades down. The room lights come up on TERRY, DUSTY, GAVIN, MELISSA, FRED, CHARLOTTE, DOUGLAS *and* LIZ.

TERRY The thing is, it is actually real value for money. Now this is a very, very unusual thing. It is an extremely unusual thing these days to find that you are getting real value for money. You take your hand out of your pocket and you put your money down and you know what you're getting. And what you're getting is absolutely gold-plated service. Gold-plated service in all departments. You've got real catering. You've got catering on all levels. You've not only got very good catering in itself – you know, food, that kind of thing – and napkins – you know, all that, wonderful, first rate – but you've also got artistic catering – you actually have an atmosphere – in this club – which is catering artistically for its clientele. I'm referring to the kind of light, the kind of paint, the kind of music, the club offers. I'm talking about a truly warm and harmonious environment. You won't find voices raised in our club. People don't do vulgar and sordid and offensive things. And if they do we kick them in the balls and chuck them down the stairs with no trouble at all.

766

MELISSA Can I subscribe to all that has just been said?

Pause.

I would like to subscribe to all that has just been
said. I would like to add my voice. I have belonged to
many tennis and swimming clubs. Many tennis and
swimming clubs. And at some of these clubs I first met
some of my dearest friends. All of them are now dead.
Every friend I ever had. Or ever met. Is dead. They are
all of them dead. Every single one of them. I have
absolutely not one left. None are left. Nothing is left.
What was it all for? The tennis and the swimming
clubs? What was it all for? What?

Silence.

But the clubs died too and rightly so. I mean there is a
distinction to be made. My friends went the way of all
flesh and I don't regret their passing. They weren't my
friends anyway. I couldn't stand half of them. But the
clubs! The clubs died, the swimming and the tennis
clubs died because they were based on ideas which had
no moral foundation, no moral foundation whatsoever.
But *our* club, *our* club – is a club which is activated,
which is inspired by a moral sense, a moral awareness,
a set of moral values which is –-1 have to say –
unshakeable, rigorous, fundamental, constant. Thank
you.

Applause.

GAVIN Yes, I'm terribly glad you've said all that. (*To
the others.*) Aren't you?

767

DOUGLAS First rate.

LIZ So moving.

TERRY Fantastic.

FRED Right on the nail.

CHARLOTTE So true.

DUSTY Oh yes.

She claps her hands.

Oh yes.

DOUGLAS Absolutely first rate.

GAVIN Yes, it was first rate. And it desperately needed saying. And how splendid that it was said tonight, at such an enjoyable party, in such congenial company. I must say I speak as a very happy host. And by the way, I'll really have to join this wonderful club of yours, won't I?

TERRY You're elected forthwith. You're an honorary member. As of today.

Laughter and applause.

GAVIN Thank you very much indeed. Now I believe one or two of our guests encountered traffic problems on their way here tonight. I apologise for that, but I would like to assure you that all such problems and all related problems will be resolved very soon. Between ourselves, we've had a bit of a round-up this evening.

This round-up is coming to an end. In fact normal services will be resumed shortly. That is, after all, our aim. Normal service. We, if you like, insist on it. We will insist on it. We do. That's all we ask, that the service this country provides will run on normal, secure and legitimate paths and that the ordinary citizen be allowed to pursue his labours and his leisure in peace. Thank you all so much for coming here tonight. It's been really lovely to see you, quite smashing.

The room lights go down.

The light from the door intensifies, burning into the room.

Everyone is still, in silhouette.

A man comes out of the light and stands in the doorway. He is thinly dressed.

JIMMY Sometimes I hear things. Then it's quiet.

I had a name. It was Jimmy. People called me Jimmy. That was my name.

Sometimes I hear things. Then everything is quiet. When everything is quiet I hear my heart.

When the terrible noises come I don't hear anything. Don't hear don't breathe am blind.

Then everything is quiet. I hear a heartbeat. It is probably not my heartbeat. It is probably someone else's heartbeat.

What am I?

Sometimes a door bangs, I hear voices, then it stops.
Everything stops. It all stops. It all closes. It closes
down. It shuts. It all shuts. It shuts down. It shuts. I see
nothing at any time any more. I sit sucking the dark.

It's what I have. The dark is in my mouth and I suck
it. It's the only thing I have. It's mine. It's my own.
I suck it.

MOONLIGHT

Moonlight was first performed at the Almeida Theatre,
London, on 7 September 1993. The cast was as
follows:

ANDY	Ian Holm
BEL	Anna Massey
JAKE	Douglas Hodge
FRED	Michael Sheen
MARIA	Jill Johnson
RALPH	Edward de Souza
BRIDGET	Claire Skinner

Directed by David Leveaux
Designed by Bob Crowley

Characters

ANDY
a man in his fifties

BEL
a woman of fifty

JAKE
a man of twenty-eight

FRED
a man of twenty-seven

MARIA
a woman of fifty

RALPH
a man in his fifties

BRIDGET
a girl of sixteen

Three Main Playing Areas

1 Andy's bedroom – well furnished

2 Fred's bedroom – shabby

(*These rooms are in different locations.*)

3 An area in which Bridget appears,
through which Andy moves at night and
where Jake, Fred and Bridget play their scene.

BRIDGET *in faint light.*

BRIDGET I can't sleep. There's no moon. It's so dark. I think I'll go downstairs and walk about. I won't make a noise. I'll be very quiet. Nobody will hear me. It's so dark and I know everything is more silent when it's dark. But I don't want anyone to know I'm moving about in the night. I don't want to wake my father and mother. They're so tired. They have given so much of their life for me and for my brothers. All their life, in fact. All their energies and all their love. They need to sleep in peace and wake up rested. I must see that this happens. It is my task. Because I know that when they look at me they see that I am all they have left of their life.

ANDY'*s bedroom.*

ANDY *in bed.* BEL *sitting.*

She is doing embroidery.

ANDY Where are the boys? Have you found them?

BEL I'm trying.

ANDY You've been trying for weeks. And failing. It's enough to make the cat laugh. Do we have a cat?

777

BEL We do.

ANDY Is it laughing?

BEL Fit to bust.

ANDY What at? Me, I suppose.

BEL Why would your own dear cat laugh at you?
That cat who was your own darling kitten when she
was young and so were you, that cat you have so
dandled and patted and petted and loved, why should
she, how could she, laugh at her master? It's not
remotely credible.

ANDY But she's laughing at someone?

BEL She's laughing at me. At my ineptitude. At my
failure to find the boys, at my failure to bring the boys
to their father's deathbed.

ANDY Well that's more like it. You are the proper
target for a cat's derision. And how I loved you.

  Pause.

What a wonderful woman you were. You had such a
great heart. You still have, of course. I can hear it from
here. Banging away.

  Pause.

BEL Do you feel anything? What do you feel? Do you
feel hot? Or cold? Or both? What do you feel? Do
you feel cold in your legs? Or hot? What about your
fingers? What are they? Are they cold? Or hot? Or
neither cold nor hot?

ANDY Is this a joke? My God, she's taking the piss out of me. My own wife. On my deathbed. She's as bad as that fucking cat.

BEL Perhaps it's my convent school education but the term 'taking the piss' does leave me somewhat nonplussed.

ANDY Nonplussed! You've never been nonplussed in the whole of your voracious, lascivious, libidinous life.

BEL You may be dying but that doesn't mean you have to be *totally* ridiculous.

ANDY Why am I dying, anyway? I've never harmed a soul. You don't die if you're good. You die if you're bad.

BEL We girls were certainly aware of the verb 'to piss', oh yes, in the sixth form, certainly. I piss, you piss, she pisses, et cetera.

ANDY We girls! Christ!

BEL The term 'taking the piss', however, was not known to us.

ANDY It means mockery! It means to mock. It means mockery! Mockery! Mockery!

BEL Really? How odd. Is there a rational explanation to this?

ANDY Rationality went down the drain donkey's years ago and hasn't been seen since. All that famous rationality of yours is swimming about in waste disposal turdology. It's burping and farting away in the cesspit for ever and ever. That's destiny speaking, sweetheart! That was always the destiny of your famous rational intelligence, to choke to death in sour cream and pigswill.

BEL Oh do calm down, for goodness sake.

ANDY Why? Why?

Pause.

What do you mean?

Fred's bedroom.

FRED *in bed.* JAKE *in to him.*

JAKE Brother.

FRED Brother.

JAKE sits by the bed.

JAKE And how is my little brother?

FRED Cheerful though gloomy. Uneasily poised.

JAKE All will be well. And all manner of things shall be well.

Pause.

FRED What kind of holiday are you giving me this year? Art or the beach?

JAKE I would think a man of your calibre needs a bit of both.

FRED Or nothing of either.

JAKE It's very important to keep your pecker up.

FRED How far up?

JAKE Well . . . for example . . . how high is a Chinaman?

FRED Quite.

JAKE Exactly.

Pause.

FRED You were writing poems when you were a mere child, isn't that right?

JAKE I was writing poems before I could read.

FRED Listen. I happen to know that you were writing poems before you could speak.

JAKE Listen! I was writing poems before I was born.

FRED So you would say you were the real thing?

JAKE The authentic article.

FRED Never knowingly undersold.

JAKE Precisely.

Silence.

FRED Listen. I've been thinking about the whole caboodle. I'll tell you what we need. We need capital.

JAKE I've got it.

FRED You've got it?

JAKE I've got it.

FRED Where did you find it?

JAKE Divine right.

FRED Christ.

JAKE Exactly.

FRED You're joking.

JAKE No, no, my father weighed it all up carefully the day I was born.

FRED Oh, your father? Was he the one who was sleeping with your mother?

JAKE He weighed it all up. He weighed up all the pros and cons and then without further ado he called a meeting. He called a meeting of the trustees of his estate, you see, to discuss all these pros and cons. My father was a very thorough man. He invariably brought the meetings in on time and under budget and he always kept a weather eye open for blasphemy, gluttony and buggery.

FRED He was a truly critical force?

JAKE He was not in it for pleasure or glory. Let me make that quite clear. Applause came not his way. Nor did he seek it. Gratitude came not his way. Nor did he seek it. Masturbation came not his way. Nor did he seek it. I'm sorry – I meant approbation came not his way –

FRED Oh, didn't it really?

JAKE Nor did he seek it.

Pause.

I'd like to apologise for what I can only describe as a lapse in concentration.

FRED It can happen to anybody.

Pause.

JAKE My father adhered strictly to the rule of law.

FRED Which is not a very long way from the rule of thumb.

JAKE Not as the crow flies, no.

FRED But the trustees, I take it, could not, by any stretch of the imagination, be described as a particularly motley crew?

JAKE Neither motley nor random. They were kept, however, under strict and implacable scrutiny. They were allowed to go to the lavatory just one and a half times a session. They evacuated to a time clock.

FRED And the motion was carried?

JAKE The motion was carried, nine votes to four, Jorrocks abstaining.

FRED Not a pretty sight, by the sound of it.

JAKE The vicar stood up. He said that it was a very unusual thing, a truly rare and unusual thing, for a man in the prime of his life to leave – without codicil or reservation – his personal fortune to his newborn son the very day of that baby's birth – before the boy had had a chance to say a few words or aspire to the unknowable or cut for partners or cajole the japonica or tickle his arse with a feather –

FRED Whose arse?

JAKE It was an act, went on the vicar, which, for sheer undaunted farsightedness, unflinching moral resolve, stern intellectual vision, classic philosophical detachment, passionate religious fervour, profound emotional intensity, bloodtingling spiritual ardour, spellbinding metaphysical chutzpah – stood alone.

FRED Tantamount to a backflip in the lotus position.

JAKE It was an act, went on the vicar, without a vestige of lust but with any amount of bucketfuls of lustre.

FRED So the vicar was impressed?

JAKE The only one of the trustees not impressed was my Uncle Rufus.

FRED Now you're telling me you had an uncle called Rufus. Is that what you're telling me?

JAKE Uncle Rufus was not impressed.

FRED Why not? Do I know the answer? I think I do. I think I do. Do I?

  Pause.

JAKE I think you do.

FRED I think so too. I think I do.

JAKE I think so too.

Pause.

FRED The answer is that your father was just a little bit short of a few krugerrands.

JAKE He'd run out of pesetas in a pretty spectacular fashion.

FRED He had, only a few nights before, dropped a packet on the pier at Bognor Regis.

JAKE Fishing for tiddlers.

FRED His casino life had long been a lost horizon.

JAKE The silver pail was empty.

FRED As was the gold.

JAKE Nary an emerald.

FRED Nary a gem.

JAKE Gemless in Wall Street –

FRED To the bank with fuck-all.

JAKE Yes – it must and will be said – the speech my father gave at that trustees meeting on that wonderfully soft summer morning in the Cotswolds all those years ago was the speech either of a mountebank – a child – a shyster – a fool – a villain –

FRED Or a saint.

  MARIA *to them,* JAKE *stands.*

MARIA Do you remember me? I was your mother's
best friend. You're both so tall. I remember you when
you were little boys. And Bridget of course. I once
took you all to the Zoo, with your father. We had tea.
Do you remember? I used to come to tea, with your
mother. We drank so much tea in those days! My three
are all in terribly good form. Sarah's doing marvellously
well and Lucien's thriving at the Consulate and as for
Susannah, there's no stopping her. But don't you
remember the word games we all used to play? Then
we'd walk across the Common. That's where we met
Ralph. He was refereeing a football match. He did it,
oh I don't know, with such aplomb, such command.
Your mother and I were so . . . impressed. He was
always ahead of the game. He knew where the ball
was going before it was kicked. Osmosis. I think that's
the word. He's still as osmotic as anyone I've ever
come across. Much more so, of course. Most people
have no osmotic quality whatsoever. But of course in
those days – I won't deny it – I had a great affection
for your father. And so had your mother – for your
father. Your father possessed little in the way of
osmosis but nor did he hide his blushes under a barrel.
I mean he wasn't a pretender, he didn't waste precious
time. And how he danced. How he danced. One of
the great waltzers. An elegance and grace long gone.
A firmness and authority so seldom encountered. And
he looked you directly in the eye. Unwavering. As he

swirled you across the floor. A rare gift. But I was young in those days. So was your mother. Your mother was marvellously young and quickening every moment. I – I must say – particularly when I saw your mother being swirled across the floor by your father – felt buds breaking out all over the place. I thought I'd go mad.

ANDY's *room*. ANDY *and* BEL.

ANDY I'll tell you something about me. I sweated over a hot desk all my working life and nobody ever found a flaw in my working procedures. Nobody ever uncovered the slightest hint of negligence or misdemeanour. Never. I was an inspiration to others. I inspired the young men and women down from here and down from there. I inspired them to put their shoulders to the wheel and their noses to the grindstone and to keep faith at all costs with the structure which after all ensured the ordered government of all our lives, which took perfect care of us, which held us to its bosom, as it were. I was a first-class civil servant. I was admired and respected. I do not say I was loved. I didn't want to be loved. Love is an attribute no civil servant worth his salt would give house room to. It's redundant. An excrescence. No no, I'll tell you what I was. I was an envied and feared force in the temples of the just.

BEL But you never swore in the office?

ANDY I would never use obscene language in the office. Certainly not. I kept my obscene language for the home, where it belongs.

Pause.

Oh there's something I forgot to tell you. I bumped
into Maria the other day, the day before I was stricken.
She invited me back to her flat for a slice of plum duff.
I said to her, If you have thighs prepare to bare them
now.

BEL Yes, you always entertained a healthy lust for her.

ANDY A *healthy* lust? Do you think so?

BEL And she for you.

ANDY Has that been the whisper along the white
sands of the blue Caribbean? I'm dying. Am I dying?

BEL If you were dying you'd be dead.

ANDY How do you work that out?

BEL You'd be dead if you were dying.

ANDY I sometimes think I'm married to a raving
lunatic! But I'm always prepared to look on the sunny
side of things. You mean I'll see spring again? I'll see
another spring? All the paraphernalia of flowers?

BEL What a lovely use of language. You know, you've
never used language in such a way before. You've
never said such a thing before.

ANDY Oh so what? I've said other things, haven't I?
Plenty of other things. All my life. All my life I've been
saying plenty of other things.

BEL Yes, it's quite true that all your life in all your
personal and social attachments the language you

employed was mainly coarse, crude, vacuous, puerile, obscene and brutal to a degree. Most people were ready to vomit after no more than ten minutes in your company. But this is not to say that beneath this vicious some would say demented exterior there did not exist a delicate even poetic sensibility, the sensibility of a young horse in the golden age, in the golden past of our forefathers.

Silence.

ANDY Anyway, admit it. You always entertained a healthy lust for Maria yourself. And she for you. But let me make something quite clear. I was never jealous. I was not jealous then. Nor am I jealous now.

BEL Why should you be jealous? She was your mistress. Throughout the early and lovely days of our marriage.

ANDY She must have reminded me of you.

Pause.

The past is a mist.

Pause.

Once . . . I remember this . . . once . . . a woman walked towards me across a darkening room.

Pause.

BEL That was me.

Pause.

ANDY You?

Third area.

Faint light. BRIDGET.

BRIDGET I am walking slowly in a dense jungle. But I'm not suffocating. I can breathe. That is because I can see the sky through the leaves.

> *Pause.*

I'm surrounded by flowers. Hibiscus, oleander, bougainvillea, jacaranda. The turf under my feet is soft.

> *Pause.*

I crossed so many fierce landscapes to get here. Thorns, stones, stinging nettles, barbed wire, skeletons of men and women in ditches. There was no hiding there. There was no yielding. There was no solace, no shelter.

> *Pause.*

But here there is shelter. I can hide. I am hidden. The flowers surround me but they don't imprison me. I am free. Hidden but free. I'm a captive no longer. I'm lost no longer. No one can find me or see me. I can be seen only by eyes of the jungle, eyes in the leaves. But they don't want to harm me.

> *Pause.*

There is a smell of burning. A velvet odour, very deep, an echo like a bell.

> *Pause.*

No one in the world can find me.

Fred's bedroom.

FRED *and* JAKE, *sitting at a table.*

JAKE What did you say your name was? I've made a note of it somewhere.

FRED Macpherson.

JAKE That's funny. I thought it was Gonzalez. I would be right in saying you were born in Tooting Common?

FRED I came here at your urgent request. You wanted to consult me.

JAKE Did I go that far?

FRED When I say 'you' I don't of course mean you. I mean 'they'.

JAKE You mean Kellaway.

FRED Kellaway? I don't know Kellaway.

JAKE You don't?

FRED Yours was the name they gave me.

JAKE What name was that?

FRED Saunders.

JAKE Oh quite.

FRED They didn't mention Kellaway.

JAKE When you say 'they' I take it you don't mean 'they'?

FRED I mean a man called Sims.

JAKE Jim Sims?

FRED No.

JAKE Well, if it isn't Jim Sims I can't imagine what Sims you can possibly be talking about.

FRED That's no skin off my nose.

JAKE I fervently hope you're right.

  JAKE *examines papers.*

Oh by the way, Manning's popping in to see you in a few minutes.

FRED Manning?

JAKE Yes, just to say hello. He can't stay long. He's on his way to Huddersfield.

FRED Manning?

JAKE Huddersfield, yes.

FRED I don't know any Manning.

JAKE I know you don't. That's why he's popping in to see you.

FRED Now look here. I think this is getting a bit out of court. First Kellaway, now Manning. Two men I have not only never met but have never even heard of. I'm going to have to take this back to my people, I'm afraid. I'll have to get a further briefing on this.

JAKE Oh I'm terribly sorry – of course – you must know Manning by his other name.

FRED What's that?

JAKE Rawlings.

FRED I know Rawlings.

JAKE I had no right to call him Manning.

FRED Not if he's the Rawlings I know.

JAKE He is the Rawlings you know.

FRED Well, this quite clearly brings us straight back to Kellaway. What's Kellaway's other name?

JAKE Saunders.

Pause.

FRED But that's your name.

RALPH *to* JAKE *and* FRED.

RALPH Were you keen on the game of soccer when you were lads, you boys? Probably not. Probably thinking of other things. Kissing girls. Foreign literature. Snooker. I know the form. I can tell by the complexion, I can tell by the stance, I can tell by the way a man holds himself whether he has an outdoor disposition or not. Your father could never be described as a natural athlete. Not by a long chalk. The man was a thinker. Well, there's a place in this world for thinking, I certainly wouldn't argue with that. The trouble with so much thinking, though, or with that which calls itself thinking, is that it's like farting Annie Laurie down a keyhole. A waste of your time and mine. What do you think this thinking is

793

pretending to do? Eh? It's pretending to make things
clear, you see, it's pretending to clarify things. But
what's it really doing? Eh? What do you think? I'll tell
you. It's confusing you, it's blinding you, it's sending
the mind into a spin, it's making you dizzy, it's making
you so dizzy that by the end of the day you don't
know whether you're on your arse or your elbow, you
don't know whether you're coming or going. I've
always been a pretty vigorous man myself. I had a
seafaring background. I was the captain of a lugger.
The bosun's name was Ripper. But after years at sea
I decided to give the Arts a chance generally. I had
tried a bit of amateur refereeing but it didn't work out.
But I had a natural talent for acting and I also played
the piano and I could paint. But I should have been an
architect. That's where the money is. It was your mother
and father woke me up to poetry and art. They changed
my life. And then of course I married my wife. A fine
woman but demanding. She was looking for fibre and
guts. Her eyes were black and appalling. I dropped
dead at her feet. It was all go at that time. Love,
football, the arts, the occasional pint. Mind you,
I preferred a fruity white wine but you couldn't actually
say that in those days.

Third area.

JAKE (*eighteen*), FRED (*seventeen*), BRIDGET (*fourteen*).

BRIDGET *and* FRED *on the floor,* JAKE *standing.*

A cassette playing.

FRED Why can't I come?

JAKE I've told you. There isn't room in the car.

BRIDGET Oh take him with you.

JAKE There's no room in the car. It's not my car. I'm just a passenger. I'm lucky to get a lift myself.

FRED But if I can't come with you what am I going to do all night? I'll have to stay here with her.

BRIDGET Oh God, I wish you'd take him with you. Otherwise I'll have to stay here with him.

JAKE Well, you are related.

FRED That's the trouble.

BRIDGET (*to* FRED) You're related to him too.

FRED Yes, but once I got to this gig I'd lose him. We wouldn't see each other again. He's merely a method of transport. Emotion or family allegiances don't come into it.

BRIDGET Oh well go with him then.

JAKE I've told you, he can't. There isn't any room in the car. It's not my car! I haven't got a car.

FRED That's what's so tragic about the whole business. If you had a car none of this would be taking place.

BRIDGET Look, I don't want him to stay here with me, I can assure you, I actually want to be alone.

FRED Greta Garbo! Are you going to be a film star when you grow up?

BRIDGET Oh shut up. You know what I'm going to be.

FRED What?

BRIDGET A physiotherapist.

JAKE She'll be a great physiotherapist.

FRED She'll have to play very soothing music so that her patients won't notice their suffering.

BRIDGET I did your neck the other day and you didn't complain.

FRED That's true.

BRIDGET You had a spasm and I released it.

FRED That's true.

BRIDGET You didn't complain then.

FRED I'm not complaining now. I think you're wonderful. I know you're wonderful. And I know you'll make a wonderful physiotherapist. But I still want to get to this gig in Amersham. That doesn't mean I don't think you're wonderful.

BRIDGET Oh go to Amersham, please! You don't think I need anyone to stay with me, do you? I'm not a child. Anyway, I'm reading this book.

JAKE You don't want to be all on your own.

BRIDGET I *do* want to be all on my own. I want to read this book.

FRED I don't even have a book. I mean – I have books – but they're all absolutely unreadable.

JAKE Well I'm off to Amersham.

FRED What about me?

BRIDGET Oh for God's sake take him with you to Amersham or don't take him with you to Amersham or shut up! Both of you!

Pause.

JAKE Well I'm off to Amersham.

He goes. BRIDGET *and* FRED *sit still. Music plays.*

ANDY's *room.* ANDY *and* BEL.

BEL I'm giving you a mushroom omelette today and a little green salad – and an apple.

ANDY How kind you are. I'd be lost without you. It's true. I'd flounder without you. I'd fall apart. Well, I'm falling apart as it is – but if I didn't have you I'd stand no chance.

BEL You're not a bad man. You're just what we used to call a loudmouth. You can't help it. It's your nature. If you only kept your mouth shut more of the time life with you might just be tolerable.

ANDY Allow me to kiss your hand. I owe you everything.

He watches her embroider.

Oh, I've been meaning to ask you, what are you making there? A winding sheet? Are you going to wrap

797

me up in it when I conk out? You'd better get a move on. I'm going fast.

Pause.

Where are they?

Pause.

Two sons. Absent. Indifferent. Their father dying.

BEL They were good boys. I've been thinking of how they used to help me with the washing-up. And the drying. The clearing of the table, the washing-up, the drying. Do you remember?

ANDY You mean in the twilight? The soft light falling through the kitchen window? The bell ringing for Evensong in the pub round the corner?

Pause.

They were bastards. Both of them. Always. Do you remember that time I asked Jake to clean out the broom cupboard? Well – I *told* him – I admit it – I didn't ask him – I told him that it was bloody filthy and that he hadn't lifted a little finger all week. Nor had the other one. Lazy idle layabouts. Anyway all I did was to ask him – quite politely – to clean out the bloody broom cupboard. His defiance! Do you remember the way he looked at me? His defiance!

Pause.

And look at them now! What are they now! A sponging parasitical pair of ponces. Sucking the tit of the state.

Sucking the tit of the state! And I bet you feed them a
few weekly rupees from your little money-box, don't
you? Because they always loved their loving mother.
They helped her with the washing-up!

Pause.

I've got to stretch my legs. Go over the Common,
watch a game of football, rain or shine. What was the
name of that old chum of mine? Used to referee
amateur games every weekend? On the Common?
Charming bloke. They treated him like shit. A subject
of scorn. No decision he ever made was adhered to or
respected. They shouted at him, they screamed at him,
they called him every kind of prick. I used to watch in
horror from the touchline. I'll always remember his
impotent whistle. It blows down to me through the
ages, damp and forlorn. What was his name? And now
I'm dying and he's probably dead.

BEL He's not dead.

ANDY Why not?

Pause.

What was his name?

BEL Ralph.

ANDY Ralph? Ralph? Can that be possible?

Pause.

Well, even if his name was Ralph he was still the most
sensitive and intelligent of men. My oldest friend. But

799

pathologically idiosyncratic, if he was anything. He
was reliable enough when he was sitting down but you
never knew where you were with him when he was
standing up, I mean when he was on the move, when
you were walking down the street with him. He was a
reticent man, you see. He said little but he was always
thinking. And the trouble was – his stride would keep
pace with his thoughts. If he was thinking slowly he'd
walk as if he was wading through mud or crawling
out of a pot of apricot jam. If he was thinking quickly
he walked like greased lightning, you couldn't keep
up with him, you were on your knees in the gutter
while he was over the horizon in a flash. I always had
a lot of sympathy for his sexual partner, whoever she
may have been. I mean to say – one minute he'd be
berserk – up to a thousand revolutions a second – and
the next he'd be grinding to the most appalling and
deadly halt. He was his own natural handbrake. Poor
girl. There must be easier ways of making ends meet.

Pause.

Anyway, leaving him aside, if you don't mind, for a
few minutes, where is Maria? Why isn't she here? I
can't die without her.

BEL Oh of course you can. And you will.

ANDY But think of our past. We were all so close.
Think of the months I betrayed you with her. How can
she forget? Think of the wonder of it. I betrayed you
with your own girlfriend, she betrayed you with your
husband and she betrayed her own husband – and

me – with you! She broke every record in sight! She was a genius and a great fuck.

BEL She was a very charming and attractive woman.

ANDY Then why isn't she here? She loved me, not to mention you. Why isn't she here to console you in your grief.

BEL She's probably forgotten you're dying. If she ever remembered.

ANDY What! What!

Pause.

I had her in our bedroom, by the way, once or twice, on our bed. I was a man at the time.

Pause.

You probably had her in the same place, of course. In our bedroom, on our bed.

BEL I don't 'have' people.

ANDY You've had me.

BEL Oh you. Oh yes. I can still have you.

ANDY What do you mean? Are you threatening me? What do you have in mind? Assault? Are you proposing to have me here and now? Without further ado? Would it be out of order to remind you that I'm on my deathbed? Or is that a solecism? What's your plan, to kill me in the act, like a praying mantis? How much sexual juice does a corpse retain and for how long, for Christ's sake? The truth is I'm basically innocent. I know little of women. But I've heard dread tales. Mainly from my old mate, the referee. But they were probably all fantasy and fabrication, bearing no relation whatsoever to reality.

BEL Oh, do you think so? Do you really think so?

FRED's *room.*

FRED *and* JAKE, *at the table.*

JAKE The meeting is scheduled for 6.30. Bellamy in the chair. Pratt, Hawkeye, Belcher and Rausch, Horsfall attending. Lieutenant-Colonel Silvio d'Orangerie will speak off the record at 7.15 precisely.

FRED But Horsfall *will* be attending?

JAKE Oh, Horsfall's always steady on parade. Apart from that I've done the placement myself.

FRED What are you, the permanent secretary?

JAKE Indeed I am. Indeed I am.

FRED Funny Hawkeye and Rausch being at the same table. Did you mention Bigsby?

JAKE Why, did Hawkeye tangle with Rausch at Bromley? No, I didn't mention Bigsby.

FRED They were daggers drawn at Eastbourne.

JAKE What, during the Buckminster hierarchy?

FRED Buckminster? I never mentioned Buckminster.

JAKE You mentioned Bigsby.

FRED You're not telling me that Bigsby is anything
to do with Buckminster? Or that Buckminster and
Bigsby –?

JAKE I'm telling you nothing of the sort. Buckminster
and Bigsby are two quite different people.

FRED That's always been my firm conviction.

JAKE Well, thank goodness we agree about something.

FRED I've never thought we were all that far apart.

JAKE You mean where it matters most?

FRED Quite. Tell me more about Belcher.

JAKE Belcher? Who's Belcher? Oh, Belcher! Sorry.
I thought for a moment you were confusing Belcher
with Bellamy. Because of the 'B's. You follow me?

FRED Any confusion that exists in that area rests
entirely in you, old chap.

JAKE That's a bit blunt, isn't it? Are you always so
blunt? After all, I've got a steady job here, which is
more than can be said for you.

FRED Listen son. I've come a long way down here to
attend a series of highly confidential meetings in which
my participation is seen to be a central factor. I've
come a very long way and the people I left to man the
bloody fort made quite clear to me a number of their
very weighty misgivings. But I insisted and here I am.
I want to see Bellamy, I want to see Belcher, I need to

see Rausch, Pratt is a prat but Hawkeye is crucial. Frustrate any of this and you'll regret it.

JAKE I can only hope Lieutenant-Colonel Silvio d'Orangerie won't find you as offensive as I do. He's an incredibly violent person.

FRED I know Silvio.

JAKE Know him? What do you mean?

FRED We were together in Torquay.

JAKE Oh. I see.

Pause.

What about Horsfall?

FRED Horsfall belongs to you.

ANDY'*s room.* ANDY *and* BEL.

ANDY Where is she? Of all the people in the world I know she'd want to be with me now. Because she I know remembers everything. How I cuddled her and sang to her, how I kept her nightmares from her, how she fell asleep in my arms.

BEL Please. Oh please.

  Pause.

ANDY Is she bringing my grandchildren to see me? Is she? To catch their last look of me, to receive my blessing?

  BEL *sits frozen.*

Poor little buggers, their eyes so wide, so blue, so
black, poor tots, tiny totlets, poor little tiny totlets,
to lose their grandad at the height of his powers, when
he was about to stumble upon new reserves of spiritual
zest, when the door was about to open on new ever-
widening and ever-lengthening horizons.

BEL But darling, death will be your new horizon.

ANDY What?

BEL Death is your new horizon.

ANDY That may be. That may be. But the big question
is, will I cross it as I die or after I'm dead? Or perhaps
I won't cross it at all. Perhaps I'll just stay stuck in the
middle of the horizon. In which case, can I see over it?
Can I see to the other side? Or is the horizon endless?
And what's the weather like? Is it uncertain with
showers or sunny with fog patches? Or unceasing
moonlight with no cloud? Or pitch black for ever and
ever? You may say you haven't the faintest fucking
idea and you would be right. But personally I don't
believe it's going to be pitch black for ever because if
it's pitch black for ever what would have been the
point of going through all these enervating charades
in the first place? There must be a loophole. The only
trouble is, I can't find it. If only I could find it I would
crawl through it and meet myself coming back. Like
screaming with fright at the sight of a stranger only to
find you're looking into a mirror.

Pause.

But what if I cross this horizon before my grandchildren get here? They won't know where I am. What will they say? Will you ever tell me? Will you ever tell me what they say? They'll cry or they won't, a sorrow too deep for tears, but they're only babies, what can they know about death?

BEL Oh, the really little ones I think do know something about death, they know more about death than we do. We've forgotten death but they haven't forgotten it. They remember it. Because some of them, those who are really very young, remember the moment before their life began – it's not such a long time ago for them, you see – and the moment before their life began they were of course dead.

Pause.

ANDY Really?

BEL Of course.

Half-light over the whole stage.

Stillness. A telephone rings in FRED's *room. It rings six times. A click. Silence.*

Blackout.

Third area.

Faint light, ANDY *moving about in the dark. He stubs his toe.*

ANDY Shit!

He moves to an alcove.

Why not? No fags, no fucks. Bollocks to the lot of them. I'll have a slug anyway. Bollocks to the lot of them and bugger them all.

Sound of bottle opening. Pouring. He drinks, sighs.

Ah God. That's the ticket. Just the job. Bollocks to the lot of them.

He pours again, drinks.

Growing moonlight finds BRIDGET *in background, standing still.*

ANDY *moves into the light and stops still, listening.*

Silence.

Ah darling. Ah my darling.

BEL *appears. She walks into moonlight,* ANDY *and* BEL *look at each other. They turn away from each other.*

They stand still, listening. BRIDGET *remains still, in background.*

Silence.

Lights fade on ANDY *and* BELL.

BRIDGET, *standing in the moonlight.*

Light fades.

Fred's room.

JAKE *and* FRED. FRED *in bed.*

JAKE How's your water consumption these days?

FRED I've given all that up.

JAKE Really?

FRED Oh yes. I've decided to eschew the path of purity and abstention and take up a proper theology. From now on it's the Michelin Guide and the Orient Express for me – that kind of thing.

JAKE I once lived the life of Riley myself.

FRED What was he like?

JAKE I never met him personally. But I became a very very close friend of the woman he ran away with.

FRED I bet she taught you a thing or two.

JAKE She taught me nothing she hadn't learnt herself at the feet of the master.

FRED Wasn't Riley known under his other hat as the Sheikh of Araby?

JAKE That's him. His mother was one of the all-time-great belly dancers and his father was one of the last of the great village elders.

FRED A marvellous people.

JAKE A proud people too.

FRED Watchful.

JAKE Wary.

FRED Touchy.

JAKE Bristly.

FRED Vengeful.

JAKE Absolutely ferocious, to be quite frank.

FRED Kick you in the balls as soon as look at you.

JAKE But you know what made them the men they were?

FRED What?

JAKE They drank water. Sheer, cold, sparkling mountain water.

FRED And this made men of them?

JAKE And gods.

FRED I'll have some then. I've always wanted to be a god.

JAKE (*pouring*) Drink up.

FRED Listen. Can I ask you a very personal question? Do you think my nerve is going? Do you think my nerve is on the blink?

JAKE I'm going to need a second opinion.

FRED We haven't had the first one yet.

JAKE No, no, the second is always the one that counts, any fool knows that. But I've got another suggestion.

FRED What's that?

JAKE What about a walk around the block?

FRED Oh no, I'm much happier in bed. Staying in bed suits me. I'd be very unhappy to get out of bed and go out and meet strangers and all that kind of thing. I'd really much prefer to stay in my bed.

Pause.

Bridget would understand. I was her brother. She understood me. She always understood my feelings.

JAKE She understood me too.

Pause.

She understood me too.

Silence.

FRED Listen. I've got a funny feeling my equilibrium is in tatters.

JAKE Oh really? Well they can prove these things scientifically now, you know. I beg you to remember that.

FRED Really?

JAKE Oh yes. They've got things like light meters now.

FRED Light meters?

JAKE Oh yes. They can test the quality of light down to a fraction of a centimetre, even if it's pitch dark.

FRED They can find whatever light is left in the dark?

810

JAKE They can find it, yes. They can locate it. Then they place it in a little box. They wrap it up and tie a ribbon round it and you get it tax free, as a reward for all your labour and faith and all the concern and care for others you have demonstrated so eloquently for so long.

FRED And will it serve me as a light at the end of the tunnel?

JAKE It will serve you as a torch, as a flame. It will serve you as your own personal light eternal.

FRED Fantastic.

JAKE This is what we can do for you.

FRED Who?

JAKE Society.

Pause.

FRED Listen. I'd like – if you don't mind – to take you back to the remarks you were making earlier – about your father – and about your inheritance – which was not perhaps quite what it purported to be, which was not, shall we say, exactly the bona-fide gold-plated testament deep-seated rumour had reckoned but which was – in fact – according to information we now possess – in the lowest category of Ruritanian fantasy –

JAKE Yes, but wait a minute! What exactly is being said here about my dad? What is being said? What is this? What it demonstrably is not is a dissertation upon the defeated or a lament for the lost, is it? No,

no, I'll tell you what it is. It is an atrociously biased and
illegitimate onslaught on the weak and vertiginous. Do
you follow me? So what is this? I am entitled to ask.
What is being said? What is being said here? What is it
that is being said here – or there – for that matter? I
ask this question. In other words, I am asking this
question. What finally is being said?

Pause.

All his life my father has been subjected to hatred and
vituperation. He has been from time immemorial
pursued and persecuted by a malignant force which
until this day has remained shadowy, a force resisting
definition or classification. What is this force and what
is its bent? You will answer that question, not I. You
will, in the calm and ease which will come to you, as
assuredly it will, in due course, before the last race is
run, answer that question, not I. I will say only this:
I contend that you subject to your scorn a man who
was – and here I pray for your understanding –- an
innocent bystander to his own nausea. At the age of
three that man was already at the end of his tether. No
wonder he yearned to leave to his loving son the legacy
of all that was best and most valuable of his life and
death. He loved me. And one day I shall love him. I
shall love him and be happy to pay the full price of
that love.

FRED Which is the price of death.

JAKE The price of death, yes.

FRED Than which there is no greater price.

JAKE Than which?

FRED Than which.

Pause.

Death –

JAKE Which is the price of love.

FRED A great great price.

JAKE A great and deadly price.

FRED But strictly in accordance with the will of God.

JAKE And the laws of nature.

FRED And common or garden astrological logic.

JAKE It's the first axiom.

FRED And the last.

JAKE It may well be both tautologous and contradictory.

FRED But it nevertheless constitutes a watertight philosophical proposition which will in the final reckoning be seen to be such.

JAKE I believe that to be so, yes. I believe that to be the case and I'd like to raise a glass to all those we left behind, to all those who fell at the first and all consequent hurdles.

They raise glasses.

FRED Raising.

JAKE Raising.

They drink.

FRED Let me say this. I knew your father.

JAKE You did indeed.

FRED I was close to him.

JAKE You were indeed.

FRED Closer to him than you were yourself perhaps.

JAKE It could be argued so. You were indeed his youngest and most favoured son.

FRED Precisely. And so let me say this. He was a man, take him for all in all, I shall not look upon his like again.

JAKE You move me much.

Pause.

FRED Some say of course that he was spiritually furtive, politically bankrupt, morally scabrous and intellectually abject.

Pause.

JAKE They lie.

FRED Certainly he liked a drink.

JAKE And could be spasmodically rampant.

FRED On my oath, there's many a maiden will attest to that.

JAKE He may have been poetically downtrodden –

FRED But while steeped in introversion he remained proud and fiery.

JAKE And still I called him Dad.

  Pause.

FRED What was he like in real life? Would you say?

JAKE A leader of men.

  Pause.

FRED What was the celebrated nickname attached to him by his friends with affection, awe and admiration?

JAKE The Incumbent. Be at the Black Horse tonight 7.30 sharp. The Incumbent'll be there in his corner, buying a few pints for the lads.

FRED They were behind him to a man.

JAKE He knew his beer and possessed the classic formula for dealing with troublemakers.

FRED What was that?

JAKE A butcher's hook.

  Pause.

FRED Tell me about your mother.

JAKE Don't talk dirty to me.

ANDY's *room.* ANDY *and* BEL.

BEL The first time Maria and I had lunch together – in a restaurant – I asked her to order for me. She wore

815

grey. A grey dress. I said please order for me, please,
I'll have whatever you decide, I'd much prefer that.
And she took my hand and squeezed it and smiled and
ordered for me.

ANDY I saw her do it. I saw her, I heard her order for
you.

BEL I said, I'll be really happy to have whatever you
decide.

ANDY Fish. She decided on fish.

BEL She asked about my girlhood.

ANDY The bitch.

BEL I spoke to her in a way I had never spoken to
anyone before. I told her of my girlhood. I told her
about running on the cliffs with my brothers, I ran so
fast, up and down the heather, I was so out of breath,
I had to stop, I fell down on the heather, bouncing,
they fell down at my side, and all the wind. I told her
about the wind and my brothers running after me on
the clifftop and falling down at my side.

  Pause.

I spoke to her in a way I had never spoken to anyone
before. Sometimes it happens, doesn't it? You're
speaking to someone and you suddenly find that
you're another person.

ANDY Who is?

BEL You are.

816

Pause.

I don't mean you. I mean me.

ANDY I witnessed all this, by the way.

BEL Oh, were you there?

ANDY I was spying on you both from a corner table, behind a vase of flowers and *The Brothers Karamazov.*

BEL And then she said women had something men didn't have. They had certain qualities men simply didn't have. I wondered if she was talking about me. But then I realised of course she was talking about women in general. But then she looked at me and she said. You, for example. But I said to myself, men can be beautiful too.

ANDY I was there. I heard every word.

BEL Not my thoughts.

ANDY I heard your thoughts. I could hear your thoughts. You thought to yourself, Men can be beautiful too. But you didn't dare say it. But you did dare think it.

Pause.

Mind you, she thought the same. I know she did.

Pause.

She's the one we both should have married.

BEL Oh no, I don't think so. I think I should have married your friend Ralph.

ANDY Ralph? What, Ralph the referee?

BEL Yes.

ANDY But he was such a terrible referee! He was such a hopeless referee!

BEL It wasn't the referee I loved.

ANDY It was the man!

Pause.

Well, I'll be buggered. It's wonderful. Here I am dying and she tells me she loved a referee. I could puke.

Pause.

And how I loved you. I'll never forget the earliest and loveliest days of our marriage. You offered your body to me. Here you are, you said one day, here's my body. Oh thanks very much, I said, that's very decent of you, what do you want me to do with it? Do what you will, you said. This is going to need a bit of thought, I said. I tell you what, hold on to it for a couple of minutes, will you? Hold on to it while I call a copper.

BEL Ralph had such beautiful manners and such a lovely singing voice. I've never understood why he didn't become a professional tenor. But I think all the travel involved in that kind of life was the problem. There was a story about an old mother, a bewildered aunt. Something that tugged at his heart. I never quite knew what to believe.

ANDY No, no, you've got the wrong bloke. My Ralph was pedantic and scholastic. Never missed a day at night school. Big ears but little feet. Never smiled. One day though he did say something. He pulled me into a doorway. He whispered in my ear. Do you know what he said? He said men had something women simply didn't have. I asked him what it was. But of course there was no way he was going to answer that question. You know why? Because referees are not obliged to answer questions. Referees are the law. They are law in action. They have a whistle. They blow it. And that whistle is the articulation of God's justice.

MARIA *and* RALPH *to* ANDY *and* BEL.

MARIA How wonderful you both look. It's been ages. We don't live up here any more, of course.

MARIA Years ago.

RALPH Ten. Ten years ago.

MARIA We've made friends with so many cows, haven't we, darling? Sarah's doing marvellously well and Lucien's thriving at the Consulate and as for Susannah, there's no stopping her. They all take after Ralph. Don't they darling? I mean physically. Mentally and artistically they take after me. We have a pretty rundown sort of quite large cottage. Not exactly a château. A small lake.

RALPH More of a pond.

MARIA More of a lake, I'd say.

ANDY So you've given up refereeing?

RALPH Oh yes. I gave that up. And I've never regretted it.

ANDY You mean it didn't come from the heart?

RALPH I wasn't born for it.

ANDY Well, you were certainly no bloody good at it.

Pause.

RALPH Tell me. I often think of the past. Do you?

ANDY The past? What past? I don't remember any past. What kind of past did you have in mind?

RALPH Walking down the Balls Pond Road, for example.

ANDY I never went anywhere near the Balls Pond Road. I was a civil servant. I had no past. I remember no past. Nothing ever happened.

BEL Yes it did.

MARIA Oh it did. Yes it did. Lots of things happened.

RALPH Yes, things happened. Things certainly happened. All sorts of things happened.

BEL All sorts of things happened.

ANDY Well, I don't remember any of these things. I remember none of these things.

MARIA For instance, your children! Your lovely little girl! Bridget! (*She laughs.*) Little girl! She must be a mother by now.

Pause.

ANDY I've got three beautiful grandchildren. *(To* BEL*)* Haven't I?

Pause.

BEL By the way, he's not well. Have you noticed?

RALPH Who?

BEL Him.

MARIA I hadn't noticed.

RALPH What's the trouble?

BEL He's on the way out.

Pause.

RALPH Old Andy? Not a chance. He was always as fit as a fiddle. Constitution like an ox.

MARIA People like Andy never die. That's the wonderful thing about them.

RALPH He looks in the pink.

MARIA A bit peaky perhaps but in the pink. He'll be running along the towpath in next to no time. Take my word. Waltzing away in next to no time.

RALPH Before you can say Jack Robinson. Well, we must toddle.

RALPH *and* MARIA *out.*

BEL *goes to telephone, dials. Lights hold on her.*

Lights up in Fred's room.

The phone rings, JAKE *picks it up.*

JAKE Chinese laundry?

BEL Your father is very ill.

JAKE Chinese laundry?

Silence.

BEL Your father is very ill.

JAKE Can I pass you to my colleague?

FRED *takes the phone.*

FRED Chinese laundry?

Pause.

BEL It doesn't matter.

FRED Oh my dear madam, absolutely everything matters when it comes down to laundry.

BEL No. It doesn't matter. It doesn't matter.

Silence.

JAKE *takes the phone, looks at it, puts it to his ear.*

BEL *holds the phone.*

FRED *grabs the phone.*

FRED If you have any serious complaint can we refer you to our head office?

BEL Do you do dry cleaning?

FRED *is still. He then passes the phone to* JAKE.

JAKE Hullo. Can I help you?

BEL Do you do dry cleaning?

JAKE *is still.*

BEL *puts the phone down. Dialling tone.*

JAKE *replaces phone.*

JAKE Of course we do dry cleaning! Of course we do dry cleaning! What kind of fucking laundry are you if you don't do dry cleaning?

Andy's room. ANDY *and* BEL.

ANDY Where are they? My grandchildren? The babies? My daughter?

Pause.

Are they waiting outside? Why do you keep them waiting outside? Why can't they come in? What are they waiting for?

Pause.

What's happening

Pause.

What is happening?

BEL Are you dying?

ANDY Am I?

BEL Don't you know?

ANDY No, I don't know. I don't know how it feels. How does it feel?

BEL I don't know.

  Pause.

ANDY Why don't they come in? Are they frightened? Tell them not to be frightened.

BEL They're not here. They haven't come.

ANDY Tell Bridget not to be frightened. Tell Bridget I don't want her to be frightened.

FRED's *room.*

JAKE *and* FRED.

FRED *is out of bed. He wears shorts. They both walk around the room, hands behind backs.*

JAKE Pity you weren't at d'Orangerie's memorial.

FRED I'm afraid I was confined to my bed with a mortal disease.

JAKE So I gather. Pity. It was a great do.

FRED Was it?

JAKE Oh yes. Everyone was there.

FRED Really? Who?

JAKE Oh . . . Denton, Alabaster, Tunnicliffe, Quinn.

FRED Really?

JAKE Oh yes. Kelly, Mortlake, Longman, Small.

FRED Good Lord.

JAKE Oh yes. Wetterby, White, Hotchkiss, De Groot . . .
Blackhouse, Garland, Gupte, Tate.

FRED Well, well!

JAKE The whole gang. Donovan, Ironside, Wallace,
McCool . . . Ottuna, Muggeridge, Carpentier, Finn.

FRED Speeches?

JAKE Very moving.

FRED Who spoke?

JAKE Oh . . . Hazeldine, McCormick, Bugatti, Black,
Forrester, Galloway, Springfield, Gaunt.

FRED He was much loved.

JAKE Well, you loved him yourself, didn't you?

FRED I loved him. I loved him like a father.

Third area.

BRIDGET Once someone said to me – I think it was
my mother or my father – anyway, they said to me –
We've been invited to a party. You've been invited too.
But you'll have to come by yourself, alone. You won't
have to dress up. You just have to wait until the moon
is down.

Pause.

They told me where the party was. It was in a house at the end of a lane. But they told me the party wouldn't begin until the moon had gone down.

Pause.

I got dressed in something old and I waited for the moon to go down. I waited a long time. Then I set out for the house. The moon was bright and quite still.

Pause.

When I got to the house it was bathed in moonlight. The house, the glade, the lane, were all bathed in moonlight. But the inside of the house was dark and all the windows were dark. There was no sound.

Pause.

I stood there in the moonlight and waited for the moon to go down.

ASHES TO ASHES

Ashes to Ashes was first presented by the Royal Court at the Ambassadors Theatre, London, on 12 September 1996. The cast was as follows:

DEVLIN   Stephen Rea
REBECCA   Lindsay Duncan

Directed by Harold Pinter
Designed by Eileen Diss
Lighting by Mick Hughes
Costume by Tom Rand
Sound by Tom Lishman

Characters

DEVLIN

REBECCA

both in their forties

Time: now

A house in the country.

Ground-floor room. A large window. Garden beyond.

Two armchairs. Two lamps.

Early evening. Summer.

The room darkens during the course of the play. The lamplight intensifies.

By the end of the play the room and the garden beyond are only dimly defined. The lamplight has become very bright but does not illumine the room.

DEVLIN *standing with drink.* REBECCA *sitting.*

Silence.

REBECCA Well . . . for example . . . he would stand over me and clench his fist. And then he'd put his other hand on my neck and grip it and bring my head towards him. His fist . . . grazed my mouth. And he'd say, 'Kiss my fist.'

DEVLIN And did you?

REBECCA Oh yes. I kissed his fist. The knuckles. And then he'd open his hand and give me the palm of his hand . . . to kiss . . . which I kissed.

Pause.

And then I would speak.

DEVLIN What did you say? You said what? What did you say?

Pause.

REBECCA I said, 'Put your hand round my throat.' I murmured it through his hand, as I was kissing it, but he heard my voice, he heard it through his hand, he felt my voice in his hand, he heard it there.

Silence.

DEVLIN And did he? Did he put his hand round your throat?

REBECCA Oh yes. He did. He did. And he held it there, very gently, very gently, so gently. He adored me, you see.

DEVLIN He adored you?

Pause.

What do you mean, he adored you? What do you mean?

Pause.

Are you saying he put no pressure on your throat? Is that what you're saying?

REBECCA No.

DEVLIN What then? What are you saying?

REBECCA He put a little . . . pressure . . . on my throat, yes. So that my head started to go back, gently but truly.

DEVLIN And your body? Where did your body go?

REBECCA My body went back, slowly but truly.

DEVLIN So your legs were opening?

REBECCA Yes.

Pause.

DEVLIN Your legs were opening?

REBECCA Yes.

Silence.

DEVLIN Do you feel you're being hypnotised?

REBECCA When?

DEVLIN Now.

REBECCA No.

DEVLIN Really?

REBECCA No.

DEVLIN Why not?

REBECCA Who by?

DEVLIN By me.

REBECCA You?

DEVLIN What do you think?

REBECCA I think you're a fuckpig.

DEVLIN Me a fuckpig? Me! You must be joking.

REBECCA *smiles.*

REBECCA Me joking? You must be joking.

Pause.

DEVLIN You understand why I'm asking you these questions. Don't you? Put yourself in my place. I'm compelled to ask you questions. There are so many things I don't know. I know nothing . . . about any of this. Nothing. I'm in the dark. I need light. Or do you think my questions are illegitimate?

Pause.

REBECCA What questions?

Pause.

DEVLIN Look. It would mean a great deal to me if you could define him more clearly.

REBECCA Define him? What do you mean, define him?

DEVLIN Physically. I mean, what did he actually look like? If you see what I mean? Length, breadth . . . that sort of thing. Height, width. I mean, quite apart from his . . . disposition, whatever that may have been . . . or his character . . . or his spiritual . . . standing . . . I just want, well, I need . . . to have a clearer idea of him . . . well, not a clearer idea . . . just an idea, in fact . . . because I have absolutely no idea . . . as things stand . . . of what he looked like.

I mean, what did he *look like*? Can't you give him a shape for me, a concrete shape? I want a concrete image of him, you see . . . an image I can carry about with me. I mean, all you can talk of are his hands, one hand over your face, the other on the back of your neck, then the first one on your throat. There must be more to him than hands. What about eyes? Did he have any eyes?

REBECCA 'What colour?

Pause.

DEVLIN That's precisely the question I'm asking you . . . my darling.

REBECCA How odd to be called darling. No one has ever called me darling. Apart from my lover.

DEVLIN I don't believe it.

REBECCA You don't believe what?

DEVLIN I don't believe he ever called you darling.

Pause.

Do you think my use of the word is illegitimate?

REBECCA What word?

DEVLIN Darling.

REBECCA Oh yes, you called me darling. How funny.

DEVLIN Funny? Why?

REBECCA Well, how can you possibly call me darling? I'm not your darling.

DEVLIN Yes you are.

REBECCA Well I don't want to be your darling. It's the last thing I want to be. I'm nobody's darling.

DEVLIN That's a song.

REBECCA What?

DEVLIN 'I'm nobody's baby now'.

REBECCA It's 'You're nobody's baby now'. But anyway, I didn't use the word baby.

Pause.

I can't tell you what he looked like.

DEVLIN Have you forgotten?

REBECCA No. I haven't forgotten. But that's not the point. Anyway, he went away years ago.

DEVLIN Went away? Where did he go?

REBECCA His job took him away. He had a job.

DEVLIN What was it?

REBECCA What?

DEVLIN What kind of job was it? What job?

REBECCA I think it had something to do with a travel agency. I think he was some kind of courier. No. No, he wasn't. That was only a part-time job. I mean that was only part of the job in the agency. He was quite high up, you see. He had a lot of responsibilities.

Pause.

DEVLIN What sort of agency?

REBECCA A travel agency.

DEVLIN What sort of travel agency?

REBECCA He was a guide, you see. A guide.

DEVLIN A tourist guide?

Pause.

REBECCA Did I ever tell you about that place . . .
about the time he took me to that place?

DEVLIN What place?

REBECCA I'm sure I told you.

DEVLIN No. You never told me.

REBECCA How funny. I could swear I had. Told you.

DEVLIN You haven't told me anything. You've never
spoken about him before. You haven't told me
anything.

Pause.

What place?

REBECCA Oh, it was a kind of factory, I suppose.

DEVLIN What do you mean, a kind of factory? Was it
a factory or wasn't it? And if it was a factory, what
kind of factory was it?

REBECCA Well, they were making things – just like
any other factory. But it wasn't the usual kind of
factory.

DEVLIN Why not?

REBECCA They were all wearing caps . . . the
workpeople . . . soft caps . . . and they took them off
when he came in, leading me, when he led me down
the alleys between the rows of workpeople.

DEVLIN They took their caps off? You mean they doffed them?

REBECCA Yes.

DEVLIN Why did they do that?

REBECCA He told me afterwards it was because they had such great respect for him.

DEVLIN Why?

REBECCA Because he ran a really tight ship, he said. They had total faith in him. They respected his . . . purity, his . . . conviction. They would follow him over a cliff and into the sea, if he asked them, he said. And sing in a chorus, as long as he led them. They were in fact very musical, he said.

DEVLIN What did they make of you?

REBECCA Me? Oh, they were sweet. I smiled at them. And immediately every single one of them smiled back.

Pause.

The only thing was – the place was so damp. It was exceedingly damp.

DEVLIN And they weren't dressed for the weather?

REBECCA *No.*

Pause.

DEVLIN I thought you said he worked for a travel agency?

REBECCA And there was one other thing. I wanted
to go to the bathroom. But I simply couldn't find it.
I looked everywhere. I'm sure they had one. But I never
found out where it was.

  Pause.

He did work for a travel agency. He was a guide. He
used to go to the local railway station and walk down
the platform and tear all the babies from the arms of
their screaming mothers.

  Pause.

DEVLIN Did he?

  Silence.

REBECCA By the way, I'm terribly upset.

DEVLIN Are you? Why?

REBECCA Well, it's about that police siren we heard
a couple of minutes ago.

DEVLIN What police siren?

REBECCA Didn't you hear it? You must have heard it.
Just a couple of minutes ago.

DEVLIN What about it?

REBECCA Well, I'm just terribly upset.

  Pause.

I'm just incredibly upset.

  Pause.

Don't you want to know why? Well, I'm going to tell you anyway. If I can't tell you who can I tell? Well, I'll tell you anyway. It just hit me so hard. You see . . . as the siren faded away in my ears I knew it was becoming louder and louder for somebody else.

DEVLIN You mean that it's always being heard by somebody, somewhere? Is that what you're saying?

REBECCA Yes. Always. For ever.

DEVLIN Does that make you feel secure?

REBECCA No! It makes me feel insecure! Terribly insecure.

DEVLIN Why?

REBECCA I hate it fading away. I hate it echoing away. I hate it leaving me. I hate losing it. I hate somebody else possessing it. I want it to be mine, all the time. It's such a beautiful sound. Don't you think?

DEVLIN Don't worry, there'll always be another one. There's one on its way to you now. Believe me. You'll hear it again soon. Any minute.

REBECCA Will I?

DEVLIN Sure. They're very busy people, the police. There's so much for them to do. They've got so much to take care of, to keep their eye on. They keep getting signals, mostly in code. There isn't one minute of the day when they're not charging around one corner or another in the world, in their police cars, ringing their sirens. So you can take comfort from that, at least.

Can't you? You'll never be lonely again. You'll never be without a police siren. I promise you.

Pause.

Listen. This chap you were just talking about . . .
I mean this chap you and I have been talking about . . .
in a manner of speaking . . . when exactly did you
meet him? I mean when did all this happen exactly?
I haven't . . . how can I put this . . . quite got it into
focus. Was it before you knew me or after you knew
me? That's a question of some importance. I'm sure
you'll appreciate that.

REBECCA By the way, there's something I've been
dying to tell you.

DEVLIN What?

REBECCA It was when I was writing a note, a few
notes for the laundry. Well . . . to put it bluntly . . .
a laundry list. Well, I put my pen on that little coffee
table and it rolled off.

DEVLIN No?

REBECCA It rolled right off, on to the carpet. In front
of my eyes.

DEVLIN Good God.

REBECCA This pen, this perfectly innocent pen.

DEVLIN You can't know it was innocent.

REBECCA Why not?

DEVLIN Because you don't know where it had been. You don't know how many other hands have held it, how many other hands have written with it, what other people have been doing with it. You know nothing of its history. You know nothing of its parents' history.

REBECCA A pen has no parents.

Pause.

DEVLIN You can't sit there and say things like that.

REBECCA I can sit here.

DEVLIN You can't sit there and say things like that.

REBECCA You don't believe I'm entitled to sit here? You don't think I'm entitled to sit in this chair, in the place where I live?

DEVLIN I'm saying that you're not entitled to sit in that chair or in or on any other chair and say things like that and it doesn't matter whether you live here or not.

REBECCA I'm not entitled to say things like what?

DEVLIN That that pen was innocent.

REBECCA You think it was guilty?

Silence.

DEVLIN I'm letting you off the hook. Have you noticed? I'm letting you slip. Or perhaps it's me who's slipping. It's dangerous. Do you notice? I'm in a quicksand.

844

REBECCA Like God.

DEVLIN God? God? You think God is sinking into a
quicksand? That's what I would call a truly disgusting
perception. If it can be dignified by the word
perception. Be careful how you talk about God. He's
the only God we have. If you let him go he won't
come back. He won't even look back over his shoulder.
And then what will you do? You know what it'll be
like, such a vacuum? It'll be like England playing
Brazil at Wembley and not a soul in the stadium. Can
you imagine? Playing both halves to a totally empty
house. The game of the century. Absolute silence. Not
a soul watching. Absolute silence. Apart from the
referee's whistle and a fair bit of fucking and blinding.
If you turn away from God it means that the great
and noble game of soccer will fall into permanent
oblivion. No score for extra time after extra time after
extra time, no score for time everlasting, for time
without end. Absence. Stalemate. Paralysis. A world
without a winner.

Pause.

I hope you get the picture.

Pause.

Now let me say this. A little while ago you made . . .
shall we say . . . you made a somewhat oblique
reference to your bloke . . . your lover? . . . and babies
and mothers, et cetera. And platforms. I inferred from
this that you were talking about some kind of atrocity.
Now let me ask you this. What authority do you think

you yourself possess which would give you the right
to discuss such an atrocity?

REBECCA I have no such authority. Nothing has ever
happened to me. Nothing has ever happened to any
of my friends. I have never suffered. Nor have my
friends.

DEVLIN Good.

Pause.

Shall we talk more intimately? Let's talk about more
intimate things, let's talk about something more
personal, about something within your own immediate
experience. I mean, for example, when the hairdresser
takes your head in his hands and starts to wash your
hair very gently and to massage your scalp, when he
does that, when your eyes are closed and he does that,
he has your entire trust, doesn't he? It's not just your
head which is in his hands, is it, it's your life, it's your
spiritual . . . welfare.

Pause.

So you see what I wanted to know was this . . . when
your lover had his hand on your throat, did he remind
you of your hairdresser?

Pause.

I'm talking about your lover. The man who tried to
murder you.

REBECCA Murder me?

DEVLIN Do you to death.

846

REBECCA No, no. He didn't try to murder me. He didn't want to murder me.

DEVLIN He suffocated you and strangled you. As near as makes no difference. According to your account. Didn't he?

REBECCA No, no. He felt compassion for me. He adored me.

Pause.

DEVLIN Did he have a name, this chap? Was he a foreigner? And where was I at the time? What do you want me to understand? Were you unfaithful to me? Why didn't you confide in me? Why didn't you confess? You would have felt so much better. Honestly. You could have treated me like a priest. You could have put me on my mettle. I've always wanted to be put on my mettle. It used to be one of my lifetime ambitions. Now I've missed my big chance. Unless all this happened before I met you. In which case you have no obligation to tell me anything. Your past is not my business. I wouldn't dream of telling you about my past. Not that I had one. When you lead a life of scholarship you can't be bothered with the humorous realities, you know, tits, that kind of thing. Your mind is on other things, have you got an attentive landlady, can she come up with bacon and eggs after eleven o'clock at night, is the bed warm, does the sun rise in the right direction, is the soup cold? Only once in a blue moon do you wobble the chambermaid's bottom, on the assumption there is one – chambermaid not bottom – but of course none of this applies when you have a wife. When you have a wife you let thought, ideas and reflection take their course. Which means you never let the best man win. Fuck the best man, that's always been my motto. It's the man who ducks his head and moves on through no matter what wind or weather who gets there in the end. A man with guts and application.

Pause.

A man who doesn't give a shit.

A man with a rigid sense of duty.

Pause.

There's no contradiction between those last two statements. Believe me.

Pause.

Do you follow the drift of my argument?

REBECCA Oh yes, there's something I've forgotten to tell you. It was funny. I looked out of the garden window, out of the window into the garden, in the middle of summer, in that house in Dorset, do you remember? Oh no, you weren't there. I don't think anyone else was there. No. I was all by myself. I was alone. I was looking out of the window and I saw a whole crowd of people walking through the woods, on their way to the sea, in the direction of the sea. They seemed to be very cold, they were wearing coats, although it was such a beautiful day. A beautiful, warm, Dorset day. They were carrying bags. There were . . . guides . . . ushering them, guiding them along. They walked through the woods and I could see them in the distance walking across the cliff and down to the sea. Then I lost sight of them. I was really quite curious so I went upstairs to the highest window in the house and I looked way over the top of the treetops and I could see down to the beach. The guides . . . were ushering all these people across the beach. It was such a lovely day. It was so still and the sun was shining. And I saw all these people walk into the sea. The tide covered them slowly. Their bags bobbed about in the waves.

DEVLIN When was that? When did you live in Dorset? I've never lived in Dorset.

Pause.

REBECCA Oh by the way somebody told me the other day that there's a condition known as mental elephantiasis.

DEVLIN What do you mean, 'somebody told you'? What do you mean, 'the other day'? What are you talking about?

REBECCA This mental elephantiasis means that when you spill an ounce of gravy, for example, it immediately expands and becomes a vast sea of gravy. It becomes a sea of gravy which surrounds you on all sides and you suffocate in a voluminous sea of gravy. It's terrible. But it's all your own fault. You brought it upon yourself. You are not the *victim* of it, you are the

cause of it. Because it was you who spilt the gravy in
the first place, it was you who handed over the
bundle.

Pause.

DEVLIN The what?

REBECCA The bundle.

Pause.

DEVLIN So what's the question? Are you prepared to
drown in your own gravy? Or are you prepared to die
for your country? Look. What do you say, sweetheart?
Why don't we go out and drive into town and take
in a movie?

REBECCA That's funny, somewhere in a dream . . .
a long time ago . . . I heard someone calling me
sweetheart.

Pause.

I looked up. I'd been dreaming. I don't know whether
I looked up in the dream or as I opened my eyes. But
in this dream a voice was calling. That I'm certain of.
This voice was calling me. It was calling me sweetheart.

Pause.

Yes.

Pause.

I walked out into the frozen city. Even the mud was
frozen. And the snow was a funny colour. It wasn't
white. Well, it was white but there were other colours

in it. It was as if there were veins running through it.
And it wasn't smooth, as snow is, as snow should be.
It was bumpy. And when I got to the railway station
I saw the train. Other people were there.

Pause.

And my best friend, the man I had given my heart
to, the man I knew was the man for me the moment
we met, my dear, my most precious companion,
I watched him walk down the platform and tear all
the babies from the arms of their screaming mothers.

Silence.

DEVLIN Did you see Kim and the kids?

She looks at him.

You were going to see Kim and the kids today.

She stares at him.

Your sister Kim and the kids.

REBECCA Oh, Kim! And the kids, yes. Yes. Yes, of
course I saw them. I had tea with them. Didn't I tell
you?

DEVLIN No.

REBECCA Of course I saw them.

Pause.

DEVLIN How were they?

REBECCA Ben's talking.

DEVLIN Really? What's he saying?

REBECCA Oh, things like 'My name is Ben'. Things like that. And 'Mummy's name is Mummy'. Things like that.

DEVLIN What about Betsy?

REBECCA She's crawling.

DEVLIN No, really?

REBECCA I think she'll be walking before we know where we are. Honestly.

DEVLIN Probably talking too. Saying things like 'My name is Betsy'.

REBECCA Yes, of course I saw them. I had tea with them. But oh . . . my poor sister . . . she doesn't know what to do.

DEVLIN What do you mean?

REBECCA Well, he wants to come back . . . you know . . . he keeps phoning and asking her to take him back. He says he can't bear it, he says he's given the other one up, he says he's living quite alone, he's given the other one up.

DEVLIN Has he?

REBECCA He says he has. He says he misses the kids.

Pause.

DEVLIN Does he miss his wife?

REBECCA He says he's given the other one up. He says it was never serious, you know, it was only sex.

DEVLIN Ah.

Pause.

And Kim?

Pause.

And Kim?

REBECCA She'll never have him back. Never. She says she'll never share a bed with him again. Never. Ever.

DEVLIN Why not?

REBECCA Never ever.

DEVLIN But why not?

REBECCA Of course I saw Kim and the kids. I had tea with them. Why did you ask? Did you think I didn't see them?

DEVLIN No. I didn't know. It's just that you said you were going to have tea with them.

REBECCA Well, I did have tea with them! Why shouldn't I? She's my sister.

Pause.

Guess where I went after tea? To the cinema. I saw a film.

DEVLIN Oh? What?

REBECCA A comedy.

DEVLIN Uh-huh? Was it funny? Did you laugh?

REBECCA Other people laughed. Other members of the audience. It was funny.

DEVLIN But you didn't laugh?

REBECCA Other people did. It was a comedy. There was a girl . . . you know . . . and a man. They were having lunch in a smart New York restaurant. He made her smile.

DEVLIN How?

REBECCA Well . . . he told her jokes.

DEVLIN Oh, I see.

REBECCA And then in the next scene he took her on an expedition to the desert, in a caravan. She'd never lived in a desert before, you see. She had to learn how to do it.

  Pause.

DEVLIN Sounds very funny.

REBECCA But there was a man sitting in front of me, to my right. He was absolutely still throughout the whole film. He never moved, he was rigid, like a body with rigor mortis, he never laughed once, he just sat like a corpse. I moved far away from him, I moved as far away from him as I possibly could.

  Silence.

DEVLIN Now look, let's start again. We live here. You don't live . . . in Dorset . . . or *anywhere else*. You live here with me. This is our house. You have a very nice sister. She lives close to you. She has two lovely kids. You're their aunt. You like that.

Pause.

You have a wonderful garden. You love your garden. You created it all by yourself. You have truly green fingers. You also have beautiful fingers.

Pause.

Did you hear what I said? I've just paid you a compliment. In fact I've just paid you a number of compliments. Let's start again.

REBECCA I don't think we can start again. We started . . . a long time ago. We started. We can't start *again*. We can end again.

DEVLIN But we've never ended.

REBECCA Oh, we have. Again and again and again. And we can end again. And again and again. And again.

DEVLIN Aren't you misusing the word 'end'? End means end. You can't end 'again'. You can only end once.

REBECCA No. You can end once and then you can end again.

Silence.

(*Singing softly.*) 'Ashes to ashes' –

DEVLIN 'And dust to dust' –

855

REBECCA 'If the women don't get you' –

DEVLIN 'The liquor must.'

Pause.

I always knew you loved me.

REBECCA Why?

DEVLIN Because we like the same tunes.

Silence.

Listen.

Pause.

Why have you never told me about this lover of yours before this? I have the right to be very angry indeed. Do you realise that? I have the right to be very angry indeed. Do you understand that?

Silence.

REBECCA Oh by the way there's something I meant to tell you. I was standing in a room at the top of a very tall building in the middle of town. The sky was full of stars. I was about to close the curtains but I stayed at the window for a time looking up at the stars. Then I looked down. I saw an old man and a little boy walking down the street. They were both dragging suitcases. The little boy's suitcase was bigger than he was. It was a very bright night. Because of the stars. The old man and the little boy were walking down the street. They were holding each other's free hand. I wondered where they were going. Anyway, I was about to close the curtains but then I suddenly saw a woman following them, carrying a baby in her arms.

Pause.

Did I tell you the street was icy? It was icy. So she had to tread very carefully. Over the bumps. The stars were out. She followed the man and the boy until they turned the corner and were gone.

Pause.

She stood still. She kissed her baby. The baby was a girl.

Pause.

She kissed her.

Pause.

She listened to the baby's heartbeat. The baby's heart was beating.

The light in the room has darkened. The lamps are very bright.

REBECCA *sits very still.*

The baby was breathing.

Pause.

I held her to me. She was breathing. Her heart was beating.

Devlin goes to her. He stands over her and looks down at her.

857

He clenches his fist and holds it in front of her face.
He puts his left hand behind her neck and grips it.
He brings her head towards his fist. His fist touches
her mouth.

DEVLIN Kiss my fist.

She does not move.

He opens his hand and places the palm of his hand
on her mouth.

She does not move.

DEVLIN Speak. Say it. Say 'Put your hand round my
throat.'

She does not speak.

Ask me to put my hand round your throat.

She does not speak or move.

He puts his hand on her throat. He presses gently.
Her head goes back.

They are still.

She speaks. There is an echo. His grip loosens.

REBECCA They took us to the trains

ECHO the trains

He takes his hand from her throat.

REBECCA They were taking the babies away

ECHO the babies away

Pause.

REBECCA I took my baby and wrapped it in my shawl

ECHO my shawl

REBECCA And I made it into a bundle

ECHO a bundle

REBECCA And I held it under my left arm

ECHO my left arm

   Pause.

REBECCA And I went through with my baby

ECHO my baby

   Pause.

REBECCA But the baby cried out

ECHO cried out

REBECCA And the man called me back

ECHO called me back

REBECCA And he said what do you have there

ECHO have there

REBECCA He stretched out his hand for the bundle

ECHO for the bundle

REBECCA And I gave him the bundle

ECHO the bundle

REBECCA And that's the last time I held the bundle

ECHO the bundle

Silence.

REBECCA And we got on the train

ECHO the train

REBECCA And we arrived at this place

ECHO this place

REBECCA And I met a woman I knew

ECHO I knew

REBECCA And she said what happened to your baby

ECHO your baby

REBECCA Where is your baby

ECHO your baby

REBECCA And I said what baby

ECHO what baby

REBECCA I don't have a baby

ECHO a baby

REBECCA I don't know of any baby

ECHO of any baby

Pause.

REBECCA I don't know of any baby

Long silence.

Blackout.

CELEBRATION

Celebration first published by
Faber and Faber Ltd 2000
© Fraser52 Limited, 2000

Celebration was first presented in a double bill with *The Room* at the Almeida Theatre, London, on 16 March 2000, with the following cast:

LAMBERT   Keith Allen
MATT   Andy de la Tour
PRUE   Lindsay Duncan
JULIE   Susan Wooldridge
RUSSELL   Steven Pacey
SUKI   Lia Williams
RICHARD   Thomas Wheatley
SONIA   Indira Varma
WAITER   Danny Dyer
WAITRESS 1   Nina Raine
WAITRESS 2   Katherine Tozer

Directed by Harold Pinter
Designed by Eileen Diss

Characters

LAMBERT

MATT

PRUE

JULIE

RUSSELL

SUKI

RICHARD

SONIA

WAITER

WAITRESS 1

WAITRESS 2

A restaurant.

Two curved banquettes.

Table One.

WAITER Who's having the duck?

LAMBERT The duck's for me.

JULIE No it isn't.

LAMBERT No it isn't. Who's it for?

JULIE Me.

LAMBERT What am I having? I thought I was having the duck?

JULIE (*to* WAITER) The duck's for me.

MATT (*to* WAITER) Chicken for my wife, steak for me.

WAITER Chicken for the lady.

PRUE Thank you so much.

WAITER And who's having the steak?

MATT Me.

He picks up a wine bottle and pours.

Here we are. Frascati for the ladies. And Valpolicella for me.

LAMBERT And for me. I mean what about me? What did I order? I haven't the faintest idea. What did I order?

JULIE Who cares?

LAMBERT Who cares? I bloody care.

PRUE Osso Bucco.

LAMBERT Osso what?

PRUE Bucco.

MATT It's an old Italian dish.

LAMBERT Well I knew Osso was Italian but I know bugger all about Bucco.

MATT I didn't know arsehole was Italian.

LAMBERT Yes, but on the other hand what's the Italian for arsehole?

PRUE Julie, Lambert. Happy anniversary.

MATT Cheers.

They lift their glasses and drink.

Table Two

RUSSELL They believe in me.

SUKI Who do?

RUSSELL They do. What do you mean, who do? They do.

SUKI Oh, do they?

RUSSELL Yes, they believe in me. They reckon me.
They're investing in me. In my nous. They believe in
me.

SUKI Listen. I believe you. Honestly. I do. No really,
honestly. I'm sure they believe in you. And they're
right to believe in you. I mean, listen, I want you to
be rich, believe me, I want you to be rich so that you
can buy me houses and panties and I'll know that
you really love me.

They drink.

RUSSELL Listen, she was just a secretary. That's all.
No more.

SUKI Like me.

RUSSELL What do you mean, like you? She was
nothing like you.

SUKI I was a secretary once.

RUSSELL She was a scrubber. A scrubber. They're all
the same, these secretaries, these scrubbers. They're
like politicians. They love power. They've got a bit of
power, they use it. They go home, they get on the
phone, they tell their girlfriends, they have a good
laugh. Listen to me. I'm being honest. You won't find
many like me. I fell for it. I've admitted it. She just
twisted me round her little finger.

SUKI That's funny. I thought she twisted you round
your little finger.

Pause.

RUSSELL You don't know what these girls are like. These secretaries.

SUKI Oh I think I do.

RUSSELL You don't.

SUKI Oh I do.

RUSSELL What do you mean, you do?

SUKI I've been behind a few filing cabinets.

RUSSELL What?

SUKI In my time. When I was a plump young secretary. I know what the back of a filing cabinet looks like.

RUSSELL Oh do you?

SUKI Oh yes. Listen. I would invest in you myself if I had any money. Do you know why? Because I believe in you.

RUSSELL What's all this about filing cabinets?

SUKI Oh that was when I was a plump young secretary. I would never do all those things now. Never. Out of the question. You see, the trouble was I was so excitable, their excitement made me so excited, but I would never do all those things now I'm a grown-up woman and not a silly young thing, a silly and dizzy young girl, such a naughty, saucy, flirty, giggly young thing, sometimes I could hardly walk from one filing

cabinet to another I was so excited, I was so plump
and wobbly it was terrible, men simply couldn't keep
their hands off me, their demands were outrageous,
but coming back to more important things, they're
right to believe in you, why shouldn't they believe
in you?

Table One.

JULIE I've always told him. Always. But he doesn't
listen. I tell him all the time. But he doesn't listen.

PRUE You mean he just doesn't listen?

JULIE I tell him all the time.

PRUE (*to* LAMBERT) Why don't you listen to your
wife? She stands by you through thick and thin.
You've got a loyal wife there and never forget it.

LAMBERT I've got a loyal wife where?

PRUE Here! At this table.

LAMBERT I've got one under the table, take my tip.

He looks under the table.

Christ. She's really loyal under the table. Always has
been. You wouldn't believe it.

JULIE Why don't you go and buy a new car and drive
it into a brick wall?

LAMBERT She loves me.

MATT No, she loves new cars.

LAMBERT With soft leather seats.

MATT There was a song once.

LAMBERT How did it go?

MATT Ain't she neat?
Ain't she neat?
As she's walking up the street.
She's got a lovely bubbly pair of tits
And a soft leather seat.

LAMBERT That's a really beautiful song.

MATT I've always admired that song. You know what it is? It's a traditional folk song.

LAMBERT It's got class.

MATT It's got tradition and class.

LAMBERT They don't grow on trees.

MATT Too bloody right.

LAMBERT Hey Matt!

MATT What?

LAMBERT *picks up the bottle of Valpolicella. It is empty.*

LAMBERT There's something wrong with this bottle.

MATT *turns and calls.*

MATT Waiter!

Table Two.

RUSSELL All right. Tell me. Do you think I have a nice character?

SUKI Yes I think you do. I think you do. I mean I think you do. Well . . . I mean . . . I think you could have quite a nice character but the trouble is that when you come down to it you haven't actually got any character to begin with – I mean as such, that's the thing.

RUSSELL As such?

SUKI Yes, the thing is you haven't really got any character at all, have you? As such. Au fond. But I wouldn't worry about it. For example look at me. I don't have any character either. I'm just a reed. I'm just a reed in the wind. Aren't I? You know I am. I'm just a reed in the wind.

RUSSELL You're a whore.

SUKI A whore in the wind.

RUSSELL With the wind blowing up your skirt.

SUKI That's right. How did you know? How did you know the sensation? I didn't know that men could possibly know about that kind of thing. I mean men don't wear skirts. So I didn't think men could possibly know what it was like when the wind blows up a girl's skirt. Because men don't wear skirts.

RUSSELL You're a prick.

SUKI Not quite.

RUSSELL You're a prick.

SUKI Good gracious. Am I really?

RUSSELL Yes. That's what you are really.

SUKI Am I really?

RUSSELL Yes. That's what you are really.

Table One.

LAMBERT What's that other song you know? The one you said was a classic.

MATT Wash me in the water
Where you washed your dirty daughter.

LAMBERT That's it. (*To* JULIE.) Know that one?

JULIE It's not in my repertoire, darling.

LAMBERT This is the best restaurant in town. That's what they say.

MATT That's what they say.

LAMBERT This is a piss-up dinner. Do you know how much money I made last year?

MATT I know this is a piss-up dinner.

LAMBERT It is a piss-up dinner.

PRUE (*to* JULIE) His mother always hated me. The first time she saw me she hated me. She never gave me

874

one present in the whole of her life. Nothing. She wouldn't give me the drippings off her nose.

JULIE I know.

PRUE The drippings off her nose. Honestly.

JULIE All mothers-in-law are like that. They love their sons. They love their boys. They don't want their sons to be fucked by other girls. Isn't that right?

PRUE Absolutely. All mothers want their sons to be fucked by themselves.

JULIE By their mothers.

PRUE All mothers –

LAMBERT All mothers want to be fucked by their mothers.

MATT Or by themselves.

PRUE No, you've got it the wrong way round.

LAMBERT How's that?

MATT All mothers want to be fucked by their sons.

LAMBERT Now wait a minute –

MATT My point is –

LAMBERT No my point is – how old do you have to be?

JULIE To be what?

LAMBERT To be fucked by your mother.

MATT Any age, mate. Any age.

They all drink.

LAMBERT How did you enjoy your dinner, darling?

JULIE I wasn't impressed.

LAMBERT You weren't impressed?

JULIE No.

LAMBERT I bring her to the best caff in town –
spending a fortune – and she's not impressed.

MATT Don't forget this is your anniversary. That's
why we're here.

LAMBERT What anniversary?

PRUE It's your wedding anniversary.

LAMBERT All I know is this is the most expensive
fucking restaurant in town and she's not impressed.

RICHARD *comes to the table.*

RICHARD Good evening.

MATT Good evening.

PRUE Good evening.

JULIE Good evening.

LAMBERT Good evening, Richard. How you been?

RICHARD Very very well. Been to a play?

MATT No. The ballet.

RICHARD Oh the ballet? What was it?

LAMBERT That's a fucking good question.

MATT It's unanswerable.

RICHARD Good, was it?

LAMBERT Unbelievable.

JULIE What ballet?

MATT None of them could reach the top notes. Could they?

RICHARD Good dinner?

MATT Fantastic.

LAMBERT Top notch. Gold plated.

PRUE Delicious.

LAMBERT My wife wasn't impressed.

RICHARD Oh really?

JULIE I liked the waiter.

RICHARD Which one?

JULIE The one with the fur-lined jockstrap.

LAMBERT He takes it off for breakfast.

JULIE Which is more than you do.

RICHARD Well how nice to see you all.

PRUE She wasn't impressed with her food. It's true. She said so. She thought it was dry as dust. She said –

what did you say darling? – she's my sister – she said she could cook better than that with one hand stuffed between her legs – she said – no, honestly – she said she could make a better sauce than the one on that plate if she pissed into it. Don't think she was joking – she's my sister, I've known her all my life, all my life, since we were little innocent girls, all our lives, when we were babies, when we used to lie in the nursery and hear Mummy beating the shit out of Daddy. We saw the blood on the sheets the next day – when nanny was in the pantry – my sister and me – and nanny was in the pantry – and the pantry maid was in the larder and the parlour maid was in the laundry room washing the blood out of the sheets. That's how my little sister and I were brought up and she could make a better sauce than yours if she pissed into it.

MATT Well, it's lovely to be here, I'll say that.

LAMBERT Lovely to be here.

JULIE Lovely. Lovely.

MATT Really lovely.

RICHARD Thank you.

PRUE *stands and goes to* RICHARD.

PRUE Can I thank you? Can I thank you personally? I'd like to thank you myself, in my own way.

RICHARD Well thank you.

PRUE No no, I'd really like to thank you in a very personal way.

JULIE She'd like to give you her personal thanks.

PRUE Will you let me kiss you? I'd like to kiss you on the mouth?

JULIE That's funny. I'd like to kiss him on the mouth too.

She stands and goes to him.

Because I've been maligned, I've been misrepresented. I never said I didn't like your sauce. I love your sauce.

PRUE We can't both kiss him on the mouth at the same time.

LAMBERT You could tickle his arse with a feather.

RICHARD Well I'm so glad. I'm really glad. See you later I hope.

He goes. PRUE *and* JULIE *sit.*

Silence.

MATT Charming man.

LAMBERT That's why this is the best and most expensive restaurant in the whole of Europe – because he *insists* upon proper standards, he *insists* that standards are maintained with the utmost rigour, you get me? That standards are maintained up to the highest standards, up to the very highest fucking standards –

MATT He doesn't jib.

LAMBERT Jib? Of course he doesn't jib – it would be more than his life was worth. He jibs at nothing!

PRUE I knew him in the old days.

MATT What do you mean?

PRUE When he was a chef.

LAMBERT's *mobile phone rings.*

LAMBERT Who the fuck's this?

He switches it on.

Yes? What?

He listens briefly.

I said no calls! It's my fucking wedding anniversary!

He switches it off.

Cunt.

Table Two.

SUKI I'm so proud of you.

RUSSELL Yes?

SUKI And I know these people are good people. These people who believe in you. They're good people. Aren't they?

RUSSELL Very good people.

SUKI And when I meet them, when you introduce me
to them, they'll treat me with respect, won't they?
They won't want to fuck me behind a filing cabinet?

SONIA *comes to the table.*

SONIA Good evening.

RUSSELL Good evening.

SUKI Good evening.

SONIA Everything all right?

RUSSELL Wonderful.

SONIA No complaints?

RUSSELL Absolutely no complaints whatsoever.
Absolutely numero uno all along the line.

SONIA What a lovely compliment.

RUSSELL Heartfelt.

SONIA Been to the theatre?

SUKI The opera.

SONIA Oh really, what was it?

SUKI Well . . . there was a lot going on. A lot of
singing. A great deal, as a matter of fact. They never
stopped. Did they?

RUSSELL (*to* SONIA) Listen, let me ask you something.

SONIA You can ask me absolutely anything you like.

RUSSELL What was your upbringing?

SONIA That's funny. Everybody asks me that. Everybody seems to find that an interesting subject. I don't know why. Isn't it funny? So many people express curiosity about my upbringing. I've no idea why. What you really mean of course is – how did I arrive at the position I hold now – maîtresse d'hôtel – isn't that right? Isn't that your question? Well, I was born in Bethnal Green. My mother was a chiropodist. I had no father.

RUSSELL Fantastic.

SONIA Are you going to try our bread-and-butter pudding?

RUSSELL In spades.

SONIA *smiles and goes.*

RUSSELL Did I ever tell you about my mother's bread-and-butter pudding?

SUKI You never have. Please tell me.

RUSSELL You really want me to tell you? You're not being insincere?

SUKI Darling. Give me your hand. There. I have your hand. I'm holding your hand. Now please tell me. Please tell me about your mother's bread-and-butter pudding. What was it like?

RUSSELL It was like drowning in an ocean of richness.

SUKI How beautiful. You're a poet.

RUSSELL I wanted to be a poet once. But I got no encouragement from my dad. He thought I was an arsehole.

SUKI He was jealous of you, that's all. He saw you as a threat. He thought you wanted to steal his wife.

RUSSELL His wife?

SUKI Well, you know what they say.

RUSSELL What?

SUKI Oh, you know what they say.

The WAITER *comes to the table and pours wine.*

WAITER Do you mind if I interject?

RUSSELL Eh?

WAITER I say, do you mind if I make an interjection?

SUKI We'd welcome it.

WAITER It's just that I heard you talking about T. S. Eliot a little bit earlier this evening.

SUKI Oh you heard that, did you?

WAITER I did. And I thought you might be interested to know that my grandfather knew T. S. Eliot quite well.

SUKI Really?

WAITER I'm not claiming that he was a close friend of his. But he was a damn sight more than a nodding acquaintance. He knew them all in fact, Ezra Pound,

W. H. Auden, C. Day Lewis, Louis MacNeice, Stephen
Spender, George Barker, Dylan Thomas and if you go
back a few years he was a bit of a drinking companion
of D. H. Lawrence, Joseph Conrad, Ford Madox
Ford, W. B. Yeats, Aldous Huxley, Virginia Woolf and
Thomas Hardy in his dotage. My grandfather was
carving out a niche for himself in politics at the time.
Some saw him as a future Chancellor of the Exchequer
or at least First Lord of the Admiralty but he decided
instead to command a battalion in the Spanish Civil
War but as things turned out he spent most of his
spare time in the United States where he was a very
close pal of Ernest Hemingway – they used to play gin
rummy together until the cows came home. But he
was also boon compatriots with William Faulkner,
Scott Fitzgerald, Upton Sinclair, John Dos Passos –
you know – that whole vivid Chicago gang – not to
mention John Steinbeck, Erskine Caldwell, Carson
McCullers and other members of the old Deep South
conglomerate. I mean – what I'm trying to say is –
that as a man my grandfather was just about as all
round as you can get. He was never without his
pocket bible and he was a dab hand at pocket
billiards. He stood four square in the centre of the
intellectual and literary life of the tens, twenties and
thirties. He was James Joyce's godmother.

Silence.

RUSSELL Have you been working here long?

WAITER Years.

RUSSELL You going to stay until it changes hands?

WAITER Are you suggesting that I'm about to get the boot?

SUKI They wouldn't do that to a nice lad like you.

WAITER To be brutally honest, I don't think I'd recover if they did a thing like that. This place is like a womb to me. I prefer to stay in my womb. I strongly prefer that to being born.

RUSSELL I don't blame you. Listen, next time we're talking about T. S. Eliot I'll drop you a card.

WAITER You would make me a very happy man. Thank you. Thank you. You are incredibly gracious people.

SUKI How sweet of you.

WAITER Gracious and graceful.

He goes.

SUKI What a nice young man.

Table One.

LAMBERT You won't believe this. You're not going to believe this – and I'm only saying this because I'm among friends – and I know I'm well liked because I trust my family and my friends – because I know they like me fundamentally – you know – deep down they trust me – deep down they respect me – otherwise

I wouldn't say this. I wouldn't take you all into my
confidence if I thought you all hated my guts – I
couldn't be open and honest with you if I thought you
thought I was a pile of shit. If I thought you would
like to see me hung, drawn and fucking quartered –
I could never be frank and honest with you if that
was the truth – never . . .

Silence.

But as I was about to say, you won't believe this, I fell
in love once and this girl I fell in love with loved me
back. I know she did.

Pause.

JULIE Wasn't that me, darling?

LAMBERT Who?

MATT Her.

LAMBERT Her? No, not her. A girl. I used to take her
for walks along the river.

JULIE Lambert fell in love with me on the top of a
bus. It was a short journey. Fulham Broadway to
Shepherd's Bush, but it was enough. He was trembling
all over. I remember. (*To* PRUE.) When I got home
I came and sat on your bed, didn't I?

LAMBERT I used to take this girl for walks along the
river. I was young, I wasn't much more than a nipper.

MATT That's funny. I never knew anything about
that. And I knew you quite well, didn't I?

LAMBERT What do you mean you knew me quite well? You knew nothing about me. You know nothing about me. Who the fuck are you anyway?

MATT I'm your big brother.

LAMBERT I'm talking about love, mate. You know, real fucking love, walking along the banks of a river holding hands.

MATT I saw him the day he was born. You know what he looked like? An alcoholic. Pissed as a newt. He could hardly stand.

JULIE He was trembling like a leaf on top of that bus. I'll never forget it.

PRUE I was there when you came home. I remember what you said. You came into my room. You sat down on my bed.

MATT What did she say?

PRUE I mean we were sisters, weren't we?

MATT Well, what did she say?

PRUE I'll never forget what you said. You sat on my bed. Didn't you? Do you remember?

LAMBERT This girl was in love with me – I'm trying to tell you.

PRUE Do you remember what you said?

Table Two.

RICHARD *comes to the table.*

RICHARD Good evening.

RUSSELL Good evening.

SUKI Good evening.

RICHARD Everything in order?

RUSSELL First class.

RICHARD I'm so glad.

SUKI Can I say something?

RICHARD But indeed –

SUKI Everyone is so happy in your restaurant. I mean women *and* men. You make people so happy.

RICHARD Well, we do like to feel that it's a happy restaurant.

RUSSELL It is a happy restaurant. For example, look at me. Look at me. I'm basically a totally disordered personality, some people would describe me as a psychopath. (*To* SUKI.) Am I right?

SUKI Yes.

RUSSELL But when I'm sitting in this restaurant I suddenly find I have no psychopathic tendencies at all. I don't feel like killing everyone in sight, I don't feel like putting a bomb under everyone's arse. I feel something quite different, I have a sense of equilibrium,

888

of harmony, I love my fellow diners. Now this is very unusual for me. Normally I feel – as I've just said – absolutely malice and hatred towards everyone within spitting distance – but here I feel love. How do you explain it?

SUKI It's the ambience.

RICHARD Yes, I think ambience is that intangible thing that cannot be defined.

RUSSELL Quite right.

SUKI It is intangible. You're absolutely right.

RUSSELL Absolutely.

RICHARD That is absolutely right. But it does – I would freely admit – exist. It's something you find you are part of. Without knowing exactly what it is.

RUSSELL Yes. I had an old schoolmaster once who used to say that ambience surrounds you. He never stopped saying that. He lived in a little house in a nice little village but none of us boys were ever invited to tea.

RICHARD Yes, it's funny you should say that. I was brought up in a little village myself.

SUKI No? Were you?

RICHARD Yes, isn't it odd? In a little village in the country.

RUSSELL What, right in the country?

889

RICHARD Oh, absolutely. And my father once took me to our village pub. I was only that high. Too young to join him for his pint of course. But I did look in. Black beams.

RUSSELL On the roof?

RICHARD Well, holding the ceiling up in fact. Old men smoking pipes, no music of course, cheese rolls, gherkins, happiness. I think this restaurant – which you so kindly patronise – was inspired by that pub in my childhood. I do hope you noticed that you have complimentary gherkins as soon as you take your seat.

SUKI That was you! That was your idea!

RICHARD I believe the concept of this restaurant rests in that public house of my childhood.

SUKI I find that incredibly moving.

Table One.

LAMBERT I'd like to raise my glass.

MATT What to?

LAMBERT To my wife. To our anniversary.

JULIE Oh darling! You remembered!

LAMBERT I'd like to raise my glass. I ask you to raise your glasses to my wife.

JULIE I'm so touched by this, honestly. I mean I have to say –

LAMBERT Raise your fucking glass and shut up!

JULIE But darling, that's naked aggression. He doesn't normally go in for naked aggression. He usually disguises it under honeyed words. What is it sweetie? He's got a cold in the nose, that's what it is.

LAMBERT I want us to drink to our anniversary. We've been married for more bloody years than I can remember and it don't seem a day too long.

PRUE Cheers.

MATT Cheers.

JULIE It's funny our children aren't here. When they were young we spent so much time with them, the little things, looking after them.

PRUE I know.

JULIE Playing with them.

PRUE Feeding them.

JULIE Being their mothers.

PRUE They always loved me much more than they loved him.

JULIE Me too. They loved me to distraction. I was their mother.

PRUE Yes, I was too. I was my children's mother.

MATT They have no memory.

LAMBERT Who?

MATT Children. They have no memory. They remember nothing. They don't remember who their father was or who their mother was. It's all a hole in the wall for them. They don't remember their own life.

SONIA *comes to the table.*

SONIA Everything all right?

JULIE Perfect.

SONIA Were you at the opera this evening?

JULIE No.

PRUE No.

SONIA Theatre?

PRUE No.

JULIE No.

MATT This is a celebration.

SONIA Oh my goodness! A birthday?

MATT Anniversary.

PRUE My sister and her husband. Anniversary of their marriage. I was her leading bridesmaid.

MATT I was his best man.

LAMBERT I was just about to fuck her at the altar when somebody stopped me.

SONIA Really?

MATT I stopped him. His zip went down and I kicked him up the arse. It would have been a scandal. The world's press was on the doorstep.

JULIE He was always impetuous.

SONIA We get so many different kinds of people in here, people from all walks of life.

PRUE Do you really?

SONIA Oh yes. People from all walks of life. People from different countries. I've often said, 'You don't have to speak English to enjoy good food.' I've often said that. Or even understand English. It's like sex isn't it? You don't have to be English to enjoy sex. You don't have to speak English to enjoy sex. Lots of people enjoy sex without being English. I've known one or two Belgian people for example who love sex and they don't speak a word of English. The same applies to Hungarians.

LAMBERT Yes. I met a chap who was born in Venezuela once and he didn't speak a fucking word of English.

MATT Did he enjoy sex?

LAMBERT Sex?

SONIA Yes, it's funny you should say that. I met a man from Morocco once and he was very interested in sex.

JULIE What happened to him?

SONIA Now you've upset me. I think I'm going to cry.

PRUE Oh, poor dear. Did he let you down?

SONIA He's dead. He died in another woman's arms. He was on the job. Can you see how tragic my life has been?

Pause.

MATT Well, I can. I don't know about the others.

JULIE I can too.

PRUE So can I.

SONIA Have a happy night.

She goes.

LAMBERT Lovely woman.

The WAITER *comes to the table and pours wine into their glasses.*

WAITER Do you mind if I interject?

MATT What?

WAITER Do you mind if I make an interjection?

MATT Help yourself.

WAITER It's just that a little bit earlier I heard you saying something about the Hollywood studio system in the thirties.

PRUE Oh you heard that?

WAITER Yes. And I thought you might be interested to know that my grandfather was very familiar with a

894

lot of the old Hollywood film stars back in those days. He used to knock about with Clark Gable and Elisha Cook Jr and he was one of the very few native-born Englishmen to have had it off with Hedy Lamarr.

JULIE No?

LAMBERT What was she like in the sack?

WAITER He said she was really tasty.

JULIE I'll bet she was.

WAITER Of course there was a very well-established Irish Mafia in Hollywood in those days. And there was a very close connection between some of the famous Irish film stars and some of the famous Irish gangsters in Chicago. Al Capone and Victor Mature for example. They were both Irish. Then there was John Dillinger the celebrated gangster and Gary Cooper the celebrated film star. They were Jewish.

  Silence.

JULIE It makes you think, doesn't it?

PRUE It does make you think.

LAMBERT You see that girl at that table? I know her. I fucked her when she was eighteen.

JULIE What, by the banks of the river?

  LAMBERT *waves at* SUKI. SUKI *waves back. She whispers to* RUSSELL, *gets up and goes to* LAMBERT's *table followed by* RUSSELL.

895

SUKI Lambert! It's you!

LAMBERT Suki! You remember me!

SUKI Do you remember me?

LAMBERT Do I remember you? *Do* I remember you!

SUKI This is my husband Russell.

LAMBERT Hello Russell.

RUSSELL Hello Lambert.

LAMBERT This is my wife Julie.

JULIE Hello Suki.

SUKI Hello Julie.

RUSSELL Hello Julie.

JULIE Hello Russell.

LAMBERT And this is my brother Matt.

MATT Hello Suki, hello Russell.

SUKI Hello Matt.

RUSSELL Hello Matt.

LAMBERT And this is his wife Prue. She's Julie's sister.

SUKI She's not!

PRUE Yes, we're sisters and they're brothers.

SUKI They're not!

RUSSELL Hello Prue.

PRUE Hello Russell.

SUKI Hello Prue.

PRUE Hello Suki.

LAMBERT Sit down. Squeeze in. Have a drink.

They sit.

What'll you have?

RUSSELL A drop of that red wine would work wonders.

LAMBERT Suki?

RUSSELL She'll have the same.

SUKI (*to* LAMBERT) Are you still obsessed with gardening?

LAMBERT Me?

SUKI (*to* JULIE) When I knew him he was absolutely obsessed with gardening.

LAMBERT Yes, well, I would say I'm still moderately obsessed with gardening.

JULIE He likes grass.

LAMBERT It's true. I love grass.

JULIE Green grass.

SUKI You used to love flowers, didn't you? Do you still love flowers?

JULIE He adores flowers. The other day I saw him emptying a piss pot into a bowl of lilies.

RUSSELL My dad was a gardener.

MATT Not your grandad?

RUSSELL No, my dad.

SUKI That's right, he was. He was always walking about with a lawn mower.

LAMBERT What, even in the Old Kent Road?

RUSSELL He was a man of the soil.

MATT How about your grandad?

RUSSELL I never had one.

JULIE Funny that when you knew my husband you thought he was obsessed with gardening. I always thought he was obsessed with girls' bums.

SUKI Really?

PRUE Oh yes, he was always a keen wobbler.

MATT What do you mean? How do you know?

PRUE Oh don't get excited. It's all in the past.

MATT What is?

SUKI I sometimes feel that the past is never past.

RUSSELL What do you mean?

JULIE You mean that yesterday is today?

SUKI That's right. You feel the same, do you?

JULIE I do.

MATT Bollocks.

JULIE I wouldn't like to live again though, would you? Once is more than enough.

LAMBERT I'd like to live again. In fact I'm going to make it my job to live again. I'm going to come back as a better person, a more civilised person, a gentler person, a nicer person.

JULIE Impossible.

Pause.

PRUE I wonder where these two met? I mean Lambert and Suki.

RUSSELL Behind a filing cabinet.

Silence.

JULIE What is a filing cabinet?

RUSSELL It's a thing you get behind.

Pause.

LAMBERT No, not me mate. You've got the wrong bloke. I agree with my wife. I don't even know what a filing cabinet looks like. I wouldn't know a filing cabinet if I met one coming round the corner.

Pause.

JULIE So what's your job now then, Suki?

899

SUKI Oh, I'm a schoolteacher now. I teach infants.

PRUE What, little boys and little girls?

SUKI What about you?

PRUE Oh, Julie and me – we run charities. We do charities.

RUSSELL Must be pretty demanding work.

JULIE Yes, we're at it day and night, aren't we?

PRUE Well, there are so many worthy causes.

MATT (*to* RUSSELL) You're a banker? Right?

RUSSELL That's right.

MATT (*to* LAMBERT) He's a banker.

LAMBERT With a big future before him.

MATT Well, that's what he reckons.

LAMBERT I want to ask you a question. How did you know he was a banker?

MATT Well, it's the way he holds himself, isn't it?

LAMBERT Oh, yes.

SUKI What about you two?

LAMBERT Us two?

SUKI Yes.

LAMBERT Well, we're consultants. Matt and me. Strategy consultants.

MATT Strategy consultants.

LAMBERT It means we don't carry guns.

MATT *and* LAMBERT *laugh*.

We don't have to!

MATT We're peaceful strategy consultants.

LAMBERT Worldwide. Keeping the peace.

RUSSELL Wonderful.

LAMBERT Eh?

RUSSELL Really impressive. We need a few more of you about.

Pause.

We need more people like you. Taking responsibility. Taking charge. Keeping the peace. Enforcing the peace. Enforcing peace. We need more like you. I think I'll have a word with my bank. I'm moving any minute to a more substantial bank. I'll have a word with them. I'll suggest lunch. In the City. I know the ideal restaurant. All the waitresses have big tits.

SUKI Aren't you pushing the tits bit a bit far?

RUSSELL Me? I thought you did that.

Pause.

LAMBERT Be careful. You're talking to your wife.

MATT Have some respect, mate.

LAMBERT Have respect. That's all we ask.

MATT It's not much to ask.

LAMBERT But it's crucial.

Pause.

RUSSELL So how is the strategic consultancy business these days?

LAMBERT Very good, old boy. Very good.

MATT Very good. We're at the receiving end of some of the best tea in China.

RICHARD *and* SONIA *come to the table with a magnum of champagne, the* WAITER *with a tray of glasses. Everyone gasps.*

RICHARD To celebrate a treasured wedding anniversary.

MATT *looks at the label on the bottle.*

MATT That's the best of the best.

The bottle opens. RICHARD *pours.*

LAMBERT And may the best man win!

JULIE The woman always wins.

PRUE Always.

SUKI That's really good news.

PRUE The woman always wins.

RICHARD *and* SONIA *raise their glasses.*

902

RICHARD To the happy couple. God bless. God bless you all.

EVERYONE Cheers. Cheers . . .

MATT What a wonderful restaurant this is.

SONIA Well, we do care. I will say that. We care. That's the point. Don't we?

RICHARD Yes. We do care. We care about the welfare of our clientele. I will say that.

LAMBERT *stands and goes to them.*

LAMBERT What you say means so much to me. Let me give you a cuddle.

He cuddles RICHARD.

And let me give you a cuddle.

He cuddles SONIA.

This is so totally rare, you see. None of this normally happens. People normally – you know – people normally are so distant from each other. That's what I've found. Take a given bloke – this given bloke doesn't know that another given bloke exists. It goes down through history, doesn't it?

MATT It does.

LAMBERT One bloke doesn't know that another bloke exists. Generally speaking. I've often noticed.

SONIA (*to* JULIE *and* PRUE) I'm so touched that you're sisters. I had a sister. But she married a foreigner and I haven't seen her since.

PRUE Some foreigners are all right.

SONIA Oh I think foreigners are charming. Most people in this restaurant tonight are foreigners. My sister's husband had a lot of charm but he also had an enormous moustache. I had to kiss him at the wedding. I can't describe how awful it was. I've got such soft skin, you see.

WAITER Do you mind if I interject?

RICHARD I'm sorry?

WAITER Do you mind if I make an interjection?

RICHARD What on earth do you mean?

WAITER Well, it's just that I heard all these people talking about the Austro-Hungarian Empire a little while ago and I wondered if they'd ever heard about my grandfather. He was an incredibly close friend of the Archduke himself and he once had a cup of tea with Benito Mussolini. They all played poker together, Winston Churchill included. The funny thing about my grandfather was that the palms of his hands always seemed to be burning. But his eyes were elsewhere. He had a really strange life. He was in love, he told me, once, with the woman who turned out to be my grandmother, but he lost her somewhere. She disappeared, I think, in a sandstorm. In the desert. My grandfather was everything men aspired to be in those days. He was tall, dark and handsome. He was full of good will. He'd even give a cripple with no legs crawling on his belly through the slush and mud of a country lane a helping hand. He'd lift him up, he'd show him his way, he'd point him in the right direction. He was like Jesus Christ in that respect. And he was gregarious. He loved the society of his fellows, W. B. Yeats, T. S. Eliot, Igor Stravinsky, Picasso, Ezra Pound, Bertholt Brecht, Don Bradman, the Beverley Sisters, the Inkspots, Franz Kafka and the Three Stooges. He knew these people where they were isolated, where they were alone, where they fought against savage and pitiless odds, where they suffered vast wounds to their bodies, their bellies, their legs, their trunks, their eyes, their throats, their breasts, their balls –

LAMBERT (*standing*) Well, Richard – what a great dinner!

RICHARD I'm so glad.

LAMBERT *opens his wallet and unpeels fifty-pound notes. He gives two to* RICHARD.

LAMBERT This is for you.

RICHARD No, no really –

LAMBERT No no, this is for you. (*To* SONIA.) And this is for you.

SONIA Oh, no please –

LAMBERT *dangles the notes in front of her cleavage.*

LAMBERT Shall I put them down here?

SONIA *giggles.*

No I'll tell you what – you wearing suspenders?

SONIA *giggles.*

Stick them in your suspenders. (*To* WAITER.) Here you are son. Mind how you go.

Puts a note into his pocket.

Great dinner. Great restaurant. Best in the country.

MATT Best in the world I'd say.

LAMBERT Exactly. (*To* RICHARD.) I'm taking their bill.

RUSSELL No, no you can't –

LAMBERT It's my wedding anniversary! Right? (*To* RICHARD.) Send me their bill.

JULIE And his.

LAMBERT Send me both bills. Anyway . . .

He embraces SUKI.

It's for old times' sake as well, right?

SUKI Right.

RICHARD See you again soon?

MATT Absolutely.

SONIA See you again soon.

PRUE Absolutely.

SONIA Next celebration?

JULIE Absolutely.

LAMBERT Plenty of celebrations to come. Rest assured.

MATT Plenty to celebrate.

LAMBERT Dead right.

MATT *slaps his thighs.*

MATT Like – who's in front? Who's in front?

LAMBERT *joins in the song, slapping his thighs in time with* MATT.

LAMBERT *and* MATT Who's in front?
Who's in front?

LAMBERT Get out the bloody way
You silly old cunt!

LAMBERT *and* MATT *laugh.*

SUKI *and* RUSSELL *go to their table to collect handbag and jacket, etc.*

SUKI How sweet of him to take the bill, wasn't it?

RUSSELL He must have been very fond of you.

SUKI Oh he wasn't all that fond of me really. He just liked my . . . oh . . . you know . . .

RUSSELL Your what?

SUKI Oh . . . my . . . you know . . .

LAMBERT Fabulous evening.

JULIE Fabulous.

RICHARD See you soon then.

SONIA See you soon.

MATT I'll be here for breakfast tomorrow morning.

SONIA Excellent!

PRUE See you soon.

SONIA See you soon.

JULIE Lovely to see you.

SONIA See you soon I hope.

RUSSELL See you soon.

SUKI See you soon.

They drift off.

JULIE (*off*) So lovely to meet you.

SUKI (*off*) Lovely to meet you.

Silence.

The WAITER *stands alone.*

WAITER When I was a boy my grandfather used to take me to the edge of the cliffs and we'd look out to sea. He bought me a telescope. I don't think they have telescopes any more. I used to look through this telescope and sometimes I'd see a boat. The boat would grow bigger through the telescopic lens. Sometimes I'd see people on the boat. A man, sometimes, and a woman, or sometimes two men. The sea glistened.

My grandfather introduced me to the mystery of life and I'm still in the middle of it. I can't find the door to get out. My grandfather got out of it. He got right out of it. He left it behind him and he didn't look back.

He got that absolutely right.

And I'd like to make one further interjection.

He stands still.

Slow fade.